ELTON'S SONG

A Wicce Novel

MIRIAM CUMMING

Cover design by Vanesa Garkova

Edited by Tochi Biko

Rendezvous technology by Peter Mieras and Kathy Johnson

First printed 2022 ISBN: 978-0-6483921-8-7
eBook ISBN: 978-0-6483921-7-0

For my niblings;

May you be surrounded by steadfast family and loyal
friends;

Find fulfilling work and chase your passions;

Be loved and respected in equal measure;

And never lose the magic.

Love,

Enty Miri x

Contents

1.	Two of Cups	1
2.	The Tower	27
3.	These Three Kings	53
4.	Come All Ye Faithful	82
5.	Cadenza	121
6.	The Lovers	156
7.	The Star	194
8.	Chromatic	220
9.	Amoroso	250
10.	Death Rx	269
11.	Temperance	296
12.	Tacet	316
13.	Paean	347
14.	Duet	376

15. Eight of Wands 405

16. Coda 429

17. Ten of Quavers 457

18. Last Christmas 478

TWO OF CUPS

MORRIGAN

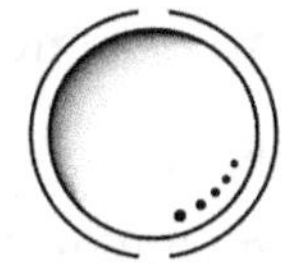

"Never have I ever kept a secret from my best friend," Meddy said, laying a jack of hearts on the table. I tucked in a finger, unable to agree with the statement, and she quirked an eyebrow at me. Card games like these were tough for witches doing their best to be honest when life necessitated lies. If she asked later, I'd remind her how, for the first decade of our friendship, she hadn't known there was an underground library in my house—though that wasn't the worst of what I'd covered up. Across from me, Viridis Thimberry—Viri—tucked his finger away too. Was I the only person here not crushing on the tall, handsome witch? Probably. With his gleaming smile, dark, unblemished skin and resonant voice, he left guys, girls, and enbies alike salivating. But not me, of course.

Meddy nudged Astrid, who followed with, "Never have I ever kissed a man."

I snorted. Good one. Astrid Ursache was a lesbian. Still, I got to keep my last finger untucked. I hadn't kissed a guy either. Or anyone, for that matter. Probably never would. The thought wasn't utterly abhorrent, like the idea of sex, but I couldn't imagine loving someone enough to let them put their tongue into my face. The height of my romantic fantasies stopped at snuggling under a warm blanket, sipping hot chocolate, and nuzzling the crook of their neck.

Astrid had filled out in the last couple of months, the rest of her body growing into proportion with her broad swimmer's shoulders. She was one of those white people whose skin glowed red at the slightest provocation, and she was flushed now. She pushed her long black hair off her forehead with her twiggy fingers and laughed.

Viri drank, having run out of fingers, and Meddy murmured to Astrid, keeping her up to speed on what went on at my banged-up kitchen table.

"Four." Eliss laid down zir card, and we dove for the floor, Brooke falling out of her chair in her haste. Meddy, the slowest to react, drank. Traditionally, Kings was a drinking game, but none of us had alcohol so we'd modified a few of the cards to accommodate.

Astrid fingered the Braille on the corner of her card, played the second three of the deck, and poured a slug of her Fanta into the central glass. Eliss and I shared a disgusted look—Fanta wasn't going to compliment the splash of iced chai already in there.

A wave of almost-cool air washed over me as Mum set up another fan.

I lifted my curls off my sweaty neck. "Thanks."

She placed a cutting board on the bench and piled tiny tomatoes into a colander before rushing off down the hall, probably to pick herbs from the garden.

Eliss waited until zir turn rolled around to ask, "Do you think this is the year your parents will finally get a reverse cycle?"

"Hah! Doubtful." They were saving hard to buy out Arcane Industries—the company we all worked for. Besides, air cons used way more electricity than fans.

Eliss pulled a king. "Every time someone pours a drink, everyone else needs to stand and twirl." Ze demonstrated. Eliss was what Meddy would call 'visibly queer'. Ze kept zir bleached hair buzzed short—save for a sweeping fringe streaked with fantastical colours that fell over one eye—and dressed eclectically in pieces that only went together because ze said so. Today ze wore bright blue rectangular glasses with no lenses in them.

Dad poked his head through the kitchen door. "Merry meet." He waved to my friends. "Morrigan, with me please."

He left, expecting me to drop everything and follow, though I was clearly busy. And I did. We passed through the lounge room to Dad's home office, where I was surprised to find Liam Kendren, AI's head of Logistics, waiting.

For me, full names were default. I had to practice people's preferred names, teaching myself to think of them how they wanted to be addressed, but I'd never mastered that for Liam Kendren. There were some people that, no matter how hard I tried, I couldn't break their names into segments or deconstruct the image I had of them in my head. Not their physical form; something deeper. Whatever made them who they were couldn't be summarised without the entirety of their name. Liam Kendren was one of them.

We'd worked together when I was a kid, but these days I only saw him at Arcane Industries' bi-annual solstice parties. Sneaky Witch Private Investigators, the division I worked with, operated on a different floor from the parent company.

He offered a short mocking bow. "Miss Larue." His lank brown hair flopped over his prominent forehead.

"Hi, Liam."

His cheek twitched. "Mr Kendren, please."

Ah, nothing changed with this stick-in-the-mud.

Dad and I sat while *Mr* Liam Kendren leaned on the wall by the window, looking outside.

"What's up?" I asked Dad.

Liam Kendren butted in before Dad could respond. "Cause for celebration, Miss Larue. Our mutual—" he gestured to Dad— "Is officially the vice president of Arcane Industries, in training to take the throne. I expect big upgrades will come with him."

"Nice one." I pantomimed applause. Curiously, he assumed Dad wouldn't have told me, when it was as much my future as Dad's. But who had told Liam Kendren? Had our CEO announced the change to the company and I'd missed it, or had Dad shared his plans privately?

"First though," Dad said, "Mr Kendren has enlisted our help contacting as many local Selkies as possible. AI's donor stores are running low, Selkie skins especially." Dad tidied his desk, as if he hadn't realised how chaotic it was until outsiders entered his office. "We need Selkies who are willing to donate their skins before death."

"They can do that?" I hated sounding inexperienced, but the question asked itself.

"Oh yes." Liam reached overhead, swinging his arms back to crack his shoulders, emphasising his towering height. "Their furs are a burden to them, even a liability. With the poor quality of water and shortages of food due to overfishing, who'd live in the ocean if they had the choice?" He smiled, no-doubt content to have schooled me.

Dad's gaze never left Liam Kendren, who continued to stare outside like he'd never seen lawn gnomes before. "Our scientists are teetering on the edge of a medical breakthrough, holding their breath for a shipment from Perth that we confirmed missing today. AI needs these furs—Selkie skins—if we're to continue providing healthcare to the aquatic fae community."

"And to get elders like Aoidh Vess off our backs," Liam added.

I'd never met a Selkie—or if I had, I hadn't picked them for one—but it made sense they'd turn to Arcane Industries for their medical needs. Meddy did as well. A person had a better chance of holistic care if they didn't have to keep secrets like 'I'm not human' or 'I have forty-five snakes living under my hijab' from their doctor.

Tired of the window, Liam Kendren strode to Dad's cabinet. If he expected to find a decanter of brandy, he'd be disappointed. "Surely you can see why we'd appreciate your unique skills, Miss Larue."

Indeed. But why show up at my house on a Sunday afternoon, instead of emailing, or making an appointment through Sneaky Witch PI's reception? Was this a *feed two birds with one scone* situation? Had he been celebrating with Dad and decided asking me now would be most efficient?

"Will you require anything, beyond compensation, to track down Selkies in the Sydney region and encourage them to come forth?" The High Priest of Logistics pointedly admired the framed photographs and artworks that covered Dad's walls. I bet it galled him to need my assistance.

Wrapping my necklace around my hand, I pinched the Celtic salmon pendant between finger and thumb. "Is this..." I couldn't ask if it was legal. That wasn't a consideration we at AI had much regard for. "...moral?"

"Anyone you contact will believe they had a premonition, unless you tell them who you are and that you've dream-travelled to them specifically. They're not going to feel like we cold-called them."

Except that's exactly what we would be doing. Which, no, that wouldn't be moral. It wasn't okay to step into a person's dream and urge them to donate a kidney either. I made a long "Hmmm," to signal I was weighing their words.

"Time is of the essence." Liam Kendren pressed. "If you make contact tonight while you sleep, AI can go back to saving lives. As it stands, we have delayed most surgeries until we can source skins and stem cells."

"I'll do my best." It was rare for me to astral travel to a stranger without an item of clothing or some DNA to anchor my magick, but this wasn't the first time I'd done it. Perhaps if I focused on travelling to a beach, I'd find Selkies hanging out on the sand. "Draw up a contract and email—"

"No need." Liam crossed to my seat and picked up his briefcase from the floor, balancing it on the corner of Dad's desk to pop the latches. He laid a thin sheaf of stapled sheets in front of me, with my name and the compensation Arcane Industries would offer on top of my regular wage from Sneaky Witch. No way! I fought to keep my expression neutral, wanting to whistle in appreciation. Liam Kendren was offering two hundred dollars a night, plus a bonus fifty dollars for every Selkie that stepped forward and mentioned compelling dreams. He planted a non-disclosure agreement on top, and pressed a pen into my hand.

Dad rocked gently in his padded office chair, watching through his thin-framed reading glasses. His eyebrows kissed in the middle. "Doing things the old-fashioned way, huh?"

As much to annoy Liam Kendren as to be a responsible adult, I read both the NDA and my contract, ignoring the murmur of their voices. Curiously, the NDA focused on not gossiping in the office about the donor program or my participation, rather than restricting who in my personal life knew. I signed. Liam Kendren shook my hand to thank me, then tucked the paperwork back into his briefcase.

I sanitised my hands. "It's a pleasure to work with you again, L— uh, Mr Kendren."

When I returned to the kitchen, Eliss was gone, Viridis was raiding the fridge and Meddy had her tongue halfway down Astrid's neck. Puke-worthy, but when I caught Meddy's gaze I gave her a thumbs-up anyway. It was good to see her happy. Perhaps she'd realise what advocating for yourself achieved and stop being a gutless wonder.

With the exceptions of Brooke and Viri, none of my friends knew I was employed by Arcane Industries. Meddy knew I helped my parents occasionally, doing paperwork or taking calls, but not that I worked nights on my own assignments or that my money wasn't from the Bank of Dad.

It'd been a secret for so many years, it'd cause more trouble than it was worth to admit I'd hidden my career. It hadn't been all that long since I'd disclosed my supernatural abilities to Meddy, and though she'd taken it well—more relieved by not being the only one with "powers" than upset I hadn't told her sooner—dropping another truth bomb wasn't on my agenda. Better to let her believe I'd signed my first real independent gig. That way, we'd avoid any awkwardness, and it was one less lie I needed to tell going forward.

I put my palms on the tabletop, leaned in, and dropped my voice, "Guess who's got a contract with Arcane Industries, talking Selkies out of their skins?"

ELTON

"No! I'm not ready for Elton to have his fur back." Mother's voice shrilled then fell into sobs. "Not even if it's only a couple of months early." I hovered at the kitchen threshold, on the verge of fleeing. Mother turned to grab a tissue off the counter behind her and spotted me.

"Oh, Elton," she cried, snatching at the tissues as she lurched out of her chair to enfold me in a fierce hug. I wrapped my arms around her and rested my cheek on her grey curls.

"Can someone tell me what is going on?" I asked Papa, who rose from his seat at the far side of the round table.

"I best put the jug on, aye?"

Mother snuffled an affirmative. I patted her shoulders, my guts turning to knots. The plan had always been that I'd be given my fur on my twenty-first birthday, and with it the choice to return to the ocean or stay ashore. Were they discussing withholding that from me? My identity? The key to my life as yet unlived?

I drew Mother back to the table and sat beside her, holding her plump, speckled hand.

Like my own, her human form was dappled. Her marks appeared closer to age spots, while mine resembled freckles. They cascaded abaft my ears from hairline to jaw, and sprayed across my back, darkening my brown skin.

She rubbed at her face, sniffling. When she lowered her head, the softened skin below her eyes pooled on her cheekbones.

Papa slid steaming cups in front of us and seated himself.

When it was clear Mother wouldn't open the discussion, he said, "Arcane Industries contacted us again. A recent breakthrough by their medical scientists has presented a unique opportunity. Your mother and I, we're already registered as organ donors after we die, but there's something we could give before then to change the lives of many."

I cupped my lips, my fingers curling under my tense jaw.

"Are you up to date with the news, Elton?" Mother asked.

I shrugged one shoulder. News was plentiful.

"Arcane Industries think they might be able to grow furs in their labs. They've had some promising successes."

The nerve! What right did they have to experiment on us? "And what good would our involvement do, beyond gifting our secrets to human witches?" I kept a beat in my words, underlining how we weren't like them, lest my parents forget. We were graceful and poetic, the stuff of legends.

Papa's brow lowered.

I cringed at my carelessness. "For Raeyn?"

My sister Raeyn had been born without a fur, as good as human, save for the webbing doctors cut from between her fingers and toes. If it weren't for her, the lot of us may have returned to the sea long ago.

"Yes." Mother smiled, though the water in her eyes and the discolouring of her skin didn't ebb. "Our aid will also benefit Selkies caught in nets or wounded by sharks.

There's no limit to the miracles Arcane Industries' doctors may perform once they've mastered these procedures."

Humans saving us from other humans. Great.

"But first," Papa said, "they need donations."

My breath quickened. I dug my fingernails into my knees, waiting for the noble suggestion that mun come next. Mother made clear she didn't want to lose "her baby"—me—but surely, to pressure me in my early man-hood to donate my freedom and stay close to home would be too much. "Our magick camouflage and songs divine, you'd sacrifice more than transformation. It—" My voice was too loud, losing its lilt to desperation. "It's dangerous to hand away that which makes one powerful."

Mother stroked a line down the centre of her forehead to the bridge of her nose, releasing the tension there. "The risks aren't lost on us."

They knew better than anyone the power an individual held over a Selkie via their fur. They'd hidden each other's before I'd been born. And then they'd taken mine.

"Realistically, AI won't enslave Selkies." Wisps of white hair poked out of Papa's ears, below his French style wool cap. "There will be no forced marriages. These witches are honourable and kind; this isn't the eighteen hundreds. Our elders have vouched for them. The risks are minimal, maybe non-existent. No, we wouldn't be able to channel the sea's energy through our songs, or blend into the environment anymore, but it's been a decade since we needed do any of those things." He breathed in steam from his tea. "Your mother and I have made our choice. Even if we miss those abilities, it's a small price to pay to be liberated of the water's call and the *oidhirp anabarrach* that accompanies it."

The water's song, *gairm gu uisge*, lured me too, but as I'd never put on my seal skin in answer, my *oidhirp anabarrach*—"the storm", witches liked to call it—lacked the violence of my parents'.

I smiled encouragingly. "Relief so sweet, most deserved."

Papa's eyes shone with hope. "For us as well as others."

"And if they create a fur for Raeyn?" Mother leaned back in her chair and gestured with her tea, "She wouldn't be bereft by your goodbye. When we die, she'll have better options."

"Abandon her, I would never. So harsh the words you speak." It was hardly desertion when I'd been upfront about my plans since forever.

As if synchronised, my parents drained their cups. How odd that they wanted badly to be rid of their own furs, yet to keep their children together, they'd open their daughter to a world of conflict she'd thus far avoided.

Pulling my hair into a low pony, I confirmed, "You'll donate now instead of after death?"

Mother bobbed her head. "We don't need them. We made our decision long ago."

"And hiding each other's fur strains our marriage when *oidhirp anabarrach* descends. If Arcane Industries can't use them for whatever reason, they'll safely destroy our skins for good."

That they didn't encourage me to follow suit spread a lightness across my shoulders. I sat straighter. "Will you each donate for the other?"

Mother shook her head. "We'll have Raeyn pick them up from their respective hiding places and drop them off with our consent forms. It's all arranged."

"What we were discussing," Papa said, "was whether we should have her bring your fur to the house while she's running errands."

Oh. The kitchen brightened, alive with slivers of blue and green glinting off the hanging crystals Mother kept by the windows. I gathered her hands between mine. "I'm strong. I can resist the call to sea, an' it should be a choice I make freely."

"You're not that strong," she whispered, "None of us are. Only accept your skin if you're ready to say goodbye."

I kissed the back of her hand, considering my reply. How much of her fear was manipulation rather than truth? She was not above weaponizing her tears, when voice alone would not do. "I'll prove my fortitude, you'll see. Believe."

The tapping of Raeyn's feet, as she danced an excited jig around the faded lino floor of her tiny apartment's kitchen, reached into mine bedroom. She was too jittery to sit for our phone call. "This is my chance to fit in with the rest of you! Oh, oh Elton, I've dreamt of this night after night. You and me, swimming into the moonrise."

She had? "But what about Papa and Mother dear?" I held my phone away from my face to protect it from sweat. "Where are they in this vision you're having?" She ought to stay and care for them, as their eldest. As their daughter.

"They're not going to live forever, Bro." So morbid. They were only in their sixties. "Besides, it's not like we'll never return home."

"When stars align in seven years' time," I corrected.

She needed to cease arguing a breath and allow me to process this fantasy I'd never dared dream. Desires neither of us were allowed. I'd hardly given a thought to having

Raeyn with me when I returned to the sea. It wasn't home to her, that was here on land, but it would be home to me.

"You don't know it's seven years, there are a lot of myths. There weren't seven years between my sweet sixteenth and yours, but Daikon made both."

And hadn't been back since. "Papa and Mother wouldn't have buried their furs if they could whenever come ashore. An' I can feel it, Raeyn, our magick high. When Venus kisses Neptune thrumming nigh. The sacred cycle complete on the seventh year when Saturn's birthday tremors through the sky."

"In storage is hardly buried, brother. I still hear *gairm gu uisge*, you know. The sea sings to my blood. Desperate rage does not a Selkie make."

Had I said it did? Never. She was different than us—a fact. She ought to appreciate the freedom from desperation triggered by the stars or the proximity of one's fur. Her lack of *oidhirp anabarrach* didn't make her human, it merely made her insecure.

The summer heat vexed me with its prickles. I cracked the window for a breeze and hot air rolled over my shirtless skin. Reconsidering, I shut and closed the blinds, thrusting my bedroom into darkness. What if AI really did conjure her a fur from pieces of our parents'? Would the song grow overpowering? Would a fabricated fur fabricate a storm?

"You really believe they can do it?" Raeyn's question mimicked my thoughts. "These human witches?"

"Who's ever worked as hard for magick than they?"

She snorted softly, as if I was joking. "True."

"To shift together, oh..." A grin crept over my face, though I couldn't quite comprehend the possibility.

Raeyn took a deep, audible breath and held it, the way she did when she was about to broach an uncomfortable subject. I waited.

"You want me to retrieve your skin when I go for mum's and dad's, I imagine?"

My grip on the phone tightened. "I do, yeah. Or even just tell me where."

"Can't do that. Promises, you know. But I can pick it up for you."

She'd gather it, but then what? Would she make me wait until my twenty-first, as per my parents' desire?

"My thanks," I murmured. But when? Oh, when? I held the question in, wary of upsetting her, as my longing for the sea tended to do to those around me.

"I'll text the moment I have it. Work's intense with the Christmas rush, and it's a bit of a drive, but I'm on it the second I get a chance. Vested interest, and all that. Promise me a dinner, tonight or tomorrow, in case the pull's too strong and you cannot say goodbye?"

My precious Raeyn, not asking me to linger. I agreed, thanking her again, and changed the subject, making small talk until we hung up, each of us giddy and somewhat terrified.

I paced from driveway to mailbox, looking both ways along the street, until the crushing heat and sense of exposure overcame me, and I retreated inside to watch out the window.

The past four days lasted an aeon. Dinner last night with Raeyn, ten years past. My parents' house chafed me. We lived together peaceably, but the sand-coloured paint, white draperies, and crystals didn't jive. Why venerate an environment you'd wilfully cast aside? I got a drink for my vigil, passing Mother at the table working puzzles and pretending today wasn't happening.

On the way back to the window, I checked my phone. Nothing new. Raeyn's last message read, *Leaving now, see you in an hour.* It had been fifty minutes.

"By salt and stars, I need to get a grip," I muttered, tossing the device onto the couch and heading upstairs to wash my face.

I missed Raeyn's approach when she finally arrived. Mother answered the knock. I bounded down the stairs, sailed through the kitchen buoyed by joy, and leapt the couch. "Hello Raey—"

Mother slammed Raeyn into the wall. The door shut, jamming Raeyn's skirt and barely missing her hand. The signs of *oidhirp anabarrach* were clear, but it wasn't time. I kept careful watch upon the skies; the moon wasn't slivered, the stars had no trine.

Squeezing Raeyn's throat, Mother wrestled with her shoulder bag, pinning it against Raeyn's thigh with her own to yank the zipper. Raeyn froze, her too-round eyes tracking me as I came abreast of them. It would've been nice to say we'd never seen our mother like this, but it'd also be a lie.

Words were too humane for Mother, she growled and sobbed as she freed my fur from Raeyn's bag. Mother clutched the fur to her chest and backed away. They both gasped, Raeyn for breath, hers morphing into a cough; Mother's as though she were in pain. Eyes never leaving us, Mother unrolled the thick pelt. Its living juices dripped upon the floor. Tears streaked her weathered face. A smile broke her apart as the tail fin slapped her ankle.

"Oh fuck," Raeyn whispered.

Guilt gnawed me to see Mother so, shattered at the very thought she'd have to let me go. I'd imagined my fur darker—brown and black like my speckled skin, less grey. As I opened my arms to it, her lip curled and she jerked away. The belly would be white where I'd step through the vertical slit to pull it on. Oddly, I felt no compulsion to do so.

They'd claimed I'd become mindless in the thrall of my skin, that the song would be too strong, the storm would set in. Resisting would crush me, the world would be pain, yet the ocean's gravity remained the same.

Cold realisation slipped in close. "Raeyn, heavens no! That's not my fur, it's but her own."

Mother bolted, making for the back door, grey curls bobbing. Her keys rattled as she slammed her thumb onto the fob, triggering the garage roller and unlocking the car.

I gave chase. Tackled her. The back door's latch scratched the papery skin of her face as we tumbled. She could thank me later. I wrapped an arm around her, trapping her arms against her sides and pressing her spine to my chest. Mother bellowed and kicked her heels at my shins. We rolled on the unforgiving linoleum. I seized the fur with my other hand and yanked, but between her desperate grip and my prone position, I progressed naught.

Raeyn rushed over and straddled Mother's hips, pinning us both to the floor. "Get her hands."

Mother swung her arms from the elbow, attempting to punch Raeyn without releasing her fur.

"Sweet shit on a sandwich," my sister cursed, her décolletage red and sweaty. Bruises were surfacing on her throat. Now wasn't the time to tell her that their weight was crushing me.

Mother used Raeyn's shirt for leverage, lifting her torso and head before crunching backwards. My nose popped. Blood flooded my eyes and ran into my mouth. My brain throbbed as I coughed.

"Elton," Raeyn hissed. She held Mother's wrists, striving to separate them. Eyes shut against the blood, I scrabbled the fur free for all my worth. Papa would be shattered if we failed. Mother would be too, when she came to her senses. We couldn't let her return to the sea, not after everything they'd been through to stay here together. They'd never forgive us.

The fur slapped the floor at my side as Mother bashed in the rest of my face with her skull. I heaved, shifting enough that she pounded my chest instead. I spat pink. "Get. Her. Off."

Raeyn complied, hauling our mother to her feet.

I swooned, but got my knees beneath me, scooped up the fur, and darted for the living room. On my second step, my foot caught on the empty fur's jaw, my toes going in through the gaping slit at the collar, up through the throat and out through the mouth. I stumbled. Shouting and the clamour of smashing crockery followed me onto the carpet. Mother's fur stared up at me with its empty eye sockets as I shook my foot, trying to dislodge it without slowing. A resounding crash in the kitchen sent glass spraying into the living room. Raeyn's boots crunched over what remained of the china display. She snatched the fur, wrenching my ankle in her haste and landing me square on my arse.

"I'll be back!" Raeyn slammed the front door behind her.

Quiet intruded as my pulse eased off. Crawling to the sofa for support, I gingerly regained my feet and peeked into the kitchen. Mother's legs were pinned under a fallen display cabinet. Cold shuddered through me. I scrutinised her chest for the ebb and flow of breath. It seemed measured.

I fetched the first-aid kit and a wet facecloth for each of us from the upstairs bathroom. When I returned, Mother was sitting up, examining her wounds. Rage forbade me assist her. Adrenaline pooled in the bottom of my stomach, making me queasy. I grabbed a packet of peas from the freezer and iced my face by the sink until it stopped oozing. When it did, I rinsed the pea packet and returned it to the freezer. Only then did I feel stable enough to aid Mother.

The cabinet ought to have been light. The glass shelving and wooden drawers had given in to the seduction of gravity and sprayed over the tiles alongside the cabinet's contents; treasures from bygone days, or garage sale junk my parents ought to have purged years past, depending on who you asked. The doors had shattered. Yet, the weight proved too much for me alone.

I grabbed a face cloth and winced as I dabbed my swollen skin. "To set you free, Pa's help I'll need. Sorry." Recovering my phone from the couch, I dialled Papa. His phone rang out on the first attempt, but he picked up the second. We kept it direct, both content to belay discussion in favour of releasing Mother's legs before permanent damage was done.

"My thanks." Mother's voice was full of tears.

I crouched, setting the first-aid kit beside her and unsnapping it. "Together as family we face our trials."

When Papa arrived, it was with Raeyn, their voices proceeding them up the path to the cottage.

"They're similar sizes, but I was sure..." Raeyn was saying.

"Thank the seas it wasn't mine." Though Papa avoided building muscle, he was still broad and strong. If it'd been him in Mother's place, Raeyn and I would've lost a parent this day. I was fit from running on the beach, but I'd taken their warnings to heart and never beefed up for fear of doing damage to someone during my own periodic *oidhirp anabarrach*.

They kept on their boots, coming straight into the kitchen. I'd given Mother pain relief and a cuppa, then swept, but not yet vacuumed.

Papa rushed over and kissed her fiercely, holding her head; their lips made a wet smack. Raeyn and I took up position on the other end of the china display.

The three of us righted the cabinet, then Raeyn knelt to check Mother's legs, while Papa kissed me on my battered forehead. "Have you called a doctor?"

"No, not I." To an outsider we'd look like domestic violence victims, I'd only call in a life-or-death situation.

Raeyn helped Mother peel off her glass-covered shorts. "I've got to call Arcane Industries anyway; I may as well request a healer while I'm at it."

She avoided my gaze as she passed me, going to the hooks by the front door for her cell. I folded my lips into my mouth and pinched them between my teeth. Why did she need to phone AI?

Mother donned a clean skirt and Papa settled her at the table. They picked over the few items I'd salvaged while I strained my ears, unable to catch enough of Raeyn's words to make sense of her conversation. It ended sooner than it should.

She returned to the kitchen, flipping on the light. The sun had sunk behind the neighbouring homes. "They're closed. I left a message on their voice mail and tried the emergency number, which nobody answered." Her dramatic brows made a concerned V.

"I'm fine anyway," Mother said. "Nothing broken, except my heart for hurting you both. Where's my fur now?"

"Not at home, not in my car. Not anywhere you'd think to look or pass by accidentally. It's safe." Raeyn went to rub her neck, then snatched her hand away. "We're safe."

Mother visibly relaxed, but Raeyn held herself stiffly, turning to face me as if in slow motion.

"An' where's mine?" I asked.

"AI tower, in the CBD." She swallowed audibly. "I'm sorry brother; I donated it."

THE TOWER

ELTON

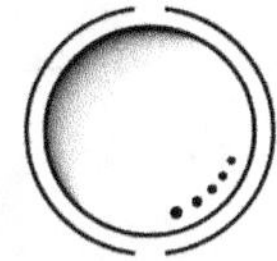

The sandstone base of the witches' skyscraper cooled my shoulder where I leant against it, a pleasing contrast to the stink of Sydney's central business district. It wasn't yet 8 am, but the hot air leeched the moisture from my eyes. My phone beeped.

'*Don't hate me Bro,*' Reayn sent. '*My car won't start. I'm waiting on roadside assist. I've called in sick to work and I'll get your skin today like I said I would, but I won't be at AI right when they open.*'

'*Your absence I know, as I'm here alone, appearing quite the vagabond with my ruined nose.*'

'*Aw shit, Elton. I said I'd do it! You didn't have to come. Hold on.*'

I kicked at a discarded bottle on the ground, sending it rolling in parallel to a family sedan pulling an illegal U-turn in front of AI's central office. The driver flicked on their hazards. The bottle rolled to a stop by a post box. I ambled over to pick it up, ignoring the scrutiny of the sedan's passengers; two middle-aged white gents, one taking a call. In the backseat, a fiery redhead. I tucked the bottle into my messenger bag—man bag, as Raeyn liked to say—to recycle later, extremely conscious of the bruising and swelling marring my face.

The redhead exited the sedan, nodding impatiently at whatever the men were saying. Both were older, neither attractive enough to capture such a mortal goddess's attention, so I supposed they were her dads. I got the impression she'd ridden into the city with them and was being dropped off for a day of shopping as they proceeded to their boring office jobs. She had wide hips with anime thighs, rounded arms, and a strong back laid bare by her knitted tank top. Her curple, encased in jean shorts, enraptured me as she slammed the car door. She then stepped onto the footpath to fight her mane into a bandanna.

Her dads drove off, turning into an underground car park further down the block.

The beauty closed the distance between us and thrust her hand forward to shake. "You must be Elton Abercrombie." Her hands were chapped and her grip firm. "Your sister told us to expect you. I'm Morrigan Larue, nightwalking PI." She didn't look the part, which was all the more captivating. "Come in, we'll get this mix-up sorted immediately."

Perhaps not all was lost. I fought for words. Any language would do to stop me appearing the bamboozled schoolboy. "My thanks," I managed.

The men Morrigan had travelled with approached us across the expansive, marble-floored foyer. One was tall and weedy, with sad brown hair. His suit was worn, giving him a sloppy appearance. He was probably the company's computer guy. The other had Morrigan's ocean-coloured eyes and was closer to her height, but with straight grey hair. He'd paired his suit with canvas shoes and wire-framed glasses—the kind of guy who attended meditation retreats and never lost his temper.

Morrigan indicated the computer guy. "This is Liam Kendren, High Priest of Logistics. He manages the intake of all our donations." The other man stopped beside her. "And this is Matthias Larue, HP of the Director's Board and municipal liaison for Gulgadya and Baludarri wards."

So confident and professional. Were the shorts a ploy to have people underestimate her?

"This way, please." Liam directed me toward an elevator wherein Morrigan discretely sanitised her hands with a travel-sized bottle from her pocket.

The elevator let out on the 20th floor. Liam charged forward and I followed; the Larues brought up the rear. The modern decor clashed with the purpose of the building, and my expectations of what witchcraft entailed. AI put me in mind of the specialist's rooms in the medical centre where Mother worked; many offices had the same glass doors. Not the one Liam selected, however, room 270. He covered the pin pad with his left hand while he input the access code. A chime sounded, then he tapped his ID to another panel. The door unlocked with a clunk.

Fluro lights flickered on. Liam gasped before my eyes had a chance to adjust. The room was tidy; groups of boxes stacked and awaiting sorting to our left and either side of the sole entrance. The back wall featured a bank of metal lockers and to the right was a wooden display case such as one expected in a museum. In the centre was a table so bare, one couldn't even call it a desk.

"They're gone!" Liam laced his fingers through his hair. "Matthias, this proves it! I've been telling you we need better security measures."

"Breathe, Mr Kendren." Mr Larue said. "There are multiple shipments here—"

Liam stamped a foot, his face contorting as he dragged his palms down his cheeks. "I left them right here on the desk."

I rubbed my eyebrow, behind which the first seeds of a headache took root. "No, really? Serious you're not." Liam left me on shifting sand, but the Larues' confidence provided something to lean on. They'd find my fur in a moment.

Morrigan drifted around the office, inspecting the labels on the top of each box. She bent over a row of hip-high boxes to check the contents of those against the wall, her back arching just so. Her rump—

I smiled appreciatively as she glanced my way, but she didn't hold the contact, instead scrutinising her father and this man who was having some kind of breakdown.

"There are a handful of other explanations." Matthias kept his tone even. "Let's not jump to conclusions."

"They're gone!" Liam wailed.

My heart throbbed with such intensity, it cracked a new rib with every quaking pulse. Morrigan locked gazes with me and spread her hands before herself, then pantomimed letting steam out of her collar.

Liam approached, an apology on his lips. I didn't care for his empty words.

"I got nothing," Morrigan reported to the older Larue.

"Let's check with reception, put a ticket in with security." He stepped between Liam and I, turning Liam toward the door by his shoulder. "Fire up the system in your office, Mr Kendren. We'll investigate the paper trail." Matthias ushered us out. "Connie might have processed them—"

"She left before I did!" Liam snapped. "I know where I left them. This is why you need to review my proposal."

Morrigan put space between us and made a hurried call.

Matthias pulled level with Liam, looking him straight in the face. "Now's not the time. Calm down."

Liam straightened his tie, nodded, and reigned it in.

Matthias checked the computer system and led us through several rooms. Each new failure added a rock to my tender stomach and slowed my steps. Liam now seemed almost bored. Morrigan stayed with me, flexing her jaw, stepping away whenever Liam moved within a metre of her. I wanted badly to step her aside and ask if he was always hot and cold like this.

At last, Matthias looked at his watch and heaved a sigh. "I'm sorry Elton, there's no point in you and Morrigan hanging around while Mr Kendren and I sort this out. I've put a freeze on any new skins being dissected until we locate yours and will personally see to it that Arcane Industries rights this wrong. We'll keep you updated." He withdrew a business card from his wallet and passed it to me. "These are my personal lines. Contact me directly instead of through reception."

I thanked him from a place of disconnection, all at once not believing they'd lost my magick, yet accepting the inevitability of it, as though I'd always known I'd never sink into my fur and swim free.

Morrigan saw me out, holding the heavy glass door wide. Would she question other employees? She'd introduced herself as a PI, but maybe that acronym meant something else to witches. I hovered by the exit biting my lip. Once I left, I'd be entrusting my future to these strangers.

"Presumptuous I may seem, but I must ask, d'you've one of these?" I flashed Matthias's business card. "Your voice would soothe my anxious nerves, belay my troubled thoughts, an act I'd find utmost kind; my loss denies me words."

She frowned for a long moment. Perhaps I ought to do as Raeyn suggested, talk more human, act more bland. Kill the art and poetry of my ocean soul to fit in with the land.

Morrigan's sweet strawberry lips quirked up at the corners. "I'm ace, so, uh, quell any wild ideas you're getting. Right?"

Ace? Like the card? Or was that a detective joke? Was she saying she didn't date clients? Sweat tickled my temple.

She rested against the open door, releasing air-conditioned relief while she dug out her contact details. "I empathise with you. It's a rotten situation. Something's off for sure. If you need a friend on the inside, you can text."

Her card was dog-eared and smelled faintly of bergamot. "My thanks. An' trust, I'll bother you naught." I let myself get drawn away by the pedestrian stream.

When I glanced over my shoulder, Morrigan was watching through the glass with her cute half-smile. I soon lost sight of her. To give myself something to focus on, I read over their business cards, but the wax-coated paper had no gravity to anchor me. Shoulders jostled me as their owners rushed by. All my life, others held power, keeping me from my magick. From my choices! Raeyn's disability mattered more than anything I desired. More than me. Playing human trumped all for my parents. They'd forgotten who we were. A briefcase hit my leg as a woman bustled past. I'd missed the bus stop and was halfway to Wynyard train station. Losing my way in the city would be poetic for the day I lost my future. I blinked hard, shoving the cards deep into my pocket. I wasn't being fair to my family. This was AI's mistake. But they'd given our furs to witches who specialised in cutting them up, and if those witches succeeded, I'd be trapped here, as my family always dreamed.

MORRIGAN

Sitting in my parked car, a block away from the Abercrombie residence, I logged my whereabouts with AI's system. I held my work cell in one hand and texted Brooke with my personal phone in the other. *'You know him then?'*

GPS tracking flickered on. Someone at AI was playing guardian angel. Not that I'd need it.

'"Know" is too strong a word.' Brooke replied. *'More like "am acquainted." His sister was my guidance buddy when I started high school, and our families gravitate toward each other at Faery Festivals, but I wouldn't say we're mates or anything.'*

I tucked my work cell into my slacks and tugged one of my gemstone bracelets to the tips of the fingers of that hand, stretching the elastic and clicking the stone chips together. *'Does he play contact sports?'* Or was I entering a domestic violence situation? I glanced over my shoulder, as if an AI employee might materialise in the back seat while I was discussing a client with my friend. I rolled my shoulders uneasily. It'd be stupid to make this house call alone if the family were dangerous, though Liam Kendren assured me they weren't and alluded that I was racist. Or specisist. The memory chafed me. It was one thing to be called out by Viri when my activism went too far or my privilege blinded me, and quite another to take shit from Liam Kendren. I should have hit back with his ageism. He'd given me grief for no reason when I first started at AI, but it was too late now. He'd assigned me this visit and here I was. Elton had texted for an update, and anyway, the Abercrombies deserved the comfort of ongoing contact.

'They were both in soccer as kids, why?' Brooke sent.

My bracelet went stretch-clink. Stretch-clink. *'Are they rowdy? Loud? He seemed a bit flirtatious.'* Perhaps a jealous lover had messed up Elton's face. Or a soccer ball.

There was a long pause, so I expected a lengthy text, but all Brooke sent was *'What do you know about Selkies?'*

What was that supposed to mean? Was it that obvious I'd never worked with fin folk before and most of my knowledge came from web searches?

'They're a type of water faery,' I sent. *'When they pull on their skins they shape-shift into seals. There are sacred restrictions around when they can transition. AI is more concerned with medicinal uses of donated furs than family dynamics.'* That wasn't entirely fair. I added, *'At least in logistics. Other divisions have a more personal approach.'*

'*Like the seas, Selkies are attuned to the heavens. Certain astrological events compel Selkies to return to the ocean. The longer they've been on land, the harder it becomes to resist the compulsion. It can send them mad. Think zombie on espresso, or werewolf.*'

I glared at my phone. She was having me on. '*Please, Brooke, be serious—*'

Brooke's next message popped through. '*This uncontrollable frenzy, called oidhirp anabarrach or 'the storm' may also be triggered if a captive selkie senses their skin nearby, giving them extra strength to recover it when necessary. Selkies have a long history of being oppressed by humans.*'

Wow. Okay, so they were violent, albeit not deliberately. I pulled up Astro Tracks on my phone to double check today's celestial positions. Nothing seemed exciting about tonight's disseminating moon, but Jupiter would trine with Mercury in a few days. Did it matter which planets were aligned? Probably.

I swiped to the next screen for my horoscope. Apparently, I was radiating compassion and would feel inspired to work out later. I snorted. I wouldn't call necessity particularly inspiring, but all right.

Another message came through from Brooke. '*The Selkie community here in Sydney are all very aware of their oidhirp anabarrach. You'll notice they don't take visitors at that time. I wouldn't worry.'*

'Why don't they just go swimming and call it good?'

'Because they can't return until a particular alignment between governing planets, which can be as long as seven years. Life would get complicated if you tried to rock up to work on Monday as a seal.'

I'd meant why didn't they swim in their human forms, but that didn't seem to be a consideration. I sighed and swung my legs out of the car. If witch academies were real, I'd have learned about this in high school and my head wouldn't be throbbing, but noooo, fitting into society was *so much more* 'essential'. I closed the car door with my butt, thanked Brooke, switched off my personal phone, and put my business face on.

The Abercrombie residence had a Scottish cottage feel, lumpy whitewash with a blue roof and a low stone fence that held the neighbours at bay. The family's AI profile recorded Mr and Mrs Abercrombie receiving grant money to get them started, before their children were born, which they'd used to buy land. Back when working class people could do that in Sydney. The lawn was high enough to offend nearby homeowners and lacked flowerpots or ornaments of any kind. The garden gate had a padlock hanging open from the latch; an intruder could easily step over the short fence anyway. The pebble path crunched under my sensible office shoes, footwear that previously served as part of my school uniform.

A broad-bellied older man answered my knock and smiled warmly.

"Yes, I'd love some Girl Scout biscuits! Let me get my wallet." He shut the door and returned seconds later, wallet in hand.

"There seems to be a misunderstanding." I adjusted my green chiffon scarf— which might have been the catalyst for his assumption—loosening it around my neck in hopes of a breeze. "My name is Morrigan Larue, I'm here on behalf of Arcane Industries, touching base with you and thanking you for your generous donation."

"That you lost." His face clouded. He stepped aside, indicating I should enter.

I bit my tongue to stop myself refuting his words. I didn't lose a damned thing, but I was here as a representative, so...

Elton smiled, tight-lipped, from where he was sprawled on the sofa, then stood abruptly and fled through a door on the far side of the room, his long hair swishing like a cape. What was I supposed to make of that?

Thick turquoise carpet sank under my feet as I waited for Mr Abercrombie to invite me to sit. They had three plush loveseats packed into the modest room, a driftwood coffee table, and on the far wall, two reverse cycle air conditioners, both running.

He moved into the kitchen instead, beckoning me to follow. Elton was pulling out a chair at their circular dining table.

"Why, hello again, Morrigan." Elton practically sang my name. If he was holding a grudge about his lost skin, he wasn't harbouring it against me personally. Raeyn, however, glared at me from across the table as I sat where Elton directed—right beside him.

Poorly-concealed bruises encircled Raeyn's neck and her wavy hair kinked to a stop above her shoulders. She wore a long-sleeved blouse and there was scar tissue between her fingers.

Mr and Mrs Abercrombie made coffee and set out a cheesecake that I assumed wasn't vegan, while I tried not to gawk at the broken blood vessel marring Raeyn's eye. Elton's face had lost a lot of its swelling, enough that I could tell he was otherwise quite handsome, in a windswept way. And his smile... His smile told me I was staring. Shitsticks.

When her parents finally sat, Raeyn gripped the edge of the table, her hands matching the scrabble of her voice. "Have you recovered the lost furs?"

"Not yet. Including yours, thirty-two Selkie skins have been recorded missing." I forced myself to speak evenly. To face the facts and not rush my delivery. "The potential loss of lives and freedom from this incident is unacceptable. I wanted to run you through—"

"Wait, how are you in charge of this?" Raeyn stared me down. "You can't be any older than Elton."

Ugh. Thankfully, most of my work was intelligence gathering, at night, alone, in secret. Every time I dealt with clients, I got this question. There was a fine line between sharing my credentials and bragging; a line that galled me to walk. I took a mouthful of coffee. "I'm nineteen. What I lack in age, I make up for with experience. If you would like to see my portfolio, references, or request a new consultant, I can provide my supervisor's num—"

"Your dad, you mean?" Raeyn cut in. "We can call your daddy and tell him you've been a bad girl?"

"Oh Raeyn." Elton gave her a long-suffering look.

I pressed my molars together and drew a long breath through my nose. "I'm answering to Mr Liam Kendren, HP of Logistics, for this contract. I'm a Private Investigator, working in a completely different department to my dad. That Matthias and I are both on this case, shows how serious Arcane Industries is taking the issue."

"It matters not." Elton glared at his sister.

I held up a hand to stall him defending me. "My whole family is employed by AI and have filled a variety of roles through the generations since its inception. I apologise if that makes you uncomfortable." I let that sink in, then prepared to turn the conversation around. "In just twenty-four hours, we've—"

Raeyn tossed a notepad in my direction. "For those phone numbers."

Breaking eye-contact, I readjusted my suit jacket and withdrew a pen from the pocket. I'd worried that I'd be uncomfortable wearing office attire on this house call but was now relieved I had. The cranked air conditioning and chilly reception raised the hairs on the back of my neck. On the pad I wrote *Liam Kendren, Matthias Larue, Silver Moontread (CEO)* in a list and copied their numbers from my work cell, wary of speaking.

"What of your donation drive?" Mrs Abercrombie asked. "Your advertisements continue to run, urging faerie donors to step forward. Don't you feel the continuation of this campaign to be dishonest?"

This is above my paygrade. I licked my teeth. "Matthias Larue suspended our donation drive this morning, but I'm not in marketing; I can't say how long those orders take to filter through social media channels or other advertising." The tar-like coffee Mr Abercrombie provided rattled through my veins. Satisfied to let his family grill me, he glared from under thick greying brows. No one had touched the cheesecake.

Mother and daughter shared a look.

Raeyn nodded sharply, as if something had been communicated. "What of compensation? How will your people make amends if my brother's fur can't be located?"

Elton's hands tightened around his cup.

I passed the notepad back to Raeyn. "I'm not putting energy into a future where these skins go unrecovered. Every missing fur represents a live donor at risk." I met the eyes of each Selkie in turn. "Compensation, however, is your right as our victims, and I am prepared to advocate for you to secure whatever you seek."

"That's unnecessary. How would that help me?" Elton fussed with his perfectly straight hair; blue-green light reflecting off mirror-black strands as he released the tie. "My soul seeks the sea; I don't want your money. Please." His voice captivated me. Elton could make the dictionary enchanting with his lilting inflection. His expression was open, so much less hostile than the rest of his family. "Let's hear what Miss Larue has come to say; what progress made?"

My cheeks burned, fighting the cottage's chill. I cleared my tight throat and addressed him as though not looking at his sister would stop her interrupting. "There are no identifiers on the actual pelts, and the sheer number of skins stolen indicates that whoever took them isn't after a domestic servant or worse. Additionally, all attempts at scrying have been unsuccessful, which Mr Larue believes is a sign they're still on the premises. Arcane Industries has wards in place to block second sight."

"Excuse me, dear," Mr Abercrombie said, "you lost me at wards and scrying."

"Wards are a stationary metaphysical construct that block incoming energy or hide areas from metaphysical detection." I waited for him to nod his understanding. "And scrying is a type of divination, wherein a witch can see lost objects or visions of the future. A reflective surface is generally used."

His thundercloud eyebrows lowered. "You're saying you still don't know where our son's fur is. That it's misplaced somewhere in your witches' tower?

"She's saying they've got no leads," Raeyn snapped.

The old man tapped his fingertips on the table. "Why are you here?"

I asked myself the same question.

Elton cut Mr Abercrombie a slice of cheesecake, then moved on to serve his mother.

"I'm here supporting your family because I recognise this is a difficult time, and that emails are cold comfort." I wouldn't let them see me shaken. "All staff members connected to the donation drive and everyone who worked that evening are being interviewed. All security footage is being reviewed. Access cards traced. I'm here to assure you that Arcane Industries is taking decisive action."

Raeyn sneered. "Instead of taking decisive action yourself."

Elton slid a slice to Raeyn, then bumped my elbow and pointed at the cake with his knife.

"No thank you, I'm dairy free."

Raeyn held a forkful to her lips. "Shame."

I swirled the dregs of my tar-coffee. Manners decreed that I swallow them, but if I drained the cup, Mrs Abercrombie might pour me another. My jaw ached. "Technically Raeyn, today is my day off, as was the day I met Elton at AI tower. This is a courtesy visit, made on my free time, without pay, because the comfort of your family is important to me." And because Liam Kendren insisted my personal touch would smooth relations between this family and the company. Was Raeyn's disdain for me personal? Did she dislike humans in general? Maybe she was projecting the anger she felt for herself onto me. Either way, coming here was a mistake. I slid my chair back from the table, careful not to scrape the feet on the tiles. "I deeply regret that my presence has done more harm—"

"Spare me, witch." Raeyn slapped another slice of cheesecake onto her plate and made for the door behind her.

Mrs Abercrombie watched her exit the cottage with a concerned expression, then turned to me. "I appreciate your visit. Please, don't feel unwelcome here."

It was a bit late for that.

I toed off my shoes and socks, dumped my jacket and scarf on the sofa, and found Dad in his home office, playing a computer game.

"What are you doing?" The words shot out of my mouth.

He spared me only a glance. The lounge room clock ticked three loud seconds.

"Uh, I mean... It's hot, can I get you a drink?" I said.

He indicated the glass of iced soft drink beside his keyboard. "I'm ganking people." He clicked frantically, dodging to the side as a missile flew toward his character. "Do we still say ganking?"

"I don't know, Dad." I flopped into one of the spare seats and waited until a scoreboard filled his screen.

"Something bothering you, Morri? How was your visit with the Abercrombies?"

"They pretty much hate me, except Elton, who arguably has the most right to hate me." I scratched at my sweaty scalp. "Went to the tower after, but Liam said I wasn't needed."

"Huh, I thought he had the weekend off. At any rate, I'm glad he sent you home. Don't you have a circle tonight?"

Damn, I did. Was it too late to cancel? No, that was just slack. They'd never organise a venue in time. Poe's was usually our coven's second home, but when we gathered there, we had to wait until after the twins were in bed to start the ritual, making for a very late night. I rubbed the back of my neck. "Dad, is there something more we could do? Have we called in any of the donors to give additional DNA to help with tracking?"

"Morri..."

"Elton was asking. After I left, he messaged that we should meet up without his family."

"Ah yes, he's offered his amateur detective services to me too. I switched my phone off."

My eyebrows dropped low, framing my vision orange. "Seriously?"

"Yes." He scooted his chair toward me. "We're all concerned, but it's important not to bring your work home. Not to let it taint your family life. If you internalise every case you take on, this job will destroy you."

"But time could be everything."

"Or it could be nothing. Some janitor moved the furs down to the basement thinking they were a seasonal decor thing. They come back from holiday leave in a few days, read their emails, and have the whole mess sorted by 10am. And then what? You've turned your hair grey and damaged your friendships by blowing your mates off for no reason."

"I enjoy helping people."

"So do I. And we'll help them on Monday. Leave your work at work."

As if I could. I fulfilled most of my contracts in bed at night.

He stood, glancing at his watch. "Do you have any ideas for dinner? Are we feeding your coven?"

Dinner turned out to be a nacho feast for around twenty people, as Mum had invited her friends over before their pre-Christmas drinks. We moved the dining table into Mum and Dad's bedroom to make floor space, and everyone ate standing. Bowls of toppings marched across the kitchen benches. It was crowded and loud, and I kept watch on Meddy, in case her anxiety spiked and she needed me to get her out.

"This cheese tastes like the real deal!" Faun exclaimed, plucking shreds from her bowl with her fingers, much to an older woman's chagrin. I hid my mirth behind a corn chip.

"Still equally as bad for you as the dairy version," Meddy reminded, right on cue. She'd sprinkled her nachos with nooch and extra garlic.

You could never have too much garlic, but I wasn't going to pass up an opportunity to rib her. I got a glob of melted cheese on my fork. "What'd you say?" I asked, laying the oily deliciousness on my tongue and rolling my eyes back in exaggerated bliss.

"Dead sexy." She shoved me playfully. "Nothing turns a woman on more than heart disease."

"Hey, I drink my tea with the antioxidants intact, thank you very much!"

She laughed, "That's not—"

"Ay, you pair," Indra stabbed the air with his bean-laden fork and thickened his Indian accent for effect. "I'm trying to enjoy these fart capsules in peace, thanks all the same."

He was as done-up as Mum's friends, with his crest freshly gelled, nails painted, and his silver jewellery polished.

"Ohmigawd." Eliss half-chuckled, half-choked, "You didn't just—" ze coughed, washed down zir mouthful with juice, then said, "Tell me you're not wooing Vanessa with your manly fart nuggets."

"Vanessa's not here, it's you I woo."

What would Elton make of my friends? Probably more than Mum's ladies did. They'd spread out into the lounge room to put space between themselves and us.

"Thinking of," Indra continued, "we're holidaying with Vanessa's parents over Christmas, then mine will join us for New Years. I'll be gone several weeks."

"Half your luck," Poe said. "My idea of a holiday is being alone in the bathroom for three minutes."

Viri casually rested his cheek against Poe's head while he chewed and swallowed. "So that's two of you abandoning us. Tazmin's camping down at Gundungurra"

Poe looked up at him. "You're not?"

"Nah. Mum's unwell. Lana went though. I practically threw her in the truck. She needs a break."

"Less exciting than a holiday." Faun scraped the last of her beans up with a chip. "But I'll be gone too. Got a job picking stone fruit at Forbes." Faun was the youngest member of our coven and busting to work. Not an easy feat for a weed-thin thirteen-year-old.

Eliss pulled a face. "Crappy way to spend your birthday."

"I'll buy myself a cupcake. At least I'll have money; they don't care I'm underage." Faun headed to the bench for seconds. "And a lot of those backpackers are super-hot."

An image of Elton—up a ladder, surrounded by leaves, blue sky peeking through from behind him—intruded on my thoughts with its absurdity. Imaginary Elton smiled. "Want to make sorbet later?" He wouldn't say it like that, though; his words had rhythm. Had he texted? I could duck into the toilet before circle and check. Not that our texts wouldn't be case related of course. And if they weren't, it wouldn't do me any good. My peers hadn't yet emerged from that phase where dating was a thinly veiled tactic to explore unfamiliar bodies; a pastime I shared no interest in. I wouldn't date for years yet, if ever. Perhaps I'd find a companion after retirement, when our parts stopped functioning. Then he'd share my desires: love and companionship. Snuggles, laughter, and a deep abiding respect for physical privacy. What would Elton be like in old age?

A hand flashed in front of my face, jerking me out of my revere.

"Welcome back," Brooke said.

Mum had left for her ladies' night, and it was quiet enough that ambient music—for ganking—reached us from Dad's office.

My cheeks heated. "Sorry. Thinking about work."

"I'm sure glad work makes you this happy."

Dad breezed into the room. "It's not the work." He wove between us to grab juice from the fridge. "It's the client!"

"Daaaaad!"

He chuckled, returning to his office.

Brooke quirked an eyebrow. "Speaking of, Elton's invited me to some sculpting class with him, you know? Like we're mates of old."

Guy was bold! What did he want with Brooke?

Poe and Viri carried the table back into the kitchen. As they set it down, Poe said, "Nothing suss."

"Right?" I agreed. I caught Brooke's gaze. "You gonna go?" I hoped I didn't look too eager for her to spend some time with Elton, to help me understand him better.

"Maybe." She shrugged one shoulder, then flipped her long blond hair and strode toward the hall and the covenstead beyond. "If I think up a good prank for him."

These Three

Kings

MORRIGAN

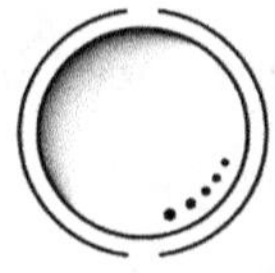

When I dragged my arse home after hitting the gym with Brooke Monday afternoon, Dad was torrid. The force of his agitation pinned me in place. I clutched my sneakers, unable to lift the lid of the storage bench and dump them in because even that much noise might be intrusive. His cheeks were mottled. He stood in the middle of the lounge room, holding Mums thin red hands, something furry curled in one of his palms. He clicked his jaw. She anchored, waiting for the first rock to proceed his avalanche. Or perhaps they both waited for me to leave.

The work line rang from his office. Mum tightened her hands on his, pulling them close.

"Felicia." Dad's expression was pleading. "I made assurances that their biggest fears would never occur on my watch." His voice shook. "But they have." Had he been acting tough for my benefit, or had he really believed a janitor had lost the furs?

The phone kept ringing. He glanced toward his office, undecided. Had something happened at Arcane Industries while I was working out?

"Leave it," Mum said.

"You're right," He embraced her. "What can I say to them?" He shook the scrap of fabric. Cream-coloured fur with black spots. She released him to pace our pristine, unused lounge room, passing where I hovered by the entranceway. "What do I train our girl to say to their justifiable anger?"

I shot Mum a look, hoping she might fill me in on what I'd missed. She held up her hand, palm out. *Just wait.*

She was in her office wear, probably hadn't got home long before me. "Our daughter isn't on this case."

He clenched his fists, resting them, then his forehead, on the false wall to the right of the front door. Beyond sat my baby sister's nursery, preserved all these years. I'd never been in there. I found the concealed latch once; that'd been the extent of my morbid curiosities. He tapped his head on the panel, sighed, then took his restless energy to the kitchen, where he made himself a cup of instant coffee.

Mum and I sat together at the table, waiting. I likely imagined Dad's approval, his silent acknowledgement of our support.

He stirred the coffee, having put in so many spoonfuls, my hair began to straighten from the fumes, then rested his backside against the bench, facing us. His spoon clinked inside the mug. *Tink. Tink. Tink.*

"Morrigan, you're correct. The Selkie skins are not in Arcane Industries' tower. I've checked every last cubicle, at the behest of Ms Moontread. That's how I found this." He held up the scrap. "This and Liam Kendren's old pass card, that's what we've got. Whoever stole the Selkie skins is cutting them up. The room I discovered this in—an un-used office at the end of the hall on Enchanted Glamour's level—smelled of chemicals - to clean and preserve would be my best guess. Perhaps to tan."

I sat straighter and tightened my core.

He scrunched his eyes shut a moment. *Tink Tink tink.* "The paper trail led me to the cubicle of the warlock in our midst. Fur the same colour as this covered his keyboard; his desk drawers too."

"Liam Kendren?"

The steam from dad's coffee gave the impression of smoke coming out his nostrils. "No. Your disdain of the man doesn't make him guilty."

I tried not to wince.

Dad took a deep whiff of coffee. "I sent samples of this fur and the desk fur to the lab for testing, but the mess in that spare room is incriminating." He tucked the scrap into his pocket, to better cradle the cup of undrinkably-strong instant. "Be patient with me; I want to see if you reach the same conclusions I did. The pass reader on Enchanted Glamour's floor recorded Ms Moontread as the only person moving around after hours the day the Abercrombies' skins came into our care. Earlier that morning, shipments arrived from Kati Thanda and Darwin. I hadn't set eyes on them personally—" made sense, Dad was a Municipal Liaison and ran on the board. He had no business accepting deliveries, "—but we're talking two tea chests, maybe more. I have records of the boxes being opened by Dan—runner Dan, you remember him? Now, those orders came through front desk during Leslie's shift, but she denies requesting the boxes unpacked."

Runner Dan made great drinks and ordered the finest pastries. His counterpart at Sneaky Witch wasn't half as good. Which was for the best. Meddy's favourite climbing gym had put in monkey bars and other arm-intensive activities; I didn't need to embarrass myself.

"And those lost deliveries from Perth? Not lost at all. The courier emailed me proof they'd been signed for." He swept a hand through his hair, then bounced that fist on the bench top in frustration. "The signature was Ms Moontread's. She doesn't remember signing."

I frowned. "So, Ms Moontread is the thief?" And everything we worked for was a lie? No. "What about the security footage?"

Dad stirred his instant some more, trying to dig a hole in the mug with his spoon. "That's the thing. The lobby camera picked up a mere two seconds of footage. Someone in a wide-brim Akubra, oversized trench coat, and scarf—in the middle of bloody summer!—shut the door and slipped straight into the blind spot, knowing it was there. The under-awning camera showed the hand holding the key. To me, it didn't look as withered as Ms Moontread's. But the image is pixelated to hades."

Mum drew a random pattern on the table with her finger, using a thread of her energy to light it up. "Do I have access to the footage?"

"No love, but I can show you on my machine."

I needed to call my supervisor at Sneaky Witch, if Dad hadn't already. But if Ms Moontread was truly at fault, would using a child company of AI to investigate her be the wisest course? I tugged the hair at my temple. "How tall was the thief?"

Dad lowered his brows. "Average height. Taller than Ms Moontread, but it's easy to fudge a few inches with a hat and boots."

"It's not Silver." Mum used our boss's first name. "I don't buy it. She's the CEO for crying out loud."

She was also in her eighties. She seemed fit, but hauling mounds of heavy furs?

"I don't want to think that of her either," Dad agreed. "And though the pass reader recorded Ms Moontread accessing Enchanted Glamour after hours, the reader by storage room 270 said only Liam and Dan entered that room."

I opened my mouth to speak.

Dad held one hand palm out, "Don't get excited. Liam had mentioned he needed to get a new card from IT. If I was going to break into my place of employment, I'd use a lost card I found on the floor instead of my own."

"Was there any other footage?"

"Basement car park, elevators, fire escape. I've checked them all. Nobody dressed out-of-season left the building, nor did any laundry trolley, tea chests, or other shipment-sized equipment. I assessed the faces of every person and group exiting. None of them were Dan or Liam. And neither Silver nor Dan worked the Saturday we discovered the furs missing."

I fidgeted with my bracelets. "And we gave Liam a lift that morning. He wasn't there before opening."

"Right."

Mum's doodling turned to list-keeping. The details her finger traced onto the table glowed softly against the damaged wood. "Have you spoken to IT?"

"No, that slipped my mind. We need to do that." Dad set the still full cup on the bench but didn't join us at the table. "Following that train of thought, what if Kendren's card wasn't lost, but stolen? Bruce Morwen, Kendren's assistant, shares Kendren's office but also works out of his own cubicle. He left the tower six separate times that Friday afternoon. He had his backpack and briefcase each time. Four trips to the car park and two out the front door."

I sucked a breath past my teeth. "He smuggled the skins out a couple at a time?"

Mum made a thoughtful noise and wrote *Bruce Morwen* on the table. "Leslie complained he kept popping by reception for small things all day."

"I bet he was waiting for an opportunity to log the request that Dan open the shipment," I said in a rush.

"Has he been interviewed?" Mum tapped the table with her jewel encrusted nail. She'd gone all out for Litha with purple polish and garnet diamantes.

"Not yet." Dad massaged the wrinkles on his forehead. "I've emailed all those I recognise from the footage with an appointment time tomorrow, and I've sent screenshots of those I don't recognise to you, love, in the hopes you can match them to their employee files."

To her credit, Mum didn't groan at the huge task the way I'd have done.

Dad continued, "But Morwen's on leave this week." The muscle in his jaw flexed. "I suspect he's not returning."

Mum lit Morwen's column in orange. "Easy access to Liam's card. Frequent trips to his car. Leslie's testimony. Convenient holiday." There wasn't much in Silver's column, but it was still there, glowing faintly blue on the table's surface. Her signature on a delivery reported missing, accessing odd floors after hours.

But Morwen was such a nice old guy. Clean. Completed his work without a fuss. Respected personal space. "What's his motive, then? And what about Liam Kendren's tanty?" The words ate their way out of my mouth. "I've never seen him act so highly strung. You have to admit it was suspicious."

Dad didn't admit a damn thing, he just stood there glaring at me.

I elaborated. "His reaction was so fast, like he'd prepared for it. He didn't want us to search. He seemed panicked - caught out."

"He was panicked, Morrigan. I was panicked! This is worth panicking over." Was he implying I wasn't taking this seriously enough? He looked at Mum. "I've requested PIs from Sneaky Witch—day trackers—and CC'd you. Sneaky Witch will conduct the interviews."

Mum had made Liam Kendren a list and written *tantrum* underneath. "I'll coordinate with whoever they send us, and I'll contact IT."

"Thank you."

The phone in Dad's office trilled.

The conversation was closing against my will. "Why would Morwen take them? Why would Ms Moontread? Answers are found within motives."

Mum wrote *retiring soon* on Bruce Morwen's list. "Maybe he's unsatisfied with his long-service pay-out and this is his chance to take his retirement to the next level. There's a market for exotic furs, if he's been tanning them. There's a buyer for pretty much everything." Mum pursed her lips. "For all that he rubs you the wrong way, Liam has always advocated for the ocean. He's a conservationist. He's volunteered for fundraisers and home-building projects and donation drives for the Selkie community. Don't forget it was Liam that ran the bycatch information evening, and he oversees our monthly beach clean-up parties. He's not their enemy."

"I've worked with Mr Kendren forever." Dad sighed. "Why would he pour effort into designing presentations, running petitions and submitting essays detailing improvements he wants AI to make if his master plan was to become a smuggler? At any rate, the paper-trail leads to Mr Morwen. Everything else is fluff. It's Morwen." Dad picked up the still-full coffee, strangling it. "And he's skipped town. Probably cutting up more priceless donations."

I glanced at Mum's lists and tapped the table. "It was Liam who insisted we—"

"Morrigan." Dad flexed his jaw again and his nostrils flared. "You are letting bias blind you."

"No, you're completely ignoring my intuition because you want me to stay your baby!"

He didn't seem to hear me. "On the strength of one man not in control of his emotions, by the old Gods. One man's tanty. I'll give you a damn tanty!" Dad's arm extended at shoulder height. Staring me down, he tipped the cup. Liquid frustration poured forth; splattering the floor, table leg, oven, and the wall. "Patience has abandoned me, Morrigan. Men have feelings. And I have this mess to clean." He righted his cup and placed it in the sink, then gestured to the two available exits. "If you please…"

Mum and I fled upstairs.

"You weren't fair on him back there," she said, pausing at the door to the rooftop patio as I reached for my doorknob. "When have we ever babied you?"

Done with talking, I shut myself in my bedroom and flopped down for a nap. I'd be working tonight, digging into the truth of a family law dispute for Sneaky Witch. Dream travel wasn't restful. Best to recharge now.

The sky was dark when Dad came into my room. The grumble of my stomach suggested I'd slept past dinner. He'd changed into his gym tights and a long-sleeved black shirt, looking somewhere between a man misplaced in time and a burglar.

"You robbing a bank?" A heartbeat later, my brain woke up and I tensed. Was he still mad from before? Would my joke set him off?

Cracking a grin, he replied, "Maybe. You want to come?"

"Belinda agreed with you," Dad said. I assumed he meant my manager at Sneaky Witch, Ms Coolman, and not the kid he'd hired to tend the garden once a month. "Without further evidence against Bruce Morwen, it's an unfortunate case of 'bad optics'. Nothing more." He parked in the visitor's area of a posh residential estate I had fuzzy memories of. I'd been here, but the why and when escaped me.

"So, we're doing what? Arresting him?"

"No!" Dad gave me the cobra face. "Sweet sheets Morri, we're here to prove his innocence."

"By breaking in?"

"Exactly."

I slow-blinked until he elaborated.

"If he's been honest about his vacation, nobody's going to be home. If not, maybe we'll find a stack of skins in the kitchen, shipping boxes awaiting a courier, or documentation pointing to his purpose."

Or maybe Morwen was taking a staycation and we'd find him on the lounge in his undies, eating chips, oblivious to work-related drama.

We shut our doors as quietly as possible and kept to the shadows as we approached Morwen's house. Ten o'clock wasn't really that late, but the windows were dark. I checked over my shoulder again, sure a car would drive into the estate any second.

Dad hugged the hedge as he flitted across the grass. "We'll cut up the side of the yard and hop the railing at the porch to avoid triggering the security light."

Security? "What about an alarm?" I hissed, grabbing for his shirt and missing as he leapt the wooden rail. His feet thudded on the decking.

He smiled as I clambered over, my shorter legs sticking out every which way, then produced a key from within a plastic rock. "I cared for his cat one time."

"Uh-huh."

In a moment, we were in. Retro Christmas lights tinted the lounge room. The security alarm beeped unnervingly, confirming the Morwens weren't home. Dad keyed the code into the pin pad as I locked the door behind us.

"I'm going to head upstairs to his office." Dad flicked on the stairwell light. "You dig around down here—carefully, mind!—look for travel itineraries—that might clear his name—or anything related to Selkies that might incriminate him. Keep an eye out for phone bills and business cards." He disappeared up the stairs, stopping my heart with "Well hello, John!"

A bell tinkled.

I took a steadying breath and caught a whiff of catnip. If Dad was at all concerned Bruce Morwen would bust us, he hid it well.

The Morwens had a landline on a phone stand. I snapped photos of every piece of paper I happened across, from invoices to post-it notes. Then I rifled through the pockets of coats hanging from the antique hat-stand in the corner. Morwen reminded me a bit of Meddy; old-fashioned even among his own generation.

An ugly mustard coat produced folded insurance papers for a rental van. The dates pegged it for pick-up tomorrow morning. A low whistle escaped me. What did Brian Morwen need with a large, hired vehicle, on Christmas Eve, when he was supposed to be vacationing? At the top sat the licence plate number. I snapped a photo. What else must he have taken, if he needed to rent a van to haul it all? Maybe he'd been smuggling from AI for decades.

I kept searching, putting everything back where I found it, but came across nothing else before Dad returned, a fluffy cream cat on his heels.

"Can you please gather in while I check the kitchen?"

I nodded and then cast the spell, removing the lingering traces of our presence, eager to return to the car and show Dad what I'd uncovered.

At ten past nine, I woke in a panic and ran downstairs with one sock on, yelling for Dad. I passed the bathroom and slipped, arms windmilling, into the kitchen.

Mum hid her grin behind her mug. "He already left." On the table in front of her sat the smallest cauldron I'd ever seen. In place of a handle, it had a long silver chain for wearing. Wisps of green smoke puffed from within.

"But Bruce Morwen's got the skins in the rental truck and we—"

"Woah." Mum held up her hands as if to deflect a projectile. "I know. Your Dad and I talk. It's fine. Belinda worked her magick at the rental company. Those trucks have tracking devices "

"So, Dad's gone after the truck? Not alone, surely."

"What are you talking about?" Mum slid her chair back and stood to face me. "The rental manager mentioned Bruce being excited for his new property at The Entrance, and GPS puts him on the Pacific Motorway. We can assume that's where he's going."

"But we should stop him before he gets there! I was at his house; he's clearly not packing to move."

"Ground yourself, love. We'd only take that kind of direct action if the proof was irrefutable."

How wasn't this irrefutable? I grabbed a hunk of my hair, steadying myself as the last of the haze in my brain burned off. Mum embraced me.

"It's okay," she murmured. "Your dad's got this."

I released my scalp to hug her back. There was nobody I trusted more than Dad, not even Meddy, but this was my case. I couldn't just sit back and do nothing. Or worse, deal with Liam Kendren's email asking why I hadn't logged any time this week visiting Selkies in their dreams.

"I've got a date with Meddy this morning," I fibbed, "then I'll head into the office. Hopefully, by noon, there'll be some concrete way to help."

Mum rubbed my upper arms vigorously, then planted a kiss on my third eye. "Whatever you need, just make sure you're getting paid for your time. Wish Medusa a Merry Christmas Eve for me." She shooed Miriam, one of our black, domestic shorthairs, away from the tiny cauldron. "Is she celebrating Christmas this year?"

"Hey, thanks for hanging out at such short notice."

Meddy settled into the passenger seat, dumped her bag between her feet and slammed the door. "'Short notice' would have been last night. This is 'spur of the moment.'"

"That, then." I merged into the light Tuesday traffic. "I appreciate it. Mum says Merry Christmas."

"Don't remind me. Dad's dragging me to Midnight Mass tonight."

Meddy's parents thought she was still finding herself, dabbling in Islam and Wicca after which she'd ultimately return to Jesus. It was a safe belief for them to cling to while Meddy lived under their roof.

"So where are we going?" she asked.

"On an adventure, as Poe would say."

Meddy shot me a look and I sighed.

"The Selkie skins are in a removalist van heading up the Pacific Motorway to The Entrance. We're going to intercept them."

"But the van has already left?"

My cheeks heated. "Dad has no intention of doing anything with the information."

"But you can't just sit around."

"Exactly."

"Do we have a plan?"

"I dunno, Meddy. Do we?"

She pulled a notepad and pen from the back of her planner. "Tell me everything we know."

Bruce Morwen might have had a head-start, but we hadn't needed to fill any paperwork or load stolen goods. Not knowing where the skins had been stored for the weekend, Meddy concluded we'd have to ambush him at his destination, which hadn't been too difficult to determine.

Oz Real Estate kept a web page dedicated to recent sales. Only three newly sold properties in The Entrance weren't units. As the Morwens' lived in a two-story house in Dover Heights, one of the most expensive suburbs in Sydney, a reasonable downsize would be a single-story waterfront home, not an apartment. Besides, one of the properties was a discreet bayside fixer-upper; exactly the kind of place I'd buy if I was going into shady business. I drove faster than strictly legal to beat Bruce Morwen to the cul-de-sac where the house was located, enjoying Meddy's company.

I pulled over. "Hop out."

Sprawling new homes shared the single-lane street with older, more modest dwellings. All had front lawns or gardens, some unfenced. Between the houses to my right, I caught glimpses of sparkling blue coast. A few cars lined the street and sat in driveways further along, but I had the road to myself. "I'll park a few blocks away and jog back here, all right?"

"I'll meet you..." Meddy cast around, then pointed. "There, under that bottle brush." The wild native hung over a dilapidated fence a little way ahead. "I'll make sure the van isn't already parked out the front."

"You know the plates?"

She flashed her inner wrist, where she'd scrawled both the plate number and the address.

"Nice."

I chucked a Uey the moment she hopped out.

Not five minutes later, I clutched the stitch in my side as I stumble-ran the last half-block to where Meddy crouched, completely concealed by the flowering bottle brush tree. She withdrew her hand from under her head-scarf as I ducked in beside her, and I tried not to think about the snakes living under there. Yuck.

"We either beat him here, or he's made the drop and gone. Place is nicer than in the photo. Artsy studio vibes." Her cheek sucked in where she chewed it.

"Let's wait a bit."

Meddy settled in. "To confirm: if he comes, I stop the truck. Then when he goes to get help from his crime buddies at the house, we'll grab the Selkie skins?"

"Right. Try to stop the van about there." I pointed at a lavish brick home with a wide lawn and matching brick fence about a metre tall. "We'll dump the skins behind that fence. With any luck, the removalist van will be between us and Morwen, providing cover. We'll have to make several trips."

"That's someone's home."

"It's a workday. You can't buy a house like that on a single income."

"It's also the festive season." She studied the road a moment, weighing the risks. "We should've asked Brooke along to unlock the truck."

"Damn it." I slapped my knee in irritation. Too late now. We'd have to hope Bruce Morwen left his keys in the ignition.

When we were both clear on the plan and my restlessness became unbearable, I jogged to the corner and stopped in the shade of a bus stop on the adjacent street, and fished out my phone. Splitting up kept me safe. I didn't want to distract Meddy or get caught in the cross-fire of her powers. I'd just pressed *call,* when a maxi taxi rounded the corner, catching me unprepared. I'd expected a cube truck or some such. Bruce Morwen had the window rolled down; his forearm sunburnt where it rested on the door.

"He's here!" I squeaked, ducking behind the bus shelter's advertisement panel. My ancient Gods, why hadn't I at least worn a hat to hide my bright orange hair? What if he recognised me? It wasn't like we didn't work in the same building. He'd seen me at every other office function and Yule party since before I could walk.

I peeked around the corner in time for the van's back tyres to become stone, cracking the tarmac as they rolled on down the road; slowed but not stopped.

Seriously?

Morwen leaned out his window, swearing. Meddy Flint-stoned the front tyres too. A bus I hadn't signalled pulled over to my corner.

I put my back to it, but the door opened anyway.

"Lass?" The driver called.

I spoke over my shoulder. "Sorry, wrong bus."

"This is the only bus on this route." He looked me up and down. "Where you headed?"

"Uh, never mind. I think I'm confused. Big party last night." I rubbed my head for effect, wishing I'd thought to say I was just enjoying the shade. "Thanks anyway." I ambled into the cul-de-sac.

Twenty odd metres away, Meddy threw open the van's backend. Morwen had left the vehicle, not even shutting the driver's door. Perfect. I put on a burst of speed.

"Oh no, no no no," Meddy chanted, backing up past me as I huffed to a stop. She hugged herself, looking like she was about to vomit, but it wasn't the sight of seal leather handbags or half-cured skins that sent her into a spiral. Materials designed for kitchen instalment stared back at us. Complete with double-sided metal sink.

Meddy hissed. "He's coming."

"Go!" I shoved her to get her moving and stretched up to close the boot.

"Leave it!" She grabbed my wrist to haul me away.

She was right. If Bruce saw the boot open, he might pause to check everything was there instead of giving chase. Hopefully. Keeping the van between him and us, we made it to the footpath.

I squatted behind a parked car. "Turn the wheels back!"

Meddy's eyes bugged out of her head. "You know I can't!"

We crouch-ran into the nearest front garden. "I thought you'd been working on it."

The rattle of a trolley was followed by cussing and a woman's exclamations of awe over the four solid tyres. We scurried along the side of the house. When we reached the backyard—thankfully devoid of pets—we climbed the fence, crossing into another yard and from there into a parallel street, to make the long, circuitous route to my car. My hands shook and I swallowed a cackle. Meddy pressed her lips tight and hugged her middle.

Morwen would report our rogue magick to AI for sure. It was only a matter of time before my parents heard the story of the rental van's stone wheels and concluded Meddy and I were to blame. I needed to get home and fess up.

As we arrived at my car, my phone vibrated. I dug it out alongside my keys. It was Dad.

'The Selkie skin sample doesn't match the fur on Morwen's keyboard. That's cat hair.'

I smacked my forehead on the car roof in frustration.

ELTON

I grabbed a soft drink from the display fridge and placed it on the conveyor belt.

"Uhm, what else?" Brooke asked herself, tucking a wayward strand of sunshine-gold hair behind her ear. "Oh, always message before you arrive at her house, otherwise she'll probably be naked."

"I wouldn't mind." I laughed at her hyperbole. "But please, guide me true."

"I'm full serious, it's a Wiccan thing. I dropped in on Morr on a Saturday morning once and Felicia, her mum, was doing some nude yoga on the roof."

"You're Wiccan too, is this something you do?" I asked.

"We're an all-girl household, we have the same parts."

When I'd purchased our drinks, we left the crowded shopping complex, weaving through the last-minute holiday rush, heading for Sydney's best soapstone studio, Rockin' Polish. The sun blasted down. I imagined stretching on the beach, my body joining sand to the sky. Instead Brooke and I were hitting it off like we'd done this a hundred times. I'd have called her a social butterfly, but butterflies don't slip plastic bugs into your drink when you weren't looking.

Turning onto a quieter street brought me an opportunity to ask, "What, pray tell, be my chances she'll consent to a date? Morrigan, that is, not her mo—"

Brooke gave me flat stare. "Really, Elton? Really? You're not gonna continue pretending that this isn't a fact-finding mission about my friend?"

The flowers on the council strip provided no reprieve. My face aflame, I fumbled to deny.

"The stereotype is true then," Brooke said. "You lust after the human maids; break their hearts. Free some from unhappy homes?"

"Salt, no!" Fire burbled through my torso. "Morrigan is no conquest. She's... I swear she hears my heart song."

"Morr doesn't date. Let's head that off at the pass."

"I—"

Brooke held up a hand, stalling my rebuttal. "She gets me too; I know how you feel. She doesn't care we're not entirely human. Or I suppose in your case, not human at all. I would date her if I swung for women! But I've known her since she was thirteen, Elton, and she's never dated. I've never seen her flirt with anyone other than Medusa, and I reckon that's an in-joke. There's no attraction there."

So, they weren't sisters then. Morrigan had mentioned Medusa in her texts; I'd definitely gotten more of a family vibe than a flirty one.

"She doesn't have a dream wedding dress," Brooke said. "She's never had a celebrity crush..."

But Morrigan would have told me outright if she didn't date. If she wasn't interested, why did I have the sense she was? We reached Rockin' Polish.

Brooke hammered her point home. "She doesn't so much as understand why nakedness is sexual. Why being nude during circle differs from being nude at the doctor's or taking a shower. Be her friend, let her help you, play with magick together, whatever. But if you're hoping for a summer romance before you return to sea, you've swum into the wrong harbour."

I held open the studio door and ushered her in, neither agreeing nor disagreeing. Cool air and stone dust greeted us. I rented a workbench in the artist studios upstairs, but for today I'd booked Brooke and I into a guided workshop, beginner style. Brooke's acrylic nails said she didn't work with her hands all that often. We settled into our seats, waiting while the instructor welcomed the rest of the attendees.

As a kid, Papa would tell us enchanting stories featuring stone carvings at the bottom of the ocean. Great monoliths, sculptures that stretched for miles. Raeyn and I dreamed of visiting them together, back before we understood she wasn't like me and would never dive into the depths. She hadn't carved with me since, and I'd let her think my fascination had died alongside that fantasy.

Doubt's insidious tentacles writhed inside me, worming their way around my core. If Morrigan and her team of witches failed me, mine and Raeyn's futures would once again converge.

Then what? I pictured us doing a roast at our parents' house. Tried to imagine a future where I'd be grateful for what she'd done to me. Where I'd forgiven her mistake. Eventually, I'd have to. Maybe if I summoned the same career drive as humans tended to and fell in love with camping or abseiling. If I had human children and they loved their school and their cousins and sewing little Faery Scouts badges to their uniforms. Morrigan might teach me to forget the ocean, given time.

My face grew hot and I loosened my collar. It was crazy and embarrassing to be caught in ponder, we hardly knew one another. Settling down with a witch my family disliked, a girl who didn't date? Brooke said Morrigan didn't eat fish, or any meat at all. Morrigan and I had naught in common. I'd mistaken her professional courtesy for attraction.

And yet...

Brooke put on her dust mask and clear goggles. "You going to make her a gift?"

I feigned innocence. "Who? Mother?"

"What? No. Morrigan."

"A thank you gift? Indeed, she will have earned one when my fur returns to me." When she discovered where the furs had been taken and who had taken them. If they hadn't been sold onward. Or altered. Or destroyed. Cold sweat dampened my hairline. I focused on the instructor like I needed this lesson more than breath.

Soon, we were carving. The stone exposed its secrets, and my panic receded. I would do as I'd always done—live it up while I waited for my real life to begin.

Throughout the afternoon, I peppered Brooke with questions, not only about Morrigan, but what she knew of AI, about herself and about their coven—the things she was allowed to reveal anyway.

"I met Morrigan through AI." Brooke said. "Kind of. She fell into my dream and helped me escape the angry hor—actually, never mind that." Brooke brushed the conversation off with a flick of her tiny hands, sending up an equally small cloud of dust. "There were five people in our coven, including me, when I joined. Morrigan, Poe, Viridis, and a witch named Taliesin who moved away that same year. Said not to keep contact. The magick, the synchronicities... It was too much for them."

The name rang a bell. I wondered if Brooke had brought Taliesin to a faery gathering some time. I changed to a file, having coaxed a rough fish shape from the stone. Scales would provide some challenge to this beginner lesson. "Any other fae folk in your coven?"

"Yeah, Oberon. You remember him? Spiky blond hair, pale skin, effeminate voice?"

"Wears skinny jeans. Short?" I had fond childhood memories of Oberon. It was fitting he'd joined a coven.

"That's him." She put her tools down to glare at her sculpture, a simple sleeping puppy.

I nudged the best rasp for the job toward her and she took it up.

Come All Ye Faithful

MORRIGAN

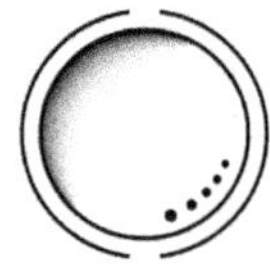

Raeyn Abercrombie was nothing like her brother. She could've used some poetry in her texts to soften her endless disdain. Manners wouldn't have gone astray either.

I stopped outside my front door and replied. *'Anything I tell you at this point would be speculation. When we have something concrete, I'll contact you immediately.'* I really wanted to say 'get off my arse' but there were rules.

The door was unlocked but Dad wasn't in his office. Nor the kitchen, his bedroom, or the back garden. I discovered Mum on the roof patio, talking to her Blue Star Jasmine. She didn't garden as much as Dad, but she had a select few "plant babies" that were hers alone.

"Have you seen Dad?"

She cupped a flower in her hand, but the tone of her voice changed, lifting to a false youth. "'Hi Mum, how are you?' 'Good, but I miss my daughter,'" she used her own voice to imitate herself. "'she only ever wants her dad. At least Medusa visits m—'"

"Mum!" My bare feet slapped the flagstones. "It's not like that."

She sniffed the flower and let it re-join the whole. "Feelings don't have to make sense."

"They just are." She'd been telling me my whole life. "You look tired."

"Good. I'd hate to look something I'm not."

I took her in my arms, hugging her light frame. She was fitter than me, more wiry. Did I feel soft and vulnerable to her? "You're right though. We haven't spent much time together. I'll be home for dinner, at least."

The skin around her eyes still drooped, but the rest of her face lifted. "Let's order in then. Your Dad won't be home."

"Girl's night!" Something she said earlier clicked in my brain. "Wait... have you been hanging out with Meddy?"

Mum wrapped her arm over my shoulder and steered me toward the deck chairs. "Not intentionally. I just find her in the kitchen randomly, and I'm hardly going to ignore her. She has a lot of questions about Wicca and her powers, and it's nice that she turns to me. Coming to witchcraft late isn't something you and Matthias relate to."

"Mmm, I suppose." Meddy looking after Mum took the pressure off me. I'd never been quite enough for two parents. "I do need to talk to Dad though. To both of you."

She lounged on her deck chair, pulling her straw hat low over her eyes. I perched on the side of mine while I filled her in on my morning's grand failure. Her lips twitched and danced when I got to the part where Meddy stoned the van's tyres, but she didn't interrupt. When I finished, she let out a long exhale. "Thank you for telling me."

That was mum-code for *I want to throttle you.*

I fiddled with my bracelets while she digested everything. My phones buzzed in my pockets. The hot tub's cover was firmly in place, luckily, because the urge to toss them in and be done taunted me.

"Were you seen?" Mum asked.

"I'll do a card reading to confirm, but I don't think so. The street was pretty quiet. The bus driver saw me, but he'd only be questioned if the police got involved, and Morwen won't call the cops."

She shook her head. "No, he'd recognise it for witch business. At worst, he'd contact Independent Coven Review, but seeming they never prosecuted Meddy for retaliating against Ceannas, I doubt they'll be able to track the tyres back to her. And if they did? No one was hurt." She took off her shirt and wiped her sweaty face with it.

Meddy wouldn't be concerned about whatever fine the ICR might dish out so much as the discovery of her powers. Neither of us knew what ICR—or even AI—would do if they knew she was lethal, but it wouldn't be good.

Mum tossed her shirt in the direction of the patio door and resettled her hat. "That said, if Bruce describes either of you to Arcane Industries, it won't take a crystal ball to divine you girls are the culprits."

I mashed my face with my hands. "That occurred to me. Not the stuff about ICR, but the rest." I snatched my hands away from my face to sanitise them, then sanitised my forehead and cheeks where I'd been rubbing. "It scares me. I love my job. Our company. Even now with everything going on."

"Don't put that on your face, Morrigan. You need good bacteria for healthy skin." Mum scrutinised me from under her hat. "Do what you can to make it right, before you talk to your dad. His plate is full. Word won't get back to him today, I should think. Half the office took the day off."

Right, because it was Christmas Eve. That bought me a grace period of a few hours at least. "Thanks Mum. I'll get started." I stood and went for the door, then thought better of it and returned to plant a kiss on the top of her hat. "I appreciate you. Sorry if I don't show it enough."

She squeezed my hand. "Talk to you at dinner."

It was blissfully cool inside. I stopped on the landing between my bedroom and the stairs to let my eyes adjust. Magdalene came up, mewing, and rubbed against my ankles. When I bent over to pat her, she ran for the patio door and mewed again.

"That's all I am to you people." I went and held the door for her. Emmanuel tore across the carpet and bolted past us, out into the sunshine. Would my parents let me take any of the cats when I finally moved out? If whatever rental I got allowed pets.

Heading downstairs, I checked my phones, expecting more grief from Raeyn. Instead, Liam Kendren had sent me a link to a research paper published by Mages Anon, AI's Canadian counterpart. *Thought you'd find this interesting.* The title was *Otherkin return home thanks to medical development* and nothing in his tone exuded his usual arrogance. I'd read it later, when I needed a feel-good story.

Viri and Brooke had both messaged my personal mobile.

'Can I invite Elton to Boxing Day's circle?' Brooke sent.

Viri's text was easier to deal with, so I hit reply to that one first. He'd run out of slippery elm bark and wanted to know a substitute.

'I'd use Burdock. Or dandelion leaf, short term.'

I badly needed a nap. I rummaged in the kitchen for something to snack on while I figured out my damage-control strategy. The corn chips and salsa positively had my name on them, and I hovered between them and the container of lychees. Though most of my private investigator work was carried out in other people's dreams, my physical fitness mattered. My strength mattered. The ability to summon almost any object into a dreamscape was limited by my real life ability to use it. I couldn't keep up with a car chase if I couldn't drive, or replace a ship rat if I didn't have the muscle to climb rigging. My job required me to follow wherever a client or mark's dream went, find the truth, and bring myself out alive. I glared at the lychees, slapping them onto the table. Meddy would be proud of me. She'd begun studying to be a nutritional scientist before most of our grade knew which high school they'd attend, and her voice spoke in the back of my mind as I fetched a bowl for the salsa. "If you're craving something, eat it. Even if it's a red-light food. But before you do, eat a salad. The salad might fill you and then you don't want the red-light anymore, but even if you're not that lucky, you've eaten a salad, so you still win."

Salad required effort, but fruit was a good choice. Maybe I ought to ask Meddy about Elton coming to our circle. Or Poe— she'd be hosting.

I navigated back to Brooke's message and sent, *'Have you asked Poe? It's her house.'* then portioned out some chips and settled in to peel lychees.

Did I want Elton to come to circle? I wanted to see him. And hear our incantations in his musical voice. I'd been fairly successful keeping my friends separate from my work life, a massive endeavour, considering Brooke had been my first client, Meddy worked for Enchanted Glamour—one of AI's child companies—and Viri was on our payroll. Arcane Industries had a financial safety net for witches who, due to their magickal abilities or spiritual service to the community, found themselves unable to hold down regular jobs. Poe had also freelanced for AI a time or two. But Elton sharing our sacred space was different, some-how.

Lychee juice ran down my arm, drying into sticky trails as sweetness blossomed over my tongue. Brooke was al-ready Wiccan when I met her; her inclusion hadn't invad-ed anyone's privacy. But Meddy wasn't Wiccan when she started attending circles. The skin on my forearms clung to the table each time I rested them, grating on me like my thoughts. Meddy was doing spells with us before her initiation. In a huff, I took the lychee skins to the bin, wiped down the table, and washed the lychee juice off my skin.

If anyone had asked, I'd have said I was following Dad's advice, trying not to bring my work home, but I couldn't twist it like that for myself. Unlike Australia's current pollies, Arcane Industries was a governing body I believed in. We actively improved people's lives. Some structure and regulation were healthy. We had our own charities. Stocks. Superannuation. We had our own lawyers. Scientists. Doctors. Priests. And in AI's child companies, we had so much more. Sneaky Witch Private Investigators had day walkers—who used regular investigator training combined with specialised forms of divination—and night walkers, hedge witches like me, who astral travelled or moved through people's dreams. We decoded recurring nightmares, unravelled hexes, and soothed the faery beings who lived in those planes of existence. Enchanted Glamour, the branch Meddy worked for as a social media influencer, produced powerful cosmetics that drastically altered a witch's appearance and brought a touch of magick to the broader community. Aradia's Sacred Gardens specialised in horticulture, protecting and recreating faeries natural environments. As a company, we had heaps to be proud of, and working there was intrinsic to my identity. Yes, some things needed improvement and I pushed for those changes when possible. But I was glad my friends finally knew what I did.

Elton probably wouldn't understand that. I snapped a corn chip in half. His family thought witches untrustworthy. He saw me as, what? Professional, I hoped. Capable. A wild creature tamed, perhaps. If he joined us in a casual setting, would that damage his perception of me? Of AI? I stirred the salsa with a chip. Hanging out casually would certainly make things more complicated.

"If you're going to practise pyrokinesis on the salsa, maybe take it outside?" Mum joked. How long had she been watching me daydream?

I shoved the soggy chip into my face and covered my mouth with my hand to talk. "Just thinking. Brooke wants to invite Elton to a circle."

"What do you want?"

"To say yes. But also to do the appropriate thing, which is probably not saying yes."

She went to her Thermomix on the counter and looked in. Its emptiness confirmed, she began piling spices into the metal bowl. "You're not on the Abercrombie's case. He's not your client. And after what you and Meddy did to

Bruce's rental this morning, there's no way you'll be signed on." She held her palm out to stop me arguing. "Hey, don't. You wouldn't hire you after that stunt either."

I crammed a whole handful of chips into my mouth. The salt stung my lips. She didn't have to be so right.

"All I'm saying is, if you want to see him casually, see him. I'm not stupid enough to think you've never had Elouera do spells on the side that benefit whatever case you're working on." She pitted a couple of dates and threw them in with the spices.

"Do you think he wants us for our magick? Is that why he's randomly asked to hang with Brooke?"

Expression indecipherable, she scrutinised me as she crossed to the fridge for some milk. Finally, she said, "You won't know what he wants until you ask." The carton gurgled as she poured it. "What are you doing to rectify this morning's mistakes?"

My face warmed at the mention of what I should've been agonising over. "I've got to pay for new tyres. But if I do it online or over the phone, the rental company will have my name. Shitsticks. I'll need to go in person, before Morwen returns." I pictured the stone tyres clunking down the pacific motorway. "Before the tow truck gets to the rental place, too, I suppose. I'll have to leave money to cover that, somehow. But I'll also need to alter my appearance." My curls were too wild for a wig, but Meddy kept a spare hijab here. And I had Enchanted Glamour samples. Hopefully they weren't expired. I was on my feet and halfway out of the kitchen before the crumbs on the table and empty salsa bowl got my attention.

Mum shooed me. "I'll do it. Go."

The bliss of resting permeated my being as I sank into my mattress. I didn't have a PI assignment tonight and it'd been a crazy long day. Christmas music drifted at the edge of my awareness, buoyed by the collective excitement of children dreaming.

Tomorrow night, we'd have a barbeque on the lawn, welcoming anyone who wandered in, as per our tradition.

Would I have a chance to hit the post-Christmas sales with Viri and Brooke this year?

Crashing ocean waves swallowed the Christmas music.

I walked out of the shopping centre onto a warm sandy beach where the absurdness had me pause and pinch my nose shut.

It did nothing to hamper my breathing. That confirmed it: I was asleep. In a dream that, judging from the clothes

I wore—shorts from which the bottom of my butt cheeks hung exposed—wasn't mine.

I willed myself into a baby-blue sun dress.

What brought me here?

A colony of seals basked on the sand nearby.

Holding my focus, I wandered down to the water. My footfalls left no prints. The utter lack of other humans was both unnerving and wondrous. I'd never have this opportunity in the waking world. Where was the dreamer, then? Was it a seal? Had I slipped into this dream by accident—a rooky mistake I rarely made these days—or had I been drawn here?

With nothing better to do, I imagined a stick in my hand and wrote my name in the sand. Then I skipped through the surf, singing. The seals didn't mind my choice of ancient song, à la Medusa Capatos. A song about riding horses; though if it was intended for lovers, or from a dad to his daughter, I wasn't sure.

I jumped the next wave that rolled in. Cool water splashed over my knees.

A giggle interrupted my song. In the way of dreams, I assumed it was my own, until the dreamer began to sing with me, revealing himself.

"Riding those horses, yeah-eh." Elton caught one of my hands and lifted both of his overhead, "Way up high, my darling.'"

I swallowed my surprise and sang along. "Tumbled in the sand? I'll pick you up."

"Pick you u-up."

And he did. He gripped me around the waist and swung me over the foam.

I squealed out my weightless joy, flinging my stick seaward, then held his shoulders to steady myself as he set me down in the waves.

"That's all I know from this song so old." His smile was tight-lipped but genuine. The dream space laid out his intent, making his convoluted words easier to understand. "A pleasure it is to dream of you, but this beach is fin-folk only."

No humans. Damn. It was no wonder the fae would exclude us. Or his subconscious. "Sorry for my intrusion." I smoothed my dress. "It was nice seeing you. I'll, uh, go back to my own dream now." I shut my eyes to focus but they flew open again when he grabbed my shoulder.

"Wait!" He glanced at the herd of seals—probably Selkies—who remained unmoved by my presence, then squinted at me. "Are we dream things?"

"They are." I motioned with my head. "You're real, just asleep. Me too. I guess we were thinking of each other."

He leant toward me as if to impart a secret. "You *are* uniquely captivating."

I willed my cheeks to remain milk-pale. "Yes. Well. You too." I reached for my bracelets and they appeared for me to fidget.

He ran a thumb over my turquoise beads. "You mean to say you're real as day?"

I bit my lip. What was the harm in telling him? "Yes. This is my... talent. I'm a hedge witch. When my conscious mind separates from my body, I can move through other people's dreams. It's called 'jumping the hedge'. I can astral travel when I'm awake too." I left out the part about moving objects through the universal subconscious; taking real things from their owner's dreams to my bedroom. Nobody likes a bragger.

"Indeed." He caressed my arm with the backs of his fingers. "Far be it for me to request proof from a lady. I usually ask for their phone numbers."

Betrayed by my imagination, a scrap of paper materialised in his hand, robbing me of the chance to rebuke his antiquated "lady" comment.

He read my number aloud, eyes wide, then whistled in surprise. "Salt. I suppose I owe the same. Witness then my claim to fame."

But there was nothing to witness. He'd disappeared.

"Cool, no?" He materialised behind me.

Was this a trick? Was he saying he'd also mastered lucid dreaming, or was this a talent carried over from life?

He grinned at my confused expression and disappeared again. Unlike mine, his feet imprinted the sand as he dashed up the beach.

When he reappeared, I clapped. "Impressive!"

In a blink, he stood before me again, all mischief and charm. "Do you know modern songs for us to croon? That I might romance you throughout this afternoon?"

I wasn't about to remind him it was night, and he was dreaming.

ELTON

Even without Brooke's forewarning, I'd watched enough Halloween movies to know what to expect of a witch's circle—candles, power of three, maybe some possession if the evening went well—but when I stepped into

Poe's living space cradling Mother's fresh-baked rosemary bread, I froze, unprepared for the veritable party. I'd over-dressed. Brooke said to choose dark green natural fabrics, which had narrowed my options to a collared dress shirt with wooden buttons, and brown chino shorts.

Morrigan wasn't here yet. She'd sent a curt text to Raeyn about her official banishment from our case, inspiring a rant of epic proportions from my beloved sister. Despite Morrigan's demotion, her coven put aside whatever they'd originally planned for this gathering to aid me. Giving up was "not her jam", Morrigan had said. Whether she'd meant jam as in music, or jam as in the spread was not clear, however.

I hovered in the doorway until a rough-cut gem noticed me, offering her smile from where she was sprawled on the floor. She had deep tanned skin with warm under-tones, and long brown hair tied back in a ponytail. Her jeans—cut off at the bottom and fraying over her bare feet—ripped across the thigh as she stood. "Dang it," She muttered, brushing her hand over the tear, through which fine white scars showed.

I smiled reassuringly. "Girls splurge their savings on jeans with tears; yours increased their value, thanking use-ful years." Her cheeks blossomed pink as we shook hands. "I'm Elton." Not that she couldn't have guessed, but for want of her name in return. "Please accept this salted loaf. May we compose a friendship sturdy through."

"Poe." Extensive scarring was visible through the gauze of her overshirt, too. Hundreds of raised lines from the middle of her forearms to her shoulders. What kind of twisted magick had she worked that needed her to maim herself so? "Thanks for coming, and for the bread. Bathroom is up the hall to the right. Try not to make any sudden or loud noises, I'm putting the twins to bed. Uhm, and if you need anything, ask." The youth in Poe's voice warred with the fatigue on her face. She had to be ten years older than Morrigan. I wondered how they'd met. She smiled ruefully. "I'm an awful host; you *will* need to ask."

She left me there, hovering on the outside of a ring of strangers deep in conversation. I'd have appreciated some introductions; no one else appeared to notice my presence. Brooke and Oberon were the only familiar faces, so I dodged my way over and sat on the floor between the recliners they occupied. Oberon and I had been close as primary-schoolers, but then we'd attended different high schools. We were both too lazy or unmotivated to follow up on our promises to hang out. And yet, I needed help and here he was. Here they all were.

"Hey, you made it," Oberon greeted me as the person he'd been speaking to disengaged and went to their bag, pulling out a bundle of green fabric.

Brooke peered over the edge of the plump recliner cocooning her slight frame. "Not what you expected, is it?"

Was I so easy to read? "A gathering vast; but alas I find my hopes are dashed. The song of the sea pulls from within, how can these witches anchor me?" As if my acknowledgement were an invite, *gairm gu uisge* swelled louder, tugging eastward.

Brooke sprayed me with faery glitter that twinkled through the air and disappeared upon landing. "Strangers are just friends you haven't met yet."

Oberon put his legs up the back of his recliner and dangled his head beside mine. "That's Eliss." He pointed to his previous companion, who was heading up the long hall, past the kitchen. "Eliss's pronouns are ze/zir." Oberon gestured to two women sitting on the floor, who I'd stepped around on my way over. One was wearing a hijab. She was opening a stack of mail—sheets of stickers—and showing the other, a sweet, clean-faced beauty with thick eyebrows and a strong jawline who feigned interest. "On the right there is Trinity. We were in a coven together before we merged with this one."

I kept my voice low, "An who's your Muslim friend, delighting in the simple?"

"She's Wiccan like the rest of us, just really likes her privacy. That's Medusa."

Medusa? As in Meddy?

The way Morrigan had spoken of her best friend over text, I'd expected Medusa to be about six feet tall with designer clothing and ravishing good looks. In truth, her face disquieted me and her style was dated; a singlet top over a flowing skirt that didn't quite hide her hairy calves.

"Got it. Eliss, Trinity, Medusa."

The downstairs door slammed and footsteps echoed up to the unit. "Time to get changed," Brooke said. Oberon flipped upright as Morrigan and an imposing Blackfella shuffled into the crowded lounge room, already dressed in floor-length green robes.

A delightful flutter coursed through me at the sight of her, warming my cheeks. In my dreams, she sang with me on the beach and delighted me with her rich laughter. It was as though I knew her better than I in fact did.

Poe hadn't returned, so I played the role of greeter, going over to welcome them in. To my surprise, the big guy—Viridis—hugged me, as did Morrigan.

Her body melded to mine, filling my nose with the scent of vanilla, berries, and an undercurrent of something spicy. "I'm glad you came." Her heartbeat raced against my chest.

Viridis excused himself but Morrigan stayed with me, lowering her voice. "If at any point you're overwhelmed, or the storm is coming and you need me to make an excuse so you can leave, let me know, like…" She tugged her hair. "Okay?"

The storm she mentioned had to be *oidhirp anabarrach*, but what was she saying? Like what? "Oh!" I rubbed my foolish face.

Morrigan chuckled. "I feel like facepalming might give a mixed signal."

Laughing, I tugged my hair how she had done. Tonight's waning moon and its confusing, compelling power had nothing on this witch.

We stepped aside as Viridis began to rearrange Poe's furniture. Trinity and the supposedly private Medusa changed into their robes right there in the living room, completely unperturbed when Oberon joined them, stripping off his shirt. He was a graceful snowflake beside muscular Medusa with her olive skin. Trinity's soft curves were quickly hidden beneath her forest-green robe. Now, my clothing fit the coven's tone.

Morrigan dropped her thongs on the shoe rack, then returned for me. "Help me get the wine and biscuits while the circle is constructed?"

Within half an hour, Poe's run-down rental full of teens transformed into sacred space. The last rays of sunlight sliced golden through the wide glass doors to the balcony, haloing Morrigan in orange and pink. A spooky pattern had been chalked onto the carpet and an altar set up toward the east, with space enough to pass behind without stepping out of bounds.

The candles I'd anticipated sprang from nowhere and clustered over Poe's desk. Stacks of books, plastic milk crates, and the windowsill between this room and the kitchen. Ocean sounds played through a portable speaker. A nod to my heritage, or was this common to their practice? Did they think me merely a creature of the sea, hollow of personality?

The shin-high altar hosted the biscuits and goblet of wine, a deck of tarot cards, a black mirror, a bowl of salt, cauldron of water, cones of incense, a pointy rock on a chain, and even more candles. Alongside the altar, on the floor, sat a wooden box and a long, bejewelled stick.

Most of the coveners were armed, daggers tucked into their cord belts. Medusa had a knife and another stick, both in sheaths, on hers. She took the place to Morrigan's right, so I shuffled to Morrigan's left, beckoning Brooke to follow.

"Thanks for coming," Poe said. "Let's be kind to ourselves and forgive in advance any fumbles we make while so many of us are absent."

Salt, there were more of them? How big did these covens get?

Morrigan took my right hand and instructed us to breathe—like we weren't already—and Brooke's tiny hand burrowed into my left. An irrational urge to guffaw came over me. I shut my eyes to quash it and *gairm gu uisge* asserted its tug on my mind. Around me, the witches slowed their breathing. Mine tore in and out of my throat. I needed to swim. This was the wrong place. These people were wrong. The city an affront to nature. The skin over my chest stretched, aching and dry. I would crack open, dissolve to dust—

"Now we cast circle," Morrigan murmured.

Casting circle could best be described as a stage play for the invisible beings they invited into the space, or their Goddess. Each step and turn was carefully choreographed; whatever fumbles they might have made in the absence of their missing members were undetectable. The oddness of their drama provided me a point of focus. I put my trust in them. I'd expected a massive spell book, possibly on a lectern, but everything had been meticulously rehearsed—the players acting from memory and shared instinct. They knew their magick.

"We gather here this evening to honour the moon Goddess who controls the seas. Lady of the night, queen of the stars. You who call upon our souls to rise and come unto you; we have answered." Viridis's voice vibrated with total conviction, conflicting with everything I knew to be true. The Moon—their Goddess if I understood right—was my enemy. Her stars sowed my life with chaos. Now I stood in her church? My hand twitched toward my hair.

Morrigan bowed her head, praying, "Goddess, we ask your blessing upon our new friend, Elton. Guide us to find that which has been stolen from him."

At a signal I missed, the coven sat. I hurried to follow. Those who'd been on the other side of the altar came forward to sit in front of it, including Viridis, who reached behind himself to pull the cards, a white handled knife, and the black mirror into his lap.

"Using these, we're going to make a map, of sorts." Viridis surveyed the circle as he spoke, but I alone needed the instruction. "We'll find the skin with the scrying mirror, and then the cards will become a bridge back to Elton." Viridis turned the handle of the knife toward me and leant forward. "May we have a lock of your hair or a few drops of blood? It'll make it easier to locate your specific skin, instead of a random fur in a wardrobe somewhere."

I accepted the knife and ran my fingers through my hair. I'd left it loose today and it fell to the middle of my back.

Morrigan tickled close to the nape of my neck. "If you cut under here, it'll be less noticeable."

"Experience you possess, beyond mine fanciful dreams, t'would honour me if you'd assist, less a mess I be com-mixt."

She blinked thrice rapidly, golden candlelight flashing in her irises. "Umm, all I got from that was 'assist', and sure." She lifted the bulk of my hair away, pinning the topmost layers against my skull with her forearm to slice off a chunk I wouldn't miss. Viridis tacked the strands to the velvety back of the mirror while Brooke withdrew a stack of notes from her robe.

"Here's our chant, sorry it's a bit of a rush-job. I'm not much of a songwriter." Brooke handed the stack to me. "Take one, pass it on."

Eliss asked, "Songwriter?"

"Water faeries and aquatic mammals like Selkies are often musically inclined. We'll have a better chance of hitting the right vibe if we sing," Brooke explained.

"Viri is our focus for the mirror and will steady the vision while we perform the spell's second stage," Morrigan said.

"I'll be our focus for the second stage, so when you see something in the mirror, start channelling your power to me."

A murmur of agreement flowed through the circle. Morrigan picked up the cards and shuffled. Viridis held the black mirror so that everyone could see its face, though he and the witches either side of him, Poe and Trinity, would view the image upside down.

Brooke sang alone and unabashed, her voice clear, "May we see the lights in the distance, trembling on the ocean of night,

Future before us, parting parting, removing the cloak with our second sight.

Seals in the distance swim toward us, graceful in their playful flight,

Lead us back to the skin we're seeking, harness the storm that comes in the night.

I can see my magick around me, I can feel the cloak's true weight.

I can see intents and outcomes, answering the call of a Selkie's fate."

Morrigan joined in at "Seals in the distance," more speaking than singing. For the next two lines, I listened as she relaxed into it; not matching Brooke's ethereal tinkle but not killing any cats either. Her jaw moved gracefully, her neck elongating as she gained confidence. I ripped my gaze away, and focused on the paper in my hands.

By the end of the first repetition, my voice put Brooke's to shame. By the third, it was war.

Viri's bass, rich and full, underlined all else.

The others sang with us, the threads of their voices pulling power from the air, weaving it to a crescendo. My *oidhirp anabarrach* flared, taunted by their strange human magick. I balled my hands into fists. Energy was everywhere. The moon rising behind the unit amplified *gairm gu uisge* and my own debilitating longing. Strength rushed through me, zipping around the circle. I could scale any building, tunnel into a bunker, drive my fist though whatever blocked the path to my fur. The air trembled. We'd do everything necessary, me and my witches. *I'm coming*, I told the sea. *I'm coming home.*

Morrigan tapped my knee and pointed toward the mirror.

I sang, my throat vibrating with my need. "I can see!" The weight of our combined energies spilled down my face in a wave of tears. Then I really could see. My fur. There. In a pile, sandwiched between others, dry nose and drooping whiskers framed by my flippers. Scissors glinted from atop the stack, but we were too close to see the surrounding room.

A bombardment of power passed through me, slamming into Morrigan. The force of it rocked her. I reached to steady her, one hand on her shoulder, the other on her lower back. At my touch, the surge became a roaring torrent. Sweat ran down my forehead, stinging my eyes. Morrigan pressed her hand over mine, holding our contact. The chant continued, grating out of my throat like so many broken shells. Morrigan pulled me through the pain, the tarot deck cupped in her free hand.

Pick one, she urged, unspeaking. I hesitated, looking into her face for confirmation, but her eyes were sealed, deep lines of concentration etched into her brow.

I took the top card. Viridis had said we'd use them as a bridge, so I threw it at the mirror. By some miracle, it landed face up just in front of the black glass. I drew another and another, my hope growing with every draw, every steppingstone laid between now and the future.

Not knowing how I knew, I sensed the next card would be the last, so I scooped the deck from Morrigan's hand, reverently laying it in front of us with the topmost card turned up. As the deck touched the carpet, Viridis boomed, "We see the path, it is done!"

The chant halted mid-line.

"Praise the Goddess, it is done!" Trinity echoed.

"So mote it be," mumbled Morrigan, her eyes searching the cards for clues.

Pen and paper came counter-clockwise along the circle until they reached her. She scrawled the card names even as she declared them. "Justice reversed."

"Slow legalities," Medusa said, her voice as ghastly as her face. Sweat had run her makeup, leaving dirty streaks. "An allied person deliberately slowing our progress. Card one is linking to card three."

How did she know? They weren't touching. They weren't even the same colour.

"I see it too," Morrigan said. "The lovers."

Her and me? Heat prickled down my neck. She was so smart and interesting and inclusive—but no. Brooke had been adamant I didn't stand a chance. Morrigan was "ace" and didn't date clients. But we were here in her friend's house, reading tarot cards in a chalk circle.

Morrigan answered herself. "An idyllic union. Question the method of achieving the ideal." She scribbled that down.

Leaning forward to see, Poe read the third card. "The Emperor."

"An authority figure or superior," Medusa said. "It's someone at AI. A person who always seeks positions of leadership."

Brooke glanced between Viridis and Morrigan. "It's that tall skinny dude with the attitude. Liam! Is anyone else thinking it's Liam?"

Morrigan sucked her teeth, her tongue flicking between her lips. "I did at first. But what if I just want it to be him? It's too easy." She poised her pencil. "Five of Wands."

"Learn how to fight," Trinity responded, her voice mousey. That was all well and good, but it told me nothing.

"Two of Wands," Morrigan said. The card showed a fearsome warrior holding a pair of electrified staves. Something was being conjured in the static between. The palette exuded Frankenstein vibes. "Prosperous partnerships. Creative energy." She shook her head. "What do yous reckon?"

"It's a good omen for buying investment properties," Medusa said. "If it's not talking about poor Bruce Morwen, it might be worth looking at recently sold listings."

Who? I grit my teeth.

Eliss flipped zir pastel-streaked fringe. "Doubtful. Probably means whoever's got the skins is making bank."

Of course they were! "What locale? Which card tells us where to seek?"

Morrigan's cheek curved up in gentle sympathy. "They all do, in their own way. Do you feel it?"

I felt many things, a million drops of water passing through each other, slamming into the shore, becoming one. Breaking the rocks. Wearing me away. Not all my feelings were even my own, how did she feel any one sensation enough to be guided?

"Last card is the Eight of Cups," Medusa said.

"That's your answer," Oberon spread his hands, palms up. "Clear as day."

The picture on the card showed a merman, empty cups falling through the water as he swam away into a harsh light.

I clasped my hands in my lap to contain my frustration. "Won't you please explain? I see only bane."

"I don't read tarot," Oberon prefaced his comment, "but if the image is anything to go by, it's got something to do with litter. We should find the most polluted beach in Sydney and start there."

Morrigan shook her head. "That's not what that card means, usually. It's about moving away from trauma, getting on with your life. Sometimes heralds a break-up."

Oberon's tone was insistent. "It feels true."

Morrigan was wrong. I was not moving on with my life, I was getting my birthright back, whatever the cost. "My heart unwon cannot grieve, thus that meaning I dinae believe."

Poe hummed. "Eight of cups can represent a lack-luster environment, that's the message I'm getting. We can double check with the pendulum?"

Trinity retrieved the pointy rock on a chain from the altar and passed it to Poe, but as Poe slid the Eight off the deck, she revealed a seventh card, stuck by static to its back. Trinity squeaked.

I froze. Had I bungled everything by missing that card? My gaze snapped around the circle, gauging people's reactions. Medusa's jaw moved as if she were chewing gum.

"It's face up. Do we read it?" Poe asked Morrigan.

"Always."

"Reversed Page of Pentacles." Poe laid it down, and all but Viridis rocked forward to observe the artwork and symbolism. Which, in this case, was painfully clear. The being on the card pulled the pentacle apart. Destroyed it. I began to rise, but Morrigan held me.

"Don't break the circle, we'll lose it all."

"A misunderstanding of the magickal nature of a sacred object," Medusa recited, seeming to have memorised the cards meanings rather than hearing their message on the same level Morrigan did.

Brooke's words were muffled by her hand over her mouth, "The making of small pieces. To cut or tear."

Morrigan wasn't nearly as alarmed as one ought to be. "Dad found an off-cut in an empty office. We know the skins are being processed—that's why we're here, not putting our feet up for the holidays."

Hot nausea roiled me.

She traced the card with a finger. "The Page takes the pentacle apart, but she puts it back together again."

Living things did not *go* back together.

Medusa scratched at her scalp, pushing her scarf in between what must have been thick braids and digging hard. "It's linking to the Two of Wands, you see that?"

My hair stood on end, as though infused with static. I needed to do something, not sit here talking. I tapped my fingers against my thigh, but it didn't help.

"If they were making something, what would it be?" Viridis asked. "What good are Selkie skins to humans?"

Poe picked up the Two of Wands and Page of Pentacles, holding them side-by-side to search their imagery. "Not everything's about humans," she muttered.

MORRIGAN

"Flirting with Elton?" Brooke asked as I responded to a text. We were heading to brunch with what was left of Elouera. The holidays, and possibly adult life in general, had ravaged our number, and—I feared—some coveners' priorities. Not only were we in that hazy time between Christmas and New Year's, but most of us had graduated, catching us in that awkward place between high school and the rest of our lives. It was somewhat expected that spirituality took a back seat after high school. Mum reckoned she was the only person in her teen coven to remain Wiccan, and even she stopped practising until she got together with Dad.

I met Brooke's gaze. "Not every time you have a positive interaction with someone does it have to be considered flirting." My words came out mangled. Hopefully she wouldn't notice.

"But it is Elton, isn't it?"

I wished. "Dad, actually. He's still fuming. Funny how when I do something dodgy, I'm irresponsible but when he does, it's a necessary risk. Wish I'd said that to him." I shook my head in annoyance. "Anyway, he wants to make sure I'm really going to brunch." Paying for new tyres and the tow truck had depleted my savings. It soothed my guilt but hadn't placated my father half as much as I'd hoped. "He doesn't trust me anymore, and he's not trying to hide it." The sun pounded us as we reached the zebra crossing, reminding me to reapply my sunblock. I sanitised my hands in preparation for touching my face.

"Don't check in with your Dad, you're nineteen!" Brooke flicked her hair. "You won't catch me dead telling Aunt Annis my business when I'm your age."

Brooke didn't work at the same company as her guardian though. And there were two of them, Brooke and her cousin, to look after her aunt. Our situations weren't comparable. Nor worth making a fuss over. "So rebellious!" I teased, offering her a squeeze of sunblock before slathering my pale skin with protection.

I tucked the tube back into my handbag as we rounded the corner onto Norton Street. Meddy waved at me from Nutty North's patio. A Sweet Cup of Joanne's, our favourite cafe, was closed until New Year.

"Oh really," Brooke muttered.

Huh? I followed her gaze and spied Astrid sitting demurely beside Meddy. I hadn't realised she'd be here, but in hindsight it was obvious. Meddy organised this brunch, of course she'd invite her girlfriend. She wanted people to stop making a big deal about their relationship, so she wouldn't be shouting from the rooftops that the most despised witch in the suburb was coming to tea. At least Faun and Tasmin wouldn't be here to make a stink.

Brooke wasn't Astrid's biggest fan, but she wouldn't say anything catty. How could she? This wasn't coven business. Poe had her kids, and if he wasn't away, Indra would have brought his girlfriend. I greeted everyone with hugs, including Astrid, then pulled a chair over from a nearby table and parked it in-between Viri and Brooke. As they read their menus, I checked my messages and sent Dad photo proof of my innocent gathering. A bandage for our broken trust.

Elton had messaged me too; he'd remembered my personal number from our shared dream. *'Raeyn's answering no messages, calls, knocks on her doors. The guilt and shame, too much to bear my blame. But mother's comforted, though she tries to hide; she ever wanted my fur denied.'*

I rubbed my head and reread it. Raeyn felt guilty and knew he blamed her, was that what he was saying? But his mum was happy because she wanted them all stuck on land together? My reply would have to wait. I tucked my phone into my bag so I wouldn't be tempted to look at it and tuned into the conversations around me.

"—and then ze invited us to dinner in the new year." Meddy was telling Poe.

"Wait, Eliss did?" I clarified.

"Yeah. Just me and Astrid. It's..." She scrunched her brow and laced her fingers with Astrid's where they rested on the table.

"It's weird," Astrid said. "But everyone deserves a second chance."

Brooke made a face at that.

Astrid smiled at Meddy, oblivious. "It'll be fun. We're meeting some of zir other friends."

"Oof," Poe grunted as Apollo scampered over her to sit on Meddy.

"Did you bring stickers?" Apollo asked. His red-blond curls were getting long; they bounced even when he'd stopped moving.

Poe tilted her head to see around the little boy. "Eliss has matured these past few months. I'm happy for all of you."

For a while, Poe and I thought Eliss and Meddy were going to hook up, but it'd ended badly and wounded the coven.

Meddy slapped the table, startling me and making the twins giggle. "Oh! Thinking of growing up! Poe, I texted Radia your number, I hope that's okay. Her kid is going through a stage and I thought you'd have advice."

That Radia even had kids was news to me. Meddy's planner friend was older than us, probably older than Poe too, but I'd never realised.

A waitress appeared, eyeing our misfit party. "We don't split bills, just so you know."

"Welcome to Australia," Brooke muttered.

"No worries." Viridis gave the 30-something lady his winning smile. She didn't smile back.

We ordered, Poe and Astrid competing for the title of hottest, strongest, largest coffee. As the waitress went inside, Brooke grinned wickedly.

"What?" I asked her.

"Oh, nothing." She failed to straighten her face. "That waitress needs someone to brighten her day."

"Leave her alone," I warned. There weren't rules forbidding use of magick on normal folk; who would police that anyway? But it wasn't worth the risk. Witches had made leaps and bounds, being afforded protections under the Religious Freedom Act, but that didn't stop 'good, god-fearing people' getting hysterical. Not that Brooke needed magick to prank someone.

Viri looked between Brooke and I. "Any news on those missing Selkie furs? Did you tell Matthias your suspicions and what the cards said?"

I groaned. "Dad's put out by my 'unprofessional metho dology.'" I made air quotes. "If I had half a chance, I'd have told him about the reading, but I need solid proof that it's

Liam Kendren, too. Not just because Dad won't believe me, but so he can take that evidence to his superiors."

"Anything in Liam's file?" Viri asked. "Past misdemeanours?"

I spread my hands. "Dunno, that's above my pay grade."

Brooke's eyes twinkled. "Bet your dad has remote access." It made sense; how else would Dad be able to work from home? "Go clean up his office like the wonderful daughter you are, and if you stumble upon something useful..."

My fingers itched with temptation but I shook my head. "He'll know. And if I don't find anything... I've already broken my parents' trust."

"Gather in?" Astrid suggested.

"He's a witch. There's no way he isn't going to sense an intrusion."

"Take my kids then," Poe said.

"What?"

"Take my kids. I'd love someone to watch them while I'm at the doctor's. If they accidentally got into the office while you were making them a snack..." She spread her hands. "I'll apologise profusely when I pick them up, of course."

I eyed the pre-schoolers. What were the chances they'd dob me in? "I'll watch them for you anyway. When's your appointment?"

She used her hand as a shield, hiding her sheepish face. "In a couple of hours."

Well, at least I wouldn't spend my afternoon sweating over my mistakes.

The waitress returned, balancing our orders on a large round tray, and this time she spared a smile for us. I glanced at Brooke, who beamed.

We each thanked her as she set our drinks and snacks on the table. All except Artemis.

She stood on her chair, trying to get a better look at the tiny skink riding on the waitress's neck, behind her ear. "Cuuuute!"

The waitress blushed. "You're welcome, and thank you little miss. Holler if yous need anything else." She'd given me extra sauce, and a wedge of lemon for my water.

Poe side-eyed Brooke as the waitress went back inside. "What did you do?"

Brooke chomped on a complimentary biscuit. "I asked Mother Nature to send her a friend." Spraying her faery glitter over the children, she added, "I'm not all pranks and envious beauty you know."

CADENZA

MORRIGAN

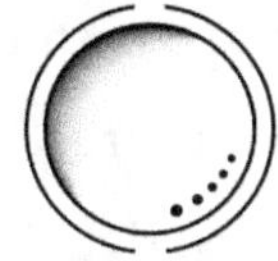

After brunch, Brooke and I pulled out our phones on the way back to my car. I had another message from Elton.

"School next year is gonna be weird," Brooke said. "It'll be just Indra, me and Faun."

"It's already weird, the great unknown stretching before us. Meddy and Astrid wanting a hermit cottage. The others talking about moving away or studying abroad. Trinity, Oberon, Tasmin… Is this the beginning of the end?"

"Not for us. Not for Elouera's core."

I sighed. I'd never wanted any kind of division in my coven, but it had happened anyway. Viri, Poe and I had founded Elouera. Indra and Brooke joined a couple of years after; Eliss and Tasmin near the end of that same year. For ages, we didn't initiate any new members. We'd been so complete—so balanced—until a rival coven began hexing people, through which Elouera experienced an influx of initiates, giving us a less-experienced tier of coveners. Was this our peak? Was it downhill from here?

My thoughts were so consuming, I had to read Elton's message three times instead of the usual twice. A tingle started at the base of my spine and grew upward. "Oh my ancient gods, Brooooke!" I thrust my phone at her. "Is he asking me on a date? He is, right?" How had coming out to him as an ace woman not scared him off? It rendered me an instant reject the one other time I dared mention it to a guy.

Brooke let out a giddy squeal, her eyes scanning the screen. "Yes! Wow. I told him not to bother you, but..." Her thought trailed off as she scrolled to the bottom of his message. She giggled. "'Radiant' and 'poised'? That's a high-key flirt. Are you... interested?"

I took my phone back and scrunched my nose. "Pretty sure there's nothing I can eat at Nell's Seafood and Grill. Should I suggest somewhere else?"

"Eat before you go, and buy a fancy drink."

"Mmm. Where there's fish, there'll be chips. That's okay." We reached my car. "Might be fun."

Brooke smiled approvingly. "What are you going to wear?"

At home, I had a more pressing dilemma: how to get Dad back on-side. I parked my car and crossed our yellowing lawn. I wasn't giving up on Elton, or any Selkie, but how was I supposed to recover anything without Arcane Industries' resources? Could I make do with half a coven and my old banger?

Liam Kendren was both my number one suspect and my link to the case. If I hadn't been in his employ as a nocturnal liaison for the donation drive, I mightn't have heard a thing. Ms Coolman, my supervisor at Sneaky Witch PI, wouldn't have—and didn't—choose me for the investigation.

My only recourse was to find the information AI needed, locate the skins, and show Dad he'd been wrong to doubt me.

As I unlocked the front door, Poe pulled up and her children spilled out, shouting my name like we hadn't seen each other twenty minutes ago.

"Mum? Dad?" I called through the door. That it'd been locked was evidence I had the house to myself, but it didn't hurt to check.

I waved to Poe, letting her know I'd take it from here. The pre-schoolers missed her blown kisses as they barrelled past me into the lounge room.

"Is Matthias here?" Artemis rubbernecked as she kicked off her shoes, leaving them in the middle of everything.

"No, but—"

Apollo cut me off, "Is you got any lollies?"

"Umm..."

"Lol-ly! Lol-ly!" Artemis chanted. I liked them better before they learned to talk.

But the opportunity was right there, screaming at me. I pointed at Dad's office, triggering a tiny stampede, then followed at a more sedate pace.

During my childhood, I found out the hard way that Dad used wards throughout his office, particularly on the door, the top drawer of his desk, and his mouse. Taking a deep breath I stepped inside, careful not to touch the doorframe with my skin.

Artemis had knocked Dad's mouse clear off the desk and was clicking furiously, while Apollo wrestled with the locked filing cabinet.

"Little Arrow," I said, "I don't think there's lollies in the computer." Artemis's eyes went wide as she remembered what they'd come for. She scurried to Dad's shelves.

It looked like Dad had left in a hurry; a cup of tepid coffee sat by the haphazard stack of papers off to the right. There was an inbox under there somewhere.

I skimmed the report on his screen, but the jargon was indecipherable, at least whilst making sure the pre-schoolers didn't break anything and listening for the sound of Dad's engine. I snapped a quick photo and clicked the AI icon on his action bar. The connection to his AI office was still running and several tabs opened at once.

Liam Kendren's profile was in Dad's recent views. The heading asked, *Return again?*

"Don't mind if I do," I muttered.

"Ooo Kewlminties!" Artemis waved the pack at her brother. "Come get a minty mint."

Tiny white balls rolled across the carpet and the twins squealed with joy.

Liam Kendren's file loaded with big black lines all over the pages. I refreshed and tried paging forward, but the marks remained. Was the damn file corrupted? No, redacted. I flexed my jaw and began reading Liam Kendren's history.

He'd won conservation awards. Team projects with Aradia's Sacred Gardens blah blah. 17th June—black line—International Coven Review prosecuted Liam Kendren. For what? The page ended, and the start of the next page was blacked out.

Was this why dad was gone? Was he looking for paper records?

I closed the tab. Hopefully the redactions raised Dad's suspicions. That'd be progress.

A folder popped up with one file still highlighted, showing it was open. *Muldjewangk 572 LSK*, the title read. I brought that document to the front.

By extracting chromatophores from the dermis and combining them with ground calcite and peacock ore, partial obscurity can be achieved. Enchanted Glamour rejected this formula [1] falsely labelling it an animal-based product.

Of course! Meddy wouldn't have taken the job with them if Enchanted Glamour's cosmetics weren't vegan. I skimmed until another line caught my attention.

This facilitated land movement in addition to hypox breathing. Full concealment from the naked eye and cohesion. The Kendren method suggests combining the ore and chromatophores within a calcite rhombohedron, the clear advantage being we can field ten times as many Muldjewangk.

My head pounded. Full concealment? Like Elton's invisibility talent? Calcite was a stone, and dermis was skin; the second layer or something. I scribbled a quick translation on Dad's notepad in an attempt to unravel what was being said. Liam had created a substance that provided invisibility and the ability to come up onto land, presumably from the sea. The dermis referenced had to be Selkie skins. I wrote *Hypox breathing* and *Muldjewangk* and circled them to research later.

Scrolling further, past scientific element stuff—the only parts of which I recognised were Calcite $CaCO_3$, and water H_2O—and a metaphysical pattern breakdown which Poe would appreciate, I fussed with my bracelets. *What are you doing, old man?* I'd underestimated the guy. The rattle of metal charms and clicking of gemstones filled the silence.

Silence?

Shitsticks! The twins had abandoned me. I grabbed my phone to take a photo of the sciencey part for Poe, shaking the device as the camera app took forever to load. I needed to full screen whatever dad had been reading and get out. The house was too quiet. I'd shut the front door, right?

I leaned back to get a view of the entryway from Dad's desk and froze, my neck twisted.

Dad rested against the doorframe, arms crossed over his chest. "This is a new low for you, isn't it?"

"Uh…"

"Using the children was genius. If you'd been faster, I'd have fallen for it."

Shit. On. A. Stick.

He lifted an eyebrow. "I'm waiting."

I aimed my camera at his screen and mashed the button.

Dad didn't move.

I pocketed my phone and picked up the notepad. If I was going to have this conversation, I'd do it on my feet, facing him. "The big words slowed me down." A casual shrug would have been perfect, but my rigid muscles didn't comply. I swallowed and ploughed on. "This confirms everything we saw in our circle last night. I've been wanting to go over the reading we did with you. Want me to make a brew and we can hash it out?"

His brows made to grab his honey brown hair.

I frowned. "You dyed your hair!"

"Yes." His tone offered no hint to how much trouble I was in. "And do you want to know a secret?"

My knees quivered. "I'm in the business of knowing secrets."

"This isn't the first time. I'd feel hurt you never noticed, but well…" he waved it away. "Parenting and being precious don't go together."

If I apologised now, something would shift. It wouldn't be about me creeping into his office or acknowledging his hair. I'd be admitting defeat.

He studied my face, blue eyes intent. Finally he sighed, cradled his forehead in his long fingers and huffed as he did when I was little—when he was holding in laughter because he was supposed to be angry. "You always were cute, Morrigan. Trying to bluster your way through every mess. Fine. Make coffee, and put all your love into it. I'll print some things off and meet you in the kitchen."

I scrambled past him, turning at the kitchen door to look back. He hadn't moved. "I'm sorry I never noticed your hair," I said. "It looks good."

"Thanks." His gaze fixed me to the spot. "We are going to discuss this, when I figure out what to say."

My response came out squeaky. "I understand." Would he conjure a punishment for me, his adult daughter? Would he take this to the company and have me fired? I'd probably deserve as much.

I got the milk from the fridge. A streak of movement through the foliage on the windowsill snagged my attention. Artemis and Apollo were naked, shooting water pistols at each other in the back yard. The neighbours would enjoy their playful shrieks—a novelty compared to our late-night rituals.

While the kettle boiled, I sent photos of Liam's redacted file and my notepad to Viri. I'd show the other photo to Poe later, when she collected the twins.

I set Dad's French press and cup on the table, poured myself a drink, then dashed to the covenstead for Elouera's Book of Shadows. *Keeping the silence* didn't apply to my dad; never would.

He was watching the kids through the window when I returned. "I miss that age." He sighed. "It all went too quick." He sat in the chair closest to the stove—electric now, unlike during my childhood—and I joined him, moving purposefully, as though I felt confident and unashamed. "Reckon we should log this conversation on company time?"

Dad levelled his gaze. "I admire you, Morrigan, but save your sass for someone else."

I tucked my chin, breaking eye contact. Another year had passed where the kitchen table hadn't been sanded and refinished—a thousand new scratches decorated the top. I ran my finger along one of the deeper groves.

"I'm getting the impression you believe I'm unfit for my job. That you're wanting to replace me already."

"No, I..."

"Think about it," Dad said. "What conclusion would you come to if you were me?"

Tears stung my eyes. The implication was there. "We need to move fast, before the skins are destroyed." *Before Elton's skin is destroyed.*

"For all your speed, what have you achieved? And how much has it cost?"

My parents' respect and most of my savings. My throat tightened. What had I got for that?

"There's a line between confidence and arrogance, Morrigan. There's a difference between being passionate about a cause, and recklessness."

I'd crossed both.

"I ought to tell Ms Moontread. How do you think Arcane Industries deals with wayward witches who abuse their positions? There would be sanctions for me too, for not having kept my office secure. Perhaps I'd no longer be able to work from home. You're a woman grown; I don't need to supervise you while I work anymore." There was a faint undertone of *or I shouldn't have to.* "You're not even on this case. You could have applied for it, put forward your credentials and been considered for the team, but you didn't. The gods know why Mr Kendren sent you to parley, or why you thought doing it off the books was acceptable. At no point have you followed protocol. If you were anyone else, I would fire you."

I met his gaze. I expected him to be red-faced, to see his hair standing up the way it did when he raked his fingers through in frustration. Instead, deep lines spidered over his temples and circled his mouth. His eyes were as watery as my own.

"I should fire you," he murmured. "But I won't. That's my arrogance. I want to believe we raised you to make good choices, to think before you act. Worse, I want someone to pass my legacy to; I can't do that if I end your career now. Know this: your unique gift, your talents, and work ethic mean nothing. The only reason you still have a job is that you're my daughter."

I pulled my feet up onto the chair and hugged my knees. His words twisted in my guts. He required a reply. If I said nothing for too long, the command would come. Respond. He needed confirmation that I'd listened and understood. "Okay," I croaked.

Dad poured his coffee and cradled the glass cup in his hands, steadying himself. "Did you find what you were seeking on my computer?"

I shook my head. How was I supposed to focus now? Why did he even want to work with me? I wouldn't want to work with me. My voice came out dry. "I didn't have the time—" or the knowledge "—to put the pieces together. What I found is important though." I managed to look up. "I thought if I proved we had a case against Liam Kendren—found something solid—you'd take what I've been saying seriously." Again I sounded like I didn't trust him to get results. Didn't trust his judgement about Liam Kendren. Was it bad if I didn't? I clenched my fists in my lap. "And no, it's not a grudge. I've done my shadow work on this, Dad. The cards point to him. And I know there are other clues in our reading, things I haven't unravelled. So, I've got nothing, essentially. Nothing to prove I'm worth your grace." Nothing to show for all my efforts. My throat tightened. "But it *is* suspicious that Liam's file is redacted. There must be a reason."

That the redactions might not be connected to the skins occurred to me a moment later. I braced myself for Dad to point out the flaw in my logic.

"Your mum used to believe that privacy is only necessary if you have something to hide." He breathed deeply of his coffee and took a sip. "She changed her stance after you were born, but it always stuck with me. In this case, it's true."

"But why? What's so terrible that tell-tale blank patches become preferable?"

Dad tugged his goatee. "Once I read the un-butchered version, I got the impression Kendren hadn't known what was in his file, saw it, and panicked. Most of the information was decades old. Youthful foolishness. Nevertheless, Ms Moontread and I got our lead, including a short list of possible accomplices."

My phone danced in my pocket. I relaxed my legs and linked my hands together on the tabletop.

"As you suspected," Dad continued, "he did take those skins. We've confirmed it."

I'd expected to feel victorious. To be allowed a flash of jubilation. But there was none of that. Dad hadn't needed me at all.

"Kendren's groundwork to frame Mr Morwen and cover his own involvement was thorough. Continuing to stay and work beside us opened up opportunities for him to warp proceedings to his advantage too—which is clever, no matter what you think of him." Dad straightened his print-outs.

I nodded once, conceding the point. "So, where are the Selkie skins? Has Liam been arrested? Are the other suspects employees of AI? What about—"

Dad raised his hands to stall my barrage. "We don't know, no, and no." My phone vibrated again. Dad took a drink as he found the paper he required. "This is the report you were taking notes on. It details what Kendren is doing with the skins and I'm hoping if we make heads or tails of it, we'll discern the whereabouts of his operations. Best I can tell—"

My mobile's merry tune cut Dad off. Viri had given up trying to get my attention over text.

"Sorry." I hunched guiltily but answered the call anyway. "Hello?"

"How could you not respond to that?" Viri's exasperation filled the line. "Just drop a photo and go?"

"I haven't read the message: Dad and I are discussing... stuff."

"Do you know what a Muldjewangk is?"

I shook my head even though he couldn't see me. "No, I—"

"Then open my damn text!" The squeal of his caravan door drew him away. "I've got to go. I sent you a photo. Show your dad." He hung up.

I shuffled to Dad's side of the table. "Viri says we both need to look at this." I clicked on the image. Viri's personal Book of Shadows boasted pressed flowers on tea-stained, annotated pages. He often used it in artful flat-lay photos to accompany his blog posts, but I'd never seen this partic-ular entry.

Dad squinted. "Handwriting is a bit rough."

I read, "'The presence of Muldjewangk, (pronounced with a silent e) is characterised by large clumps of floating seaweed. These water spirits inhabit the Murry River, or any lake, stream, or sea affected by hypoxic dead zones.'"

Dad ran his finger down the paper and tapped the words hypox breathing. I paused.

"I'm still listening," he said.

"'Originally thought a myth to scare Aboriginal children away from dangerous waters, the Muldjewangk are related to Undines and other Fin Folk, with the exception that they do not breathe oxygen, and have never displayed sentience.'" I snorted, disbelieving, "Well they reckon that about a lot of creatures. Hmm, oh. 'Caution is urged when dealing with Muldjewangk; they wield a deathly curse.' There's nothing more on this page."

Dad rubbed his chin. "We need to know what the curse entails. Ask Viridis. And give him my thanks too."

"You believe it then?" I asked. "You don't think it's slander? Dangerous curses, stealing children... People say that about witches too. These Muldjewangk should be more friend than foe."

"Maybe, but First Nations people know their land and the spirits who live here." Dad grabbed his work tablet. "Either way, if they're being controlled by Kendren, it doesn't bode well for us." He typed *Hypoxic zone Sydney* into a search engine.

I thumbed my circle notes, focusing on the meanings of the last two cards Elton had drawn. *Lack-lustre environment* my scribble said. *Pollution.* Dead zones would certainly fall into that category; I'd read that they were one of the reasons many Selkie families had opted to settle on land.

"Here." The map showed the New South Wales coast, a large dead zone highlighted near Tamarama beach.

Air hissed through my teeth.

"What?" Dad asked.

"I'll be there tomorrow night. Well, not *there* there, but here," I pointed to Nell's Seafood Bar and Grill. "I have a date."

"A date?" He jerked aside and blinked like I'd shone a torch in his eye.

"Freaky coincidence."

"Uh, well. If you're thinking of swimming after, drive south to Bronte."

"I reckon. Holy crap." My gaze roamed over the documents on the table. "Next question: what's a rhombohedron?"

Elton appeared completely at ease waiting out front of Nell's Seafood Bar & Grill, greeting people who stared too long and smoothing his hair when the coastal breeze threatened to muss him. I took a minute, semi-concealed by greenery on the hillside, to compose myself. He looked sharp with his long hair straightened. It was dark grey, not black as I'd thought at first. He wore suit pants and a light pink shirt open at the throat, making me glad I'd put in the extra effort myself. Meddy had enhanced my face with her paints and powders, despite Elton being well aware what my real face looked like. Apparently, that was beside the point. "I dress nice for Astrid when we have a date, it's a sign of respect," she'd said, lending me a sheer top with chrome zippers that I'd never seen her wear. I completed my outfit with form-fitting high waisted pants and Mum's black pumps.

He passed a small blue and white cooler from hand to hand as I approached, and embraced me with one arm when I reached him.

Below us, Tamarama Beach was a U stamped into the coastline; smaller than I'd imagined. From my vantage-point on Marine Drive, I couldn't see any buildings at the water level.

"Uhm, hi," I said when we pulled apart. I probably should've complimented him on his outfit, instead I blurted, "What's with the Esky?"

"Brooke had me know of sea life you partake none. It is not food to you but friend." We turned and started up the steps to Nell's. "An' so mock fish and pretwans I sourced, most discreet."

I tilted my head. "Pretwans?"

"Pretend prawns." He grinned in a way that constricted my breathing. "So, from the flavours of the menu, get your fill."

"Thoughtful." *Yet mortifying.* "Thank you."

He offered his elbow to escort me through the restaurant's entrance. "I considered changing venues, when at last I heard. But Leonard's—" Elton paused as another couple passed close by us in a cloud of perfume. "—one like me, and so I did defer."

Leonard must have been the chef or owner.

The ambiance inside was all but overwhelming. "No problem," I murmured as a host stepped forward to greet us.

"Reservation name?"

The restaurant was hardly a bar *or* a grill. Set out over three tiers, all tables had a clear view of the bay below. The dining room boasted both openness and privacy. Mermaid sculptures and portraits of grizzled captains decorated the space. The floor was carpeted blue, the tablecloths crisp white, and the railings between tiers gleamed silver like the cutlery.

When we'd been seated, on the second level in the centre of all the fancy people and excessive wealth, I thanked him again.

Elton touched my hand where it curled on the padded menu. "Think nothing of it, my lady."

I snorted. "I'm not a lady. The concept's offensive. Sitting properly, looking pretty, speaking only when spoken to... Hard pass."

His eyebrows pinched together and he leaned forward over the table. "A truly awful job you're doing of not looking pretty." He rested his cheek on his hand and admired me openly.

I bit my lip, but my smile escaped regardless. He was welcome to take me to dinner and blow smoke up my arse anytime.

"Hello, my name is Samira and I'll be taking care of you this evening." Our server appeared on silent feet while I was still grinning like a fool. "Can I get you anything to drink?"

I hadn't even opened the dinner menu, never mind the drinks one.

Elton shone through. "A Caesar for me, please. And if you can let Leonard know we're here?" He passed her the miniature Esky.

"Sure thing, Mr Abercrombie." The server turned to me. She had wide brown eyes and lipstick the exact same shade. "And for you?"

"Something fruity with no animal products, please."

"I'd recommend the blue island splash."

I agreed, trusting luck, or whatever spirits were guiding me.

When she bustled off, I flicked my gaze conspiratorially and whispered. "This is super fancy. Do you think they can tell I'm a fraud?"

"They see only our beauty, manner an' graces in their endless sea of changing faces." He opened his menu like a newspaper.

I laid mine flat on the table, careful not to knock over the water or disturb the hundred different forks. "So, what else did Brooke tell you?"

"Since you ask"—His eyebrows popped above the padded screen— "She said you do not date, an' you said you are ace, yet here we sit. So, I beseech, provide the answers that I seek."

Oh my ancient gods. He didn't know what ace meant, and he hadn't searched the term either. I whipped my menu vertical so fast I just about smacked myself in the face. None of the words on the page in front of me made sense. They danced around, taunting me.

Elton cleared his throat. "D'you mean to say we must abstain until our work is done? For I fear, as a client I've your ear; we'd make this crisis fun. But once my fur we have reclaimed, my time here, it is over and all the sweetness we'd have shared lost to my departure."

"Your departure? Right. Because when we reclaim your skin, the call to the ocean will be irresistible."

"Don't underestimate my strength, as mine parents do. If they and Leonard and others have succeeded, there's no reason I couldn't too."

"Okay." So staying was possible, but he didn't want to? Or perhaps he planned to return at some point. Either way, he wasn't keen to discuss it.

Another member of the waitstaff swept by our table, a reminder that I'd need to order soon. I tried to focus, but Elton's expectation weighed the air.

"Umm, right. We are here. On a date. Yes." Eloquent. Go me.

I drew a bubble of protection around us, a smaller version of a magick circle, keeping my words for his ears only. "I'm more than happy to date you." I caught his gaze over our menus. "I'm flattered." Ecstatic, even. I swallowed hard, my eyes focusing on the scroll work beside the title *Mains*. "Ace is short for asexual. It's a sexual preference. Or lack thereof." A lump formed in my throat. "Mine, that is. I'm asexual." It hadn't been this hard to say before. Not to Meddy, when we first found a label for how I felt. Or to my parents, when I came out. It wasn't hard to talk about online to younger, confused aces. My sexuality had never been a big deal. What I didn't do in my bedroom hadn't affected most of the people I'd told. But it affected him. Sweat broke out on my forehead. I hoped Meddy's mineral powders wouldn't streak.

Samira stood at the invisible edge of my shield, shuffling her feet in confusion. I let it drop so that she could settle our drinks onto the table and flee. Apparently, a Caesar was tomato juice with pickled vegetables. It didn't look at all appealing, but at least it resembled food. My blue island splash matched the swimming pool in Dad's fairy garden; bright blue with a little umbrella. Maraschino cherries dangled down the side of the glass.

Elton folded his menu and stirred his drink with the steel straw provided. "Okay, a decision I have reached. Do you know what you'd like to eat?"

So that was it then. He'd ignore what I said and we'd pretend it didn't happen. Fine. I skimmed for options. "The brothy chowder sounds nice."

Our server strode toward us. I closed my menu, only to crack it back open when Elton ordered an entree. Samira smiled down at me benevolently, pen poised.

"Chilli lime prawns," I said. "And brothy chowder for the main. Please confirm the broth is vegetable based."

"My pleasure. Your main will take slightly longer than usual, as the chowder will need to be made from scratch with the mock meat."

I repressed a groan. Of course they didn't make each bowl of soup individually. They probably had a pot bigger than my family's cauldron, bubbling away out back.

Elton passed her our menus. "There's nowhere else we'd rather be."

Soft music filled a void in the chatter around us. Elton stared at me and I stared at the table, imagining the white cloth reflecting the red of my cheeks. In truth, the lighting came from the sunset over what was once a pristine beach. *I am a real woman,* I reminded myself. *I am whole. Worthy. Independent. I can have fun tonight, even if it's a deal-breaker.* I pushed my energy out to form the bubble again.

Elton's hands hovered near mine, unsure, and I took them. They were sweaty, hopefully a sign he was as nervous as me. It was cool in here with the air-con, but nowhere near as frigid as the Abercrombies kept their house.

"You're shielding, but how? Are you kin?"

I shook my head. "It's nothing as impressive as Selkie cloaking. Everyone can still see and hear us; they just don't care to. We're unremarkable. But I have to keep a thread of concentration on it, or it'll dissipate, and if I don't keep my emotions separate, everyone who approaches the barrier will experience whatever I'm feeling. It's not perfect."

"Tell me more?"

"The same technique can be used when moving to become a trick of the light. Just a shadow, not worth investigating."

"How useful. An uncommon gift among your people, no?"

"It's not so much a gift as a learned skill. Viri taught me. My gift is rare though; the dream-travelling. And sometimes when I travel to people's dreams, I can bring objects back with me." Was I rambling?

"Ah, thus you're perfect for private detective work. That's your role at AI, correct?"

"Yep." Because Dad covered for my stupidity. "I'm not a legit spy like the day-walkers though. Dreams don't follow the logic of the waking world. Or any logic, really."

Our appetizers approached, so I dissolved my shield.

"Your coven, they're family to you, near enough?"

"I'm nothing without my friends."

Samira set our bowls in front of us and bustled away. I squeezed a wedge of lime over my steaming pretawns. Mum would think Elton's invented word was clever. My mouth watered in anticipation. "What's it like growing up with a sibling? It's just you and Raeyn, right?"

The appetizers were perfect. We filled the wait between them and the main with fluffy bread, a visit from Leonard, and comfortable conversation. I only had to ask Elton to rephrase a few times.

We'd both gone through school as misfits, carrying generational secrets. Both celebrated seasonal holidays that our peers didn't. Where I'd poured myself into drawing and meme creation, he'd carved soapstone. I'd played with the kids of my parents' covenmates and finally formed a coven of my own, while he'd done a few years of Faery Scouts and had attended a high school so close to the water that they had beach volleyball as an option for Wednesday afternoon sport.

He laughed self-deprecatingly. "Though, *gairm gu uisge* makes me swoon near the waves, thus I'm a terrible team-mate with which to play."

We ordered a fruit salad for dessert. "May I?" He offered me a strawberry so shiny it might have been glazed.

Sharing a dish was one thing, but to eat from his fork? That had been in his mouth? Cherries had stained his lips, which sat slightly parted. I ought to have been disgusted.

"Sure." I leaned forward to accept the strawberry, then found a piece of rock melon to feed him in return. It was weird. But it was fun too: like re-enacting a cheesy movie.

Elton pressed the last bite to my lips: a chilled cube of watermelon, leaving the bowl empty, save a bit of rose-coloured juice in the bottom. This would've been the moment he'd have invited me back to his place, if I were a normal girl. Not that I'd ever wanted to be normal. I swallowed the sweet fruit, then dabbed my lips with the napkin. We'd had fun. It didn't matter if we never went out again. I had my coven and my cats. I didn't need him.

He cleared his throat. "Forthrightness I appreciate. Please, do not take my long consideration as rejection." He laid his fork across mine and took my hand, rubbing his thumb over my skin. I willed my hands to remain relaxed when all I wanted was to grip him tight and steady myself.

"It pains me to pry..." His usually eloquent words trailed off and began again. "How should our loves know our limits if they remain unset?" His eyes were earnest, framed by dark speckles that followed his hairline and curved around his jaw. "Mother says that marriage is a contract set to meet each other's needs."

Riiight. I'd been told plenty about 'primal needs'. My jangled feelings floated uncomfortably on my full stomach. Why mention marriage before telling me I wasn't good enough?

"Limits hey?" I glanced around, hoping our server was coming with the bill. "I'm not interested in uhm, ever, like..." There she was, heading our way. I caught her gaze and smiled, then rushed through what I needed to say. "Sex is repulsive. That includes, uh, oral and anything penetrative or sweaty." My face was on fire, but I pushed on. "If you want to have it, I'm not the girl for you." There, done.

Elton looked away, his lips forming a little tube as he exhaled.

Samira picked up the empty dessert bowl. "Can I get you another drink?"

"Just the bill, thank you." I braced myself for her exit and Elton's inevitable response.

Elton valiantly composed himself, tracking Samira as she worked the point-of-sale machine.

He's going to tell me he had a nice night, but he remembers he has somewhere to be.

"That's swell," he croaked, wincing in shame as his voice misgave him. "Discourse crystalline we'll share as we explore th' more between us," He worried his bottom lip between his teeth. He had four cuspids flanking his incisors instead of the regular two, and they each had miniature sawtooth hooks on the back. "D'you consent?"

I rubbed my pumps together under the table, hoping he'd said we'd always be honest with each other, and that we'd find a way forward because he wanted to date me regardless. "I'd like that."

Samira paused on the steps with a handheld EFTPOS, speaking to another employee. Elton and I both got our wallets out.

He shook his head. "T'was I who selected the venue. On my honour, I pay."

"Um, okay. Thank you." My fear turned to butterflies.

When she reached us, Samira didn't seem to consider that I might pay or that we'd split the bill. She slid it straight to Elton, face down on the table.

His Adams apple did a nervous dance as he eyed the total, and for the first time in my entire life, I wanted to kiss someone. Him. Right there on his neck cherry. My brain was obviously broken.

We left, then returned to reclaim the Esky, laughing. Still holding hands. I dared let myself hope as he suggested we drop the cooler off at his car and take a walk. It was so... normal. Almost like *I* was normal. This was what my friends talked about when they said they felt seen. Validated.

The sea breeze was refreshing, casting off the humidity like a blanket after a nightmare. Clouds striped the sky purple and gold. A ramp took us from Marine Drive down the beach-side park.

"As babes, we—Raeyn and I—buried treasure here. Many visits had we. Come, I'll show you our rock art." Elton strode across the grass toward the bluff at the southern end of the pocket beach.

I hesitated. Was the dead zone off the north point or the south? Was Liam Kendren experimenting nearby? There were few buildings: a Surf Life Saving Club halfway up the northern bluff shadowed by luxury apartments, a closed kiosk, change room and public toilet block down here at the park. Certainly nothing with occult vibes. Perhaps our intelligence was incorrect. There was no reason to ruin this moment with work stuff.

Flying foxes called to each other and spiralled over Marine Drive behind us. The tide was receding. My tarot cards had indicated high levels of pollution where Elton's skin was being kept, but I'd already binned the sole piece of litter I found.

Elton paused, looking back over his shoulder. Waiting for me. I swept Mum's pumps off my feet to walk properly. He beamed. I wasn't missing this for anything.

"You mentioned the sea makes you swoon," I said when I caught up. "Did you mean that literally?"

"You shared your secret, so I offered mine."

In a riddle I struggled to decipher. "Go on," I urged.

"I find myself disoriented by the sea. Its proximity and weight. The call. Instinct to don my fur. I become lost. I fall." His posture was strong and his feet sure as he followed the curve of the concrete footpath past children's play equipment. "Where's up or down? I wouldn't know; essence conflicted 'lo happiness grown."

Did he mean vertigo? He seemed steady. Perhaps it only affected him if he was in the water? We were ten odd metres from the waves. "So you can't swim, then?"

"In a pool I can." The footpath ended abruptly and he veered right, walking across exposed bedrock to rest his hand on the low cliff. I glanced behind us. We'd been walking on the top of a drain so massive, we could hide within it. A trickle of water ran out onto the sand.

Elton pulled a torch from his pocket, searching for something as we picked our way forward. I dug my phone out of my handbag. Luckily, the flashlight app worked without service, because reception down here was garbage.

"Quiet questions I asked, thinking the disorientation due to entering the sea incomplete. Never did I find another Selkie so afflicted." He spoke distractedly, focusing on his search. "Alarmed were my parents, I soon learned reticence. Perhaps if I continued to research I would have, but being regarded abnormal is uncomfortable."

He located a crude painting on the cliff, below knee height. Green algae covered the rocks underfoot, threatening the image of a stick-girl and a grey seal. "As a child I drew myself only shifted, even at school. As you may guess, concern ensued. Developmentally delayed, creative, or strange? Specialists couldn't say." He poked his tongue out and scrunched his eyes. "'Desist desist,' my mother prayed." He found the next image and another after that. Stick-Raeyn grew, as did their art style. In one painting she was crying. Elton had drawn himself human that day. "Discovered we that Raeyn was born fur-less, and the repercussions meant."

Around the corner, out of sight of Tamarama beach, the siblings were singing. "We hear the song and offer our own. Living wild we'd hit the sand. Bathe in the sun, break hearts 'neath the moon. Into the wind, songs we'd croon."

He steadied me as we picked our way across the slippery stones.

My head throbbed with the effort of following his musings against the ocean's constant boom, but I was enraptured. "What about this one?"

The next painting had been graffitied over, perhaps because it was larger and more conspicuous than the others had been.

"My cousin Devon, plus extended fam, ashore to commemorate Raeyn's sixteenth." From what I could make out, many of the partygoers had drawn themselves as seals. I couldn't tell which was supposed to be Elton.

Night had set in, blanketing everything. He moved the torchlight higher. "Up there lay others, but to climb now would be folly." He flicked the light out to sea, perhaps weighing the safety of continuing our walk versus the disappointment of saying goodbye.

A pillar of seaweed loomed in his torch beam.

I startled, a peep squeaking out of my throat, then giggled at my own ridiculousness.

The seaweed turned to regard me.

Elton and I froze, mirroring the monster's posture. Behind it were more of its kind, searching for something in the rock pools, their twiggy arms scratching the stone.

I'd told Poe's kids time and again that the only real monsters were humans, but the thing mid-scrabble in Elton's torchlight defied other labels. It was tall. Thin. Its single thick leg oozed over the ground. Only a few inches separated its puddle and my bare feet.

My mouth went dry. What had Viri called these water spirits? Muldjewangk.

More like seaweed Frankensteins, with leather pads strapped over their left shoulders instead of screws in their necks.

Some had multiple tentacle legs or long weedy hair. They all had the same sea-glass eyes and lack of visible orifices. Beyond them, a long wooden wharf extended over the waves. I edged away.

The Muldjewangk caught in the beam opened its face in a soundless scream and slapped its thin hand against its wet thigh. Blue and green eyes flashed as the others turned to observe our intrusion. The gathered Muldjewangk lurched forward, overtaking the one closest to us, which lacked the tell-tale leather pauldron and moved slower than the rest, seaweed flaking off at every step.

Elton and I bolted across the outcrop. I bloodied my toe and bruised my shins in my haste. Leaping onto the sand, I checked over my shoulder. There was a building at the end of the mysterious jetty. In moments, it was lost behind the cliff. More importantly, the Muldjewangk disappeared when our feet hit the sand.

"Elton!" I gestured, slowing my steps. The lone, pauldronless Muldjewangk crouched where we'd left it, melting in the moonlight; the only testament to my sanity.

"Just because you can't see them, doesn't mean they aren't there. Make haste!"

He kept me running until we reached my car.

The Lovers

ELTON

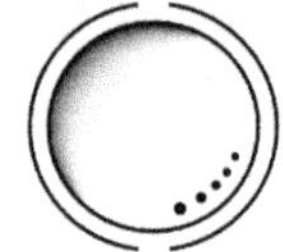

"**S**he's not your type," Raeyn protested.

How little that mattered. The human witch purged everything from my thoughts, from reason to fear. Her openness was enchanting. The way she listened intently, hanging off my every word, feeding my self-worth and putting my bluster to bed. And she was so beautiful: a sunset over ice-topped peaks.

My shoulders kissed my ears. "To woo the human is a Selkie's nature, practised since the dawn of time." It felt dishonest to say. A disservice to Morrigan. But it ought to ring true for Raeyn: she'd had scores of human boyfriends.

My sister grunted and opened the fridge. "When are Mother and Papa getting home?"

"Papa works till sundown, an' Mother's due any time."

She emerged from the fridge with a fillet of smoked cod, leftover jasmine rice and two spears of asparagus that were hardly worth the effort, then selected a frying pan. Her face was all lemons, no lemonade.

I sipped my water and watched her cook a one-woman meal in my kitchen. Something brewed inside of her, a storm unconnected to *oidhirp anabarrach*.

Raeyn shook her head. The floodgates would open any moment now.

Above the stove, the clock encouraged me to prepare for my second date with Morrigan. I rinsed the glass and placed it on the windowsill, but lingered by the door, waiting for Raeyn to mention how slow Arcane Industries was working.

Not that they were. Morrigan and Matthias would have toiled long after they sent me home. We'd sketched the monsters we'd seen, and the warehouse Morrigan vowed they'd been birthed from. I believed her. Had utmost faith in her ability. Yet there'd never in my life been a jetty there, much less a building over the waves. That I hadn't noticed it came as no surprise—the seaweed monsters captured my full attention—and yet it niggled me. Worse, from the sheer number of missing furs, Matthias theorised Liam had brought a significant force ashore, or soon would.

The old witch hadn't forbade me speak of the creatures, thus tempting me to ask my parents if they'd encountered such things in the ocean. The witches said they spawned in water that didn't have enough oxygen—"Dead zones." But wasn't water composed of oxygen? Whatever the case, those seaweed nightmares—Muldjewangk, Matthias called them—kept me awake till dawn with the chills.

My sister cleared her throat but declined to look me in the eye. "I should rejoice, I suppose. She's another reason for you to stay close. A warm body to soothe the pain of losing your skin."

"But?"

She vented her aggression on the sizzling fish, salting it with such force, I expected the shaker to come apart. "No buts."

A weak lie, befitting a child.

"Papa is ecstatic. It's all he talked about when I called in on Saturday," she said.

I suspected that was less an approval of Morrigan and more because he harboured antiquated fears about my sexual preferences. Raeyn loosened the rice and placed it in the microwave. "Mother's worried your human is a bit thin. Not soft enough, you know? I told them you can fatten her up later, if you keep her."

A growl built inside me. Although their objectification wasn't unprecedented.

"You kissed her yet? She's got nice plump lips."

"Too soon."

"Whaaa?" Raeyn flipped the cod, then made a face at me. "What decade you living in, brother?"

"One wherein women equal men in agency?" I left her there before she soured my mood further. Truth be told, Morrigan and I might never kiss. She'd made it clear there'd be no home runs. Maybe that meant never playing ball at all. I tossed my dirty shirt in the hamper and whipped off my belt. My body was plenty soft for both of us. She had no reason to avoid training. No violence danced in her blood. What did it matter how she kept herself? I kicked off my shorts and strode the three steps to my walk-in. What if we never kissed? She was a hugger, there was that. We'd snuggle. She liked the arts. We'd enjoy that together, nurture our souls. Be ourselves without judgement. Maybe massage? Massage was touching but not sexual. I pulled drawers open, pushing around the contents. What was appropriate for a mid-week date slash business catch-up? Muscle shirt? Too casual. Band tee? Too sweaty. Hemp? Ugh.

Bedecked in tighty-whities, I opened my door and bellowed, "Raeyn, I need help!"

Laughter preceded her footsteps up the stairs.

Raeyn looked me up and down. "Yes, you do." She patted my shoulder and slipped past me. "Where you going?" Coat hangers sang on their metal poles as she slid my collared shirts around.

"Rolly-polly."

She inspected a blue button-down. "The mini golf pub?"

"Can confirm." There was no false modesty between us.

"Rightio." She rejected the blue and moved deeper into my wardrobe. "Points for not making her see some boring action movie."

Morrigan struck me as a girl who'd appreciate action movies, but it didn't warrant correction.

"Start by changing your undies," Raeyn instructed. "You're just asking to be laughed at in those."

My date was never going to see my undergarments. "I don't think—"

She levelled a gaze at me. "You want my help or not?"

"Fine." I returned to my drawers, digging out the newest pair of underwear I owned.

"Teal." She nodded. "Nice. Powder up!" She tossed home-crafted talc my way, then thrust a white tee shirt at me. "This."

"Too constricting."

She raised her eyebrows in a challenge. "Fine. Throw this bright number on, but it would look better with the white underneath."

The hot pink shirt she pressed into my hands was classified as Hawaiian—though I doubted a whole island of people all dressed the same. As much as I loved the damn thing, its loudness relegated it to family Christmas barbecues and suchlike. "Is this the aid you give me? No."

"Yes. Have faith. When have I steered you wrong? You need to dress for—"

"—your body, not trends." I finished.

"Exactly." She smiled. "Put it on. Throw out those dirty undies. Don't wear your old-man sandals." She flounced out of my room and downstairs, calling, "Let me know if you want help with your hair. I can do a man bun like nobody's business."

That'd be a no from me.

The tide was coming in for trust between Morrigan and I; she'd agreed to my driving us to Rolly-Polly instead of meeting there. Between her parents and I though, I wasn't so sure. Morrigan's mum answered my knock in full ritual regalia and ushered me into the house with a rigid spine. I fumbled my greeting, then bungled my apology for my tangled tongue.

"The girls are in the co... oh, uhm." She shook her head, jingling her earrings. "I'll make you a drink while you wait."

In the light of day, their cramped kitchen appeared even more outdated. The old dining table oozed fatigue. Plants in brightly painted pots occupied much of the counter space. A roller shutter, half obscuring the window and the aggressive afternoon sun, juxtaposed the ancient feel of just about everything else. At least I wasn't out of place in my loud shirt and grandpa sandals—nothing truly harmonised in here.

Morrigan's mother had age spots instead of freckles and the same hair as Morrigan but faded, with streaks of grey. Her fingers were laden with large silver rings that hindered her as she threw dates and spices into a massive blender. She caught my scrutiny and the corner of her mouth quirked up. "I heard you came by last night. All the exciting stuff happens when I'm sleeping." She eyed the contents of her blender and added a tiny scoop of chocolate powder. "Nice to finally meet you. My name's Felicia, pronouns are she/her."

"Um, Elton. Elton Abercrombie. He/him. Sorry."

Morrigan's voice reached me from the back of the ancient house and coaxed a smile from my lips, unrelated to the conversation I was attempting with her mother. I palmed my face, suddenly aware of how little sleep I'd gotten.

Felicia poured in some plant milk. "And you're Canadian?"

"Sorry, no." Why would she think that? "I'm usually more articulate. Sorry. We're Scottish."

"Cool. It's lovely to meet you." She wrestled the lid onto her blender. "Warning, loud."

When the roar of the motor shut off, she poured us tall glasses—of what I couldn't have said—and dusted the top with cinnamon.

Morrigan entered from my right—every bit a normal teenage woman—as Matthias came into the kitchen via the door next to the stove on my left.

He looked as rough as I felt, and wore a long black robe edged in gold. "Elton?" He stopped in his tracks. "To what do we owe the pleasure?"

Morrigan put her hand on my shoulder. "No crisis, we're going mini-golfing."

"Right. Good." He rolled his shoulders. "Have fun then."

I gulped the golden potion. It was thick. Spicy but sweet. And possibly enchanted to ward Selkies away from vulnerable daughters. In the presence of Morrigan's parents, every stereotype about my people clamoured into my mind. I forced a swallow. Nothing in their voices or manner told of suspicion.

"Be with you in a sec, Elton," Morrigan said. "I just need my bag."

My neck was stiff, but I managed a nod.

Matthias kissed Felicia on the temple. "Love, I'll be setting up the altar."

Were they doing witch business on my behalf? Or for fun? Should I offer to stay and help? How often did witch business need to be done?

Matthias swept out of the kitchen. I took another gulp of the drink. It was better knowing what to expect. Felicia wouldn't be thinking that, though. Matthias either. A Selkie's reputation preceded them. I cleared my throat and Felicia paused mid-blender-rinsing.

"I assure you, I'm not my myth. They say we lure and seduce, control an' mislead. I don't want that." Not to say I didn't desire Morrigan. I did, but—

"No, you want your skin."

I crossed my arms over my chest, my too-tight tee constricting my shoulders. "The truth I cannot deny, but there does not attraction lie."

Felicia relaxed, leaning her curple against the counter's edge. "I'm glad."

Morrigan poked her head in from the hall. "Meddy and Brooke are here. Would you mind if we ran them home on our way?"

When I acquiesced, she disappeared to summon them, taking my breath with her. She was absolutely heart-stopping in a flowy, sleeveless green and brown dress, and she smelled of summer: jasmine, sunscreen, toothpaste.

Morrigan's best friend was every bit as eye-catching, for all the wrong reasons. She led the way out of the hall, a book held tight to her torso. I suppressed a shudder. Medusa's makeup—as caked on as it was—barley hid the black disfiguration on her cheek. She had one super eyebrow and grey lips. As though she noticed them right as I did, she withdrew a lipstick tube from her pocket and coloured the dead-looking flesh.

"Hey handsome." Brooke tapped the leg of my chair with her foot. "Let's go."

I rose, making the kitchen even more cramped, and thanked Felicia for her hospitality.

A dusting of shimmer powder blessed Morrigan's cheeks and collarbone. She was close enough now that her garlic undertones nipped my nose. Hemmed in by her friends, the table and the wall, she waited, twisting her many bracelets. Should I hug her? Offer her my arm? Heat rolled down my body, urging me to kiss her until her lips grew red and swollen.

In a bustle of activity, the moment passed and we crowded my car.

The drive was lively, Brooke and Medusa both grateful to not be walking in the afternoon inferno. Medusa had a dryness to her humour, which may have been incidental rather than deliberate, and the depth of her knowledge was impressive, yet I didn't feel safe with her sitting behind me. I wasn't racist or anything. It wasn't her headscarf that made me feel unsafe, nor her unfortunate visage. No, it was something instinctual. I definitely wasn't a racist. Was I?

For Morrigan's sake, I played the perfect host, driving them right to their respective front doors. Medusa lived on a hill, her drive and front yard dangerously slanted. Brooke lived in a suburban mansion.

When Brooke's door shut, I scooted an inch closer to Morrigan, such as my driver's seat allowed. Alone together at last. Would she let me hold her hand while we drove?

I backed out onto the road and glanced sideways. Morrigan was awfully quiet.

"You dislike Meddy." It wasn't a question.

"I don't know her."

Morrigan spoke with her eyebrows; they arched high.

"Perturbance hardly leaves me lonesome."

She kept her eyes on the road ahead, though the construction outside was lifeless grey.

"My nature is not shallow. Please believe my saying so."

"Meddy's a special case then?" She sagged into the seat. "She wasn't born ugly."

"You readily voice this insult?"

"I'm not being mean. She knows what she looks like. Has to live with it."

"What made her visage so?"

"A nasty curse." Morrigan pulled her phone from the tiny cross-body bag she wore and set it to silent. "I'm telling you this because I love her. Because we're a package deal. Meddy isn't going away."

I slowed with the crawling traffic. A diplomatic response failed me. "To see what you see would bring me great joy, but I cannot trust her, I sense a ploy."

"That's real."

I took my eyes from the road to scrutinise her. She'd definitely said it. She'd agreed that Medusa was hiding something; couldn't be trusted.

"I'm not afraid, because we share the same morals. I've seen who she is on the inside. But Meddy is powerful, dangerously so." She turned toward the passenger window, veiling her face. "I don't think you're shallow."

We drove the rest of the way to Rolly-Polly in silence, the venue's iconic, life-sized gingerbread cottage our beacon.

What was I plunging into with this witch?

No sex.

Terrifying best friend.

Family disapproval.

Disreputable career choice.

No sex.

Ever.

Rolly-Polly had three 18-hole courses, each themed differently. Two underground and one outside. The outdoor course sounded more interesting, being based on classic literature, but we went with the 1950's theme instead, for the air conditioning. As we putted, we compelled each other with get-to-know-you questions that set my imagination spinning.

Tears streaked my face, I panted for breath. "You jest. For real?"

Face flushed by her own laughter, Morrigan swung. The ball went into the hole way after par, but what did that matter? We passed under a vintage streetlight. The next hole was a jukebox.

"My turn."

Morrigan sat on a low bench constructed of vinyl records. I placed my ball and calculated my angle.

"What is the nicest thing you've ever done for a friend?" she asked.

Where did she get these? This was far grittier than my "Tell me a story you can't help but laugh as you recite."

Memories from high school sleepovers flooded me. I hit my ball way too hard. It bounced off a gutter and came rolling back. "Uh, no. Pass. Can I pass?"

She grinned. "It's a good one hey?"

She set her ball down then rested her head against my shoulder. "What's sayed on the course, stays on the course."

Her doe eyes made me squirm. I groaned. "I aim to impress, not appal."

She put her lips to my ear, whispering, "You can't get a girl all excited and then not tell."

My knees quivered. Her lips were nigh. It would be nothing to steal a kiss. I gripped the golf club tighter. "All right."

She flashed her flat little human teeth at me.

I surveyed our surrounds, confirming none on the course stood close enough they might overhear. "We were fifteen, my friend an' I. He's moved up the coast now, still calls to say hi."

She took her turn while I reminisced.

"At my house one night, marathon horror movies feeding our fright, my parents in bed, and us dead if they thought we'd snuck girls 'neath their guard." We cleared the hole, putting around Marilyn Monroe's legs as her real-fabric skirt flapped madly. "Then Dan, he said, 'Tina's outside, this is my chance.' An' I knew he spoke of hormones more than romance, but a slacker I'd be if I wouldna agree, so I told them to keep the noise within the hearing of us three."

"Fair. And did they?"

I nodded. "At first. They got quite handsy, so I gave them space. Was reading in bed when they picked up their pace. My worries rose, I wavered: to go downstairs or no?" I spread my hands, weighing the struggle. "Then my heart shuddered to hear mother say "What's that sound?" and Papa's footfalls, moments away from witnessing our defiled lounge."

Morrigan's lips parted in a subtle o, her eyes widening.

"No time to consider, those noises overt. I pulled up a porn site, clicked on some dirt. The first vid I found I had to let play, thus started the rumour I'm secretly gay."

Morrigan yanked the top of her dress over her face, hiding within, and made a low keening sound.

"A full thirty seconds Pa stood at my door—"

"Stop. Stooop!" Morrigan slapped at my arm and snorted with mirth. "The cringe, it hurts!" She let me steady her, a hand on the curve of her hip.

My face afire at the memory, I laughed too. "The way they stared at me over breakfast next morn—" I dried my eyes on the back of my wrist. Papa had gone back to bed, all unawares. Dan never knowing how I saved them both from being hurled from the house.

"My ancient gods, Elton. You win." She shook her wild mane from her flushed cheeks and gazed into my eyes. "You win."

"Our game of questions, maybe." But not the golf. Neither of our skills sufficed. By the last hole, neither of us could be considered the champion; we'd both done so poorly.

At the bar, we ordered wedges with sweet chili sauce. The place served a superb fisherman's basket, but I'd have a better chance at a parting kiss if I stuck to potatoes this one time.

"Will you judge me a drinker if I order us beer?" I asked.

She swirled her wedge in the sauce, "Pffft no. It's hot as death today. Besides, I work hard not to be judgemental."

"Is not death purportedly cold?"

"I'm planning on being cremated." She shrugged. "Make sure I'm really dead, you know?"

"While we're indulging morbidity," I grinned, "I'd prefer cremation too. My ashes scattered land and sea, an armistice for the woe - this mad'ning urge to roam."

"It's always there, huh?" Sadness tinged her voice, but not pity. She swivelled her bar stool till her knee rested against mine. Every conversation from every human in the bar blurred into one and faded from my awareness. They were shadows, she was fire.

"The sea's relentless, but—" My breath caught. "I told the sea she can't have me, I'm with Morrigan tonight."

She knew I bluffed, but the flattery made her glow. Her lips pinched, struggling to suppress her pleasure.

I pushed my luck. "May I... I mean..." I swallowed and then rushed on awkwardly, "Is kissing abhorrent?"

Her freckles disappeared like stars in the daytime. Biting her lip, she shook her head no, but her eyes didn't meet mine and I sat frozen.

"I'd like that," she murmured, grasping my hands.

I leaned in. She held her breath. My lips found her shy smile. Tasted it. I watched her eyes for any sign of alarm. Morrigan's eyelids fluttered shut as she tilted her head, deepening our kiss.

It might have been one minute later, or six, when a man jostled me, nearly knocking me into her lap. I shot a glare at his retreating form before giddiness swept away irritation. Morrigan stood and patted my knee. "Let's get that drink somewhere quieter."

MORRIGAN

We ended up choosing a chilled bottle of bubbly wine and heading to my place, where I threw a rug and my parents' picnic-for-two folding table on the front lawn. We drank from flutes with blue stems and kissed again and again. The bubbles, or perhaps the kissing, gave me a bad case of the giggles.

He waited as I caught my breath, smiling with his lips together. I was laying on my back, Elton's weight along my side where he'd stretched out beside me. I'd have to tell Meddy I finally understood why she always had her tongue in Astrid's face. It wasn't gross with Elton. I wanted to be consumed by him. To burrow into him somehow and wallow in his warmth. Hear the cadence of his words from the inside as he told me how enchanting I was; at least, I was reasonably sure that was what he'd been saying.

I tested what it might be like to suck his bottom lip into my mouth—utterly wonderful—then rolled onto my stomach and awkwardly slid my glass off the table. As fun as this was, my work gnawed on me. You couldn't just throw it out there like, 'you know how seaweed zombies are being made from your people's skins?' But he wasn't broaching the subject as I'd hoped.

"I've got an update on the missing skins, if you're ready?" *Let me ruin our perfectly fine afternoon.*

"Yes. What response did AI give of our report that we did submit?" He toyed with my curls as he spoke, straightening one then letting go to watch it bounce. I'd have smacked anyone else's hand away, but he didn't annoy me. Perhaps because he remained focused on what I was saying.

"Bad news first. We—AI that is, not me and Dad—uncovered how many Muldjewangk can be fielded through a single Selkie skin. The portion of skin required to raise a monster is negligible. Perhaps when Liam and his ilk started experimenting, it was one for one and that's why he sought so many skins. But we decoded a recent recipe..." I took a deep breath. "What you and I saw on the beach was nothing. He likely has hundreds of Muldjewangk under his command. A single adult Selkie skin averages twenty monsters raised from the sea, able to breathe our air and hide themselves from our sight."

Elton stared off over the lawn, his shoulders bunched.

"We only have estimates of how many donor skins Liam smuggled out, but if we lowball the numbers, there's still more Muldjewangk than Arcane Industries can deal with alone." A chill raised the hairs on my arms. Saying it out loud cemented the fact we'd been outmatched.

It had surprised me that we didn't have an army of witches specialising in this kind of thing, but this was a once-in-a-lifetime crisis. Regardless of what Hollywood would have me believe, there simply wasn't an overwhelming number of power-hungry warlocks raising armies of the dead or summoning more than a couple demons at a time. It'd never been necessary to have a large fighting force—a fact Liam Kendren was taking advantage of.

Elton's fist closed around a tuft of grass. "What is the speed at which these abominations can be called?"

"Depends how many workers and what equipment he's got. We must remember too, that he's not making the Muldjewangk. Nature makes them. Usually, they'd be confined to the dead zone off the coast and we'd never encounter them—when the zone clears, they dissipate. All Liam Kendren is making are these patches that enable the Muldjewangk to come ashore. We've been calling them pauldrons. Did you notice the Muldjewangk we encountered had a leather piece strapped here?" I ran my finger along his collarbone and down his chest, making a triangle. It was awkward because of how we were laying but touching him thrilled me.

He caught my hand and kissed it, oblivious to how germy hands were. When did I last sanitise?

"Um, anyway," I fought to stay on task, "We haven't established how many Muldjewangk there are or how quickly they... spawn?" I guessed spawn was the right word. "But we estimate working alone or in a small team, he'd produce a couple of pauldrons every day. No more than five. The chemical components need time to activate; for the crystals and the skins themselves."

His lips curled down and he swallowed audibly.

"Sorry," I murmured.

"Even five a day is quite the escalation."

I nodded. We needed to build our numbers faster than Liam Kendren built his, and apprehend him before he used his monster army. And to what end? We still hadn't discovered his purpose.

"You indicated there would be a sunny side for us to see." He squeezed my hand. "Those furs dismantled, could they be returned whole, come what may?"

"No." My throat tightened at his scrabble for hope. "I mean, if AI successfully masters lab-grown skins, as we're hoping to do for Raeyn, then reclaiming even a tiny part of a skin ought to be enough to recreate one. But research wasn't finished when this started, and no new donations are being taken. It isn't possible to deconstruct the pauldrons and sew the skins back together, though. They're being tanned, like leather." I tugged his belt for emphasis.

Elton shuddered.

"Help is on the way. We've called for support from our branches in other states, as well as international organisations. And yes, we've got the IRC—International Coven Review—involved."

His eyes narrowed. "At best, if every witch you call upon comes, how many fighters will take up arms?"

Canada promised us twenty. Five witches had already flown in from New Zealand, and we were expecting five more. Nigeria, Morocco, Scotland and Romania had all committed to sending aid. I removed my bracelets one by one, piling them on the grass. The honest answer was that we'd still be grossly outnumbered. My last bracelet clacked onto the pile. "Not enough." I met his gaze. "The best I've got is that we've divined when Liam Kendren and his monsters will be their weakest. We have a date for our attack—29th of January."

A frown etched Elton's face. He rolled onto his back and pulled me into a cuddle so that I was laying on his torso. I was probably crushing him, but the measured whoosh of his breath calmed me.

Snuggling closer, I said, "I wish I had better news."

"As do I." He ran his hand through my hair, pulling it away from my neck, his eyes lost in thought. "How... woeful."

Like I didn't know. The breeze was warm and smelled of fried onions. Christmas lights twinkled along my street. But I was failing him, and that robbed the moment of its perfection. "I don't reckon they'll let me serve, either. I quit martial arts years ago." The first day of high school, to be exact. "I'm not a fighter, in any sense of the word."

"Oh, but you are. I see it."

Pleasure bloomed in my chest. "Thank you."

"It wouldn't do for me to be correcting you, but AI needs every soul that heeds their call. Imagine: by the time help arrives, the rest of us have learned to fight. Is there no one to train us?"

The corner of my lip tugged into a smile. "I might know a guy." If I could convince her to let us risk our lives.

"I'll think about it," Mum said the next morning. She looped the tiny cauldron's chain over her neck and tucked it under her power suit.

I was sitting at the table, eating breakfast over the draft Eliss had written for our Social Live.

"We can at least gather some interested parties, contact some Selkie elders, and make a presentation." Mum threw her keys into her briefcase and grabbed a banana from the fruit bowl on the bench. As if in response to my scrutiny, she added, "I have to run into the office, Liam's impending arrest has triggered floods of paperwork. Then I've got an appointment with Silver and a rep from the IRC after lunch." She took a bobby pin from her pocket and secured a curl. "I'll bring Elton's idea up with Silver while I'm there."

Gratitude warmed me; that was one less call I'd need to make myself.

Dad tossed a little heart-shaped chocolate into Mum's case while she fussed with her shoes. "We'll turn Kendren over to International Coven Review for trial, but hopefully recovering the skins and compensating the Selkie community will remain within Arcane Industries' jurisdiction."

Mum slammed her briefcase, clipped it shut, kissed our cheeks and rushed out the door. I sat blinking at nothing. That we might lose control over the whole situation hadn't occurred to me.

Dad watched her go and sighed. "I'm glad she said no."

"To what?"

"Ms Moontread wanted your mum present for Kendren's arrest."

Despite Mum's training in de-escalation and self-defence, I wouldn't want her walking into Liam Kendren's Muldjewangk hive either. "That's today? What did she say?"

"They took him into custody at dawn, as I understand it." Dad made himself a coffee. "She said that their personal history didn't make her the best choice."

Should I remember the history Dad was referencing? Did he mean because the three of them were mates? Or was he assuming Mum had disclosed something she hadn't?

"Your mum's smarter than us. She sees a job she'd be good at and knows other people could take care of it too."

I tilted my head. "While you and I reckon we're the best man for every job?"

"We are." He grinned. "Pity we can't get to them all." Dad took a whiff of his coffee and sat opposite me. "But if all else fails, date the client."

I groaned. I should have seen that coming.

He laughed.

"That's not... I, ah." Blood rushed into my face.

"I know, I'm just ribbing. It's good to see you happy."

My phone trilled, sending an abrasive grind through the tabletop.

"Sorry," I shot him a grimace-smile. "Just Poe."

"How is she?"

I skimmed Poe's text. "Viri has her in a spin again. She's trying to analyse every inflection in each word and pose."

"She can't ask him what he means?"

Dad clearly didn't remember how dating worked. "That'd eliminate the fun, I'm sure."

There was a knock at the front door. "Hello? It's me." Eliss let zirself in.

"Hey," I called, before lowering my voice to reply to Dad. "Besides, asking directly comes with a higher chance of rejection. No one wants to make a fool of themselves."

Eliss kicked off zir shoes and dumped zir bag on the lounge.

Dad's phone blared. He snatched it up. "Hello?" He saluted Eliss as ze came into the kitchen. "I'm listening." Dad retreated to his bedroom and shut the door.

"Hey, I love where you've gone with this." I tapped the draft in front of me and stood. "Did you confirm with Viri that he can brew this recipe?" I edged toward Dad's door.

Eliss eyed me, zir reply elongated with curiosity. "Yeeeas."

I motioned for zir to keep speaking but plugged the ear closest to zir.

"... terribly suspicious," Dad was saying. "Yes. And I've never forgotten." A loose floorboard in his bedroom creaked, keeping time as he paced over it. "We've been in it together since the get-go, I don't need reminding."

My mouth went dry.

Eliss continued to ramble as ze rummaged in my fridge.

"11pm? Are you serious? I have a family." There was a pause, then Dad grunted. "I understand, yeah."

He had to be talking to Liam Kendren. Had he evaded arrest? What did he hope to get out of my Dad?

"Fine. Come around tonight then. I'll hear you out."

I tiptoed away from the door.

Eliss looked at me pointedly, wrapped up zir cover story and checked the time. "Where are Brooke and Viridis?"

"Present!" Brooke poked her head in from the lounge room.

Eliss startled, tossing a plum into the air and then fumbling zir grab. Ze pinned it against the plate cupboard with zir shin.

"Nice save." Brooke grinned.

I checked my phone. "Viri is on his way. Let's set up in the garden."

Years of practice helped our Social Live run smoothly. The hour spent with my friends talking simple magick and answering fan questions left me revitalised. I floated out the front door beside Eliss. We exchanged air-kisses and ze dashed across the lawn to zir ride. For the moment, all was right with the world.

Viri waited inside the house—to talk about Poe no doubt. To bring me into their tortured, star-crossed love, wherein no stars were crossed at all. I snorted at myself.

Elton was poetically affecting my inner voice. Poe and Viri had an argument not long before Poe gave birth, but neither told me what they'd said beyond agreeing they were better off friends. It had created a wall between them, so whilst Poe agonised over the subtleties in Viri's glances and texts, she rejected my reassurances that he liked her. It didn't matter anyway, she claimed. She had her kids, didn't need more love than that. I was confident they were different kinds of love entirely, but that was beside the point. It'd never work.

The screech of packing tape jerked me back to the present. Brooke was hovering around my dad's car.

"What are you doing?" I asked.

"Medusa helped me with this one," she said, taping a picture of a rock star I didn't recognise to Dad's hub caps. "She's adamant he'll think it's clever."

"Um, okay?"

"Yeah, I didn't get it either, at first."

"Well, nobody knows geriatric music like Meddy." I leaned down to hold the next picture in place while Brooke fussed with her tape dispenser. "I'm not sure Dad is quite this old though."

"We'll find out."

I crouched between some shrubs in the garden as Brooke ran into the house, yelling, "Matthias! Someone slashed your tyres!"

Dad flew out of the front door a moment later, Viri hot on his heels. "The nerve! In my own driveway and everyth—" he caught sight of the pictures and burst out laughing, stumbling to a stop. I laughed too, enjoying how his eyes shone, how solid my family and coven were.

"Ha! You got me." Dad slapped his knee with merriment. "Slashed, oh. I needed that today." He dried a tear from the corner of his eye then held his palm up. "Slam it."

Brooke jumped the high five, then left him to get the faces off his hubcaps, heading home for dinner. He was still chuckling when Viri and I went back inside.

"Your room?" Viri asked.

I shook my head. "Kinda hoping Dad will confirm something for me. If we hole up, I'll miss the opportunity."

Viri sat at the kitchen table. "Fair." He rubbed behind his ear and glared off into space.

"So, what's up?" I busied myself pouring drinks so the weight of my attention wouldn't silence him, not that Viri needed me to.

He pinched the skin on his forehead between his thumb and first two fingers, creating wrinkles where there were none. "Remember when Indra joined the coven? How everyone was so worried that if he and I broke up it'd cause this big rift?"

"Or at least some awkwardness."

"But it didn't."

Their relationship dissolved when the trauma of Viri's brother's death unlocked Viri's powers. It wasn't so much a true break up as a mutual understanding that the feelings between them weren't romantic. I waited for Viri to continue his thought.

"But me and Poe? Gods, it's always been her."

I passed him an iced tea with a wedge of lemon and a glass straw. "I knew before either of you realised."

"We were just kids. It would never have worked."

I didn't buy that. "You're not kids now." I sipped my tea. The urge to tell him to stop touching his face was strong. I slid my pocket hand sani toward him instead.

Viri took the hint. "It still wouldn't work. What with my calling and—"

Not this again. "You've told me your reasoning before and I still disagree." I held up a hand to stall his argument. "I'm not questioning your logic. But there's a reason logic, lust, and emotion are all represented by different elements. You can't cast a water spell with incense and expect it to do the same job."

He rested his elbow on the table and his temple in his palm, staring at the join between the kitchen cabinets and floor. "I'm leaving Elouera for a while."

I jerked, sloshing my tea over the table. "Shitsticks!" It ran off the edge onto my thigh. "Shit. Shit! No. What?" I grabbed a tea towel and pressed it to my leg. "You're not serious."

"I am." He glared at nothing. "There's no other way. I can't control myself. While she's in my coven, there's no avoiding her. I'm holding her back. Neither of us can move on."

I wiped tea off the table. "Neither of you want to move on."

"It needs to stop."

We agreed on that point.

Cleaning tea off the floor, I asked, "Does that mean you're going to move away? Change the AI office you go through? What about your Mum? The girls are still in school." He wouldn't leave his sisters while his mum was sick. I steadied myself with a hand on the table leg. "Or do you plan on just quitting circle?"

"I can't move, you're right. But if I call before I visit you..."

I flexed my jaw, not trusting myself to answer.

Dad breezed through the kitchen with his best Usher impersonation, "You got it, you got it bad."

Viri dropped his face onto the table and groaned.

"You're not helping!" I called. It did help though, just a little.

Sprawled as he was, Viri deflated. I reclaimed my seat beside him, but he didn't stir. Surely his despondency wasn't all Poe's doing. And they loved each other, what did their excuses matter? Was it their old, insurmountable argument or something else?

In addition to his impressive height, Viri was muscular. I hadn't paid attention before, but his arms had definition where Elton's were smooth. They wrapped around his skull, instead of around Poe where they belonged.

Maybe it was the twins. Viridis hated Victor Chasen. Did he see the father in the children? He was great with his younger sisters; he knew how to care for dependants. And yet, I'd never seen the twins sit on his lap or ride on his shoulders. They gravitated to Indra or Meddy. Or my parents. No, he'd have mentioned it if the twins were the deal breaker. I licked the front of my teeth. "What's triggered this? Did she say something to you?"

"No, it was my fault. I won this workshop for Apollo and Artemis, some finger-painting thing." He lifted his face momentarily to finish his thought. "She was stoked.

Said we should get lunch together while they're occupied. I agreed. And so now we have a date. I shouldn't be taking anyone on dates, Morr. She's only going to be crushed when we're friends again the next day." He wrapped his arms tighter around his head, muffling his last words. "I need to make a clean break, not play games."

I wouldn't call getting caught up in a moment of excitement and vulnerability 'playing games'. The three of us belonged together. I refused to lose either of them.

The tea's natural properties of clarity and strength infused me. "I will not give you permission to leave the coven. Elouera deserves better. And if you leave regardless of this conversation, I'll have you branded a traitor—a warlock." I clenched my fist under the table, digging my nails into my palm. Trying to be the arsehole he secretly wanted me to be. "You're not a coward, Viridis Thimberry. Come before the whole circle and give your reasons, if you're so compelled, but don't dare ask me to lie to our best friends for you."

The table absorbed his disappointment. "Okay."

Some minutes later, he added, "I guess that's fair."

How much could I tell him without betraying Poe's trust? "She loves you too."

"I know." He turned his head to face me, one tortured eye meeting my gaze over the fortress of his arm. "But love isn't all you need."

"That's something Poe would say."

"You still here solving the world's problems?" Dad called down the hall. He emerged freshly shaved and combed, and stood in the long shadow behind Viri. The day was drawing to a close. "Liam Kendren is coming here tonight. Whatever he's after will cost him Elton's skin. The question is, do I tell Ms Moontread and have her set an ambush? Or do I hear him out and keep my integrity?"

So it *was* him on the phone earlier. I tugged a fistful of my curls, shifting my scalp around. "I'm biased. Like, I literally can't answer this question."

It seemed to take him a lot of effort, but Viri twisted in his chair to look at Dad. "Brief Ms Moontread. Have her standby in case it goes poorly, but don't set something in motion you can't stop. You know this fella, yeah? Trust yourself."

Dad rubbed his chin. "I do. I want to. The planning it would require and the sheer acting skill to maintain a facade year after year..." Dad swiped a hand through his hair, mussing it.

"His disloyalty is a recent thing, yeah?" Viri said. "Possibly the desperate actions of a desperate man?"

"Must be." Dad picked at his cuticles a moment. "And haven't I betrayed him too? I could have been upfront about my intentions to buy AI."

There wasn't anything nice I could say, so I stood and fixed Dad's hair instead. Liam Kendren's actions weren't excusable, no matter how jealous he felt.

"When Ms Moontread announced that I was being trained as her replacement, he hit me with a list of suggestions to improve the company. I brushed him off."

"It's not like you haven't been absolutely swamped though. You'd have considered his proposals eventually." I hugged him around the middle and then stepped out of his space, having finished with his hair.

"Thanks." He held my gaze. We were cool. He was trusting me, Viri too. "All right." Dad nodded to Viri. "I'll go make some calls."

When the door to Dad's office snicked shut, Viri and I turned back to each other.

He rubbed the back of his neck. "When I started practising magick, I didn't anticipate it consuming my life. It was just an edgy hobby; I thought I was deadly."

"Now it's your job. It's a cornerstone of who you are. All your friends are witches and you use magick to keep your family safe. You eat and breathe it."

"Accurate. And it could take me away from everyone who depends on me." He stood and opened his arms for a hug. "I keep expecting to return to the real world, but I'm already here."

I squeezed him tight. That same feeling haunted my own line of work, but I hadn't let it stop me from living.

"Thank you for listening to me whinge." His breath ruffled my hair. "I'll stop being a sook now."

He smelled of clean linen and eucalyptus. "You're not a sook."

"I'm not being the friend you and Poe need, either."

I patted his back and steered him toward the door. "Have an early night. You'd be less overwhelmed if your eyes weren't hanging out your head."

He dropped his voice low. "You're kidding. Neither of us are sleeping tonight. Don't pretend you're not going to call Meddy and Elton after I leave, to tell them Liam will be here, safely under Matthias's watch, his warehouse full of skins unattended."

"Uh..." I had intended to make another tea and let ideas steep, and yeah, that's probably where I'd have ended up. It was perfect weather for a heist.

"Thought so. I'll nap, get some things out of the way, then I'll pick you and Meddy up and you can brief me in the car." Halfway to the footpath, he yelled over his shoulder, "And for Gods' sake, tell your parents this time!"

I would.

The Star

ELTON

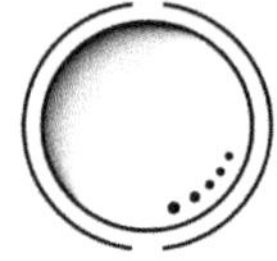

Having granted myself an interval within which to be forgotten by any I happened across on the bus, I arrived first at our rendezvous point, by an hour. Morrigan hadn't been clear who else would meet us at Tamarama Park, perhaps to protect the identities of those coveners who didn't want to support me. I'd soon learn who they were, regardless.

Three youths dressed in dark clothing approached through the shadows—the one in the front unmistakably Viridis. Medusa got out of a car on Marine Drive.

No, not Medusa. This hijabi had a perfectly normal, demure face. Trinity. Her clothes were semi-formal, including a full-length skirt. She must have left a family function.

Medusa walked with Viridis and Morrigan, their shadows solidifying as they stepped out of night's cloak.

My thoughts became unintentionally vocal, my words loud in the emptiness. "Must all witches take from cultures they've no business in?"

"I'm not appropriating anything." Trinity reached me, then checked that her ride was out of view before taking the pins out of her scarf. "This is my culture. It's just not my religion anymore."

Tamarama Park was a large grassy area dotted with picnic tables and dissected by Marine Drive. It extended downhill—encapsulating Tamarama playground—toward the beach. Local homes had, for the most part, shut off their lights for the evening, and were insulated from our discussions by native trees rimming the park.

"Apologies. I misspoke."

Trinity turned away from me and shook out her thick brown hair.

"It's a fair question, in general," Viridis said. "I've been meditating on it."

Morrigan pressed her lips flat, as if this discussion were in poor taste. When she reached my side, she entwined her fingers with mine. We fit together impeccably.

Viridis sat on an alloy table, his feet on the seat. "There's a reason Wicca is often called a salad-bar religion, and it isn't because we're all veg-heads. We're not, by the way."

Brooke snuck around behind our gathering, making Medusa jump as she stepped forward. "I prefer the term Magpie Religion. We take all the shiny parts."

"However you say it, that's the trend." Viridis slapped a mozzie on his arm. "We take what works and discard the rest, trying to evolve instead of getting bogged down in dogma. We connect to old Gods, long forgotten or with their own revivalists, and that's bound to upset people. But are we hurting anyone?"

"There's the thing," Morrigan agreed.

Brooke skipped around, weaving between trees, giving as many cares to this conversation as I did.

"Sometimes, yes," Viridis said. "We are."

Medusa clambered onto the table beside him and tilted her head back to watch the clouds scuttle over the stars.

Who else was coming? I itched to get started. Tonight, with the help of these witches, I'd reclaim my fur.

Trinity settled on a flat-topped boulder and brushed her hair. Oberon leaned beside her, one ankle crossed over the other. I did not notice him arrive. I left Morrigan's side to shake his hand, not wanting to interrupt the discussion.

Oberon smelled of summer barbeque and mint, and wore a baseball cap over his platinum blond hair.

The woman with all the scars—Paula? No, Poe—wasn't here, but I doubted she was who we waited on. She had kids. Children were a fast-track to next-level boredom.

Oberon listened to the other witches debate morals for a while before asking, "Well, you're Aboriginal. You'd be on the receiving end of appropriation, wouldn't you Viri? How would you feel if you saw a white guy playing a didgeridoo?"

Viridis rested his elbows on his knees, leaning forward. "It's a yidaki, and I'd assume he was a Blackfulla."

"Skin colour doesn't determine heritage," Morrigan said. "Not always."

"A bad example then," Oberon said.

Viridis rubbed the side of his nose. "Here's the thing: so much of my culture's been destroyed that when I see someone trying to connect with Country and learning our lore, I'm excited for them. Coloniser or not. If no one takes an interest... If people don't support our businesses and put pressure on the government to hear our voices, we'll continue to lose ourselves. But plenty of my mob disagree with me. We're not a hive mind."

"Each culture has their own, uh," Trinity's brow furrowed, "standard—I guess—of what can be shared too.

Hijab for example." She spoke directly to me. "Head covering as a sign of respect and modesty isn't owned by Islam. Look at any depiction of Mother Mary in the Catholic church. It's also cultural, not simply religious. Even before I knew why, I never cared what Meddy wore." The two girls shared a smile. "She's not stealing something from me by adopting this part of my culture."

Oberon checked his watch. "But if—"

"Hey, sorry I'm late," Eliss called, jumping one of the residential fences and pushing through the bushes to reach us. "Expected easier parking this time of night." Ze pushed zir fringe out of zir eyes. "We all here?"

"All that are coming," Medusa confirmed, readjusting her pack. "Trinity will be our lookout."

"And I'm your get-away driver." Oberon unlocked then relocked his car so we'd know where it was. "Unless you arrived here with Viridis. Then you're his problem."

We'd enter the warehouse, grab as many furs as possible, prioritising mine, and race back to the car. With the group hugging and whispering around me, it seemed easy.

Trinity would stand sentinel from Hewlett Street, where she'd have a birds-eye view of the warehouse and beach. She pulled a pair of binoculars from her side-bag. In her other hand, she held her phone. "Light to guide us," she said.

"Darkness to hide us," Medusa and Eliss chorused.

We crossed Marine Drive and the sand came into view.

"There are two floors," Morrigan said, "And two entry points on the main floor: the front door, and a small hatch on the south side. It looks like a basement hatch, but as the warehouse is built on the jetty above the water, I'm assuming it's not."

We crossed the sand, then hugged the rock-wall on our right. I wouldn't be showing anyone my childish art tonight.

Medusa stepped up beside Morrigan and I. "I'll stone the padlock. When we're inside, we'll pair up to search."

I hoped this 'stoning' wouldn't be incredibly loud. Our footfalls echoed enough.

"Meddy, I'm with you." Morrigan took Medusa's hand in her free one, making us a chain, and I had to look away, over the water, to shield them from my disappointment. They seemed to have pulled off escapades like this before, it made sense they'd work together. Perhaps that was key to our success.

As Morrigan promised there would be, a warehouse I'd failed to notice on countless visits to the shore squatted over the ocean. The tide was low. We could have walked under the jetty and broken into the warehouse via a hole in the floor, if we'd thought to bring a reciprocating saw.

Thick lumps of seaweed floated in the gentle waves. As the water ebbed, they spread over the sand like desperate claws, grabbing for the jetty's posts. My skin crawled. "Out 'o the water, we should stay."

"Shh. Shielding." Eliss shut zir eyes to concentrate, trusting Viridis not to let zir fall off the jetty. When Morrigan had shielded us, I'd recognised the magick, but I felt nothing from Eliss. Regardless, we reached the hatch unmolested.

Medusa slung her pack down and rummaged in it. "You'll want to step back."

We shuffled around. There wasn't a whole lot of clearance between the side of the building and the jetty's edge. The sea serenaded me, luring me over the ledge singing *gairm gu uisge*. I shook my head and crouched to stabilise myself.

I was level with Medusa, my line of sight clear, framed by the legs of her friends. If she held a rock at all, it wasn't big enough to do any damage, completely enclosed in her fist as it was.

Nothing happened. Time paused but for the slap of the waves, then a low crunch broke the stillness. Medusa tucked the stone into her pocket and produced a thermos. She and Eliss danced aside as boiling water sloshed onto the boards. Rinsing the broken lock's remains, I supposed.

A moment later, they pulled the short doors open and Brooke ducked into the room beyond. She switched on a flashlight.

"Safe," came her whispered assurance, and we followed her in, crawling on a cold tiled floor. To my right, there were two cubicles and a urinal. The walls were unfinished corrugated iron bolted onto recycled wooden beams. Hardened grout was splattered over the tiles. The air was hot and unfresh. Above us, the siren's song of my fur was a magnet to my soul. Below, the sea slapped at my balance. My oidhirp anabarrach would rise to meet gairm gu uisge, culminating in a glorious crescendo when I ceded; when I leapt into the sea's embrace and cast off all that bound me. The need of it set me to trembling.

Brooke was waiting for me by the restroom door. "You okay?"

I clenched my fists and forced myself to my feet. "Directly overhead, the furs are there." To pass through the door would be to move away from my goal. I stared at the chipboard cciling.

Brooke darted behind me and shoved me. I stumbled into the hall, righted myself, then turned a sharp left, where the pull felt strongest.

"I wish Poe was here," Medusa muttered.

Morrigan made a thoughtful sound. "Same."

Viridis and Eliss went right, heading for the building's rear. Everyone else accompanied me left. The hall open-ended at a T section, the right-hand path leading to the main entrance. Other closed doors in that direction betrayed no secrets. To the left, a faux wall concealed a rough wood and steel staircase leading to a cramped landing and two doors.

Vertigo struck when I was halfway up the stairs. I placed a hand against the corrugated outer wall and strove onward. The bolts were shiny new, but the beams weathered.

Medusa passed me. "Elton, can you sense which door your skin's behind?"

It was hard to hear her over the roar of the ocean and the blood pounding in my ears.

Unbearable heat flooded my system. I crumpled to my knees four steps from the top, sweating like a beast. "The ocean... I need..." I clawed my way up another step, my vision black at the edges, odd details coming into sharp focus.

Medusa unzipped her pack and handed something to Morrigan, who squeezed in beside me. "Here." She tipped a splash of icy water into my hair, then pressed the bottle into my hands. "Drink."

I did.

"Eat." She thrust a banana at me.

Who in their right mind carried bananas to a break-and-enter? I took a bite of the sickly-sweet fruit, washing it down with more water. "I can't tell, no," I answered their previous question. Morrigan tried to support me as I got to my feet, but I snatched my arm away and pushed forward. Toward my fur. My freedom. My future.

"They're locked anyway." Medusa tapped a nail against the keyhole. She had two short nails on her right hand, the rest were considerably longer, painted in bright pink and orange stripes. "Nothing I can do here."

Of course she couldn't. Useless wench.

Medusa stepped aside, pressing her spine to the wall to give Morrigan and I space as she slipped past onto the stairs. "Brooke?"

Irrationally, I wanted to give her a shove, send her flying. I balled my fist instead and slammed it into the door. The sound echoed through this end of the warehouse. My skin broke. The door remained stoic. I drew back my other fist, my lips drawn into a snarl.

"That's not helping," Brooke admonished. She bustled Morrigan off the cramped landing and stopped before me, assessing the lock.

My fist passed over her head and connected with the door again.

"Shhh!" Medusa wrung her hands, casting furtive looks over her shoulder. I'd give her shhh in her ugly face in a minute.

Brooke cowered.

Someone's phone pinged with messages.

Morrigan grabbed my wrist and spun me to face her. "Remember who you are!" Her eyes were clear. The set of her jaw determined. "Don't succumb to the storm. Not now." She towed me from the door, her body sandwiched between mine and the corrugated iron. She wrapped her arms around my hips, anchoring me. "Come back to us, Elton."

A new, more pleasant, heat welled inside me.

"We must work together," Morrigan continued. "Let Brooke focus her magick." She had a short curl at the very front that didn't reach her hair tie. I tucked it behind her ear, but it sprang free. She went cross-eyed as it fell between her eyebrows and my irrational rage subsided to a manageable level.

"You bring me—"

A shriek and the slam of a heavy door preceded measured footfalls coming in our direction. Two people, perhaps more.

Medusa froze in the middle of the staircase. Morrigan stiffened, turning to meet the intrusion.

At the bottom of the stairs, Liam Kendren stepped into view. His voice was unmistakable, despite his super-dark high-reflection sunglasses and the large, gilded mirror he carried like a shield. "Miss Larue. I'm not at all surprised." He glanced back the way he'd come, then motioned at us with his head. "Lock the ugly one in a closet with the Selkie, toss the others into the bay. Morrigan is mine." Shoulders squared, he ascended the stairs.

Medusa hugged herself.

Liam thrust his face into hers. "They said you were a smart girl. They were right."

Who was "they"? Other corrupt members of Arcane Industries?

Not that she appeared smart in the slightest; she looked ready to wet herself.

A burly woman and a wide Muldjewangk followed Liam onto the stairs. The Muldjewangk forced Medusa's arms behind her back. She yowled and thrashed, wriggling free of her backpack but not the creature's determined grip as it marched her down.

Liam leaned his mirror shield against the handrail, grinning as though Meddy's cries were music.

I stepped in front of Morrigan and Brooke.

"Naww, young love." Liam stopped a step down from us, matching my height, and reached for me, even as my bloodied knuckles flew toward his goofy face. Somehow, he was faster, wrenching my shoulder with his opposite hand and misdirecting my blow. He grabbed my shirt at the waist and threw me behind himself into the waiting arms of his strongwoman. Her forearm caught me across the small of my back as my nose met the corrugated wall.

MORRIGAN

I put my hands up. "I'll come peacefully. Don't touch me."

"As you wish."

Brooke and Elton were dragged from view, fighting every step. Meddy's wail echoed throughout the building, mingling with other cries. Eliss. Possibly Viridis too.

Meddy's bag was at the bottom of the steps. Even without any regents, I had faith in her ability to free herself and Elton. Particularly if he cooperated with her; kept her calm.

Liam Kendren sighed in a self-satisfied way as he "relieved me" of my phone and directed me to his office. "It's perfect. Matthias thinks he has Elton's skin and you're safely tucked into bed." He checked his gold and diamond watch. "And I have at least five hours before anyone notices you're missing."

As if I'd put myself in this situation, without telling anyone where I was going. No. The moment Liam Kendren had left our house, Dad would've texted me. Trinity would've called him when she saw Liam Kendren coming down the jetty. He'd know we needed help. My friends splashing in the Muldjewangk infested waters outside faced far greater risk than I did.

"Save your bragging." I rolled my eyes for effect. "This isn't a low-budget thriller."

"Rude as always."

He marched me down the hallway toward the main entrance where there was a small foyer. At some point, someone had attempted to make this area look less like an illegal shack by installing fancy lighting and covering the corrugated iron with drywall. Opposite the hallway we exited hung a wide abstract painting and below that was a bench. Large pots with fake plants taller than me brightened the corners. Two other halls branched from the foyer, one leading to the northern end of the building, the other straight down the middle into pitch darkness.

Either side of the dark hall were rooms. The one on the left was its own island—a box constructed in the foyer like an afterthought. How far into the building did it extend?

The one on the right appeared identical, save that it connected to the wall on my side instead of being flanked by corridors.

Liam Kendren stepped up beside me, now the space allowed it, and I glanced over my shoulder at the main door. It stood open, guarded by silent Muldjewangk. I'd have to brave a corridor of them on the jetty if I wanted to make a break for it.

I gestured to the display of power. "Weird flex, but okay."

He grinned. "Glad you appreciate it." He steered me toward the door on the right. "Today, if you please."

The lacky who'd taken Elton approached from the northern hall, her hard soles clacking on the concrete floor. Her expression was pinched. "There's been a slight complication, sir. A moment of your time?"

Liam Kendren paused. "Can't it wait?"

"'fraid not, sir."

"Well, I'm sure Miss Larue won't mind." He redirected me to the door on the left of the dark hall. "Join us in my office?"

The woman stepped uncomfortably close, herding me forward. She reached in front of me to turn the handle and I held my breath so I didn't have to consume hers.

The hinge squeaked. Liam Kendren rammed his boot into my arse, launching me into the unlit room. Jars clanked together at the force of the door slamming behind me. Bolts at the top and bottom slid into place.

"No hard feelings, Morrigan." The sturdy door muffled his voice. "Back in a moment." Their footfalls moved away. "What is it?"

"One of these little shits-" Another door closed and their conversation disappeared. They were likely in his office, which had to be the door he'd first steered me toward. I brushed myself off and fumbled for a light switch.

The dusty room appeared to have been a hub while the warehouse was built, now serving as a laundry and part-time break room. There was an electric kettle and jars of tea, coffee, and sugar. A mini fridge and a lime-green sticky patch. Folding chairs and a card table. Three people would have made this area crowded. Either his employees were few, or he didn't care for their comfort. The latter felt out of character, but then he wasn't the High Priest of Decorating at AI. He'd worked in logistics.

Beyond the industrial washer, drier, and folding station, metal shelves were bolted into the unfinished chipboard ceiling. Cans. Jars. Tools that had never been put away. Hands on my hips, I searched for inspiration in the tangle of exposed pipes, wires and overall neglect. He'd be back any moment, and I hardly believed he just wanted to chat. The weak bulb above me flickered. I needed a plan. A way to defend myself when he came back. If he came back. Perhaps he'd leave me to rot. I circled past the mini kitchen again. The bread on top of the microwave was solid blue-green.

The answer didn't come immediately; I was much too tired for that. When it did, it dawned slowly, like when someone has to explain their joke and then it isn't funny anymore.

Near the centre of the room, a bit across from one of the support beams, the ceiling was sagging. That was my chance. I'd either climb out onto the roof or emerge in one of the locked rooms above.

The metal shelf held firm as I scaled it, which did absolutely nothing to fuel my confidence when the part to lean backward over empty space came. Ancient Gods, Meddy would be perfect for this. She could hold her whole weight on one arm for an entire minute. I was going to fall and crack my head.

I reached out. Not far enough. My arm holding the shelf quavered. I stretched until it fully extended and my elbow locked. Meddy's voice reminded me to never lock my joints, but I ignored it. The sag turned out to be water-damaged wood, fetid and swollen. I scratched at it and flakes came away. If I had a screwdriver or a broomstick, I could open a hole and climb through.

Or, I could open a hole, attempt to climb through, fall, and break a leg. I clambered down. Meddy had broken both legs once, shattering the bones. Even with Elouera and my parents' coven casting healing spells, her recovery took months, leaving her weak and in agony. How much good would I be to Elton and my coven if I injured myself tonight? "Stop it," I muttered. Then, reaching out to the spirits around me as I scanned the shelves for something useful, I asked, "Can you help me rip through the ceiling?"

I found a crowbar on the next shelf.

Back at the soggy patch, I swung my crowbar. It sank into the sodden particle board overhead and ripped chunks free. They rained down on the floor. My hands pulsed with the strain and every sound from outside the staff storage room jolted through me. I widened the hole, even though logic said that if the wood were rotten, it wouldn't hold my weight when the time came.

What if I used the hooked end of the crowbar like a grapple, and pulled myself up into the dark above? A chuckle bubbled in my throat. No, that was absurd. I was absurd.

I arched back over the open space and prodded into the hole with my crowbar. The darkness lifted, like a blanket.

Or a rug. A rug over a dangerous, rotten patch in the floor. Who did that?

Perhaps it was carpet not a rug, and Liam—or whoever rented this shack for him—was unaware. I prayed that wouldn't be the case. Carpet wouldn't lift so easily, right?

I tugged with the crowbar as hard as my precarious angle allowed, widening the hole toward myself until I reached a place where the particle board held. What would happen when I released my grip on the shelf? Would I swing wildly on one arm until my hand slipped free and the concrete floor rushed upward? The door handle rattled. I froze. He'd laugh if he caught me like this. Great joke. I waited for the sound of bolts sliding, but it never came.

I licked my lips. How much longer did I have before he returned? Before he used me to threaten my dad, or worse, used me for some sick experiment. I readjusted my grip on the shelf in preparation. Stop over-thinking it. Meddy had taken me climbing dozens of times. Coloured handholds or no, I was strong enough for this.

If the old gods were kind, I'd be lying on my stomach in a moment, so I tucked the crowbar into my belt at the side of my hip and set my jaw. Leaning back, I grabbed the edge of the hole first with one hand then the other. Gravity hugged me around the middle. I focused on my hands, visualising how my body would move, seeing myself already where I needed to go.

I pushed off the shelf with my feet, using the momentum to carry my chest over my wrists. The rough woven backing of the floor-cover above caught my hair and scraped my cheek as I propelled my torso up and over, my legs flurrying in useless kicks behind me. With a grunt, I commando-crawled my upper body away from the hole, my heart thumping against the particle board. My breasts were crushed toward my armpits and I was grateful I had little there as the weight of my legs dragged me back. Every breath tasted of dust. My eyes began to water. A splinter sank into my elbow, but I got my hips fully onto the chipboard. Then the first sneeze hit. I didn't cover in time and more dust took flight in the restricted space. Another took me, the force of it driving my forehead into the floor. Cradling my head, I sneezed again and again, tears running down my face. If Liam Kendren didn't bust me within the next minute and pull me down from this death trap, I'd asphyxiate.

Desperate, I pushed the floor-covering up with one arm, making more room. The darkness lessened a metre or so ahead. Snot and floor grit stuck to my face as, at last, I got purchase with my feet and birthed myself into a dark laboratory. Water ran freely from my eyes. My wrists quivered as I pushed up onto my knees, found my feet, and stumbled to the nearest door.

I flicked the switch, risking the light being seen from the beach. The Muldjewangk didn't seem able to talk, and if they were capable of independent thought, I doubted they'd bother their master because a light was on.

Three long tables occupied the room: the thick-beamed white oak I'd crawled out from under, a thinner table with metal legs of the same length, and a series of portable metal tables set side-by-side against one wall. Over the weak spot where I'd made my hole, a Persian knock-off was pinned by two of the oak's legs. Linoleum off-cuts served as flooring on the other side of the room, their curled edges presenting a trip hazard.

I went to brush myself off, then thought better of it - One glance at my black tee told me I'd just fill my palms with splinters. Taking stock of the room, I re-tied my hair and blew my nose. A terrible stench assailed me, awakening the nausea coiled in my belly. Cat food. Meat. Dead things. I should've left my nose clogged.

Blood stains covered the white oak, sinking deep into the grain. The end closest to me had metre rulers painted on the tabletop, as if we were at Spotlight measuring lace. Further down the table, clumps of fur had congealed to the wood next to a diagram showing the skin's layers. Every breath was foul. I shuffled away from the oak, bumping into a pile of Selkie skins along the parallel wall, awaiting processing.

I prodded the topmost skin with my finger. When it didn't move, I ran my hand lightly over the fur. My stomach twisted again; it was warm. I shouldn't have been surprised; they were living flesh. It didn't really make sense for them to be clean, cured coats. But none of the myths mentioned the fish-market stench. No one bothered to warn me that the pelts oozed mucus or that they'd bleed when cut open. I scanned the lab for a fridge and found it next to two doors and a coat rack. Once cut, the skin would probably die, and the unprocessed pieces would need to be refrigerated to slow their decay. I tried to think clinically, to understand the process without letting it overwhelm me.

The dermal layer image was duplicated above a pair of complex machines on the metal table, alongside other instructions. I reached for my phone to take a picture, but my pocket was empty. Damn that man. I'd located what we'd come for, but alone. Stilling my thoughts, I attempted to form a telepathic message, but the assistance I required was too detailed. The most I'd ever been able to do was urge someone to pick up bread at the shops. No. This was up to me.

At my best guess, I'd have said a specific dermal layer went into the machines, somehow extracting the Selkie magick, to be combined with the semi-precious stones outlined in the documents I'd found on Dad's computer. A hurried search revealed tubs of peacock ore and calcite stowed under the metal table. How were they combined?

Shitsticks. I should have paid more attention in science class.

Rock grit covered the middle table, below which were small vats. I wasn't opening them to check, but I imagined by their placement that this was where the excess skin was cured into leather to make the backing and straps for the pauldrons. Bile rose up my throat. I had to stop this operation. But it was too big for me. Too advanced. Even with instructions on the walls, much of it was indecipherable jargon or chemical images that made no sense. I'd been a fool to involve my friends. I rubbed my naked wrists and clicked my jaw. If I didn't move, I'd be caught in here. I ought to have cleaned up the floor downstairs; it was obvious where I'd gone. Liam Kendren would barge in any moment, and I'd done nothing. Or Dad would arrive to rescue me, not knowing he was ruining my chance and I was right where I needed to be. I cast about for a sign.

Above a third door, right beside the untouched skins piled on the floor, there was one. A glowing green exit sign, complete with man running. A short manic laugh burst from me at the stupidity of it. Everything about this shack was half-arsed, but they took the time to instal proper emergency exit signs?

Grit comprised of crystal fragments and ground herbs crunched on the floor between the thin middle table and the metal ones. I passed an elaborate chemistry set, the only truly clean thing in the room, and went to try the door.

It opened out onto a fire escape that faced the ocean. "Would've been good to know," I muttered to myself. Whoever scouted this location hadn't bothered to get on a boat and investigate the rear of the building. Stepping lightly, I hung over the railing. The ocean below was calm and black, glittering with diffused gold light from behind me.

Returning inside, I lifted a flipper of the skin nearest the door. Stacked all together, the skins would be taller than I was. An eyeless socket stared up at me. The building groaned. I lifted my ponytail off my sweaty neck and assessed Liam Kendren's equipment again. Inspired, I rushed to the smaller electronic particle-separating device and unplugged it, draping the cord around my collar so it wouldn't trip me as I carried the blasted thing. It weighed about as much as a decent blender and was hopefully ruined the same when it splashed into the bay. We could recover it when this case was behind us.

Inside again, I shut and locked the door in case any Muldjewangk came to investigate. I crouched, holding my breath, but heard no disturbance on the far side.

The second machine on the metal table was bigger. I couldn't lift it, never mind hoisting it over the railing. Opening it revealed a metal drum with tubes inside, like the machines they had at the pathology for spinning blood, but they probably weren't at all similar. I pulled out a few vials. They didn't appear to have ever been used. Perhaps this method of extraction had been unsuccessful. Or maybe this was a fancy bench-top dishwasher for chemistry tubes and I didn't know what I was talking about. Damn him. Damn Liam Kendren and his cronies and their old man university degrees!

I slapped the vials I was holding onto the bench and swept some floor grit into my hands. Painstakingly, I guided it into the holes, replacing the tubes when I was done. Hopefully the machine would blow up in the face of the next person to use it.

Not my best plan, but if I slowed operations down...

I bustled back to the eerie empty seal skins and lifted one. Then two. Fish-shop-dumpster stink bloomed in the air. My eyes watered as I attempted three, but they were so awkward and heavy, I wouldn't have been able to take two steps had I succeeded. None of them resembled Elton, or how I imagined he might look. I pressed my teeth together and glanced around again. Time was running away from me. I needed help, and there was only one way to get it without a phone.

I had to fall asleep.

Chromatic

Elton

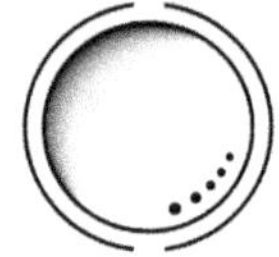

A terrible stench thickened the hallway as Medusa thrashed in the Muldjewangk's grip. She took a breath to fuel her screams and an angry hissing filled the momentary void, blocking all sense of what was happening to Morrigan.

Had she burst a noxious gas pipe to cover her escape?

No. The smell worsened as we passed the main door and headed along another hall. Medusa's wail choked the air around us. The Muldjewangk wrestled her through a door.

The strongwoman tripped me, propelling me down onto Medusa on the floor of a closet. Fumes overwhelmed me, making my eyes water despite my refusal to breathe.

The door shut behind us, then reopened to release a strip of fabric. It slithered past the frame in an instant, then darkness fell complete. The lock clicked before I managed to scramble off Medusa.

My lungs ached and my shoulder popped as I pushed up onto my knees. "One moment, I've a flashlight."

"No!" Medusa's boot scraped the rough floor as she fumbled then crashed into the supplies behind her. "No no. Don't do that. They took my hijab."

"Your grim appearance does not concern me."

She snorted. "It should."

I tested the lock and felt for a light switch that didn't exist.

"If we want to leave, I need a new head covering. Help me search."

"You want me to look an' yet I can not see?"

She sighed irritably. "Humour me."

My eyes adjusted to the darkness, revealing a stack of cheap plastic buckets in my corner, and wooden poles of varying length in hers. Who needed twenty types of broom and axe handle? The other supplies we'd been thrown in with were equally bizarre. A box of quartz points. Angle grinder discs. A dirty mop. Test tubes. Medusa picked up a short broomstick, minus the broom. Tendril-like shadows snaked around her face. The hissing had stopped, but the stank remained.

I cast my gaze away. Higher shelves held glass jars—of what eluded me—and tell-tale blue and white boxes of bicarbonate soda. The random assortment of equipment utterly lacked anything resembling cloth. Medusa assessed a deep box of corner brackets and began emptying them onto the floor with a clatter.

"What plan have you contrived?"

"Making a hat."

"You're n—" She was. She scrounged for a piece of sharp quartz with which to make eye holes. "I had to wear a paper bag once."

My stunned silence must have made her uncomfortable because she added, "It's only until I retrieve my pack. I have a spare hijab in there."

"No, I... I didn't mean..." Her determination baffled me. I took off my shirt and thrust it at her. "Try this."

She didn't so much as glance my way as she accepted. "Thank you. And I'm sorry. About the smell and every-thing."

"Sorry I am, for squashing you."

"Not really your fault." She fussed with the shirt. I hoped she didn't stretch it with whatever she was doing, whispering and cooing to herself the whole time. "Give me a minute, I'll get us out of here."

"How exactly, I do not see," I muttered.

When she finished wrapping her thick braids, she put one hand in her pocket and the other on the brass-tone doorknob.

Perhaps Brooke had taught her how to magick a lock? That'd be fortuitous.

A faint crunching sound came from the door, but it didn't open. Medusa swung an axe handle at it, fully shattering the knob. I picked up a shard while she chose a new pole.

Salt.

She'd turned the handle—the entirety of the mechanism—into rock salt. That's why she'd been pouring hot water on the side hatch! How did I miss that? Morrigan had insinuated her friend had power, but it never occurred to me she'd rival Selkie or Faerie. What exactly had Morrigan said?

I was right to be afraid.

Medusa whacked me with her pole, breaking my reverie. She hastened to apologise, explaining, "It's a little too long. I need to ram it through here, where the knob was, but I can't quite line this broom handle up because of the shelves." Speech seemed an effort to her. "The pick handles are too wide."

"Perhaps we can break it an' use only half?"

She handed the broomstick to me and spoke through clenched teeth. "Be my guest."

I leaned the pole into the corner, kicked it in the centre, and was rewarded with a satisfying crack and a long scratch on my calf.

She took the shortened stick and rammed it into what remained of the doorknob. When she removed the pole, low light from the corridor leaked in, illuminating her face as she put her eye to the hole, inspecting her work. She stuck her finger in and picked at the salt. "Doesn't look like we're guarded. Also doesn't look like I can dig this bolt out with my nails." She squinted up at me from where she crouched. "When was the last time you urinated?"

"What? You're not serious."

She stepped away from the door and faced the rear corner. "Go on. You're not going to make it stink any worse in here."

Earnest she was, indeed. I rested my hands on my zipper. That she didn't shy from the elephant in the room intrigued me. "What makes the odour? If I may be bold enough."

"It's my, uhm… hair. When I am hurt or in danger, my hair emits a disagreeable smell to dissuade attackers. High school was loads of fun."

She had ample problems without that. What a nightmare she must have survived. Was it any wonder Morrigan admired her so?

Medusa flapped her hand at me to hurry up.

"So gross," I muttered. I turned my back back to her and unzipped my fly. It was loud in that tiny space. I'd almost relaxed enough to go when Medusa spoke again.

"You're aiming for the prong that holds the door closed. So, like, point left."

The hole where the doorknob had been was higher than my crotch. I would inevitably splatter myself. And then when it ran down the door, I'd be standing in my foul water, soaking my shoes. I glanced over my shoulder. Medusa's stinky hair moved restlessly; a shifting shadow tangled in a tee shirt.

My options brought no joy: Either pee all over myself, or get naked in a cramped, dark cupboard with my girlfriend's best mate. I shut my eyes and rested my forehead against the cool door.

It was the wrong thing to do. Gairm gu uisge flared with intensity and heat pounded me. The type of heat only the ocean's embrace might subdue. I poked my finger into the sharp salt crystals, feeling for the place Medusa had indicated.

All was quiet yon the door, an auditorium for the song in my mind. Now was our chance, and I was wasting it.

I kicked off my shoes and pants and put them on a shelf. "If ambush awaits, you distract them and allow me to dress. Okay?"

"Noted." If she was disturbed by my bare curple pointed in her general direction, she didn't complain.

Despite Medusa's assertion that the stench couldn't get any worse, it did. I cringed and shut my eyes. The splash-back was awful. But it worked. Within moments, I was sitting in the corridor, hastily lacing up my shoes. I left my socks behind after I'd dried myself on them, despite Medusa protesting that a witch could 'seriously hex' me if I dropped such a convenient anchor. These witches had my fur, there wasn't a worse hex than that.

She didn't push the issue, too concerned with the angry welts covering her wrists. She drew them to her chest, tears streaming down her face, though her determined expression would have one believe she didn't notice them fall.

The instant I regained my feet, Medusa hastened back the way we'd been brought, unconcerned that we might run into a Muldjewangk or Liam's hired lackeys. She wore the neck of my tee shirt around her hairline, with a knot at the bottom hem to hold her braids, and the arms stretched and tied atop her head to keep it in place, I surmised.

"Stay behind me." Medusa produced a lump of salt from her pocket and held it tight.

The main door was open to the world. Through it a Muldjewangk, all green and stringy, caught sight of us and it spun on its heel. It pointed in our direction with its thick, dripping arm. I expected it to bellow, but it remained silent as it slow-motion charged. Mid-foyer it halted; one foot raised. Colour fled from its towering form, suddenly dry. My courage atrophied the same. The Muldjewangk teetered, light catching on its crystalline planes. A second monster, unfrozen, knocked it over as it lumbered into the warehouse, sending the first crashing to the ground. It shattered on impact. Shards of salt sprayed every direction.

Medusa gasped, distracted by her hands. The blisters on her wrists melted away. A shadow fell upon us. Medusa's gaze snapped up. This Muldjewangk also solidified, this time into an unremarkable grey stone.

The air cooled my tongue on the inhale. "Holy salt." I ought to have figured it out sooner.

"Help me," she growled. She put her shoulder to the statue, sliding it toward the hall we'd emerged from.

I jolted from my momentary stupor and joined her.

Our faces were inches apart. We heaved, managing a scant few feet. Then I flicked off the hall light for better concealment.

She nodded in approval. "That'll do."

We froze as a third Muldjewangk took a sentry position beside the door. A human guard would have had the sense to close it, but this animated seaweed creature did not. In the night yonder, a sloppy shuffling reached us over the breaking waves. More of the beasts. But how many?

As though it was nothing, Medusa solidified the third Muldjewangk, then quickly crossed the entryway. I hurried after her toward the stairs where Liam had interrupted us.

She scooped up her bag, then turned my way.

I stopped short, flinching as her gaze fell on me. "Uh, you're not going up stairs?"

Medusa peeked in her bag. "No. That'd be foolish. We can't unlock those deadbolts without Brooke. The prong is thicker than a regular doorknob and anyhow I've got no more hot water. Let's find a safe place to regroup." She checked her phone. "No messages from Morr. You?"

Mine showed no messages or missed calls, but also no service. "None."

"I bet he's taken her phone." Medusa pushed past me, heading for the exit.

"You're kidding, no?" She'd abandon her best friend?

She stopped and glared dead at me with her weird bloodshot eyes. "I don't kid. If I'm ever funny, assume it was an accident. Are you coming or not?"

Without Medusa to protect me, I was vulnerable. But my fur was at the top of those stairs, rooting me. Nor could I leave Morrigan to her fate. I put one foot on the bottom stair. Perhaps with my fur so near, I'd be able to channel *oidhirp anabarrach* to protect myself. Or I could blink out of sight and flee, if need be. If I didn't get cornered again. Yes. I had the strength. I wasn't leaving.

The doors at the top of the stairs would crumble before me. I flexed my fists. My sore knuckles told a different story.

Medusa's monobrow pinched in the middle. "We're not abandoning her, we're getting help."

At an impasse, we glowered at each other.

Her emptiness versus my noise. The roar of my furious blood, the pounding of the sea's relentless call. My need to see Morrigan safe.

At last, Medusa wrapped her arms across her chest, turned, and left me there.

I stumbled after her a few steps then stopped, biting my lip. Let Medusa rally the other witches; I needed to find a set of keys and Morrigan's location. Her presence pulled at me almost as much as my fur above and the sea below. Was that deliberate? No, she was a knight in shining armour. I wouldn't catch her sitting in a cell waiting for me.

Panicked rage surged up my neck and swirled around my molars as I slipped toward the nearest door. No light leaked out underneath. The handle turned easy. Nothing within of any import. Folding tables. A stack of plastic crates. Milk of the long-lived variety.

Listening hard, I crept along the hallway, my gaze fixed where the stone Muldjewangk stood sentinel. I tiptoed into the foyer and its presence weighed on my shoulders.

Neither the sentinel nor its fellow in the shadows moved to intercept me. Medusa's magick held. My breath ebbed and flowed, the only sound, yet I felt exposed. The need to hurry strained against caution.

I twisted the next shiny brass doorknob I happened across and eased the door inward.

Someone coughed.

I froze, drinking in the cold rush that came with flipping myself inside out. My hand on the doorknob disappeared as I became invisible, yet the metal warmed under my touch.

Footsteps scuffed over carpet inside.

Liam thrust his face through the opening, a hair's breadth from my own. He glanced at the main door, then

to his right, in a distracted way that said he expected someone in particular. His eyelid twitched.

"Nothing," he huffed.

"Told you." A brusque old-lady voice chided from within the office. "It's the presence of your sea demons messing
with my wards."

I frowned. Morrigan had spoken of wards, had she not?
Defensive spells and magickal security.

Liam stepped back to address his employee, holding the
door wide.

This wasn't the strongwoman from earlier. Where was
she now? And who was this grandma?

"Muldjewangk," Liam corrected.

"Whatever. You couldn't summon a demon with an
easier to pronounce name? You're not even Indigenous,
Kendren."

"Culture is for sharing." He paused, squinting at the
stone Muldjewangk. My heartbeat sputtered.

The woman leaked amusement through the holes between her teeth. "Did he like my old rug?"

Coaxed back into the conversation, Liam turned. The
door came at me.

I grabbed it to prevent him closing it all the way, my
knees jelly as my fingers pinched in the jam. I held my
invisibility in place through the force of my clenched jaw,

and rushed into the plush office before Liam realised the door hadn't latched. The cough sounded again as I cleared the threshold. Both witches glared. I hoped there wouldn't be other wards in here to betray my presence.

Invisibility ached.

I needed to hide.

Tiptoeing around the edge of the room, I assessed my options. A large potted plant, plastic on closer inspection, offered coverage betwixt itself and a Victorian chaise. I squeezed into the gap and held my breath as I lowered myself to the floor. My stumpy legs and torso slid under the lounge. My invisibility failed, snapping my spirit right-way in.

Let this be hidden enough, I prayed, wedging my shoulder into the space between oversized pot and striped wallpaper.

On a little sideboard under a fake window, complete with velvet curtains, a kettle reached full boil and clicked off.

Liam rubbed the back of his neck as he went to it. "If only I hadn't done Matthias dirty. Not that I can tell which pelt is the one they're so desperate to recover. But he's not going to believe me now."

"He wouldn't budge his pacifism, or consider any of the suggestions you made to the betterment of Arcane Industries. What he thinks of you is irrelevant." The woman pulled a pin from her wiry hair and began to clean under her fingernails with it. "Besides, the moment he notices the girl missing, he'll come knocking on your door, trust or no."

"I suppose." He poured boiling water on a tiny scoop of green powder and whisked it, the corner of his lip curling like a snake. "She'll ransom all the same."

"How much will he pay for her?"

"He'd give anything. He'd liquidise all his assets if I asked him to. But that's not the important part." Liam paced over to a grandfather clock as tall as he. "He'll recognise how serious I am. That I was right to petition for a witch's army. AI do need better security. He'll see that there are gaps in the system. The old hierarchy of power within the company isn't working. He's a smart man. I haven't lost faith that he'll see reason. You know what he said to me once? About his kid?"

That Matthias would discuss my beloved with this betrayer left me clenching my fists.

The old lady didn't respond. Didn't need to. Liam had a love affair with his own voice, as bland as it was.

"He said, 'She doesn't have to like me, she has to grow into a good person.' Well, he doesn't have to like me, but we both want what's best for AI. Those kids we threw in the bay, if they live, they'll go to Matthias. Not to Silver or the ICR. And I know him, he'll contact me directly. He'll do anything for his brat. Sure, he'll tell Felicia that he's seeing me, but she won't act without his say-so." He wiped a smudge off the clock face with his pocket hanky.

I was in his peripheral; one twitch and he'd spot me. If I disappeared, he'd notice the flicker. A couple more steps and he'd loom over me. What if he intended to sit on the chaise?

"It's after three," Liam said. "Morrigan's a late riser, so we've got at least four hours until Matthias notices her absence. If we're done here, her and I are due for a chat."

"You should get some rest first, my High Priest." The woman returned the pin to her hair. "I can watch over your prisoners."

"They don't need watching. That Selkie's a garden statue by now. I don't want you to join him. Leave the gorgon there to rot, she's a menace. Morrigan is the only one of value." He paced back the way he'd come. "Besides, assembly line crew will be here at six. Not sure a nap is worth it."

"Respectfully," she bowed her head, "it might not be wise to go against Matthias exhausted. Pacifist or no."

Liam huffed. "You're not wrong." Tea in one hand, he opened the door and stared pointedly at her until she rose.

As she shuffled out, he said, "While I interview our little witch, I need you to—"

She gasped.

With his back to me, I inverted myself and scrambled from my hiding place, nearly knocking the fake plant clean over. I caught and righted it, then dashed past them. The cough sounded, right on cue.

"Medusa's loose!" Liam stepped into the foyer and spun, his head whipping this way and that as he rushed his atrocious mirrored sunglasses to his face.

Salt crunched under the old woman's sensible shoes. "There's a second statue over here."

I flattened myself against a wall and focused on remaining unseen. This, too, would be rudimentary if I had my fur. The tiny hairs on my arms prickled. If they dissected my fur, this part of me would die. And would I still enrapture people with my music, or would my voice become husky dry?

"You take the southern stairs, check the rooms up there. I'll search down here, then head up. If you see her, shut your eyes. Stay alert for the Selkie too, they're violent creatures."

My hand went to my chest, to my heart. How dare he?

They split off, neither having the good sense to investigate outside, where I expected a row of stone Muldjewangk to be waiting. What had them so convinced Medusa would linger? That she'd retaliate against them? Liam withdrew a ring of keys from his trouser pocket. The keys I needed. I shadowed him a few steps, my hands going to my waistband. If I looped my belt around his neck, this would cease in a matter of minutes.

But I wasn't wearing a belt. I'd meant to buy a cloth one as leather had begun to itch my psyche. I hadn't made it to the shops yet. I hesitated. Liam's skinny appearance might belie hidden strength, or some witchcraft I was ill equipped to face.

My indecision lost him. My grip on my invisibility weakened. Medusa had been right to regroup.

Stepping carefully as to avoid the salt, I approached the main door. Liam wouldn't harm Morrigan if he needed her for ransom, but if he discovered me? Being tossed in the bay would be too great a boon to hope for.

Flickering in and out of view, I sprinted down the jetty—somehow devoid of Muldjewangk—and onto the slimy bedrock. I pushed myself harder. None of the algae stood to take humanoid form. The sand slowed me.

When I reached the dangerous current sign above the high tide mark, I puffed to a stop, giving up on my invisibility. The sea glittered with the promise of dawn.

If I tilted my head and squinted, the jetty and warehouse revealed themselves to me through the haze of Liam's stolen magick. A paddleboarder appeared, manifesting at the edge of the magick's influence and paddling hard toward the opposite point. There was a line of them, cutting across the bay. My scalp tingled with dizziness. I stumbled a few steps toward them. Two women with greying hair. Another with fiery red curls. A tall Black man. A hijabi. A grin broke over my face and I fell to my knees. What a coven. What a woman, to rally them all!

The paddleboarders each sported a brown pile on the front of their boards. Another paddleboarder rounded the edge of the warehouse. I scrambled back to my feet, sand threatening to topple me as though it had waves of its own. I was running beside them before I recognised Matthias, standing on the northern outcrop, loading skins onto a removalist trolley. Further up the hill, Eliss and Brooke bounced full trolleys up the last steps and ramps to the SLSC, where I assumed Matthias had parked.

A siren blared over the beach, warning all swimmers of a riptide.

Those few locals who frequented the small beach for their morning exercise glanced around, confused. There was no rip. But even without danger, the cacophony was unbearable. Those on the beach left and the surfers hastened toward shore.

One such came rushing onto the sand, oblivious to Liam, fuming at the end of his jetty. They passed me, jogging with their board under their arm. Liam waited for them to reach the grassy park above the beach, then raised his wand. His grin chilled the base of my spine.

The sea moved unnaturally.

Water spirits congealed, rising to Liam's summons.

I backed away.

The green rocks on the shoreline stirred, both out front of the warehouse and a hundred metres opposite, where Viridis was dragging his paddleboard and cargo onto the outcrop. Medusa moved sluggishly and was passed by the last paddleboarder. I didn't pause to figure out who they were.

Waves broke over my feet in bursts of song as I pelted across the sand toward Morrigan and the other witches on the northern point. No residents were in sight now. The sirens ceased as abruptly as they started. In the distance, out by Marine Drive, a warning played on loop that the beach was closed.

I waved my arms overhead, trying to get Matthias's attention. To warn him. But he was watching Medusa struggle, concern written large on his features. Eliss and Brooke were racing down the cliff-side ramp, their trolleys clanging. They passed Viridis as he made his way up.

The older ladies, one of whom was Morrigan's mother, held their paddles and panted, gazes locked on the warehouse. Calculating if they had time for another trip, I surmised.

"No!" I yelled, stumbling over the first rocks at the northern end. My legs wobbled, as though the beach was ten times the length of reality. Green muck stood and reached for me, a crystal on its shoulder catching the light. I dodged past, checking the others.

Morrigan was safely out of range, dragging a trolley-load of furs uphill as if all she had left was her own stalwart determination.

Medusa knelt on her board, either for a rest or because the surf was too choppy for her to stand, I wasn't sure. I yelled but the waves swallowed my wordless call to look up. To move.

With a paddle, Matthias scraped kelp that struggled to rise into the sea where it broke apart. Liam's power had limits then. It could be disrupted. At this range, Liam laboured with summoning the hypoxic spirits. Something told me he wouldn't rush over to confront us. Not with Medusa here and his bargaining chip escaped.

"Leave the boards!" the oldest lady shouted. "They don't matter." She hefted an armful of fur.

Felicia filled her own arms, freezing for a moment as she gawked at something behind me. "Ruuuuun!"

On the hill, Eliss and Brooke put on a burst of speed. Morrigan, however, stopped completely, seeking Medusa.

Matthias was shouting and reaching for Medusa, who still floated a good ten metres away. The water roiled unnaturally around her, swirls of seaweed dragging at her paddle. She was crying.

I reached Felicia and snatched up a discarded oar, swinging it as a weapon against the closest Muldjewangk. I slapped it in the face with the paddle end. Foul fluids splooshed from its head, but it kept coming. I spun my weapon and thrust with the handle, hitting the creature solidly in the shoulder and smashing the crystal. At once, the Muldjewangk collapsed in a spray of weeds and water, leaving behind a saturated leather triangle on a cross-body belt.

More grotesque Muldjewangk were closing in. My guts turned to goo. We might outrun them if we got off this beach immediately. Their odd assortment of legs, tails, and tentacles made some of them faster on land than others, but despite how spread out they were, I didn't possess the energy to finish them all. Another wave of them would reach us within a minute. Dozens more headed our way with single-minded hatred.

Matthias flattened his palms and pushed, as though the air did his bidding, then dived into the water and surfaced behind Medusa. He used her paddleboard as a giant kickboard, propelling her toward the rocks while she steered. Three Muldjewangk peeled away to intercept. I rushed to the edge of the slippery outcrop and prepared to defend their landing, while another Muldjewangk fell upon the last skins on Felicia's abandoned board, gathering them to return to its master.

I withstood the urge to prioritise my kin's furs and knelt at the water's edge, reaching for Medusa as her paddleboard bumped against the exposed bedrock. She took my hand, leapt to shore, and turned to help me drag the board to safety, despite the trembles that wracked her limbs. Matthias got a hand on the rock as a tentacled Muldjewangk got its grip on him.

He screamed the kind of scream that hurts your lungs and throat just to hear it. A shrill, tearing, mammalian cry of anguish that echoed off the very air. Medusa sobbed anew. We both dove for him, grabbing a sleeve each. A wave broke over our heads, filling my mouth with salt and grit. Matthias spluttered. When he hollered again, there was rage and determination in the pain. I pulled him onto the ground with my left hand, brandishing the oar with my right.

I aimed badly. The oar sank into the Muldjewangk's torso like a stick into mud and the Muldjewangk paid it no heed, advancing up Matthias's legs and buttocks with its octopus hold. Another took Medusa's place on the board, this one having a single serpentine tail. It stroked the skins and a flood of fire ripped through me; my anger so great I near shattered my teeth with the force which I gnashed them.

In one fluid motion I pulled my oar free, spun it over Medusa's veiled head and took the second Muldjewangk in the side of the face. Those skins weren't mine, but the fierce desire to protect them galvanised my core.

Though I hit it solidly, the Muldjewangk remained steady, tossing skins over its shoulder to its kin bobbing in the water. Matthias's screaming stopped with the oxygen flow to his brain. His attacker had its tentacles around his neck. His flesh boiled, bright blisters full of burbling blood, roiling wheresoever the Muldjewangk touched.

Medusa covered her mouth, muffling her own horrified cry. Why wasn't she doing something? She had the ability turn them all to stone, did she not? Gripping my oar in both hands, I aimed for the monster's shoulder and the magick that held it together. Perhaps I could convince it

I was the bigger threat. I lunged, stepping forward to give my attack power. The end of my oar hit, making a sharp crack as I chipped the crystal buried under the Muldjewangk's kelpy hair.

A squeal came from everywhere and nowhere as the creature burst.

Or perhaps it was a coincidence, and the sound had more to do with Medusa solidifying the Muldjewangk on the paddleboard. It hovered for a moment, almost mermaidlike with its fierce eyes and flowing stone hair, then the weight of the thing sent it crashing onto the Muldjewangk behind it. A wave broke over us, saturating our clothes. I spat saline.

Eliss rushed forward and wrapped an arm around Medusa, zir eyes firmly shut as ze squeezed the veiled witch's shoulders, then ze threw the remaining skins onto zir trolley and dashed away. Medusa drew a fold of her scarf over her lowered face, pinning it hastily. I thrust at another Muldjewangk as it stepped out of the rising tide. This one had none of the hair-like strands, making my target easier to spot, even with my opponent backlit by the newday sun. I felled it quickly. Morrigan ducked between me and Medusa, helping her dad to stand. The skin on his neck was bruised, as you might expect, but the bubbling welts were gone.

"Grab that leather triangle," he barked.

Medusa scooped it up.

They were the key to Liam's magick. Those and his wand.

We scrambled to the stairs, and I let the witches pass me, my oar at the ready, though no further attack appeared forthcoming.

"Their touch burns." Medusa's words sank into me as I brought up the rear, my focus fixed on the Muldjewangk milling on the sand. If I had to guess, I'd say they forgot about us entirely. But I didn't need to speculate. Liam had admitted defeat. This battle, anyway.

It was a long drive back to the Inner West.

Selkie heritage emanated from the cars parked out the front of Morrigan's house, singing the heartsongs of strangers. An abyss opened around me through which Morrigan's concerned voice echoed. "Elton? Hey. Look at me."

Sleep beckoned, an escape from the crushing devastation in my chest. Their empty house waited, utterly devoid of that which I sought. The furs of selkies I'd probably never meet mocked me as they passed, carried by exhausted witches over the dew-slick lawn on which I stood. Furs willingly surrendered, though not to Liam's twisted cause.

Scores of fin folk forsook the ocean. Why? I wanted to ask them. To break through the surface of polite conversation and discover the ruler of their personal tides. Why hadn't I questioned my community?

I had desired no reasons to stay.

"Let me be enough, for now," Morrigan whispered. Her eyes, clear and bright like the tropics, were rimmed red with fatigue.

Mine wasn't among them, yet the number of furs Arcane Industries had recovered with Morrigan leading them was impressive. How had she done it? As though through a mist, I searched for words to laud her. Then Felicia was there, supporting me, lifting my weight from the other side. My face was damp where it rested against Morrigan's shoulder. The couch would have welcomed me, but Felicia deposited us in the kitchen, where a kangaroo skin rug spilled out of a hessan sack on the scarred table.

Matthias took a long pull directly from the tap as Morrigan's covenmates and the old lady piled furs in the lounge room. They were joking around. Laughing. How could they laugh at a time like this?

Maybe Matthias agreed. He squint-glared at the doorway, then at the kangaroo rug. Its colour was the only similarity to a Selkie's fur. His movements heavy, he took the kangaroo to the room off the kitchen, stroking it sadly.

"I've got you." Morrigan's lips tickled my ear. "We'll get your skin back. I know it."

Did she? Through some witch sense? Or was she merely trying to make me feel better? I squeezed her leg, a silent plea for her to keep talking. To continue to anchor me with her rough, genuine voice.

"You can trust me. I've been working in the industry since I was thirteen. Did you know?"

"I did not. Is there a song honouring it?"

"Ha, no. I'd be mortified. But, late in my first mission—Gods, it wasn't even a mission as such. I was just a kid, falling out of my dreams and witnessing murders. Anyway, I didn't think Brooke and I would survive. By the end, I don't know if I even wanted to. I was so tired and scared. Waking up was the worst; failure was always there, staring at me. And then I'd have to face the victims, and my team who I was letting down. I could barely look my parents in the eye." She withdrew a pocket hand sanitiser and squirted my palms, massaging my hands as she continued. "The thing I learnt was you have to make friends with failure if you want to succeed. Disappointing people never gets easier, and it kills me that we had to leave your skin, and so many others, behind today. But we're not defeated, Elton. We'll keep trying, keep going at him. Poe tells me 'It's always okay in the end. If it's not okay, it's not the end.' and it's true. I will make that true for you."

The light of her loyalty shrunk me. I curled into her, small and vulnerable, and she wrapped me in softness, taking the sting out of my soul.

She drew me tighter, layering me with internal armour. "People like you and me, we have the power to change things. Our actions will ripple out, touching all corners of the world. We must hang on despite our losses. This is bigger than us. Bigger than Liam Kendren and his delusions of grandeur."

My voice came out raw when I spoke, as if I'd swallowed seawater. "Did you uncover his plan?" Perhaps she'd heard all I missed.

Her curls brushed the back of my hand, where it rested over hers. "No, and I don't care anymore. There's no excuse for what he's doing."

"He told me." Matthias closed the door between the lounge and kitchen, though most of the helpers had departed, and sat at the head of the table. "Yet I've got to wonder if he was lying." He spread his hands. "I'm embarrassed at how easy I was for him to fool."

My heart lamented for the old vegan, who probably had zero contact with hides of any variety throughout his life. He had to be exhausted. His eyes fairly hung from his head, yet he sat straight and spoke with conviction. "He says that the Muldjewangk are a show of force, intended to awaken Arcane Industries. He wants me to believe his actions are for the greater good; that the changes he proposes for the company are essential. If I were to agree to implement his strategies, overhaul our security systems, invest resources in schools of magick best left untouched, get some of our people into politics…" He spoke with his hand, gesturing a pile of demands ongoing. "Better, if I had Ms Moon-tread ratify the easier suggestions, and grant him a full pardon—"

Morrigan snorted.

I stiffened at the very suggestion. "None should walk free from crimes like these."

"Exactly. He can't threaten us into submission." He shook his head. "We're not beaten. Tomorrow Aoidh Vess is coming here. We'll make our case to the community and offer battle training to those who volunteer. This arvo, Morrigan will submit her report, giving us inside information about Kendren's process. We recovered a pauldron along with those skins. Today was a victory."

Yet Liam would continue to cut up Selkie furs. He still held mine, and now he had a lot less of them to choose from. Victory indeed.

AMOROSO

ELTON

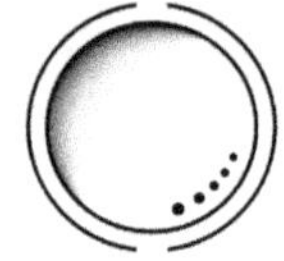

I woke in Morrigan's room to the snap of her curtains. The late afternoon breeze tickled my toes where they stuck out under the doona. Her arms still enfolded me, and her splinter-filled hair mugged my face. It smelt of dust. Dirt smeared her forehead. My soul fluttered and I pulled her closer despite my protesting muscles. She let out a pained moan, but we both smiled.

A disgusting odour washed over me, ebbing and flowing. I breathed into my hand and sniffed. Something decomposed in my mouth during our respite. I'd bet my pits smelt as terrible, but Morrigan didn't seem to mind, nuzzling my chest as the aggressive flapping curtains and their dancing shadows coaxed her to consciousness.

She groaned again. "I could sleep another ten hours." The stick of our sweat held us together for a moment too long as she rolled away, planting her face in the soft mattress. "Can't liiiiiive."

"My ray of sunshine." I lifted a mass of curls, trying to find her under the frizz to no avail. "Are you always thrilled thus, greeting the day?"

"Nah." She turned toward me to speak, the bed pulling her cheek at an adorably goofy angle. "I'm making a special effort to be nice 'cause I like you."

"You like me now?" I tried to curtail my delight. "I'm flattered."

Purple shadows lurked under her pale skin, especially around her eyes, though they sparkled. Her lips were flawless coral. "Yeah, you're all right." She picked sand out of her eye, adding, "A bit stinky."

"For yourself only speak, garlic queen."

She shoved me playfully. "I haven't been sick in years, I'll have you know."

"Nor do starved vampires dare attack. You win at life." I took her hand to kiss but paused at the damage. "Salt, you've got scratches all over. How did you win free?"

She yawned, blasting me with garlic and death. "I crow-barred a hole between the ground and first floors, dragged my arse through, and found the fire exit. Called Poe."

"But Liam had your phone."

She did that thing with her lips where they'd try to curl in amusement and she fought them. "I can talk to anyone if they're asleep. It's risky, because I might have been too tired to wake up, or it might take a while for me to fall into a REM state. But Poe's perfect. Parents sleep lightly. Anyway, I climbed up on the roof so Liam Kendren couldn't find me." She combed her hair with her fingers. "I'm surprised he wasn't more vigilant about keeping me awake."

"Delay did not match his intention, be assured."

"Mmm." Her gaze sought mine and she paused her ministrations. "How are you?"

"I haven't begun processing the ache of my chest; that any one event might be such a success and yet fail at its core. Physically fine, my heart remains sore."

She rubbed my shoulder, following the flow of my arm to my hand, where she squeezed my fingers. Her eyes were sad as she nodded her understanding. I'd have been lost without her. Hopeless, without these witches.

A twitch ran through me. I hadn't given any of her coven my gratitude as yet.

Morrigan must have been thinking the same, because she pushed up onto her knees and grabbed her phone from her desk. "Is there any way for a layperson to tell the skins apart? I wished I'd asked earlier. How will I know it's yours?"

I shook my head, guiding her to lay back down. "You did all within your power, don't be blaming yourself for this one."

"I'm just so sorry. There were stacks of them, oozing everywhere. Empty eye sockets staring." She shuddered. "I reckoned it'd be easier."

"I've not laid eye upon my fur," I murmured. "Description I cannot confer."

"It's okay." Looking beat, she woke her phone. "I'll send a blanket message to everyone, see how we're doing, if we missed anything while we slept." She withdrew a shoe box from under the bed. "Then I need to shower."

If she were another girl, I'd ask to join her, but how would that be taken? "Me, also."

The box contained a cache of dried fruits, nuts, chocolate chips and some kind of crisp that resembled cat food. "Help yourself," she invited.

As she typed the message, her jaw worked through the chewy fruits. Her cheeks glowed under my scrutiny. I crunched handfuls of her mix, the bursts of sweet and salty nothing compared to how the smooth skin of her neck would feel against my lips. I scooted closer to kiss her nape until her fingers tangled in my hair and the world receded. She might smell like garlic, but she tasted like home.

Her words against my crown were so quiet, I nearly missed them. "I think I love you, prickly pear."

My lips stopped of their own accord, and I huffed, equal parts humour and fear. "Uh. Prickly pear?" What did it mean for her to love me, beyond a world of pain? This was supposed to be fun. Memories to last a lifetime. What had I done?

She drew back to see my expression, and though she smiled, her lips were too taut for it to be wholly genuine. "You don't look like you could even grow a beard, but my neck tells a different story."

I rubbed my stubble, so precisely matched in colour to my skin as to be invisible. "My apologies, vampire slayer." Though I mocked her, the hand I placed over my heart trembled. The rush and boom inside my chest wasn't that of the ocean's doom.

She chuckled; a special kind of music. A song I wanted to hear over again until forever. I longed to see her smile and sigh with contentment. Make her laugh until she farted. More. I fancied her beside me like this, no matter where I turned.

I cupped her jaw, lifting her eyes to mine. Making it movie-perfect for her.

"I love you, too."

Her hand cocooned mine, holding me there. The fire to my water. Absolutely opposite, perfectly balanced.

"I'd kiss you right now, but we'd probably knock each other out. Shower with me?" Her expressive eyebrows lifted, as though this were a challenge.

"There's nothing I desire more."

The truth of my words, I was sure, etched my soul. Immortalising this moment wherein something separate from the sea held me in thrall.

I followed her lead, spitting toothpaste foam into the drain.

Morrigan made loving an adventure. A mystery to unfold. She challenged my general expectation of how a relationship should progress. With sex, in whatever ways she defined it, off the table—or bed, more like—where was the yardstick by which to gauge our affinity?

She handed me her loofah. "Scrub my back?"

Yes. I could manage that.

"Harder," she moaned. My face flushed. Things certainly got harder. When she turned around and saw, I didn't know what to do, save apologise.

"Don't be silly." She shook her head, "I know a compliment when I see one." She accepted the loofah and began soaping up my chest while my arms hung uselessly. "I'm not afraid of bodies."

A strangled noise squeaked out of my throat.

Valiantly, she subdued her laughter. "I'm Wiccan. A lot of our spiritual practises are done naked or in various states of undress. Nudity isn't inherently sexual. It's vulnerable, sure. Awkward and hilarious, sometimes. But naked doesn't equal sex—Oh that'd make a great meme."

Many of the times I'd had sex, my girl and I had been wearing clothes. I'd had a girlfriend who never removed her bra. Not for sex, not to sleep. Probably not in the shower either, not that she'd invited me in to confirm.

Morrigan lifted my arm and scrubbed at my pit.

"While that makes sense, my ignorance remains re the rules of... Uh." I swallowed a lump. "Engagement."

"Rule one." she raised my other arm, continuing to clean me. "There should be nothing you can't talk to your partner about." She met my gaze and grinned. "Sounds heaps mature hey? Poe taught me that." Finished with my arms, she washed my chest again, making slow circles down toward my navel. "Secondly, I might be inexperienced, but I'm not uneducated. So, if you want extra time to enjoy the shower after I get out..." With a mere heartbeat of hesitation, she swirled suds over my pubic hair, and grasped my dick with her other hand, cleaning and stroking in equal measure.

My mouth went dry and hung open. Thankfully, she wasn't looking at my face.

"All acts of love and pleasure are rituals to the Goddess, even when we're alone." She cupped my balls, cleaning beneath them.

Breathing became difficult. I gulped the damp air and closed my eyes to block out enough stimuli to speak. The soap in her hands slid in a dance. "Where though, I don't know, does romantic end and sexual dawn?" Every word I uttered was hard-won.

"That's something we've got to figure out ourselves, right? Some people think sex *is* romantic. Some people think food and genitals go together." Her visage twisted with revulsion. "For me?" Morrigan shrugged. The freckles clustered on her left shoulder resembled a fish. "I don't date. I mean, I didn't. Before you. So, give me grace to figure it out. Cool?"

She tapped my thigh, and when I didn't respond, she shoved, indicating I should spread my legs and allow her to wash between them. She crouched down. Her smooth back made a spectacular curve to her fine moon arse.

I just about passed out. She was divine. Breathless, I gasped, "Admire your confidence, I must."

"Emotions are water." Morrigan said, too consumed by her musings to respond to my comment. "The answer, then, probably shifts, depending on the situation." She stood, rinsing suds from her loofah.

Emotions are water. Ha! Indeed. My hands twitched and flexed, one against the wall, the other limp by my side. She took them, wrapping my arms around herself. "Is this okay?"

I tightened my grip, and the glory of all that was her pressed against me. "So much more." My throat strangled my words. I swallowed. "Simply okay ignores the wonder I feel."

She kissed me until the water ran cold and then she fled, filling my soul with her delighted squeals.

MORRIGAN

"What did you ever do with your love spell letter?" I asked Poe. "The one we did with Taliesin Lee for Beltane that time."

She pushed Artemis's swing, and I Apollo's. We had the playground to ourselves, because despite coming early to "beat the heat", temperatures were in the high thirties. Bees hovered over the native gardens on two sides of the playground. Cafes vied for business around the opposite edges, their chalk signs promising the suburb's best iced coffee.

We'd been talking about the force AI would need to overcome Liam Kendren's Muldjewangk army and the upcoming presentation this afternoon. It took her a moment to switch gears. She wore a loose-fitting singlet, running shorts and thongs. Some of her hypertrophic scars looked angry—possibly sunburnt—but she'd let herself tan this year, wearing her Indigenous heritage with pride instead of hiding from the sun to keep herself pale. I wished I could tell her how proud I was of her, but she'd hate the attention.

"Do you still have yours?" I prompted.

Poe turned her face into the hot wind and plucked a long strand of her brown hair out of her mouth. "No. I ended up burning it as part of my release ritual; to escape Victor way back when."

Victor. That she'd stopped calling him his preferred nickname sat well with me.

"By rights," she continued, "I shouldn't have waited till the end of the relationship. I should've burnt the damn thing the day he declared us soul mates."

I took a swig from my water bottle. The relief was short lived. I'd need a fresh shirt before Elton came over. "You can't blame yourself for what happened."

"I don't. Mostly, anyway. But maybe it would have helped if I had destroyed it earlier. I might have realised I was free to leave at any time." Artemis let go of the swing's chains, and Poe grabbed the seat to slow her decent. The little girl leapt off, her dark hair flying.

Apollo lurched forward, following his sister, but I missed whatever subtle cue Poe'd seen, seizing a handful of empty air. She caught him by the back of his tee shirt a heartbeat before he face-planted onto the playground's blue rubber flooring, and set him on his feet.

Oblivious, he ran after Artemis, strawberry blond curls sticking out in all directions. "Wait for me!"

We shadowed them. Close enough to help without in-terfering. Both wore navy blue shorts with scalloped pock-ets, their shirts featuring cartoon characters I didn't recog-nise.

"It worked out for the best." Poe wrapped her hand around her pentacle. The one Viri had bought her when she was pregnant and living at my house. Was she thinking about him? We'd all expected them to get together, but instead of getting their own place, Poe had moved back in with her dysfunctional family.

"These two are my happy ending." She leaned on the seesaw, lowering the seat for Apollo to climb on. Artemis giggled as she floated into the air. "But, like, I remember your letter being fantastical." Poe cringed apologetically. "I mean, I'm sure the words 'fairy tale romance' were in there somewhere."

"No offence taken." I'd written that if the Gods couldn't give me perfection, I wouldn't date at all; the definition of arrogance. What had perfection entailed to my thirteen-year-old mind? "So, you think I should burn my letter?"

"Yeah. Or bury it. Let the Goddess know that it's worked and you're grateful and you want free will to rule now. Or whatever." She rolled her eyes at herself. "Outside of coven stuff, I don't do a heck of a lot of spells. All my magick is sigils and prayers whispered in exhaustion." Her expression brightened. "That's heaps better now though! Been getting a bit of time to myself. And look." She put her fingertips behind her ear, highlighting dangly earrings.

Tiny clay apples. This one was whole, while its partner had been crafted with a bite taken out. "I've worn them three hours and nobody has tugged them or licked my face."

I'd intended to start the letter-burning ritual as soon as I got home, or at least set it up—New Years' Day was auspicious for releasing old magick to create a new future. But I found Mum in the kitchen drinking a turmeric latte all by herself. She didn't have her phone or a book. Her face was drawn as she jiggled the latte's foam with her spoon. Were her hands always that thin?

"Hey," I said, "want some company?"

She nodded, so I prepared my own beverage. The air crackled as I moved about. "What's going on, Mum?"

"Been thinking. You've done some bold things since you came into your power. Exciting things. Effective things. Your Dad too. And I wonder if that's because you were born into magick, or if there's some lack on my part." She gazed deep into her latte. "Am I a coward?"

I paused midway through piling ice cubes into my glass, blissfully cold air tickling my collarbones. "Why on earth would you think that?"

She seemed heartened by my knee-jerk reaction. Less slumpy. She was talking to me like a friend, not a daughter. My hands and cheeks tingled like this was important, but it was probably just the ice. I closed the freezer before she'd revert into my mother, and sat with her at the table where she waited for my secondary response. My true response.

Mum claimed everyone's first reaction was their parents and their school and their community talking. She'd often cautioned Poe not to fret too much about her initial thought, but to wait for the correction that came after. "You're your second response," she'd say.

I sipped my drink. For her to ask if I thought she was a coward, someone must have said something nasty. Had I seen her do anything particularly brave? She'd chosen a peaceful, measured life; was I supposed to believe this wasn't what she wanted? It hadn't occurred to me that either of my parents might be unhappy, except that they'd always wished for another baby. I didn't understand their grief, but it was there; a sticky web between them that they could never brush off. Yet Mum faced every day bravely, no matter the hurt she carried inside.

"Who sowed this doubt in your mind?" I asked. "I'll put a rotten banana under the driver's seat of their car."

She pursed her lips, but her smile escaped anyway. "You wouldn't dare banana your mother's car." She took a sip of her latte, her expression turning pensive. "Silver was right, and it galls me."

I tilted my head. Silver Moontread was our CEO. This must be a work thing.

"You regret not arresting Liam Kendren yourself?"

"If you want something done…" She shook her head and went back to moving yellow foam around her cup. "He might've come peacefully if I'd been there. If he didn't, I'd have dealt with that. He wouldn't have evaded me. Or had the chance to make a fool of your dad. This would be over. We'd have emptied out that place rather than leaving Liam plenty of resources to continue his power-mad plan."

"Do you ever—" I stopped. How could I ask why she avoided high risk missions without accidentally confirming her cowardice or sounding like a dick? "Are you happy? At work I mean. With what you do?"

"Because I don't break into houses or dreams, or take down rival covens like you?" She arched her eyebrow. "Morri, if I wanted a position like that, don't you think I'd have it by now?"

I felt stupid. "Yeah, you would."

"We both help people and that's the important thing. Paper pushing, losing myself in details, fundraising. Mine is good, solid work. Yes, I'm happy."

Not knowing what to say, I held her hand on the table-top.

"But, you know, somewhere along the line, I became more mother than anything else. I provide a safe haven. I take care of the background stuff, the home admin on top of my secretarial work at AI. My house is always full of kids who need nurturing. I've loved this era of my life. Shaping young people. Protecting them and helping them be their best. It's all I ever dreamed. I didn't want to travel, I partied enough in my twenties." She grinned at nothing, and I bit my lip to stop my badly timed curiosity.

"But, like Silver says, you're grown up. Most of your coven is too. I'm not needed as often at home." Mum sighed. "And I don't want my training and skills to go to waste. I haven't performed an arrest in a decade. More! Am I really the best person for the job?"

I shook her arm and pumped all my energy into a winning grin. "I'd hire ya!"

"Ha. Thanks love." She pulled me in for an awkward side-hug.

"Dad and I will be with you, at least for your first case. Us and half the community, if Elton has his way."

She released me, casting her gaze heavenward. "Gods, have you seen the numbers? I should have rented a hall for all the people he's invited."

"Guy doesn't do anything by halves." I tried to keep my lovesick swoon under control. Be professional. "He's intense about everything."

"I hope that applies to his relationships too. I'll be the one putting rotten fruit in his car if he thinks once you get his skin back he can forget you."

"He gets offended if you suggest that. Resisting the ocean's pull is a point of Selkie pride." I scratched at my scalp. Thinking about our future was hard enough without hashing it over. "There's an entire community of Selkies on land. Every one of those skins in Liam's warehouse represents a Selkie." A living one, I assumed. What happened to a Selkie's skin after they died? Did it disappear? Rot? Or did it somehow retain its power? It was probably my job to know these things. I added that to the growing list of areas I'd fallen short. "They all defy the ocean's call."

"They also flood AI the morning after a trine to get their injuries treated." She said it gently, without judgement.

My face flamed none the less. What was I getting myself into? "I haven't forgotten my jitsu training," I murmured. How fucked up was that? I shouldn't need to defend myself from my partner. I tensed, waiting for her to tell me as much.

She pressed her lips into a tight line. "Well, I should hope not; we're taking Liam's headquarters by force." Mum was a mirror of my future. Except I'd say no to the colourful 80s scrunchies she favoured. "People will start arriving soon. Have you heard from Elton or your coven?"

"My friends don't have my work number. I'm pretty disconnected from the world at the moment."

"Shoot. We need to replace your mobile. Sorry. I forgot, with everything going on."

"No shops open today anyway."

She continued to watch me, tortured lines around her eyes speaking her worry. Her disapproval was too heavy.

"I'm in love with him," I whispered. "I know the risks. How terribly wrong and dangerous this is. What I'd say to a mate in my shoes. But it feels magickal."

"He cares about you, too, I'm sure. If it comes to that, you can stay here when his storm approaches. Your bedroom is yours until the day this whole house belongs to you."

That made the future less terrifying. "Thanks Mum."

She stood to rinse out her cup, kissing the top of my head on her way to the sink. "Will you be home for dinner?"

The hope in her voice was so thick, I'd have said yes and then ran to cancel my plans if I had any.

"Yep." I stood and rubbed her back. "Do you want help cooking?"

"Pffft no." She smiled over her shoulder at me. "I'm not cooking. That's what I got married for."

"Just that, hey?" I hadn't noticed Dad in the doorway. He wove past the table, grabbed her around the waist, and kissed her like a desperate teen until she held up her hands and cried for mercy. "Not just dinner," she gasped as he released her. "My computer needs updating."

Would Elton and I be like them in thirty years? Corny and unshakable in equal measure?

Death Rx

MORRIGAN

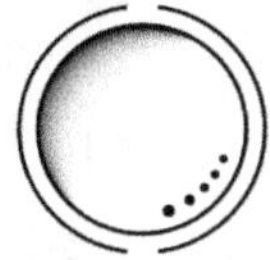

Faeries of all kinds packed my back yard, standing shoulder to shoulder with dedicated witches from AI, my coven Elouera, my parent's coven, Writtenbark, and even Brooke's aunt's coven, who clustered together to the far right, near the bird bath and garden bench. Most of the people present looked unquestionably human, and those who didn't were likely to be humans loving the alternative aesthetic.

And then there was Meddy. Her skin was a little too grey today, her shoulders stony. The jostling crowd had set off her anxiety. I wove my way over to where she stood with Astrid as Elton stepped up onto a milk crate to welcome the crowd. There must have been near a hundred listeners. Hopefully they'd bring many more to our cause.

Meddy had one hand anchoring her to Astrid and the other arm wrapped around her lower ribs. I peeled that hand off her chest, grasping it firm in my own. Her expression softened as she allowed me to protect her.

"My friends." Elton addressed the gathering against the backdrop of our hedge, shade sails stretching out over his head. He stood tall in his cheap target shoes, pressed trousers, and collared shirt. His hair was tied back, half up half down, showing off the speckles along his hairline. "Thank you. A grave injustice threatens our community. I'm heartened, though, by this show of unity. Time permitting, I'll share my personal story..."

I leaned forward to greet Astrid, then hesitated. Was I overstepping the mark, holding Meddy's hand like this when she had a girlfriend? No, both Astrid and Elton knew we were basically sisters. I was being silly.

"Hello Astrid," I whispered, "Good to see you."

She spared me a stiff nod. "Thanks."

"but first—to my great honour—allow me to introduce Sydney Selkies' most esteemed elder, Aoidh Vess." Elton pronounced it Ay, like he was trying to get someone's attention.

We applauded. Many witches had turned up in their ritual robes, their loose sleeves flapping. As tended to be the case at pagan gatherings, women vastly outnumbered men, and those not claiming binary gender were either more common or less camouflaged than in other company.

Aoidh Vess took his place on the milk crate and smiled down at Elton. "You make us sound like a football team, lad."

A chuckle fluttered through the gathering. I developed an instant fondness for the elder. He didn't seem like the hard-arse Liam Kendren had made him out to be.

"To not bore you, I'm going to assume you came today with some awareness of goings on. But *why*? You asked me in the Larue's foyer: why did Arcane Industries have these Selkie furs to begin with? How did this Kendren fellow have access? Let me begin there. For many of us—any of us!—with physiology that differs from the human standard, Arcane Industries is a safe harbour. It is our hospital. Our research centre. And like any other medical institution, it requires organ donors to provide certain services." He paused, making eye contact here and there with people in the audience, nodding to those he recognised. "And Kendren? He was our friend..."

Visually, Aoidh Vess was a kindly Asian grandfather, soft and weathered with a storytellers voice. Pain thrummed through his words, as though Liam Kendren was his wayward son. He wore plain brown slacks and a lightly patterned cream shirt, open in a V.

"My fears, and layered they are indeed, are thus," continued the elder. "This show of force Kendren has corralled; how can he keep it concealed as its numbers swell? Muldjewangk are water spirits. Fin folk in their own right. If one of them breaks Kendren's hold, what then? We can hope it would vent its anger in his direction. But what if it didn't? Muldjewangk don't belong to the surface world. Here, they upset nature's balance. More, not every psychic or sensitive person joins AI. Many faeries are cut off from their heritage. Many witches work solitary, never seeking community. There are enlightened people within mainstream religions. Any of these individuals might report Muldjewangk sightings to the police, or worse, the media." He slicked his hair back. "My children remain safe through invisibility. The general population and the authorities on the land must not discover that fin folk exist. Not Muldjewangk. Not Selkies."

Someone behind me muttered to their companion, "The mob is ruled by fear. They'll come for us."

I didn't doubt it. Faeries lived much the way witches tended to; quietly, on the edge of society with the other weirdos and misfits. Although Wiccans practised openly, healthy scepticism in the general population kept us safe. Muldjewangk, however, weren't the kind of proof anyone could ignore.

Aoidh Vess spoke on. "And don't be thinking 'It doesn't affect us who runs AI, let Kendren take it by force, if he willist.' Sure, the services might remain the same. But are you going to trust your livelihood, your medical records," his voice rose, "your personal information, or your children to a traitor? I should think not. Now I don't know this Matthias Larue half as well as I thought I knew Kendren, but I see he's given his home and personal resources over to us. His whole family is here trying to make things right. And Silver Moontread backs him. Over forty years she has served our community; brought us better technology, better access to land institutions. If she has chosen Matthias and not Kendren as her successor, well, doesn't that speak volumes?"

A twig snapped to my left, loud against the audiences' captivated silence. Ms Moontread paused, one foot raised, and grinned sheepishly. Her paper skin appeared whiter than usual against the dark green of our hedge and she carried a flat-topped wooden chest embellished with Celtic knotwork. She continued to where Elton waited with my mum.

Eliss poked zir head in-between mine and Meddy's, making me jump. When had ze got back?

"Her hair's so spunky," ze said.

"I know right?" I agreed. Ms Moontread's soft platinum spikes gave her an edge. "You'd never guess she's in her eighties."

Meddy jerked back. "She's what?"

"Shhh," Astrid said.

Aoidh Vess wrapped up his speech as Ms Moontread positioned her wooden chest beside the milk crate. "Even if we didn't care for the parts of our bodies—or our honoured dead—stolen, how can we turn from those of our own who are relying on us to recover their furs?" He invited Elton to speak and stepped down, leaning on Mum for support.

After Elton recounted what his Selkie skin meant to him, and how AI had the potential to make a skin for his sister, he said, "You see what's at stake, what we face. My hope is we combine, our skills refine, to take Liam's base, an' secure our peace. Arcane Industries have long been partners to my people. Matthias, please," He turned to Dad. "How may we overcome Liam?"

"With a more intelligent force, and cooler weapons." Dad's ritual garb swished as he stepped onto the milk crate and introduced himself. "Some of you asked me earlier whether International Coven Review is involved and why they haven't stopped Mr Kendren. In short, Mr Kendren evaded the agents ICR sent to arrest him. They have requested specialised assistance from Felicia Larue," he gestured to Mum, "to take him into custody—"

Chatter broke out across the garden. Elton murmured an observation to Viri, who grinned.

Dad raised his voice. "We'll get to the weapons shortly, I promise. What concerns me is the ICR's intent to fire the building in the event we fail."

I gasped alongside a hundred others.

"We have provided ICR with evidence that the Muldjewangk, like the Selkies whose magick they've hijacked, are affected by celestial events. For the privacy of the Selkie community, I won't disclose those details. But we believe we've narrowed down when the Muldjewangk will be easiest to defeat. This gives us roughly a month in which to train a fighting force—without which we don't stand a chance anyway. We'll have one night to stop Mr Kendren and recover the stolen skins. One opportunity to take back Arcane Industries' research and resources." Dad's gaze roved over the crowd, assessing the effectiveness of his words. "The ICR's decision doesn't consider the personal stakes, nor the years of study and the millions of dollars Arcane Industries have invested in developing new medicines and technologies specifically for Australia's growing population of Selkie refugees. I am loath to torch the place, but if we can't overcome Mr Kendren's forces, ICR will raze the site to end the Muldjewangk threat."

A shudder coursed through me. What of Liam Kendren's employees? Would they burn it down with witches inside?

Dad spread his arms to encompass the audience. "We must stop him. We will not allow Mr Kendren to threaten nor expose us, or march upon AI tower with his thralls." Dad had slipped into his ritual voice. A shiver of anticipation ran through me.

"Our mission is clear. We must see Mrs Larue safely inside Mr Kendren's warehouse, where her team will subdue him, seizing the wand he uses to direct the Muldjewangk. We'll distract and destroy the Muldjewangk on the beach. When they fall, Arcane Industries shall reclaim the donated Selkie skins, return any skins Mr Kendren illegally acquired, and deconstruct the building without alerting Tamarama's locals."

Astrid leaned toward us. "He makes it sound like a picnic."

I wanted to ask her if she was legitimately considering going—or ask her not to—but I didn't want to be ableist or suggest blind people couldn't fight.

When I looked up again, Mum was standing on the milk crate and Ms Moontread stood at her side on her wooden chest.

"I have the pleasure of introducing Ms Silver Moontread, CEO of Arcane Industries, Head Coach of Stella Jujitsu," Mum said.

There was a polite applause.

"And I am Felicia Larue. I'm an administrator at Arcane Industries—"

Ms Moontread murmured something.

Mum's eyes widened.

Silver nodded.

A proud smile overtook Mum's face. "And HP of Defence."

"Field promotion?" Meddy whispered.

Maybe. Most likely. AI didn't have a defence force, that was half our problem. I shrugged like I wasn't surprised. "Mum's a black belt."

Mum raised her voice. "Who here has a firearms licence?"

Only two people raised their hands.

"I thought as much," Mum said. "It's also illegal to carry knives. Every member of our force counts. I can't have you getting arrested while busing to the Eastern suburbs."

Some people chuckled, but it was true. A cop could search you without a warrant if they suspected you had a weapon, and we needed to prepare for the eventuality that a local might take offence to our presence in the area—or worse, spot the Muldjewangk—and call the authorities.

Elton lurched forward, a hand outstretched. "We must—"

"Laws are there for a reason." Mum sounded very parental. "Sometimes the government makes stupid laws that we protest, but this isn't one of them. When nobody's packing, everyone's safe. Besides, against the Muldjewangk, a pocketknife, or even a handgun, wouldn't be enough."

Ms Moontread cleared her throat. "Because Muldjewangk are breathing via magick, you can't suffocate them. They don't feel pain, so you can't incapacitate them with superficial wounds. Their touch inflicts a skin-boiling curse. Indigenous lore states that the Muldjewangk can curse a person at a distance, too, and as the curse only lifts when the caster dies, we're not going to risk the Muldjewangk fleeing from us." She stepped down from her box and opened it.

Mum picked up where she'd left off. "Each Muldjewangk is wearing a talisman enabling it to survive on land and become invisible."

Dad passed Mum the pauldron we'd recovered on the beach, and she held it up. The crystal in the centre was cracked and dull, but recognisable. "Look for this on your opponent's shoulder. It's hollowed calcite containing Mr Kendren's spell. Blunt force destroys it, but so too would a burst of extreme heat."

Ms Moontread held up a palm-sized silver disc.

"This device can do exactly that—store a burst of heat, electricity, wind, or gravity—and multiply the power of each spell stored within," Mum said. "Moreover, they are perfect for carrying on the streets undetected."

"Is that...? No." Meddy conversed with herself.

"What?" Astrid whispered.

"It looks like a pocket mirror. The fancy engraved ones people give out at weddings."

"Can't be."

I had to agree with Astrid.

Ms Moontread held her position a moment, rotating her wrist while the rest of us squinted in the afternoon light. "Originally designed to store and amplify spells for self-love and well-being, the Rendezvous Compact can store any enchantment, releasing it at the touch of a button." Deftly she popped the mirror open, shooting a small but loud burst of fireworks over our heads. The boom set the neighbourhood dogs barking and a startled child's cry came from within the house. Astrid's long white hands trembled in the aftershock.

"Can it store more than one spell at a time?" Someone called out.

"Yes, but spells can only be released in reverse order, so the first charge released is the last one stored, and thus the weakest." She turned the device to display its edge. "I don't know if you can see, but there are two buttons here. One that opens the compact without releasing a spell, and another that acts as the trigger. It's possible to add more triggers, however those prototypes limit the number of spells stored, whereas the model I'm holding is unlimited."

The general murmuring swelled as Ms Moontread reached into the chest for another curious weapon.

"Next, we have this sigil pen. If anyone asks you, it's eyeliner."

"She's full pullin' our legs now," Eliss muttered.

Meddy kept Astrid up to speed. "I think she's using it to make a pattern on the box, like Poe would on the floor of our circle."

I licked my teeth. Meddy needed reminding not to talk about coven business with outsiders. I didn't find the words before a spotlight shone down on Ms Moontread, creating a column of light for her to stand in with no visible light source.

"Use this to create barriers, activate sigils, detonate small objects and—yes—it really makes your eyes pop."

Eliss grinned. "Okay, I need it."

"Same," Meddy said.

No questions were forthcoming, perhaps because everyone in the audience was thinking of the sigil pen's potential uses.

"And finally…"

"It's going to be lip gloss," Eliss predicted.

"Cream," I put in.

"Bronzer brush," Meddy said, too late to guess as Ms Moontread held the soft-bristled brush high.

"Originally intended to amplify a person's best features, this innocuous powder brush reveals other hidden details, too. Mr Larue, your phone, please."

Dad's brows fled into his floppy hair, but he passed his mobile over and she held it aloft, pressing the side button to reveal the lock screen. With her other hand she swirled the bristles over the pinpad, pulling it away to a collective gasp. Glowing as though holographic, dad's fingerprints floated over the numbers.

"Five, seven, five, two. Time to change your pin, Matt."

Meddy slapped my arm in excitement. "Did you even see that?"

"Every person who stands with us against the Muldjew-angk will be equipped with these three tools—"

"Ridiculous!"

The shout came from the far side of the garden, but a man behind me backed him up. "What of us men? Will we be equipped with actual weapons, or do you expect us to rejoice over these girly toys?"

A scattering of 'yeah' and 'that's right' and 'I don't wear makeup' flared, then died as Ms Moontread's lips flattened into a duckbill.

She waited for silence. "To practise witchcraft is to enter a feminine domain—a world where not everything is about you and your towering masculinity. Simply put, you're either witch enough to fight with a woman's weapons, or you're not."

"Oooh burn," Meddy whispered.

Not a single disgruntled man left the garden.

"You'll be trained in their use," Ms Moontread continued, "able to protect yourself, reveal hidden Muldjewangk, and fell them without needing to take precise aim. Yes, these devices are small and prosaic in design. I don't blame you for being sceptical or unable to imagine their destructive potential—"

"Obliterating mindless monsters is one thing," Mum's covener said. "But you can't expect our beloved Felicia to face down that wicked man with nothing but eyeliner and her own good looks!"

Mum sighed. She could best anyone in this garden hand-to-hand, but she didn't say it. Instead, she reached into her robe and withdrew a thick chain. I didn't need to see the pendant to recognise Mum's pet project.

"It's a miniature cauldron on a necklace. Real cast iron," I said for Astrid's benefit. "She's been working with it for weeks."

Lifting the amulet above her head, Mum said, "In addition to the Rendezvous makeup kit and whatever Independent Coven Review supply me with, I have Creidwy's cauldron." She relaxed her arm, cradling the little cast iron pot between her hands. "With the Goddess's blessing, I can conjure whatever I'm focused on, as long as it's not a sentient being, and it exists on Earth in this time frame. Allow me to demonstrate." She closed her eyes, aiming the miniature cook pot away from herself, and sprayed the audience with sea water. "There are endless substances I can call, with which to defend myself." She held a hand over the opening, and a moment later pulled one of our kitchen knives from within. "I am well equipped and physically capable besides. You can count on me to bring Liam Kendren's justice swiftly."

I cheered, setting off an eruption through the crowd. How had I mistaken my mum for ordinary or boring? Or worse, cowardly?

Discussion turned to the how's and when's of training. At first, I chafed with frustration—Dad and Aoidh Vess bid us wait until the January dark moon in twenty-eight days to make our move—but then Astrid stole a sneaky kiss from Medusa and jealousy gripped my chest.

I sought Elton's gaze and spotted him weaving toward us.

Another month would give me the time I needed to solidify things with Elton, to forge ourselves a path into the future. This delay was a gift I needed to selfishly enjoy.

I whispered to Meddy, "Double date this week?"

"I'll set it up."

The garden assembly had run late, becoming an impromptu pizza party, to cater for which we ordered from three different pizza places, paying outrageous holiday surcharges. On company credit, of course. Afterwards, Dad said the mingling would make people more likely to join forces. Noble causes weren't enough; people needed to care about each other as individuals.

It was watching Mum move through that crowd as a kind of celebrity that stuck with me though. That and Meddy's words, "Your mum's always been a local hero." Her insinuation was clear: as a Daddy's girl, I hadn't noticed.

Elton's explanation had been less critical. "When standing forever in the sunlight, your eyes adjust to the brightness."

When everyone finished thanking us fifty times and the house rang with emptiness, we congregated in the lounge for a family movie night, making up for missing Christmas Eve. There was something exhausting about relaxing in front of the television, and so I hadn't undone my love letter spell afterwards, or last night either.

Mum, Meddy and one of Mum's workmates had spent the entire day yesterday organising schedules, ordering more weapons, and monopolising space at the kitchen table to ensure training sessions commenced today.

My muscles ached. We didn't even touch the makeup kits; we'd just exercised and practised defensive manoeuvres. Simple things like widening stance and disengaging from an enemy's grasp; hand-to-hand combat skills that we'd need if any of Liam Kendren's human staff resisted our advance. My jujitsu training came back to me fast. I remembered the positions, the take downs, and how to break my own fall, but my muscles did not. I'd tried to appear competent. I ought to have been helping Mum run the packed group sessions, not been counted among the trainees.

Bed beckoned me with its carefully straightened sheets. Fighting off a yawn, I dragged my arse to the window and searched the sky for the moon. Unable to find her, I checked my app instead. Dark crossing into new. Potent for the spell I intended to cast. Tomorrow night wouldn't be so auspicious, and at any rate I should let free will reign.

I washed my face and hands, then lugged everything I'd need onto the roof patio. The hot tub perfectly encapsulated mine and Elton's relationship, balancing water and fire. I uncovered it and sat my altar—the upturned wicker laundry basket I'd used to carry everything out here—in view of its shifting lights, then created a circle out of candles. Citronella. Let the mosquitos know my space was sacred too.

Within my circle, I scattered potpourri for lack of fresh rose petals. I ought to have gathered some before training, instead I'd written a report for Sneaky Witch, texted Elton for an hour, and made a meme to unwind. I sighed. Too late now. Use what you have.

My altar matched the deck furniture and took on a beach vacation quality once set with my personal chalice, candles, incense, and the tiny cherry tarts I'd raided from the fridge. Behind it all I sat pewter statues of Poseidon and Aphrodite. Pleased, I pinned my old letter spell under my altar pentacle, and then ducked inside for a quick shower. Never go before the gods dirty if you can help it.

When I returned, clad in only the sky, heavy hair tickling my back, my deep fatigue had lifted.

I cast circle meticulously, stopping to breathe between each segment of the ritual, holding my focus in a way that coven gatherings didn't allow. Everything flowed, not from practise, but from my heart.

"My circle is empowered, bound and blessed. So mote it be." I rang the bell, feeling the presence of the gods around and within me.

"Tonight, I share my circle with you to give thanks. I asked, and the universe listened. Beltane of my 13th year, I requested a partner with the spell I read aloud now." I unfolded the discoloured letter and rose petals fell onto my lap. The paper crackled as I straightened it. "O ye Goddesses and Green men of love, hear my intent, feel the enchantment etched in pen here." *Etched in pen?* I shook my head at Morrigan of the past. "Isis, Venus, Branwen, Antheia, Eros, Parvati, Lady of many names, Queen of the

Night. Lend your power to my spell, that I may attract a love of the kind fairy tales are based upon.

Call or conjure for me a partner with a voice so rich as to lure ships upon rocks; whose ancestry is timeless, and ties to the earth unparalleled. My soul's true love has kindness in their heart and magick in their veins. Every step is a dance. Every word, a poem. When I am with them, I have nothing to fear except separation. I am loved and respected so deeply, it changes how I see myself. Together we are unstoppable.

Bring me this person. Let my letter be a beacon in the dark night of my solitude. Perfection will be mine, or I shall not date at all."

The old gods had perfectly matched my request.

Above me, scattered stars; tiny reflections of the candles I'd surrounded myself with. Had Taliesin ever got their man with mismatched eyes?

"Thank you, my Lady and Lord. Without your intervention, Elton and I might never have met." Over the past six odd years, I'd done weird and absurd work assignments. Supported Poe through her break-up and the twins' early months. Watched Viri's calling take him through death's door every day for years, always wondering if he'd make it back in time. I'd brought my best friend to the Goddess after twelve long years of hoping; being there for her as she gained control of powers amid a modern-day lynching.

My high school experience had been a sleight-of-hand show where I used magick to pass each grade and pretended like I was too cool to work while I worked harder than anyone. I hadn't the time to love a partner the way they deserved until now. But the Gods? They knew that too.

"Tonight, I release the magick that brought us together. There can be no love without free will." I gathered the letter and dried petals into my cauldron, having no need to copy down the words as Poe had done. I'd originally drafted it in my Book of Shadows, memorised it, and then transcribed it during the ritual instead of making something up on the fly.

I sprinkled essential oils over the letter in my cauldron. Cyclamen, which came from a plant with heart shaped leaves and flowers like stars; Patchouli for sensuality, magnetism and to ward off malevolence; and lastly rose geranium. I couldn't remember it's correspondences, but happiness swept over me as I unscrewed the lid. Rose geranium smelt the way Elton made me feel.

Next, I poured a bloop of cooking oil, being stingy so I wouldn't have to stay up all night with it. A corner of the letter sat above the liquid, acting as a wick, and I lit it. "Elton, know the heat of my joy, the light of my devotion.

I am blessed to have you in my life; to hear your voice, breathe your scent, and taste your lips. You are not bound or beholden to me. Let us love, complete unto ourselves, one never being forced by the other."

I sat for a while, performing Cakes and Ale with a new understanding, offering my libation, and basking in the glow of my released magick. When the circle grew thin, I gave thanks, closed the elemental pentagrams and dismissed the boundary. While the oil continued to burn, I soaked in the hot tub, listening to the sound of the city and praying no neighbours called the firies thinking my roof was ablaze.

For those moments, I knew peace.

'Sworn I would, you were with me last night. Your warmth all around. Your hair unbound. Lips to mine ear, "I love you my dear" spoke unto my soul, two halves to a whole. O, say you dreamt of me too.' I screen-shotted Elton's good-morning text, grinning like a fool. I had not, in fact, dreamt of him, I'd been working. Visiting an Aradia's Garden employee on holiday in Fiji for the passcode to their secondary computer, as the main machine had died in the arse. But

hey, it was only 5am, there was still time. I took a swig of water, double checked that my email to Aradia's Sacred Gardens had sent, and snuggled into the blissful cool of my pillow.

Traffic stirred outside; the world waking up. Every moment the sky grew lighter. I pulled my sleeping mask over my eyes and breathed deeply. Elton had felt my spell.

A car door slammed, jolting down my spine. I took another slow breath, letting the irritation go. My thoughts drifted past, far above as I sank into sleep. I'd leave the keening animal crossing my front lawn to someone else. Mum was probably up already.

The front door banged.

There she goes. I rolled over, smiling.

Elton was so sweet, I'd tell him—

Thumping and dragging downstairs ended in a crash, followed by an echoing howl of pain that struck my chest. I jumped from my top bunk and raced toward the kitchen. Mum's voice, swallowed in the cry, took on an edge of panic.

Viridis Thimberry curled up on my kitchen floor, alternating between an agonised wail and panting—holding it in until he erupted all over again.

Mum spotted me entering the kitchen from the hall. "Thank the gods."

A cut on Viri's chin bled; he must have cracked it against the table as he fell.

Mum motioned at me to help lift him, draping one arm over her shoulder as she pressed her phone to her ear. "Come home," she instructed, hanging up before Dad could respond. She left her phone on the floor under the table and we hoisted Viri to his feet.

"My room." Mum wrapped her arm around his waist. His legs dragged between us; we were both much shorter than him.

He bit his lip bloody in an effort not to scream. Blisters covered his legs, weeping from the hem of his bed shorts to his ankles. Blood swirled within the largest bubbles, transforming smooth black skin into rivers of lava. It had to be the Muldjewangk curse. How though? Viri wasn't in a wet suit or boardies. Nothing implied he'd been surfing or gone for an early morning swim.

We reached Mum's neatly made bed. He buried his face in the covers and howled.

"Get a cold washcloth." Mum snapped me into action. "And pain killers."

I dashed into her ensuite and grabbed the first-aid kit, running it back to her before getting the cloth.

Viri managed to roll over. His hands crushed fistfuls of bedding.

Mum pushed painkillers between his lips. He swallowed, eyes squeezed shut.

I dabbed the cool cloth over his sweaty brow. Cold might soothe his legs too, but some of the blisters had opened. I didn't want to introduce an infection.

His wild eyes sought my gaze. "Never seen anything like it," he croaked.

But he'd been there with us when we recovered those skins. He'd seen the Muldjewangk. Fought them. What was I missing?

I wiped the tears from his temples and the dried salt trails from his cheeks. He wore a ratty Wonder Woman bed shirt, with the slogan *Heroes rest too*.

My breath caught. "You were attacked in your sleep?"

Mum answered for him. "In the Riverlands."

That was what he called the place between the worlds where he worked. I'd accessed it before, via his mind, when I dream travelled. It was a dock on the bank of the River Styx, beyond which lay the realm of the dead. Or realms. The afterlife was complicated.

Viri spoke through his teeth. "It grabbed me from the river. Return journey. Startled me awake."

"I bet." I left the washer on his forehead and slid one hand under the neck of his shirt. The other I rested on his bicep. I wasn't a skilled healer; I needed skin-to-skin contact.

"What was it doing there?" Mum asked.

Viri's head thrashed on the pillow. "Don't know." He sucked in a breath. "She was a Selkie."

Who was? My brows encroached on my vision as I tried to follow what he was saying while opening myself to receive his pain.

"My passenger. Tonight. A Selkie. Maybe that's... Why."

"Maybe." Had she died because of something Liam Kendren had done to her skin, or was her death a coincidence? It didn't matter enough to ask. Not when every word cost Viri so dearly. My legs grew uncomfortably hot as his energy flowed into me. I looked at Mum. "We need to kill it."

Dad burst in the door, took in the situation, and got his oh-shit face on. "How much pain relief did you give him?"

Mum showed him the packs while bringing him up to speed. I ignored their low, hurried voices. Viri's grimace held my full attention.

I moved my hand from Viri's arm to his fist on the bed. He wasn't squeezing so tightly anymore. "How do we kill it in the afterlife?" And how could I access the Riverlands without him?

His whisper was slurred. "Don't need to. It followed me back." His eyelids drooped. I would have to cut our connection soon or the drugs would affect me too. "Chased my car. A bit. Think it jumped in the storm drain. When it couldn't get me."

I shut my eyes and pulled with all my focus, as if I were carrying a dream item through to the waking world. My legs turned to fire.

Dad rummaged in the first-aid kit, pulling out the mortar and pestle to prepare a poultice. "The Muldjewangk will make its way back to Kendren."

Mum hustled to get the fresh ingredients.

Icy dread touched my cheeks. Imagine waking up in agony, a Muldjewangk in your bedroom. Or caravan, in Viri's case. A nightmare following you into reality. I knew too much about that.

Viri slipped into unconsciousness and I let him go, enduring the pain I'd drawn from him. I refolded the cloth for his brow. If Dad was right, we'd find the Muldjewangk that attacked Viri at Tamarama Beach.

My voice came out strangled. "But there are hundreds of them in the bay."

Temperance

ELTON

Gripping my phone, I rested my lips and chin against the back of my fingers. What an incredible woman! The breeze sighed around me. Gairm gu uisge was tempered by the pollution in the bay, the ferries and the museum's submarine. Sitting on the edge of Darling Harbour's spiral fountain enabled me to enjoy the water without being befuddled. I had this girl and the odd art of the city to inebriate me.

I typed *'You rock my world,'* into our conversation, but didn't hit send. Too kitschy.

Restlessness forced me to my feet. I'd invited Morrigan to this sculpture walk, expecting her to jump at the chance after she'd ignored my good morning text. Unforeseen, her declination became a fascinating back-and-forth.

Viridis had been attacked by a Muldjewangk at dawn and was incapacitated by its curse. I was on the cusp of hopping the tram to Morrigan's place, where he was being cared for, when she assured me there was no way I could assist, and her house was packed besides. *'There won't even be space for me soon; we're letting a family from Sudan have my room. They landed about an hour ago. Maybe we can go for a walk this arvo?'* she'd said. I took her up on it, knowing already my feet would be dead and we'd likely walk as far as the car.

'I've got to visit Viri's mum, give her his cover story, make sure they don't need anything. Heading there soon. The good news: lots of witches flying in tonight to care for him.'

'Like, flying in?' I grinned, sending her a gif of a witch riding a broom.

'Haha I wish. Think of the money we'd save on petrol.'

The harbour-side path turned from wooden dock to brick, then flagstone as it wound past cripplingly expensive restaurants to an extensive water play park.

'Hey, does Raeyn have a favourite animal?' Morrigan sent. *'I've been working on a kind of peace offering.'*

'The hare, if you'll believe.'

Beyond the water features, another art installation sprawled over the grass. Despite my expectations, not all the sculptures in the public gallery were stone. Very few were. Most were made from recycled materials. Metals and plastics pulled from the ocean; a visual plea for land folk to be conscious of their trash. Morrigan gave me hope society was changing for the better.

This piece was an anthropomorphic dog-man who sat taller than I stood. Anatomically correct. The sudden urge to take inappropriate photos gripped me and I glanced around. Nobody paid particular interest to my presence, nor the nude statue that was probably too close to the children's area for your average civilian. Coast clear.

I snapped a handful of tasteless photos, then slid in with the foot traffic like my inner twelve-year-old hadn't come out to play. Would Morrigan share my sense of humour on this? Did people who weren't interested in sex still think weird sexual things were funny? One way to find out. A half-second after I sent the photos, I realised my teeth were showing and stiffened.

The hill levelled out and I passed between skyscrapers and ancient limestone buildings, catching my reflection in the windows. Morrigan knew what I was, and I was safe with her. She wouldn't show anyone the photos, and if she did, would they really zoom in and ogle my sharp teeth with their freaky hooks? Doubtful.

'*Oh my,*' Morrigan replied. '*It's almost as big as yours!*'

I gaped at my phone, heat tingling through my cheeks. And other places.

'*His head I mean.*'

'*Ha. You got me!*' I replied.

I took a proper photo of the next sculpture for her. '*Wish you were here.*'

'*Same.*' Then, '*Update: Viri's awake. Bombed on painkillers. Mum's coven is working on him.*'

Her texts accompanied me across the city. When I looked up from my phone—really looked, instead of dodging others on the footpath—I'd returned to the sea. Judging by the wide lawns, native trees, and harbour bridge views, I'd reached Barangaroo reserve. Artfully arranged stone blocks descended into the glistening bay.

I took my miserly shoes off and stowed them under a bush, then stepped down into the water which leached the heat from my swollen toes.

'*Tell me of water spells?*' I asked.

'*They're probably not what you imagine. Water magick tends to be healing and cleansing; a bridge back to spirituality and the Goddess.*'

'*Not music magick?*'

'I reckon music would be air. Particularly singing. Music is just another form of communication.'

'It's how I reach my family.'

Gairm gu uisge thrummed through me, dancing with her words in my head. Her presence, reaching across the city. Her flat teeth and hoarse laugh. Her quirky, nonsensical, mysterious human magick. I was daylight to her darkness.

Giving in to a little madness, I held the voice message button and put my heart into song.

"The sea a queen, an ancient wife,
the sky above, twists our life.
We're compelled, alone, apart,
salty tears an' keening hearts.
Love come torn, crash of waves,
the breeze your laughter, summer days.
This song, the cadence of its flow,
connects to me w'ere I roam.
T'is the essence o' my soul,
with seven tear drops call me home."

The final words came a whisper. I compressed my lips as the recording flew through cyber space. Hopefully, she'd remember. This was as candid as I dared be, lest I betray my peoples' secrets.

My phone chimed; she'd received it. I held my breath.

Why wasn't she typing a response? Had I shared too much? Scared her off with this promise of forever?

'*Sorry that took so long,*' Morrigan sent, overcoming her apparent speechlessness. '*I made you my ring tone. Hope that's not too weird. New phone needed personalisation.*'

I covered my lips as if to make a secret of my delight. '*You flatter me, my love.*'

'*You know your offshore family? Do I understand that right? Like, you've visited with them?*'

'*"Know" may be too severe for our wide shallow bond, but they came for my sixteenth year, to party the night long. All decked out in Salvos gear, a bonfire burning high, radio blaring, seaweed on sticky rice. Don't know them from a block of salt but that stops naught.*'

'*So you show up on the beach with donated clothes and sing? Then they leave in the morning?*'

'*Less random than that, and when lucky, visits last a week before the sea calls them home. They don their skins, but I'm detained. My parents force each other just the same.*'

I sat beneath a tree, leaving my feet in the sun to dry, and tried to relax the suddenly tense muscles of my face. Daikon's sister, Rubes, would generate much mischief if she and Morrigan joined forces. Both were full of energy, spinning stories on the fly. They'd make the best of friends. I huffed, throwing a stone into the bay.

The chance they'd meet was dismal.

I sent Morrigan a picture of the glittering water. *'They're out there somewhere, not forgetting me, I hope.'*

'You're unforgettable, Elton.'

Giddiness raced over me. *'I'm pleased you think it. What about extended family? Are all Larues bold and kind?'*

'Don't really have any. Dad says it's easier to hide one thin vine of witches than a whole family tree, but I reckon it's because my fam is riddled with infertility on both sides. When the time comes, I'll struggle to have kids too.'

'An' is that a goal for you? To carry young?' My hands shook. Were we truly having this conversation?

'With the right partner? Yeah. I want the happiness my parents have.'

Were they happy though? Were mine? Or were they just committed and stubborn? No, unfairness overcame me. Before my parents donated their skins and Raeyn lost mine in the process, such thoughts wouldn't have intruded.

A cloud settled over the sun, turning the breeze from refreshing to sombre. It was time to move on.

Morrigan was typing.

People passed me, some offering smiles and the occasional "G'day", others sweated profusely as they jogged. Over the water, gulls dove for fish. How would I go eating all my food raw? I didn't mind salmon sashimi with spicy sauce, but catching wild fish would be something else. Would transformation alter my taste buds? It must.

My phone chimed.

'I don't want to do it alone. Not that it's always a choice, obviously. But I see Poe struggle, and it scares me. Mum and Dad will be there, I know. They're part of the reason I'll have a baby someday: to give them the second child they longed for. I'd have support. But first, I want what they have. The unshakeable relationship. They are each other's highest priority. Until I have that, kids are just a fun topic of conversation.'

I stepped off the path and curled protectively around my phone, in part to shield the screen from glare. I read her words again. My heart choked me. *Yes!* I wanted to shout. Yes. The kind of dedication older generations displayed, from times when things were fixed rather than thrown away.

But I couldn't give her that.

'Or kid, specifically,' She added. *'One is plenty.'*

'Because that's what you know?'

'Nah. Because I want to travel.'

My heart was the waves meeting rock, booming in the cavern of my chest. *'You speak my language, love. The world is wide, the ocean deep, far off places ours to seek.'*

A solitary child could be carried. Smaller families didn't require sprawling suites at hotels or cost as much for holiday care. One child didn't fight or cause mischief on long journeys.

But travel where I was going didn't lie in Morrigan's power, and any child we had together would be afflicted like my sister.

Morrigan's reply twisted a tear from my eye. *'Sounds amazing,'* she sent.

MORRIGAN

People expected me to have an answer. I hated that. Didn't I have the right to be as lost and confused as everyone else? Worse, usually I *did* bring the solutions. I'd set a precedent.

Poe fiddled with her sandals and scrutinised me. Waiting for some miracle. I'd finished training with the morning crowd while she'd been upstairs with Viri, now we stood in a sea of stranger's shoes by my front door, saying an amicable goodbye.

She acted like I wanted Viri to suffer for an entire month. Like I hadn't spent the last five days creeping into his room at night to syphon his pain into my body. I'd advocated to keep him at our place when he'd begged me not to let them transfer him to AI. It was me and Mum changing his sheets daily. Rolling him so he didn't get bed sores. Making offerings at dawn, begging the solar gods to give him a better day. The wait for dark moon was costing our friend, but what other option did we have?

I licked my teeth.

Poe stepped into my space, allowing a stream of witches and faeries to exit behind her, and spoke with intensity, keeping her voice low. "Why the dark moon? Why not sooner?"

"The faerie community picked the date."

"But why? If it's true the Muldjewangk will be weaker, and theirs is borrowed magick, doesn't that mean the Selkies fighting with us will also be compromised?"

I'd asked Mum that yesterday. "Even if it does, the Muldjewangk will outnumber the Selkies with us four to one."

"The longer we wait, the more there are."

"I'm aware." I stretched a hand over my forehead to rub my temples. It did nothing to ease the pounding. "Want to check some star stuff with me?" Poe was the best astrologer and astronomer in the coven. When we were younger, she considered herself a cosmic witch. Did she still identify as such?

"Are you expected to pick up the kids soon?" I asked.

Her sandals slapped the tiles as she tossed them onto the floor. "I can spare some time."

"Great. Let me see Elton and Raeyn off and we can hole up in the covenstead." My house didn't have adequate shower facilities, but that didn't seem to bother the groups chatting in the lounge room and kitchen, which had funked up like a gym after Zumba, despite exercise taking place outside. I asked Poe over my shoulder, "Reckon you can make us a snack plate?"

She gave me her signature lopsided smile. "I am overqualified for this position."

Pointedly thanking everyone loitering in the hall, I proceeded to the back yard where Elton and Raeyn chatted with Brooke's family. Aunt Annis was telling Elton a story about his parents that I hadn't caught enough of to understand, and Brooke's cousin punctuated the story with her own observations.

For once, Raeyn's expression didn't close over the moment she saw me. "This is actually perfection." She held up my sketch of a Celtic knotwork hare on A5 cardstock. The tissue paper I'd wrapped it in was crumpled in her other hand. "You see me."

"I try, at least." My core warmed in a way that had nothing to do with the humidity.

"I'll miss tomorrow," she said. "Class all morning, work in the evening. But I'll watch the training videos your Mum linked."

"No worries."

As a group, we started moving through the house, herding people ahead of us. I was keenly aware I couldn't get into the covenstead with randos hanging around.

Raeyn tapped the wood panelling beside the bathroom door and glanced up at the dusty light fixtures. "This place is exactly how I'd imagine a witch's ancestral home, you know? Super authentic."

"It's haunted too!" Brooke piped up.

It wasn't. By some miracle.

Raeyn's eyes went wide. "Is that so?" Her mouth formed a little o. "Have you made contact?"

Thankfully, we got to the front yard before Brooke had the chance to weave something truly incredulous, and I squeezed Elton's hand goodbye, not wanting to get our sticky post-workout bodies any closer.

I was wearing a track in the floor, weaving through the house so many times, but I eventually made it to the sliding wall that concealed the covenstead. A few stragglers were still getting their shoes on, but the house was calm now.

Steam seeped out of the bathroom, accompanied by Dad's humming.

Poe waited there, a wooden serving tray in her hands. Lunch was to be instant noodles and sliced fruit.

I double-checked no one was approaching, then slid aside the panel. "After you."

Her footsteps rang on the wrought iron staircase.

I waited by the open wall, listening hard. The running shower made it impossible to tell if someone was coming along the now blocked hall from the kitchen, but I'd hear the stairs creak if the family using my room started down. If someone entered via the back door though, we'd be busted. I pinched my lip between my teeth. Why hadn't my parents installed a lighting at the top of the spiral stairs?

Unable to wait longer, I plunged us into darkness.

Poe called, "I've moved away from the steps, just standing in the fiddle-de-dee."

"One sec." I activated my phone's flashlight. Sharp, eerie patterns crept over the walls as I descended. The scent of books and Nag Champa rose to meet me. The light switch was on the wall behind the staircase. I hit it. Victorian style lanterns, now with LED bulbs, sprang to life between bookshelves and over tables and couches.

Poe settled the tray on the longest table, in the far corner of the covenstead, while I withdrew a blank star chart and instruments from a drawer in the bookshelf. We'd mostly rely on our phones and my work tablet, comparing apps, but the star chart would help me solidify what we discovered. And it added to the ambience.

"The 29th at, what? 11pm?" Poe tapped her screen, inputting details, while I loaded up Space Dance on the tablet, which would yield a 3D view of the heavens on the night chosen for the attack.

"Let's go with that."

Poe whistled softly. "Busy night."

"I'll say." As I squinted at the spread of planets, looking for clues, the steam from my noodles clung to my face. Fork in one hand, phone in the other, I went to load an Aspectarian, but I hadn't finished installing my favourite apps on my new phone. I sighed. "Do you have a list of the aspects?"

Poe gulped the broth directly out of her bowl and set it back on the tray. "Yes. No interpretation though, if that's what you need."

I shrugged a shoulder. How likely were horoscopes to provide insight into the psyche of nature spirits?

Twisting a curl around my finger, I studied the 3D planets. "I'm not seeing any trines."

"That's correct, there are no trines this dark moon. Why?"

"Trines have a heightened effect on Selkies. It's when their oidhirp anabarrach flares up."

Poe tilted her head, not seeming to follow.

"Their storm. Certain times of the year, um, particular astrological events amplify their primal need to return to the sea, and they get violent if anything prevents that. It probably signals something else for Selkies in the wild, I don't know."

Poe blinked at me, her lips slightly parted while she weighed what she wanted to say. "They have dangerous turns where their rage is uncontrollable, and you're dating one of them?"

My face grew hot, but I maintained eye contact. "Yep."

"Well, all right then." She scanned her screen for anything useful. "I'd estimate that'd be a time when Muldjewangk would also be especially powerful, or at least easily agitated. We'd want to avoid that."

She had a point. Using a lead pencil, I marked the planetary locations on the star chart.

Poe turned her device toward me. "There are four sextiles that night."

"And a square."

She traced it above the tablet's screen. "Yeah, here." Mars and Jupiter were ninety degrees apart. The God of War competing with the Giver of Victory. Shitsticks.

"Do we know which aspects matter?" Poe frowned. "Or is it all of them combined?"

I drew Mars' little circle with an arrow symbol. "Nope, no idea. It's possible that the sheer chaos in the sky that evening is what works in our favour."

Poe made a sound as though she was going to speak and decided against it. When I looked up, she was focusing hard, her gaze fixed on the corner of a bookcase. Her nose reddened. She blew a slow breath between pursed lips. "I had hoped we'd find another suitable night. Sooner." She swallowed forcibly. "I can't watch Viri suffer like this for a month."

Grabbing a fistful of my curls, I joined her scrutinising the bookshelf. We had no hope of finding a similar night to the 29th.

I'd checked Viri's wounds this morning. His feet were an unwholesome charred colour along the bottoms and his nails had cracked into jagged shards. Thick veins spider-webbed toward his ankles, looking too much like blood poisoning. And still his blisters boiled inside, even as he lay motionless. If he lived, he mightn't walk again. My eyes stung.

Poe sniffed back tears, but forced levity into her voice. "You need to dust."

"I considered getting a maid, but we'd have to initiate them into the coven so they could come down here," I joked. "It'd be awkward." I could count on one hand the people who'd entered our coven space who weren't family or coveners.

She spared me a weak smile.

"We can't move the date," I said. "So what else can we do?"

Poe dry-washed her hands.

I offered her some sani. "We're not powerless."

"Let's get this star chart done. Interpreting it might give our witches an advantage."

I used her phone to check the first sextile. "After this, I'll call the coven."

"That's another thing; bring the rest of them home." Poe's gaze drilled into me. "Holidays are over, we need them here."

I didn't know where anyone was or what they were doing. Few coveners had RSVP'd for our circle in two days. Unwilling to shake her faith in me, I said "mm-hmm," stuffed an apple slice in my mouth, and focused on the chart.

Poe moved stiffly as she fetched Elouera's Book of Shadows to record her interpretations. I hadn't picked the date, yet she blamed me. I wasn't putting Elton's needs before Viri's—my beloved before hers. Was I?

She sat heavily, opening the book to a fresh page.

Venus in conjunction with Pluto and the moon in conjunction with Mercury.

Moon sextile Saturn.

Poe square me.

Between us, Poe and I made quite the masterpiece. We weren't above a little gel ink for sparkle now and then.

Poe positioned her phone over the star chart and waited a few seconds after the electronic shutter sounded, but the photo came out blurry anyway. "Lighting down here is crap."

"But atmospheric."

"Indeed." She checked the time. "Let's take this upstairs."

I finished packing the pens and instruments away, then picked up my work tablet. The solar system reacted to the movement. I tilted the device again, watching the planets spin. "We ought to check on Viri. And there's a desk in there."

Poe lifted the star chart as though it were tissue paper, careful not to touch any ink in case it wasn't fully dry, and glanced at the snack tray.

"Don't worry about it. I'll come down tonight and do a big tidy. We can leave the lights on."

At the top of the iron stairs, we listened intently, then ducked into the hall and slid the wall home. The back yard was again packed with sweaty bodies, reminding me I probably stank, but none of them had the energy to care what was happening in the house.

Poe did shifty eyes. "Mission accomplished."

Feet stopped on the stairs to the top floor. Was Viri out of bed?

"My love? Have I found you?" Elton descended the rest of the way. "Apologies if I intrude, the door lay open, I mean not to be rude. An afternoon free has been gifted to me—"

I stepped forward to hug him, but he'd stopped, staring at the technological universe in my hand and the traditional map in Poe's.

"I didn't know you were here!" My nerves lit up. Whatever I had on this evening, I'd postpone. "Were you waiting long?"

He stiffened. Had I said the wrong thing?

My heart galloped.

"You spy on me? My people?" He spluttered inelegantly. "You trust us naught; is our selected date inferior?"

I backed up a step. "It's not about that." My mouth felt slack; hard to control.

"Don't flatter yourself." Poe rolled her eyes. "Not everything is about you. I wrote up a horoscope for the Dark Moon."

"Truly? Then I'd like to see. Yet it's not here, why might that be?"

Poe glanced my way. My hesitation was incriminating. What could I say that wouldn't reveal my house's secrets? Wait with me in the kitchen, Poe will fetch her notes? Yes! I'd have to hope they were enough to convince him that horoscopes were our prime objective.

I opened my lips to form the words.

"Forget it." Elton turned on his heel, calling over his shoulder, "I've others, those more honest, with which to spend my remaining days."

My teeth clicked shut as he slammed the front door, shaking the house, its spirits, and my sense of self.

TACET

ELTON

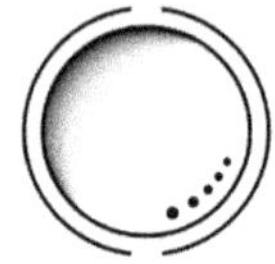

Poe's predictions appeared in my inbox that evening. Indulging the petty, I could say she conjured it the moment I left Morrigan's, but her astrology was sound and unrushed. I had to consider, too, the time it took type and format the email. They hadn't been lying; at least not in entirety. If I'd stayed another moment, I mightn't have thrown away a promising afternoon with my beloved.

'*My regret is great.*' I texted her. '*Unfairly I leapt, my conclusions harsh, so of your company I've been parched. Sorry from my deepest heart.*'

'*Don't be. It's normal to have feelings. And I do wish there was a closer date, for Viri's sake, not because I don't trust Mr Vess.*' She continued typing. I waited in stasis for the rest of her communication. *'I admit, though, I have studied the stars, trying to figure out what guides your people. What influences you. I wouldn't call it spying. I want to know how to support you, or when you may need extra consideration. Same as I expect you to be more patient when I'm on my period, because I'm drained then. It's about working together, not about mistrust. I shouldn't have gone behind your back about it though.'*

'Our love does not grant you access to my sacred truths; there are things about you I cannot know too.' One pure-hearted human did not negate the damage they'd done Selkies as a whole. Our knowledge and culture must remain separate. I brought my hair forward, as though it were a privacy screen hiding me from uncomfortable realities. *'We each deserve our privacy. To love is trusting one's lover, guarding their needs as if they're your own. I am not going to hurt you.'*

But I might come close, a tiny voice whispered. I curled around my pillow. Morrigan was delicate. Precious. I'd never raise a hand against her. It wasn't fathomable for me to lose myself so drastically; she needn't worry. It pained me she did so.

Another message chimed. *'I'm sorry my fear got the better of me. I hope you'll give me the chance to repair our trust.'*

'Time is all it takes an' it's my pleasure to spend my time on you.' I sent it, then rolled onto my stomach, crushing the pillow. *'Tell me we're still on for tomorrow?'*

Music blared from Medusa's house, our designated meeting point for this double date. Weird music. The type that made you want to clown around. Or skip. Or flat out turn it off. I pitied the girl's neighbours. None were on their verandahs, they'd taken refuge. What genre was it even? I shot Morrigan a look.

"Her parents are out." Amusement spread over Morrigan's face. Her shoulders wiggled rhythmically, making the silver threading on her dress shine in the most alluring way, leading my eye down a snowy valley—

Was that a trumpet?

It had to be. My ears were under assault. I glared up at Medusa's house.

"Don't look through the windows," Morrigan cautioned. "Meddy might be letting her hair down."

"Avert my ears I would, if only I could."

"Not a lover of the classics then?"

"I am, in fact, but this?" I shook my head, but the jaunty torment continued. "Not classical."

"No," Morrigan agreed. "This is Roy Orbinson."

"Who?"

She grabbed my hand, swinging it wildly and pulling me forward into an uphill skip as she sang along.

We mounted the porch, Morrigan snorting in joy. At her own warped humour, her friend's weirdness, or my confusion—I had no idea. None the less, gratitude infused me. We had emerged stronger for yesterday's clash.

She shut her eyes, opened the door and shouted, "Medusa Capatos!"

"It's Meddy!" The music halted. "Be right there."

Morrigan declined driving into the CBD, preferring the light rail. The waxing moon scrutinised us from the noon sky as we surfaced from the tram and headed for the restaurant Medusa had selected. She'd booked an hour for lunch, followed by a few rounds of ten pin; an admirable approach. She didn't bother us with questions or oscillate between venues; we supplied our availability and she smoothed the course.

I hadn't been convinced Astrid would much enjoy bowling, but then Medusa revealed her saucy intentions. She held Astrid from behind, pressing their bodies tantalisingly close while she guided Astrid in a couple of test swings. "The lane is directly ahead. I bet you throw as well as you swim."

Nothing about Astrid's initial throws were straight, but they weren't worse than my own. I slung my ball behind me, narrowly missing Morrigan's shins.

Giggling, she moved into place for her turn. She was using a Fluro yellow ball that reflected her disposition. "Let me show you how it's done," she teased.

"I'm watching," I said. Her dress swished as she moved, caressing her smooth thighs. It climbed as she bent at the waist.

She swung her arm, but her release came too early.

"Ay-yah!" she bunny-hopped aside, dress fluttering, as the bowling ball landed beside her foot.

I scooped the ball and capered over to her in an impersonation. "Like this?"

"You both need all the help you can get!" Medusa laughed.

On her turn, she took a running slide and released her ball, flooring nine out of ten pins.

"How is it I didn't know you bowled?" Morrigan asked.

"I don't." Medusa selected her next ball from the carousel. "Not regularly anyway." She missed the lone pin. Perhaps her mastery was more a comparison of our ineptitudes.

I gathered Morrigan onto my lap and nuzzled her neck. Summer florals tickled my senses. Astrid walked up, confident now. She must have counted the steps between the seat, ball return, and lane.

Medusa shadowed her, to further togetherness. Not to assist beyond describing how many pins stood, and in what positions. They shared a kiss, giggling at some private joke. Interestingly, they had similar disfigurements on their faces. Each had a cheek marred with dead tissue, though it was hard to determine the extent of Medusa's through her makeup.

Grinning, Medusa passed Astrid a second ball. She had straight white teeth.

I put my lips beside Morrigan's ear. "She's all right. Her appeal I understand."

"Meddy?"

"The very same."

Morrigan turned so as to sit across my lap. "I'm glad. She's a wonderful friend."

"Your people are good people." I wished she'd see my folk were worthy too.

Morrigan stood, releasing me to take my turn.

"Unbalanced it is, sadly."

She paused, tilting her head. "What is?"

"The ample time we spend in presence with your kin, yet to know my own you've yet to begin." I stepped up to bowl. Morrigan had impressed Raeyn with her artwork, but I'd have rathered those hours spent bonding in person.

As we passed each other, Morrigan said, "I'd like to change that." Then she threw two gutter balls, one after the other.

I smiled. "In that case, are you busy tomorrow?"

"I'm never not busy." She shrugged her perfectly smooth shoulders as we sat together on the horseshoe-shaped bench. "We're distributing the first lot of wea—" she glanced around. "Um, makeup kits Monday; lots of red tape to get through. And training every day."

Mrs Larue encouraged us to train six days a week where possible. I'd signed up for morning sessions.

Morrigan raised her voice to catch Medusa's ear. "I'm hoping you'll lend us your organisational skills again, Meddy. The pay is good."

"I assumed I'd be there." Medusa turned to me. "Morr is free all arvo tomorrow, she's training mornings until Wednesday."

Morrigan gathered her curls and ran her fingers through them. "What about circle?"

"That's tonight. Tell me you're prepared."

Her eyes widened. "Right. I am! Thought I had another day is all." Morrigan stepped between my feet and hugged my head. "So, tomorrow?"

She was soft and welcoming. "Mmm. Perfect." Resting my hands on her hips, I gazed up into her pink face. "Come to mine? It's a simple family afternoon playing board games."

Medusa elbowed her lightly. "No pressure."

"She laughs," Astrid said, "but Meddy's Mum put me over the fire the first time I stayed at their house, and just about had me fill in a contract when we started dating."

I sipped my drink. Their normal relationship had nothing on our fraught beginnings. "Arcane Industries sent Morri to parley, a poor first impression doomed to stay, whence my fur stolen away."

Morrigan stared at me with horror. "You're not making me feel better about this."

"I have revealed to them my feelings, how I cherish you. It'll be fine."

MORRIGAN

Nothing about this was fine.

Fives weren't rolling. Without them I couldn't get any bricks. Without bricks I couldn't build a wall. Next time the barbarians landed, I'd lose a city. Catan was complicated. Mr Abercrombie—who was far too intimidating for me to use his first name—had monopolised the brick tiles, and was trading with everyone but me, even though I had the least amount of victory points and posed no threat to his empire. Meanwhile, Mrs Abercrombie sat a massive bowl of puffed pork rinds next to me, claiming I looked "half-starved", despite being only a size smaller than her daughter who had to stand up and reach across the game board for the snacks.

Poe, I need you. I thought it with the entire force of my trained mind, the way she'd taught me, grounding myself in the greasy scent of pork and the icy air of the Abercrombie kitchen. My voice felt locked inside my mind. Trapped, like me. I wished I'd practised more often. Not that this would teach me my lesson. Telepathy wasn't the most necessary skill in a world of text messages.

"Does anyone have paper?" Elton asked. He meant in-game, not actual paper. I had some, but it was my only advantage. I scratched under my bangles. Could I spare some?

"Morrigan has paper," Mr Abercrombie said.

"I do," I admitted. "But I need it, sorry."

Elton scanned the board. "I'll give you three bricks for your paper." Paper, coin, and cloth were commodities, worth more than resources like brick and wood, but three bricks was generous.

"I'll give you a paper for a cloth," Raeyn cut in.

"Of cloth, I have none."

They mirrored each other's pug-faced shrug. It was kinda cute.

I held out my paper.

Mr Abercrombie raised his voice. "I'll give you a paper for two bricks."

Elton had received those bricks from Mr Abercrombie last round! I covered my mouth, pretending to massage my jaw or smother a yawn, hiding my incredulity.

"But bricks you have plenty." Elton seemed genuinely confused.

I'd never been more uncomfortable in my life.

Poe? Call me! Poe...

Elton and I made the trade, and I built my wall the following turn, but the awkwardness kept mounting.

When Mrs Abercrombie finished her turn, she stood. "Keep playing, I'll look on while I make monster shakes."

"Sounds impressive." I said. "What's in them?"

"Family secret my dear, but you'll love it. Everyone does."

"As you'll recall, no milk at all, for my Morrigan. Almond milk I did provide, but vegan ice cream I did not buy."

"Oh hogwash—"

I sat straighter. "Elton's right, I'm sorry."

He put a supportive hand on my arm and reassured his mother. "Ice cream aside, shakes will delight."

I managed a tiny smile of thanks. She didn't care how sick I'd be, nor how long mother cows called for their calves after farmers ripped them apart, but at some level she must have wanted to connect with me through the love language of food. She put my serve in the blender first.

As she piled the glasses high, my certainty mounted: we were all going to be ill after, regardless. Aside from milk and ice cream, the monster shakes had coffee, ice cubes, marshmallows—I recognised the brand and, thankfully, they didn't contain gelatine—pretzels, peanut butter drizzle, flaked chocolate, and—before I could ask to be spared—a huge spoonful of hazelnut spread. Even if it didn't contain milk powder, which it did, I'd have opted out because of the palm oil. How could people who'd been driven from the sea by humanity's exploitation consume products that did the same thing to land creatures, in this case orangutans?

I held my tongue between my teeth. *Poe? Come on Poe.*

As Raeyn traded me the materials I needed for a knight, which I'd use to defend my roads, Mrs Abercrombie distributed monster shakes.

"Is it okay if I snap a photo?" I asked as much to flatter her as to gossip with Meddy and Poe later.

"Oh, please do!"

Mr Abercrombie grumbled, but I was quick about it, not stalling the game longer than necessary.

Everyone else started on their spoon of spread, while I plucked pretzels from the top of my shake and waited for Mr Abercrombie to play his turn. Two fives rolled in a row, on Elton's throw then mine, and a flood of bricks came my way. Combined with the cards I held already, and a satisfying trade with Mrs Abercrombie, I got myself out of last place.

"Oh, you're catching on my girl!" Mrs Abercrombie squished me joyfully.

I didn't mention I'd played this game multiple times in the past. I smiled and returned her hug.

Mr Abercrombie pushed back his chair. "Yes, yes, very good," He agreed gruffly. "Excuse me a moment."

Mrs Abercrombie settled into her seat and scrolled her phone. Raeyn studied her cards.

Keeping my movements small and smooth, I switched my laden spoon with Elton's and grinned goofy grin that

I hoped epitomised the awkwardness inside me. He kissed me just above my hairline.

Picking up my cards, I shut my eyes and reached through the universal subconscious. *Poe?*

Maybe I should try Meddy. She'd probably laugh it off though, not trusting her intuition. And poor Viri was bombed on painkillers. I didn't want to deepen my parents' disapproval of my relationship with Elton by calling on them. It had to be Poe. Or suffer through till dinner.

When I opened my eyes, Raeyn gave me what Meddy called "the fisheye". A sideways bit of scrutiny.

Could she sense what I'd been attempting?

I turned to Mrs Abercrombie and filled the silence. "Elton tells me you're into herb gardening."

She beamed. "Yes! It fascinates me. As a kid, we took a land holiday to Italy, and I fell so in love. Every time I'm in my garden it takes me back to those two weeks with my parents." She launched into a story from that adventure, eager to share.

Mr Abercrombie returned, his face softening at the passion in his wife's voice.

"My love of gardening was one of many reasons we decided to stay," she said meeting her husband's gaze. The look of adoration they shared couldn't be feigned.

"Anyone got wheat?" Raeyn drew our focus back to the game. "Wheat for sheep."

That sounded good to me. Just as we were making our exchange, my phone rang, Elton's voice harmonising from my pocket. Mr Abercrombie let out a startled bark of laughter.

My face was on fire. There was nowhere to hide.

"My bad." I grimaced as I put the phone to my ear. "Hello?"

"Hey, thanks for your patience, the kids were..." Poe paused, "Well, it doesn't matter. You were trying to get me to call?"

I feigned a gasp, "Oh no! Will he be okay?"

"Uh, Morrigan?"

I stood, screeching the chair along the floor to cover the lack of talking on her end. "That's awful, is there anything I can do?"

"It's that bad, is it?" Poe sounded amused. "Do you need me to pick you up or do you have your car?"

"Yes, I have my car, I can come right away." I gathered up my bag and hat, which I'd hung from the back of the kitchen chair. "No, don't apologise, I understand completely. I'll be right there, it's okay."

"What a relief," Poe drawled.

"I love you. It's going to be okay." I repeated, hanging up. I rested my hand on Mrs Abercrombie's shoulder. "Sorry. Poe's little boy has been in an accident, and she needs someone to watch her daughter while they're at the ER. No dad on the scene and all that. But I had a lovely time, and the shake was amazing, I wish I had the chance to finish it."

She got up to embrace me.

"Thank you for having me in your home," I added earnestly.

I said goodbye to Raeyn and Mr Abercrombie, who didn't get up, then Elton walked me out.

"Send me a message, all is well or dire. Of your affection I never tire."

I nodded guiltily and kissed him goodbye. He tasted of chocolate and salty pretzels, which was thrilling if I didn't think too hard about how gross it was.

Elton made a longing sound and we held each other tighter.

"Drive safe, beloved."

I assured him I would, then burned out of there like my back wheels were on fire.

'You've crossed the line between wanting support and expecting me to perform miracles.'

"Nrrrgh!" I tossed my phone on the couch opposite me, and stormed upstairs from the covenstead. Meddy was right. It wasn't her fault that getting the coven together had become nigh impossible and I was having her do it on short notice. But Viri needed us to brainstorm a solution now, not wait until everyone's designated coven day rolled around again.

Part of my irritation came from arguing with Poe earlier. *'How will Elton feel when he discovers you made an excuse to leave early?'* She'd said. I'd assumed he was as uncomfortable as I'd been. That he knew from long exposure that his family—mostly his Dad—was intolerable. Poe had assured me that wouldn't be the case.

'Take this to your grave,' she'd sent, *'and don't do it again.'*

The guilt didn't sit well with me, nor did hunger.

It was around lunch time and the kitchen was full of strangers. I slipped in, grabbed a banana, a knife, and the peanut butter, then retreated to the covenstead.

Meddy had texted again in my absence. *'Our best bet is tonight at Poe's place. Eliss and Brooke can make it. You, me, and Poe. That's five. Faun is willing to sneak out if you pick her up.'*

'Tasmin got back today as well. Reckons she's beat, but Viri's her cousin, she'll come through.' I peeled the banana top and slathered it with peanut butter, took a massive bite, then added, *'You heard from Indra?'*

'He reads my messages but doesn't respond. You might have better luck.'

'I'll call him.' There was no use suggesting Meddy actually phone someone. If it wasn't her mum, it wasn't happening. I swallowed and found Indra in my contact list.

"Hey Morr, I got Medusa's text. Sorry. Just been busy."

Did he even know what busy was? I flexed my jaw as he continued.

"I don't think I can do witch stuff anymore." Voices in the background of his call faded as he changed rooms.

My eyes bugged out. I held my phone away from my face and stared at it. Yep, I'd called Indra. His name was right there on display.

"Don't be mad," he said. "I've just... outgrown it. You know?"

I did not know. My dad had been a witch his whole life. Ms Moontread was in her eighties. How could you outgrow magick once you'd seen it work?

"It makes Vanessa uncomfortable. She likes you all, but the coven takes heaps of my time. So yeah, I didn't know what to tell Medusa."

"I see." Was Vanessa to blame, or was she an excuse? How long had he considered quitting the coven?

"You're angry."

"I'm confused," I said. "You were here Saturday. Were you daydreaming when we discussed everything that happened over Christmas? Did you shut your eyes when we were in Viri's room? Didn't you see his legs and the IV and the agony on his face?"

"That's why I didn't say anything then."

You coward.

Silence filled the space between us, pushing us further apart.

"Indra, he's your friend. Are you telling me you're going to abandon him, when he's never needed you more?"

"Don't guilt me." Indra's usually warm, jovial tone hardened. "This is too big for us. There's nothing we can do for him, except bring him a world of hurt if we get it wrong—and Elouera gets it wrong a lot. Spells aren't a craft. They're an experimental science, and our attempts have blown up in our faces too many times."

That was unfair. Untrue.

Worse, he was keeping me from my lunch.

What had Meddy said last winter at Threadbo? *Witches before bitches.*

Saying that wouldn't help Viri. It wouldn't change Indra's mind or lead him to his shadow work.

I let out a calming breath. "Your fears are valid." *Even if they're not truly yours.* "If you wish to leave the coven, that's a conversation we can have. You wouldn't be the first to consider it, or even to follow through. But I'll tell you what I say to them: Come before the whole circle. I won't be your mouthpiece."

A door closed on Indra's end. He'd changed rooms again. "I understand."

"Make sure it's what you really want."

He didn't respond, but his measured breaths told me he listened.

"For now, if you want an exemption from spellcraft, fine. No one will make you train and fight beside us either. Poe's not. But you have a spiritual obligation, and there are plenty of practical things you can do for the coven and Viri that your girlfriend would be ashamed to speak against."

"She doesn't have a problem with Viri."

"Good. She can help too. Our door is always open to my coven and those they love." I necked the phone to coat my next bite of banana. "There's laundry to be done. Meals to be cooked. Supplies to be picked up and dropped off. Poe and I have been helping out Viri's family, but you could shoulder some of that pressure. Mama Thimberry needs her lawn mowed."

"I'll drop by every day after school." Indra's voice echoed, as if off tiles.

"Term doesn't start till February," I snapped. Unable to wait a moment longer, I stuffed the banana into my mouth and spoke while I chewed. "Don't pull the busy card with me. If you care about people, you make time for them."

Silence, again. I wouldn't break it for him this time. I let it get awkward.

"Tell Meddy I'll come tonight."

I glared, hoping on some level he'd feel it. "Really?" He'd done a complete one eighty. Had I been that convincing?

"Sure, sure. We can talk about, you know, future stuff, when everything settles down."

It was the best I could ask for. "I appreciate that. We'll figure this out together, okay? I won't forget."

"Thanks, Morr. See you tonight."

Poe'd left her street-level door wedged open. Faun and I were careful not to catch our bags on the handlebars of the twins' bikes and scooters as we ascended the stairs. When we got inside, Brooke was relaxing in a recliner and Tasmin was napping on the couch, apparently unconcerned by the mandarin peels in the cushion cracks or the apple core on the armrest. Meddy and Eliss were tidying: toys in the toy box, books in the nook. I started clearing dishes from the miniature table where the twins ate their meals.

We whispered greetings and waited for Poe to finish the bedtime routine, or whatever she was doing at the other end of the unit. It was just after nine.

Ten minutes later, we'd reclaimed the living area and lit linen scented candles. Poe padded down the hall in slippered feet, drying her hair on a towel. "Aww thanks sibbies. You're the best." She greeted each of us with a hug. "I made cucumber water."

I fetched it and seven glasses.

"Tell me we're not doing magick tonight," Poe said. "I haven't vacuumed under the couch in... Well, since last time."

"You've had bigger concerns." I waved away her worry. "I doubt we'll get that far. We need ideas."

Meddy slipped a coffee-zombie themed notepad from her planner while I went over Viri's condition and the ever-growing numbers of Muldjewangk.

"Dark moon is on the 29th. What can we do to stack the deck in our favour in the meantime?" I asked.

Eliss spread zir hands "Reduce the number of Muldje-wangk available to Liam? Is that a thing? If they spawn in the dead zone, and dead zones are water with low oxygen, can we dump an oxygen tank in there and call it good?"

"That doesn't help my cousin." Tasmin rolled onto her back and laid her arm over her eyes to block the light. "We ought to be healing him."

Arcane Industries already had healers working on Viri, but they didn't know him. Our spells would be stronger because our feelings for him were. I nodded, but Poe shook her head.

"It's not an illness, it's a curse. We can't heal it."

"So heal is the wrong word," Tasmin snapped. "The Muldjewangk curse is a death sentence. The longest any-one has survived it is six months, most don't make it near as long. Can we ensure Viridis lives?"

"And reduce his pain, at least?" Meddy's voice was full of gravel. No doubt she was thinking of all the failed restoration spells we'd performed on her. "Can we protect him from long-term damage? From both the curse and meds?"

Brooke leaned forward. "Here's what I don't get: You could turn the lot of them to stone. Why are we busting our arses and leaving Viridis in agony when your face is a weapon?"

Meddy hugged herself. "It doesn't work like that." Her response came out small, overshadowed by Tasmin's, but I heard her.

"She aint uglier than them," Tasmin said. "It wouldn't work."

"She's turned the Muldjewangk before," Brooke said emphatically. "When we tried to reclaim Elton's skin. That's how she escaped."

Poe pulled the thin sleeves of her summer wrap over her hands. "Too much could go wrong; some civilians on a romantic stroll, or I encounter a Muldjewangk that's blind or impervious to magick."

Faun jumped into the conversation, but her reply got tangled with Brooke's and the point Tasmin was trying to make. None of them cared Meddy was listening.

She shot me a pleading look.

"Oy!" I yelled, quieting them down.

Poe's attention snapped to her kids' bedroom door.

No sound or child emerged.

"I have turned them before, yes," Meddy said. "But I controlled it. I forced the change. And I can only focus on a single target at a time. I'd be willing to attempt to stone them en masse, but we'd need a backup plan." Her snakes stirred and she reached under her hijab to soothe them. "As Poe says, I can't guarantee my natural state would solidify them. Do they have any concept of beauty or compassion? Do they have families? Loved ones? Do they know fear? They're not mammals." She met Brooke's gaze and spread her hands. "How do we test it? I'd have to go alone. If it didn't work, I'd be screwed."

Tasmin rolled onto her side and squinted at us. "It's a bad idea anyway. We need the Muldjewangk that cursed Viridis dead. Better than dead. Destroyed. Who knows what happens to a person or thing when Medusa stones it?"

"Ceannas are dead," Poe answered. "We saw their ghosts."

I caught Tasmin's drift. "But Mayor Dawson isn't. We'll never know if the Seelie Court faeries resurrected him, or if it was simpler than that. What if it takes time for one of Meddy's victims to die?"

Colour drained from Meddy's face. Her eyes filled with tears.

"I didn't mean   "

"No no, it's okay. I wonder too." She squeezed herself tighter. "I would hate for Viri to suffer for ages after because I stoned the wrong Muldjewangk."

"There's also the matter of clean up," Poe said. "Getting a hundred monster statues off the beach before dawn would be a feat."

"Any stoning I do during the battle will be conscious. Salt most like, because we can easily shatter that."

We could easily destroy the environment by salting the earth too, but I didn't say it. Meddy would make good choices. The point was we shouldn't expect her to be our hero.

The city's silence invaded Poe's living room. Traffic on the main road below her balcony. The old white guys next door smoking on their deck chairs, laughing. Party goers singing in the park, leaning on each other and dragging themselves along fences as if it wasn't Monday night.

Faun popped her thin shoulders with an overhead stretch. "So, we need a strength spell for Viridis and to oxygenate some water. Not much to go on here." She leaned back against the wall, a life-sized rag doll beside the twin's toy box. "What say we tip off the police. Stir trou—"

"No cops!" Poe and Tasmin said together.

Tasmin snorted. "Jinx bish."

Poe rolled her eyes, then her attention settled on Faun. "No cops."

The thought of Liam Kendren getting arrested or trying to explain away the bloodstains on the table in his processing room delighted me for a few moments before logic won. "They'd think it was a prank. Unless one of them is psychic or somehow sensitive to energies, they won't see Liam Kendren's jetty shack."

Poe switched on the fan. "Nothing good would come of it either way."

"So, how do we mess up his dead zone?" Eliss grinned. "Is it like how aquariums need a pump?"

Faun cocked her head. "Isn't the sea water already sloshing?"

"Yeah, nah," Meddy replied. "Water is sedentary, like rock. Water with too many minerals sinks to the bottom, causing algae blooms. Organisms eat those blooms, consuming oxygen as they do so. Fresh water coming to the ocean from streams sits on the top, it doesn't penetrate all the way down."

Tasmin squinted at Meddy, waiting, as I was, for the science to make sense. I knew, broadly, what created dead zones: farm run-off. Fertiliser and pesticides getting into the ocean. It had never occurred to me to ask why the waves didn't re-oxygenate the water. "Wait, you're saying the dead zone is only on the sea floor?"

Meddy's lips twitched in amusement. "You didn't think the Muldjewangk were floating where any passer-by might tangle with them, did you?"

I stuck my tongue out.

"Might the dead zone clear on its own?" Brooke asked.

"Depends on how the land is being used," I said.

"And if we get any severe storms," Meddy added. "It's storm season right through till March. We could get lucky."

Brooke tossed her hair. "Witches make their own luck."

Indra's worries raced through my mind. *Spells aren't a craft. They're an experimental science and our attempts have blown up in our faces too many times.* But he hadn't bothered to attend our meeting, we owed him nothing.

I turned to Poe. Brooke was rash by nature. Faun inexperienced. Eliss didn't shy from danger and Meddy would follow where I led. But if Poe, and to a lesser extent Tasmin, seriously considered working weather magick, I trusted their judgement. More, this was their Country.

Poe had her hand around her pentacle, her gaze fixed on the cobwebs crossing the ceiling.

"Don't all talk at once," Eliss joked.

"Weather magick is dangerous, isn't it?" Faun asked.

Meddy nodded. "All the books Felicia has lent me say not to touch it with a ten-foot pole."

Brooke pulled her handbag onto her lap and dug out some lippy. "Wicca 101 says a lot of things real witches don't adhere to."

"This isn't that," Tasmin said.

"Let's think damage control," Poe told the cobwebs. "We'd be putting all those homes on the coast at risk."

Faun snorted. "Those rich bastards have insurance."

"Harm none." Meddy said what I was thinking. She flipped open her planner. Her cheek dimpled inward where she chewed it.

"What?" I asked.

She sighed. "I can't see how to fit everything in, not without ruining ourselves. We're training hard. Most of us have jobs. Poe's got kids. Oberon has competitions all month. So does Astrid—"

Brooke opened her mouth but Meddy ploughed on.

"—And if I dare suggest she help us, someone will jump down my throat, but we need everyone we can get."

Brooke's cheeks coloured and her designer eyebrows spoke volumes, but she let it go. Meddy was right anyway.

"You're hosting a bunch of families at your place, nursing Viridis, and trying to squeeze your own life out of the cracks." Meddy turned her planner around, showing a monthly spread that tracked everyone's appointments. My life was in green, nice. "So, we either need to choose a single course of action and give it our all, or we split into teams."

Faun's eyes shone with interest. "More witches means more power, doesn't it?"

"It can, yeah." Meddy tore off the top page of her notepad and wrote neat headings on the fresh page. "But it also means less focus. The bigger the coven, the more likely to make mistakes."

Poe caught my gaze and subtly pointed at Meddy. Her lips quirked as if to say *this one is turning out well*.

That was a comfort, at least. For weeks I'd been racing around, patching the holes in the hull of my relationship. Running up on shoals, making mistake after mistake. Begging for extra chances, praying those I cared about wouldn't jump overboard while I figured myself out. Poe wasn't holding a grudge though, and Meddy was every bit the witch I'd imagined she'd be. I could do this.

If we broke into smaller groups, it'd be less obvious that Indra had withdrawn his help; Elouera didn't need that added drama. And those of us summoning the storm wouldn't be worrying about the coastline and accidentally misdirect the magick.

"Sign me up for conjuring the storm," I said. "And get Astrid on that team if she's available. She's a water witch."

"And a shit stirrer," Brooke added. "If we're going to cross into chaotic territory, she's well suited."

Was that a compliment or an insult?

Meddy declined the opportunity to defend her girl-friend's honour. "I'll ask her."

"I'll do the protection spell then," Faun said.

"Same." Tasmin pushed herself into a seated position and combed her unruly hair with her fingers. "No shade on Astrid. Protecting the land is my business. You can also put me down for healing Viri, or giving him energy, whatever. I'm not training, it's the least I can do."

Meddy's pen scratched. "Got it."

I pressed my palms to my eyes and leaned back. We could handle this. Meddy and Trinity would balance their calendars and highlighters and phones. Together they'd pick the best dates for a protection spell, a storm spell, and rally for Viri. They'd assign roles: who would host, bring reagents, write the rituals. We'd cut off Liam Kendren's supply of Muldjewangk. If there weren't hypoxic water spirits to arm, his force would stop growing.

I'd arrived at Poe's unit hopeless, without direction, but as always Elouera caught me and mapped the way forward.

Tracing the edge of my phone in my cardi pocket, I wondered how much of this I could share with Elton without compromising the coven's privacy.

PAEAN

MORRIGAN

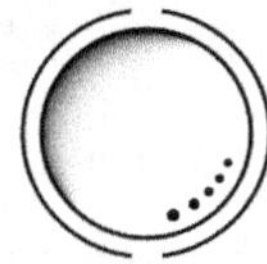

Poe set a glass salad bowl on the altar, where a map of Sydney's coast doubled as a tablecloth. Unwholesome blue-green food colouring swirled in the bowl's bottom.

"How'd you get the hypoxic water to remain separate?" Brooke tapped the glass with her acrylic nail. "Or, is it actually hypoxic?"

"Nah, it's just fresh. Fresh water sits on top of salty water. Also, cold water sinks and hot water rises."

"For real?"

Poe quirked a grin. "Clearly you've never spent a rainy afternoon with a couple of bored pre-schoolers." She opened our Book of Shadows on a folding music stand where it wouldn't get splashed, then swished away in her coven-green robes to continue setting up.

I clipped a book light to the stand. Brooke had written the ritual in diminutive lettering. We didn't typically bring plastic or electronics into circle, but her tiny print would be illegible by candlelight.

I went to the balcony doors and pushed them wide to let in the warm night. It was exciting—novel even—to go into a ritual blind when I usually led. The sky was as clear as the road below. The forecast predicted a heatwave for the weekend. Poe's children had been asleep for hours and unlikely to stir. Last night, Tasmin and her team had enacted their protection spell for the coast. Thursday was perfect to work with the Gods of thunder and lightning.

My favourite robe flared at the bottom as I turned. Where was I needed?

Around the outside of the sigil Poe had chalked onto the carpet, Meddy was placing a tight row of semi-precious stones, enabling Astrid to detect the ritual boundary. Astrid used Poe's singing bowl to fill the room with a pleasant hum, driving out negative energies. Eliss, who might have directed snark Astrid's way, was busy lighting candles. Elton shadowed Poe, helping prep the altar. His musical barrage of questions complimented the singing bowl's low hum. Everything was under control.

I went to stand with Brooke, pausing to return the Book of Shadows to the correct page. She was heaping her hair into an obscene pineapple on her head; a sure sign shit was about to go down. I adjusted mine to match.

"I understand. Hmmm," Elton replied to something Poe said. He tucked the plate of biscuits under the altar where it'd remain dry and headed back toward the kitchen, striding ahead of her. "Forgive me for not asking earlier, how fares your wee son? Morrigan was quite concerned, and not the only one."

My stomach sank.

Poe shot me a filthy look. "Parenting is a hundred heart attacks a day. Kids are always trying to off themselves. But no, he's all good now. Thanks."

I held my breath, praying none of the others asked her what she meant.

Poe switched on her old portable CD player and sat it in the hallway. The track was nature sounds; setting the mood even as it created a noise barrier for the twins.

I drew my hood up to hide my hot cheeks as Elton came back into the living room. It wasn't like I'd never lied for Poe. Deep down she wasn't judging me. She didn't care. But I cared. How was it that my experience working with people and diffusing situations wasn't carrying over into my romantic life? The more Elton and I got to know each other, the more some part of me was dedicated to messing it all up.

Astrid finished with the singing bowl and joined Meddy, who was using the book light to pin the Book of Shadows to the correct page. Why hadn't I thought of that?

Elton waited with Brooke and I. He wore borrowed robes—black with a red cord, his hair in a smooth plait down his spine.

Poe set the last piece of the spell on the altar—a cup of boiling water, tinted red.

"Feeling witchy yet?" Brooke asked Elton. Not waiting for a reply, she stepped forward to begin the ritual.

His smile was closed-lipped. He took my hand and we entered the circle.

ELTON

"Bring up those feet!" Felicia yelled, spinning into a jump where her heels struck her arse. It wasn't a polite curple, resting harmlessly at the top of her legs. No. It was a firm, bouncing rump on full display in her gym tights. At least my face was pre-reddened; a state not unique to me.

Medusa looked fit to perish, half buried beneath a make-up mudslide. She'd arrived early, snagging the patio umbrella, but that only stymied the warm summer rain, not her perspiration.

Raeyn doubled over, gasping out her new mantra. "At least it's not hot."

The grey sky imparted the morning session with a dusky feel. Last night's spell was working.

I shut my eyes as though this torture might be ignored and used the momentum of the last jump to carry me into the next, my thigh muscles burning. Should I weep for agony, none would see my tears through the wet. My braid walloped my ribcage a beat behind my feet.

"When the Muldjewangk curse you, it burns a lot worse than this!" Morrigan shouted from beside me. "Push through!"

I turned to her, incredulous that she was somehow not out of breath.

She grinned. "What?"

I didn't have the air in me to respond. My girl seemed soft. Her thighs clapped, cheering her on as Felicia led us in an aerobic lunge, cross, hop combo. I'd been fooled. Morrigan was steel inside.

Past her and Medusa, Astrid was holding her own. She had a thin build with muscular shoulders and powerful legs. The couple counted out moves to keep time.

"Plank!" yelled Ms Moontread. My cheer came out a squeak. Morrigan flowed into a downward dog first, her curple round and proud, then lowered gracefully. The rest of us in the corner—her coven, me and Raeyn—tried and failed to get into plank position, our limbs quaking on the slippery mat. The Larue's had covered their grass with blue stadium flooring that reminded me of good times. Concerts.

Raeyn laid down. She couldn't get any wetter.

"You can do anything for 30 seconds," Felicia called. "One plank, then we'll stretch it out."

Morrigan's plank dipped in the middle. She muttered an expletive.

Medusa laughed. "Pull in your core."

Astrid's hair, blacker than mine and almost as long, had come free of its tie and obscured her face. "Is it over?"

"Not yet." My neck strained with the effort. "Her watch mun be broken."

"It doesn't get easier." Raeyn shut her eyes. "Isn't it supposed to get easier? I've been coming every day for a week."

Felicia called the end of the plank and a groan rolled across the garden. I flopped down, my body making a wet slap.

"It does." Medusa leant forward to reply. "The catch is you can't tell. But if you took a long weekend, it'd be much harder when you returned."

Her words failed to inspire me.

Ms Moontread drove us to our feet and ran us through our self-defence moves. Disengage, get control, watch each other's backs. Those, at least, were sinking in.

Afterwards though, we'd practise with weapons, wherein I failed.

Beyond the shame of carrying such girly items lay my inability to use them. Morrigan and her coven knew a symbol for everything. When they used their sigil eyeliners, they looked—to borrow Poe's term—deadly. Their squiggles and runes meant nothing to me however, so I resorted to English. The chance Muldjewangk were literate was slim, but Raeyn took the micky out of me regardless. The bronzer brush was useless, and I couldn't get my mirror to charge. It wasn't broken, I'd swapped with Morrigan to be sure, but despite Morrigan's insistence that witchcraft was a craft—a practice ascertainable to all—I found myself incompatible.

Advice like "envision the result, not the process" didn't help in the slightest.

Thunder broke overhead. The weather forecast had promised clear skies by noon, but magick wasn't predictable. Our storm would continue ravaging the coast until the water was sufficiently oxygenated. Those of us on land could deal with the constant shower blowing our way. At least Sydney wasn't flooding.

Raeyn performed a double-leg takedown on me, then squinted at the sky. "Reckon they'll call it?"

"Much doubt I hold."

Ms Moontread and Felicia were discussing something up the front, but it wouldn't be abdication. They knew what Raeyn did not; we'd summoned this deluge.

"There's no saying it won't rain on the 29th." Medusa slipped out of Astrid's grip and put her in a chokehold. "We should be prepared for any eventuality."

"Let's move on to duelling," Felicia called.

I groaned softly.

Raeyn elbowed me. "I'm gonna kick your curple, little brother."

"Everyone who is ready to test their spells, please cluster on my right. Those less confident, line up for the target dummies." Felicia gestured to a row of straw people by the leftmost hedge.

"An' if you're utterly useless?" I muttered.

Morrigan rested a sympathetic hand on my shoulder, but it was Astrid that answered.

"Come inside with us."

I bristled. Sit out with the invalids?

"We'll show you how it's done."

Raeyn and Brooke peeled away to join the duels. Morrigan hesitated but followed them.

"Come on," Medusa said. "I know where they keep the towels."

We sat in the lounge room, our sopping towels and my discarded shirt in a heap against the wall. There was a plush, untouched sofa, but we settled on the tiled floor, making a triangle with our knees.

Astrid held her compact, tracing the serial number stamped on the bottom with her finger.

"We're new to magick," Medusa said. "By the Larue's standard anyway. We remember what it was like before." She twirled her hand in the air, as if I should know what came before. Morrigan said they'd been friends for life, how then was it possible Medusa had a before? She didn't elaborate. "When you came to circle at Poe's... We all raised energy and laid hands on Morrigan. Did you feel anything?" she asked.

"I can confirm I did." The memory was sharp. Energy had poured through me. "Like a live wire, it was out of my control."

"That's fine. If you recall the feeling, it gives us a place to start."

Astrid nodded. "Belief is huge in magick, and it's hard to believe what you've never experienced."

"You need to know you can do it. Your magick will work. Is already working in the future," Medusa said.

That was all very nice and uplifting, but utterly useless.

"Have you stored anything in your Rendezvous compact?" Astrid asked.

I shook my head.

"He says no," Medusa said.

"So the times you've felt magick, you were in a circle. We should replicate that. Nobody will be charging their mirrors in the heat of the moment, ain't no reason not to use every advantage." Astrid turned toward Medusa. "Can you please bring four cups of water to mark the corners?"

"Hold up." I frowned, half-remembering. "Are not the corners earth, air, fire *and* water?"

"If a successful circle can be cast by calling the four winds, or with quarter candles, or in the woods with standing stones, there's no logical reason not to cast a circle with water. All we need is to make a container for our power anyway, it's not like we're summoning the Angel of Death."

I shuddered at her flippancy.

Medusa came back with four glasses, each a different shape. She set brown in the south. The westernmost vessel had a handle like a wave. The others I didn't see, as she placed them close behind us. This circle would be tiny.

Astrid cast it without standing. Without a ritual dagger. No portals drawn in the air nor scattered salt. Damp in her workout gear. Yet she considered herself a beginner?

Medusa thumped the floor and said, "Our circle is empowered, bound and blessed."

I knew the next line. "So mote it be."

Both witches smiled.

"Let's raise energy. Can't turn the light on if there's no power," Medusa said.

People passed through the lounge room, averting their gazes to give us privacy.

"Basic chant and clap?"

"Sure. Let's use 'Magick high, blooming flower, ours to weave, drunk on power.'" Medusa tapped a three-four beat on her thigh.

"Appropriate with all this rain." I closed my eyes, listening to the patter against the front windows.

The witches began. Slow and soft at first, then louder as our heart rates picked up and the trapped air heated. We chanted until confidence unfurled within my chest. Until I believed. When I opened my eyes, I brimmed with energy, so much so I was unfazed that we weren't alone.

Astrid lifted a finger, which I took to mean one more repeat and we'd stop. I chanted louder, the tenor of my voice bouncing in the boundary.

Medusa seemed giddy, clasping her hands and rocking in place when our chant stopped.

A giggle rose in my chest.

"Yes, now there's plenty to play with," Astrid said.

"And I've got an idea." Medusa picked up my compact and handed it to me. "Trap a chant or song in your mirror. A sound to play back. Once you unlock the ability to put something—anything—in the device, it'll be simple to fill the mirror with missiles or heat bursts to release in battle." She seemed genuinely excited.

"All right." I popped open the mirror and my flushed face stared back, somewhat more handsome than usual, despite my soaking. "Uh, how?"

"Breathe deep, pulling the energy around you into your lungs. Feel it there, filling you, expanding you, desperate to break out," Astrid's voice grew wistful. "Then force that magick through the filter of your vocal cords. Hear the infinitesimal tink as your magick penetrates the mirrored glass." She leant toward me and spoke with her hands, "When you've caught it, slam the compact shut so it can't get out."

I filled my chest to bursting, concentrating on the sensation. The utter convincing of my soul that this would work. The time came to perform the magick, but I hadn't thought of any words. I sang my song; the most natural thing.

"The sea a queen, an ancient wife,

the sky above, twists our life."

The compact in my hand vibrated.

"We're compelled, alone, apart, salty tears an' keening hearts."

Thunder shook the house. Thunder we'd made.

My lungs neared empty.

"Love come torn, crash of waves,

the breeze your laughter, summer days."

My air ran out. The mirror made a delightfully crisp snap that rang with finality, capturing my voice.

I hunched over it. *Work, please.*

Curling my lips around my teeth, I snagged Medusa's gaze. My smile was pained. The hope inside me quivered. If I didn't succeed now, I had no chance. I'd be destined to wield a pool cue on Tamarama, spearing Muldjewangk the old-fashioned way.

"Well?" Astrid said. She gestured at me to get on with it. "Press the trigger."

There wouldn't be anything in there. Silence would reign. I'd been confident other times I'd tried, yet the mirror had remained dormant. "I can't."

I would cry if I'd failed, even with their guidance. When moments ago, power had thrummed through my being. It'd be too much.

Medusa's face twisted in sympathy. She nodded. "Okay, well, do you want to leave the room while we test it? We'll tell you if it worked or not?"

That sounded perfect. Yet horrible. Where would I be? In Morrigan's kitchen? I'd hear silence, perhaps some scuffling from the back yard or Medusa and Astrid's muffled amusement, then they'd come in shaking their heads?

"I'll text you later, give you some distance from it all." Medusa offered. "How about that?"

I relaxed my head back. "Your kindness is unparalleled."

"That's a yes?"

"Can confirm." I passed her my compact as Astrid dismantled the circle.

I pulled into my spot off the side of our white pebble driveway and reached for the key to turn off the ignition. The radio bid me pause.

"… we welcome Timothy Blue with the arvo surf report. Hi, Timbo. What's happening out there?"

"G'day, Rue. Our mates at the Bureau of Meteorology can't make heads or tails of this storm. It ought to 'ave blown inland by now mate, but it's hovering a couple of clicks out from Tamarama and Bronte beach. Surf conditions, not just for Tamarama—Australia's most dangerous swimming hole—but from Coogee to Bondi, are: Don't. Stay home folks. What looks like summer showers—"

I killed the engine, popped the door, and swung a leg out into the warm drizzle. My phone pinged. A video from Medusa. So soon? What of the distance she'd promised to give? I sighed, pulling my leg back in and shutting out the world. Everyone cried in their cars, where better to view her message?

Astrid stood in a library. Or perhaps Matthias's office. The wood panelling in the background was familiar. "Ready?" She asked.

"Ready," Medusa said from behind the camera.

Astrid raised the compact.

I held my breath.

She hit the trigger and the mirror sprang open, its faint metallic ring audible.

One heartbeat. Two.

Ambient noise from their side buzzed in the void.

I wasn't fool enough to hope Astrid pressed the false-trigger for spell-loading instead of the release.

"Oh." Medusa sounded defeated. The camera dipped.

"The sea a queen, an ancient wife…" My voice fluttered through my chest.

The camera lifted. Astrid smiled wide. Conscious of being filmed, she made the victory sign.

When the spell ended, Medusa cheered. The recording cut off halfway through her whoop.

"Yeah baby!" I beat my free hand on my steering wheel, blaring the horn victoriously. "Salt, yeah!" It wasn't poetic or graceful, and I didn't care who saw. I pumped my fist in the air, reignited my engine, and headed straight back to Morrigan's to collect my weapons. It was time for serious practise.

MORRIGAN

I waited on the front lawn, stretching and enjoying the first completely dry day since we'd cast our storm spell. There wasn't a quiet place inside. I'd cycled through worrying no one would show for circle—after how much I'd called on them this week, to resignation, hope, and back again.

At least Meddy would come. And Poe was already here, sitting by Viri. The twins were building a Playdoh empire on the kitchen table last I saw them. They were old enough Poe could chance a ritual and probably not get disturbed.

I rolled my shoulders. Stretching hadn't helped. Every fibre of my being ached, overworked and sore.

For today's circle, we'd give our energy to Viri. It was simple magick; we'd done it many times. The twins might even be able to join in, as we'd agreed not to shape the magick or try to force an outcome, simply giving our personal resources and allowing Viri's body to do what it needed.

He'd asked to participate, so we'd hold circle in the spare bedroom. He was "sick of the doom and gloom" so we'd planned it part ritual, part rave. I'd made a play list.

The grass was cool between my fingers and tickled my palms when I skimmed the blade tops. Magdalene trotted over and flopped onto my lap as if to say *pat me instead*.

Meddy arrived first, on foot. Tasmin and Brooke came together, and nearly got flattened by Faun as she whipped into the yard on her bike. Oberon, too, was a whirlwind. He threw his un-zipped backpack out of the passenger side of a full car as it slowed but didn't stop. Oberon followed his bag, mid-way through changing from his dance clothes into his robes. Bare chested. His shirt blew down the foot-path. The glitter in his hair caught the light.

Meddy whooped. "Way to make an entrance!"

Oberon bowed as the car sped away, then hopped in alarm before chasing his shirt.

Eliss and Trinity came down my street from opposite directions.

We waited, donning our robes and chatting on the lawn until the western clouds glowed bronze. But Indra didn't show.

Brooke stood and shook her hair free. "Let's do this."

"You putting on a spread after, Morr?" Eliss asked, "Or we going home for dinner?"

Faun's eyes lit up, but she kept a straight face while she waited for my reply. Truth was, I hadn't thought about it. When did I last eat a proper meal? We could order in pizza.

I grimaced at the thought. No, I was over pizza. Meddy wouldn't eat it anyway—too much oil and salt.

I held the door open for everyone. "I'll ask my parents what they're doing. Might be sketchy, but I'm sure we can feed yous." We piled inside, excusing ourselves as we passed through the lounge room where the out-of-towners were watching telly.

In the kitchen, Poe was serving her kids pasta and frozen peas. "Your mum said she'd watch them while we're in circle."

Mum's head snapped up at the mention. She was sitting on her bed, surrounded by paperwork, tablet in hand. I poked my head through her door so I didn't have to raise my voice.

"Hey Mum, we're headed upstairs in a minute, but it occurs to me I didn't plan for dinner, and it's dinner time, and my coven are here." I winced. "Hashtag fails at adulting."

Mum huffed in amusement. "Don't we all?" She tapped her stylus. "I was thinking sushi. How many kids? Er, coveners?"

"Like nine?"

"Ooof, this is going to hurt."

"I'll pay if you're willing to order and collect."

"Okay, moneybags," she teased. "Mmm. Brown rice for Meddy, I suppose?"

Eliss shouted from the far end of the house, "You coming, Morr?"

"I'll get my wallet," I told Mum.

I missed her muttered reply as I rushed toward Eliss.

"Just fixing dinner," I said. "Everything set?"

"Yeah, 'cept Viri's asleep."

And yet you're yelling the house down? "Might not be now."

"Poe says we go ahead but try not to wake him."

"I'll be right there."

I raced my wallet back to Mum, pausing to hug and properly thank her, then ran upstairs. On the way, I sanitised my hands.

Viri's space looked less like a sick room with witch gear strewn and candles lit. On the desk, a cheap disco light projected streaks of colour over the walls and ceiling, but the accompanying party tracks weren't playing. A devil's ivy twined around Viri's IV stand from a pot strapped to the bottom with industrial zip ties. Meddy and Poe were hanging Christmas lights across the window. The others dusted surfaces, topped-up vases with fresh water, and tried not to trip over each other in the crowded room.

I turned the music on low, gradually increasing the volume until we could understand the lyrics. It'd have to do.

Outside, the streetlights came on. Everyone arranged themselves either side and at the foot of Viri's bed. Meddy shuffled nervously. Faun watched my every move, waiting for the signal to start.

I stepped into the space between Poe and Oberon. "Let's cast circle hand-to-hand."

Oberon grabbed the hand to his right, mischief on his face. "I, Oberon, king of the faeries, cast this circle."

Eliss stared at zir plump hand, stumped for a moment. Oberon's nails were painted black, their edges filed, contrasting with zir bitten-down and chipped orange polish. Ze reached for Tasmin's hand. "I, Eliss, champion of social progress, cast this circle."

This wasn't how hand-to-hand went.

Tasmin reached to her right, and introduced herself by her craft name, Skye, a warrior of her Indigenous nation. Faun leaned across the bed to grasp Brooke's hand, continuing deosil, the path of the sun.

Brooke declared herself a style queen and showered Viri with glittering faery dust before joining hands with Trinity.

"I, Trinity, bring magick from far-off lands to cast this circle hand-to-hand."

Elouera was glowing with pride and strength. I'd have to tell Oberon how much I loved this later.

Meddy nodded at Trinity in appreciation, then took Poe's hand. "I, future Dr Medusa Capatos, nutritional scientist, cast this circle."

My breath caught. She must have accepted a university offer!

"Congratulations," murmured Poe. We clasped hands but I missed her introduction. I was busy gaping at Meddy. Did she get her first choice? Would she stay local? She'd considered so many universities, I'd lost track of which ones she'd applied to. When had she found out?

Poe jiggled my arm. *Focus, Morr.*

Right. I straightened my spine. "I, Morrigan, Celtic hedge witch, declare this circle cast! Hand-to-hand, our will is done."

We raised our arms overhead, making a fortress, then those of us standing at each of the four cardinal points invited in the elements. After Eliss delivered our opening prayer, paying homage to the living universe, we released our grips. It was time to dance. Viri slept on. Was he even home? Or was he out of his body, leading souls across the rainbow bridge? Nothing would wake him if that was the case.

"Crank up the music," I said. He wouldn't be mad.

Trinity looked ready to argue. Or, more correctly, her expression was the entirety of her argument. I smiled reassuringly.

Meddy eased the volume up until the bass thrummed through the floorboards.

Oberon found the beat and led Eliss, Tasmin and Faun in some fancy footwork. I waited until the pattern repeated and jumped in.

On the opposite side of the bed, Brooke and Trinity were singing and clapping along.

Energy thickened the air—exuded from our bright faces and churned from the earth by our stamping feet.

Without opening his eyes, Viri smiled.

"Great circle." Eliss hugged me. "We should do it like that more often."

"Maybe with our own instruments," suggested Tasmin.

The lounge beckoned me, but if I sat I wouldn't get up again. I leaned against the doorframe, arching my back to make space in my overstuffed torso. I could've sworn the sushi expanded after I ate it.

Brooke grinned up from the floor, where she was buckling her kitten heels. "I know the recorder."

Meddy laughed. "Dear lord, no."

"See you on the line," Tasmin said as she, Oberon and Eliss left.

"Shoes, please." Poe reminded her kids. She'd had her sandals on for a good ten minutes and fidgeted with impatience. "I'll be back in a sec. You'll have to carry those shoes if you're not wearing them when I return."

Somehow, carrying shoes across the lawn to the car was a valid threat. Artemis stuffed her toes into the opposite foot's sandal. I crouched down to help, my thigh muscles threatening to give way.

"There you are." Dad entered the lounge room from the kitchen, heading to his office. "Don't go anywhere."

Brooke arched her eyebrows, I shrugged in response.

She let herself out, calling over her shoulder. "See you all Monday."

Dad re-emerged, and his gaze roved over those of us by the door; waiting as Faun and Trinity said their goodbyes. It was just Meddy, the twins, and I.

"I got a report from Arcane Industries." He brandished a single-sided document. "Thought you'd be interested."

"What news?" Meddy asked.

"There's this," he waved at the paper, "But as a bonus, Kendren sent me a lovely email, apologising for his mistreatment of my daughter and requesting I *call off my dogs*." He made air quotes for the last bit. "Apparently, someone blacklisted him on TICA and that's making it very difficult for him to move his operations."

Meddy cocked her head. Her parents hadn't rented in her lifetime.

"TICA is a tenancy database," I explained. "It protects landlords from renters who damage property."

She grinned. "What a shame."

"Isn't it though?" Dad looked smug. "I told him if he hands over all the stolen Selkie skins and pauldrons, he's got a deal, but we both know negotiating is a dead end. We've talked till we're blue in the face, but the vision he has for AI and the wider metaphysical community is..." He paused, frowning, and picked a hunk of rice out of Artemis's hair. "He needs to start his own company, not mangle ours."

"That'd be expensive. Arcane Industries has the means to support itself financially. Not that I care. Anyway, we've got people on the beach monitoring him, right?"

"Watching the warehouse," Dad corrected. "Kendren himself hasn't been sighted. We assume he's holed up in that shack; groceries are delivered regularly."

"What about the storm?" Meddy asked. "Did AI confirm that the dead zone cleared?"

Dad shook his head. "Getting our hands on a research vessel to check isn't as easy as you're imagining, but Kendren's actions indicate that yes, we've cut him off." He glanced at the kids to confirm they weren't listening. The twins were occupied by tying all the shoes together and giggling. Meddy crouched to fix her laces, she'd been the first victim.

"We stopped him running," Dad said. "He can't set up base elsewhere. He knows he'll be put under citizen's arrest and handed over to ICR the moment he steps off his jetty and that's made him desperate. Look at this."

He passed me what I assumed was the report, and I leaned closer to Meddy.

The words were in English, but I couldn't make sense of them.

"Ammonium nitrate. Concentrated hydrogen peroxide." Meddy held a chunk of her inner cheek between her teeth. "I don't recognise the rest."

There were a lot of chemicals listed. "What are these for?"

"Depends who you ask." Dad took the paper back. "Ammonium nitrate, for example, is present in fertilisers—"

Meddy hissed. "He's not going to tip that into the ocean, is he?"

"Nah. No way." I didn't want to consider it. The guy was trash, but he loved the ocean. Surely he didn't believe the ends justified the means.

"He could, if he wanted to create an artificial dead zone." Dad rubbed the back of his neck. "But these chemicals are precursors for homemade explosives, too. I'd almost prefer him to pollute the ocean."

Scenes from all the war documentaries I'd watched in school flashed behind my eyelids. Fear choked my voice. "I'd hoped he'd think we gave up."

Dad stared at nothing out the window. "That would've been nicer than his gloating messages." He shook his head. "Probably wasn't hard for him to determine we were gathering a force to storm his hideaway. He's enjoying the satisfaction of proving AI needs a standing army."

"We wouldn't if he wasn't a dick."

Meddy braced herself as Artemis grabbed her hands and started walking up her legs. "Is he aware International Coven Review will burn his shack down if he repels us?" The child reached Meddy's chest, flipped to the ground and repeated her stunt.

I wasn't considering failure. Wouldn't put my energy into it. Apollo tugged on my hand, keen to replicate the climbing and flipping his sister was doing. I was grateful I hadn't changed out of my robes as his little shoes bit into my leg.

"I certainly hope he doesn't." Dad scratched his stubble. "If he feels cornered, he might march with however many Muldjewangk he has at his disposal."

I puffed air into my cheeks. Maybe he'd been stocking chemicals all along for processing the skins. But it was equally possible he felt trapped, because he was. "If he marched right now, could we stop him?"

"We've got a small, advanced force in a hotel near the beach. They'd buy the rest of us time to get there. Hopefully. But if he marches during the day, there's no hope it'll go unnoticed."

"Shit on a stick."

"Indeed." He gestured at the twins. "You need any help here?"

"Thanks, but oof—" Apollo's foot sank into my stomach. "They're just waiting for their mum."

"Poe must have fallen in the can," Meddy said.

Dad gripped my shoulder a moment, saluted Meddy, then left us to it.

I disengaged from Apollo. "I'll go see what she's doing."

"Good idea." Meddy set Artemis down and went to her messenger bag. "Who likes outer space?" She pulled out a sheet of stickers.

Poe wasn't in the kitchen and the bathroom was empty. I dragged my arse upstairs.

My bedroom door was open, the room deserted but immaculately kept.

Viri's door was closed.

At the unmistakable sound of lips pulling apart, I snatched my hand away from the doorknob.

A kiss coming to an end.

"I feel like I'm taking advantage of you," Poe murmured.

I stiffened. Sleeping people could not consent.

Viri chuckled, his voice edged in pain. My unease faded.

"Please do."

DUET

MORRIGAN

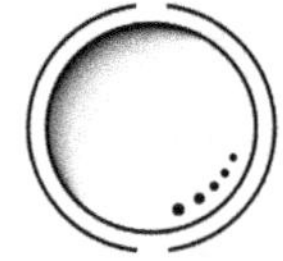

Three days out from the Dark Moon, I was the sharpest I'd been in my life, yet woefully unprepared. We'd done everything within our power to ensure success. So why did I feel like a four-year-old on the verge of tears because my favourite cup was unavailable?

Logic said fatigue. I'd attended both training sessions today and won all but two of my duels. I'd promised myself a nap, but somehow found myself in the front yard with Dad, adding new pieces to his fairy garden. I'd rest tomorrow. We were taking two recovery days so no one went into battle tired or injured.

Dad dipped a tiny tree-stump table into our bucket of soapy water and scrubbed it with a toothbrush. Grey had snuck back into his thin hair, the wisps of it flowing in the humid afternoon breeze.

I weighed my words a moment, then went direct. "Sorry I've been weird lately."

His lips twitched in amusement. "You've been weird your whole life, it's how I know you're mine."

"Daaaaad."

"Sorry, are we being serious?" He used the little table as a gear stick, jerking it through an invisible transmission. "Shifting gears." He settled the fairy table in the shelter of a blueberry bush.

I tried again. "I don't know what got into me."

"Fear?" Four matching log seats plopped into the bucket. "Even when we know people love and accept us, it's hard to believe we'll be embraced until it actually happens."

"Maybe." Insecurity was a type of fear, right?

"Or confusion," he suggested. "Lots of big changes this summer." His hands stayed busy.

I unwrapped a new fairy trellis and put it aside in favour of popping the bubble wrap. "About that. I was considering getting my own place. With some mates or something. Don't be upset. Please."

Dad made an effort not to laugh. "That's fine. I'm surprisingly okay with not cooking your dinner and doing your laundry anymore."

I hadn't thought of it that way.

"It's normal for a young person to move out of their parent's house. Your mum and I are banking on it." He finished the seating area below the blueberry by blu-tacking a tiny vase in the centre of the table. "Tell me you're not moving away, though. I mean I'll be cool and everything if you are, you can tell me the truth." He glanced at me from under his scraggly brows. "I'll cry privately if you're thinking of running away to sea with Elton, or some such. It doesn't need to be awkward." He selected a picnic basket and two wire bikes from the ornaments spread between us.

Following Elton wasn't possible. I'd considered a houseboat at one point, before I understood how disorientated the ocean made him. If he went to sea, it would be wearing his skin. And without me. I shook those thoughts from my head. "No, I'd be local. Everyone I care about is here. Work is here. Who'd look after you if I moved away?" I wasn't enough for them already.

"I'm not decrepit, Morri." He put the bikes and basket beside a resin pond. "You used to love travel."

I shifted my legs uncomfortably. "I do. Thought I'd go backpacking with Meddy after high school, but she's going straight to uni."

"That's disappointing. Have you spoken about it recently? Does she know you're still interested?"

I slid the bubble wrap through my fingers, looking for an un-popped section. It had been a while since either of us mentioned our trip. "I'll bring it up."

"Couldn't hurt." He scooted along the garden bed. "Do you worry a lot about taking care of your mum and me?"

My hands balled reflexively, the plastic crinkling as I drew them toward my core. "A bit. Yeah. There's only one of me and I miss a lot of things. Like how tight Mum is with Ms Moontread. Or how much work it is for you guys with me living at home." Really, I hadn't seen my parents as individuals at all. I wanted to make them proud of me, but they already were. It was more than that. It was how Elton changed everything. Dating took more time and energy than all my other friendships combined. My voice came out small. "I never realised how much it would matter to me that my parents liked my partner."

"We like Elton fine. He's a nice guy."

We both knew that didn't necessarily mean they wanted him as their son-in-law. Or the dating equivalent.

Dad pushed his hair away from his eyes, speckling it with soil. "Don't laugh and don't call me old—I'm not as ancient as you seem to think—but I didn't realise asexual people dated. I'm still catching up."

"I'm ace, not aro." But maybe aromantic people did date?

"Yes, well, I know that now." His cheeks coloured. "Your mum enlightened me." He tapped a tiny Victorian lamp against his chin, deciding whether to share the rest. "She also volunteered to check my network settings. Apparently, the internet is a valuable resource."

I snorted. "She uses that line on me too." I made a mental note to search aro information later.

Dad seemed to appreciate the solidarity. "Confusion aside, it's my job to worry. But if you two need my blessing in the traditional sense, I'm happy to give it."

"Yeah?" I sat a little straighter. "I'd like that."

The breeze turned cool, tickling my neck with relief.

"Hopefully the internet will tell me the best way to do that too," he joked.

We gardened in silence for a few minutes.

"You can always come to us after you move out. It's not an end. I called my mum with my problems right up until she died. I called her when I didn't have problems, too, of course." He tamped blue glass pebbles into place with a rubber mallet, as if installing a real patio. "We don't stop being your parents just because you're an adult. All that changes is—outside of work—we can't decide what you do anymore. Not that we did much of that."

My coven's trip to Jenolan Caves last winter came to mind and I nodded. Instead of telling me not to do crazy dangerous things, my parents taught me to do them better. Safer. Dad had dropped everything to help Meddy when she'd stoned men in self-defence. I'd woken him in the night to come get Brooke and I from a party where drugs and Ouija boards were being mixed. Mum had braided my frizzy hair, backed me at protests, and listened to me wonder why everyone else had feelings I didn't. Why had I worried they'd love me less for dating Elton? For dating at all?

I crawled over, avoiding the gardening supplies in the grass, and hugged Dad's sweaty neck. He rubbed my back, raining dirt on my calves, and held me until the awkwardness of the pose forced me to withdraw. "Thanks, Dad."

He took my hand. "Do me a favour?"

"Yeah?"

"Try not to be so hard on yourself. No one keeps track all the time. No one succeeds and excels at everything, especially not on the first attempt. And no one has the whole home/work/social/leisure thing in balance. If they

say they do, tell 'em they're dreaming." He tugged my fingers, sending a jiggle up my arm. "Let yourself be human,
okay?"

After I'd scrubbed the dirt out from around my nails, I
drafted a text to Elton and stared at it.

'Do you want to get a rental together?'

I added, *'After Dark Moon,'* but erased it because it was
obvious. We wouldn't inspect properties in the next three
days.

A big conversation like this should probably wait until
after the fight. He had enough to deal with. Moving in
together would be positive though, right? Not an added
stressor. Something to look forward to.

I put my phone on the kitchen bench, then picked it
back up. This was ridiculous. I wouldn't think twice about
hitting send if it was to a mate. But what if he thought I was
pushy? Or needy. We hadn't been a couple long, but I had
to move out with someone, so why not him? Shouldn't I
at least ask him before signing a year lease with... Who?

I stalled, putting my phone down again but leaving the
screen active while I surveyed the fridge. Cold boiled pota-

toes presented a no-effort snack. I put a few in a bowl and smothered them with garlic salt.

My whole life, I'd expected Meddy to be my first flatmate. Before either of us knew we were queer, we planned to marry and raise a family together.

I bit into a potato. If I asked her to flatshare she'd say yes, so long as Astrid got an invite too. Would she actually want that though? She'd never be able to leave her room before doing her makeup in the morning, couldn't whip her hijab off with one hand and her bra off with the other to relax after uni. She'd be as trapped living with me as she was with her parents. It'd be too much to ask.

Poe? No, she liked her own space. Viri had his caravan; moving wasn't a priority for him. Brooke was too young. Eliss? Eliss was perfect. Oberon might be keen too. They were both clean, outgoing people. And I was pretty sure neither was allergic to cats.

I paged away from my unsent text to message Meddy, *'Are you and Astrid getting a place together? What's she doing for uni? I imagine you're not interested in living with sighted people, yeah?'* The last thing I wanted was for Meddy to think I hadn't considered her. I shuffled along the bench as Mum came into the kitchen for a drink, then hastily sent Meddy another text. *'And are we on for back-*

packing? Can I come over so we can make real plans? In a few days, of course.'

One potato left. I hadn't tasted the others. I needed to get out of my head. I bit down and took a moment to be present. The potato skin burst, filling my mouth with a refreshing cloud. How long was it until dinner? Did I have time for another serve?

As I opened the fridge, the family borrowing my room started down the hall, loudly discussing their meal plan. It must have been around five; their family ate earlier than mine. I could wait. I collected my phone and headed to the covenstead. Meddy hadn't responded. My message to Elton remained unsent. Perhaps my oracle cards would comfort me.

Nails scrabbled on the metal stairs, meeting me on my way down. Emanuel meowed pitifully for release. I cracked the sliding wall for him, and he stalked out into the back yard, no doubt reporting my behaviour to Mum. Hopefully he hadn't been trapped in the covenstead long.

It smelled of books and Nag Champa, wood polish and home, not kitty pee, so that was a good sign. My footsteps echoed as I crossed the open space, disturbing the spirits with the slide of old wooden drawers and the scuff of chair legs on the floorboards.

My cards were thicker along the edges. Soft with use and affection, no matter how mad they might be with me. I shuffled, opening myself to their vibrations. They were tired, in need of a night under the moon.

"I'm sorry, I haven't played with you lately," I said. The cards knew a person's heart, leaving no room for excuses. "I promise the next time I draw you, we'll play solitaire and have a bit of fun." Maybe I'd invite my parents to play, and give the deck a thorough cleanse afterwards. Viri too, once we'd set him free of the Muldjewangk curse. I put the cards down to light some candles and incense.

My eyes went prickly, unconnected to the smoke. Viri had been doing so well under the care of AI's healers. After we'd held our empowerment dance party circle hybrid, there had been a few days where he'd moved around with minimal assistance. Then he plummeted again, screaming so loud I heard him from my bed on the covenstead sofa. We'd kept him sedated ever since.

I opened my Book of Shadows to a fresh page, holding my place with crystals on two corners. Passing my cards through the smoke a few times, I let my thoughts float away. I needed answers about my future. Viri was undoubtedly part of that, but I didn't want a garbled message.

"Let's begin," I murmured.

I turned the cards face-up and fanned them over the table to choose a significator: A card to show the spirits this reading was for and about me.

Throughout the deck, I had cards I related to certain people. Brooke was the Queen of Swords, never afraid to assert her boundaries. Viri was Death Reversed. I tended to pick The Star for myself, and The Star Reversed for Meddy. Not because she was my opposite, far from it, but because the card spoke to idealists. It dealt with hope and losing faith in humanity.

The Star felt wrong today.

I bit my lip. My fingertips tingled as I passed them over the deck.

Temperance offered itself to me.

Yes. Temperance was associated with Sagittarius and focused on our need to check ourselves. We required patience as much as freedom.

I set Temperance in the middle of my workspace and shuffled the other cards.

"Show me my relationship with Elton and our future beyond Dark Moon," I said.

The cards clung together, signalling their readiness.

Two of Cups—a harmonious partnership—crossed Temperance. Giddiness swept over me. Yes, this is why I'd come.

My favourite spread was the Celtic cross. No other layout consistently provided me clear assessments of whole situations. Above the two cards I'd already dealt, I laid the background card. In a general reading where the quarent hadn't asked a question, it'd tell me what situation the cards focused on. In a reading like this, it reassured me that the deck listened. Helpful, because sometimes cards would either ignore the quarent in favour of a new message or become irritated at a repetitive question.

Dread coiled my gut. Three of Swords wasn't a card I'd expected to see. I swallowed.

"Lay the cards first, then interpret them," I muttered.

Recent past—Nine of Pentacles.

I slid the next card from my deck, but the nine drew me in with a memory of a garden as lush as the one depicted.

On the last Beltane, I'd lounged with Meddy, Brooke, Eliss and Oberon, devouring a platter of summer fruit. We'd eaten blueberries, pomegranates, plums, and mangoes, enjoying the late afternoon sun. Meddy left early, taking some of our figs to Astrid's place. The carefree security of that day infused me. Abundance surrounded us and I'd had plenty to share. Everything was perfect.

I drew back into the moment. How could it have been perfect when Elton hadn't entered my life yet? I clamped my teeth together, slapping the next card down.

The High Priestess.

What was Mum doing in my spread?

Completing the cross, I laid down the near-future card in the western position.

The Knight of Swords, flying high on their winged horse. Huh. Quite the compliment if the cards meant me. An intelligent individual. Witty, confident, and reasonable. I ran a finger over the reds and golds of the art. It was probably Elton. No. A partnership where stimulation of the mind took precedence, not a specific person. Our relationship reached the future, in that case. Good.

The Three of Swords glared at me. I pressed on, laying out the seventh and eighth cards. Judgement fell into the placement that highlighted outsiders' opinions. I snorted. Others were judging. Haters loved to hate. Nice, my deck was trolling me.

A nerve in my hand twitched as I slid the ninth card from the top of the deck, and I dropped it. The Moon landed on the High Priestess, showing as reversed. Delusion. Or a person that promises false fantasies. I flipped the moon upright and moved it into ninth, the placement "for or against." When answering polar questions, the ninth card was the most important. For queries like mine, however, nine merely leaned weight into the argument.

Pins stabbed into my fingertips and shivered up to my skull as I laid the final card. Reversed Ten of Swords. I clutched my temples, holding myself together as my muscles cramped and twisted. I rubbed my arms to dispel goosebumps. It must've been colder in the covenstead than I thought.

As the shivers drained from my tail bone, I took in the spread as a whole. I relaxed my face, imagining my third eye open. Links formed between the cards, strengthening each other. The Moon was glowing, energy swirling over it in a clockwise vortex. I half expected the card to spin.

Hands grabbed at me from the Magician card in seventh place, the environment position. I picked it up.

The Magician's presence didn't surprise me. He often heralded positive beginnings for projects or relationships. But the hands in the background art, behind the magician, spoke of factors outside my control; things I couldn't ignore.

Who owned those hands? Elton? Our parents? Maybe all of Elouera. Someone had control over my relationship, other than me. I put it back and skimmed to the High Priestess, wondering again what influence Mum had on my love life. She wasn't linking to The Magician. The hands weren't hers.

The High Priestess' gaze flicked toward The Moon. *You've missed something your intuition has been telling you.*

That seemed unlikely.

I pulled my Book of Shadows closer to record the reading, starting with the question I'd asked: What would become of us after Dark Moon?

The Moon was a benevolent soul that brought to life a person's deepest fantasies. What was Elton, if not a waking dream? I pushed back my chair and crossed to the bookshelf. It'd been a long time since I'd referred to the guidebook. Were any meanings I hadn't internalised even relevant?

And Ten of Swords as the eventual outcome? Really? I envisioned Caesar's cronies stabbing him. Jon Snow betrayed by his Night's Watch brothers. Such was the violence of the card. I shook my head. Elton would never attack me, not even under the depressive effects of Three of Swords. It wasn't a card I'd apply to us at all.

The bottom shelf held all the guidebooks of every oracle, deck or bag of runes owned by my family. Some belonging to members of Elouera and Writtenbark, my parents' coven, too. I found the one I needed and knelt on the floor, flipping pages.

"Re-evaluate your circumstances," I read aloud for clarity. "Let go those aspects of your life not serving you.

Rather than dwelling on your painful past, it is essential to look ahead and realise how these events free you up to reshape your life."

I sank back onto my heels, slapping the book against my face in relief. Something traumatising would happen during the battle, and that pain would bleed into our future, causing trouble for our relationship until we overcame it. Yes. That must be it.

I moved to another cupboard and dug out my best resin incense blend. It had taken me weeks to craft, and quite a bit of money for the ingredients I could neither grow nor forage. I lit fully half the mix right then as an offering to the gods and spirits.

Perhaps Elton's skin would be destroyed. That would plunge him into misery. It was something beyond our control that affected our relationship. It would require me to become the King of Swords; to be strong and logical, and not take his sorrow as an insult. Or the King could represent the professional help he'd need. The reading had nothing to do with returning to the type of happiness I'd had before Elton completed my life, or my worries being true intuition.

So, he wouldn't be ready to live together immediately, but we were surrounded by support. We would make it through the hard times ahead. That's what mattered.

Elton looked especially beautiful this evening. He'd straightened his charcoal hair, pinned it back with a Celtic inspired clasp, and had got a manicure. Each nail was clean and square with a light gloss over top. He was wearing a deep green shirt with silhouetted leaves cascading down the chest, and black dress shorts. We'd been together all afternoon, gone for dinner, and were just now returning home, yet I couldn't stop admiring him. My throat closed around the words I'd practised as he drew me into his arms, then turned me, so I faced our reflection in my car's window.

"A stunning couple we are," he commented.

"If a little odd," I agreed.

I too wore green; a long, layered skirt I'd borrowed from Meddy, paired with a brown sleeveless blouse. Grass tickled my ankles.

My jaw quivered and I twisted, burying my face in his neck. His fresh ocean scent brought me no comfort.

"How come you smell like the sea when you don't swim there?" It wasn't what I'd wanted to ask.

"Cologne."

"I should have thought of that."

We disengaged and he crossed my lawn to where his car was parked on the street. I hurried along beside him.

"Don't you worry," he said. "Curry in a hurry is attractive too."

"Hey!" I put my hands on my hips and pouted.

He laughed.

Tomorrow everything would change. Or maybe nothing would. We'd have answers. Possibly injuries. If my cards were correct, it'd be the beginning of a long, depressive episode for him. Our honeymoon was over, and I wasn't ready.

His car keys jangled.

If I didn't speak up, I'd regret it all night. Maybe forever.

I grabbed his wrist. "Stay with me?"

His gaze met mine, full of unspoken questions.

"For the night," I added.

Elton allowed me to draw him close. His gaze searched my face, then flicked up to the house. My parent's house.

"Pyjamas I lack," he stalled. "A change of clothes also."

"Your clothes aren't dirty; you can wear them for breakfast and the drive home. And you could sleep naked, or borrow some boxer shorts." I had a pair I was pretty sure would fit him.

He nodded slowly, considering it. A teasing grin spread to his raised eyebrows. "Sleep naked on the couch?"

"You can let it all hang out on the couch if you want, but I was thinking my roo—" Shitsticks. My room was taken; I'd been crashing in the covenstead. I hadn't thought the logistics through.

"I fear your parents shall not approve."

"We're Wiccan," I reminded him. "They don't care about nudity." I didn't want to bunk in the lounge room though.

He fiddled with his keys. "Excuse my disbelief."

"Maybe we could pitch a tent in the back yard?" It was a silly idea. He didn't want to stay. I shouldn't have said anything.

He didn't respond.

"Never mind," I said. "It's too crowded, right? Fun to think about, but not practical." I hugged him goodbye and plastered on a smile.

His cartoon-red ears stalled my forcibly casual exit.

"I want to." He swallowed. "Don't think I lack desire."

Dad rounded the distant corner in his jogging tights.

Elton didn't meet my gaze. "My family would react un-favourably."

"We can ask permission, if you prefer."

Sweat dampened his hairline. "Please, Morrigan, you're killing me."

I stepped closer, rubbing his sides to soothe him.

Dad's pounding steps preceded him down the footpath. "Merry meet!" He slowed, turned to cut across our lawn, and realised he wasn't in circle. "How are ya?"

Elton lifted his hand, almost waving, and stumbled through an unintelligible reply.

Dad puffed his way to the front door.

"Hey, can Elton sleep over?" I called.

Dad gave me a thumbs up and disappeared inside.

I grinned at Elton. "See? Doesn't care."

He laughed, all adorably sheepish, and pulled me into a hug.

Fear gnawed inside me, as though this was the end, not the beginning.

I could die tomorrow.

I wouldn't though. That'd destroy my parents. And anyway, I was well trained. I needed to shake these morbid thoughts.

Elton put his keys away.

I nipped the corner of his jaw. "Can you keep a secret?"

After our shower, Elton and I lay side by side on the makeshift bed we'd created from spare blankets and doonas piled onto the covenstead floor. The cool duskiness refreshed us. A solitary fan stirred Elton's sparse body hair and coaxed our candles to dance.

"Big day tomorrow," I said.

"My love, no." He threw an arm over his eyes. "Let's not dwell on the 'morrow."

"I can't not think about it."

He took my hand and kissed my knuckles. "We've been over everything. Imagined every scenario. AI couldn't have chosen a more competent lead than your mum."

"She's amazing, but…" I rolled toward him, only to have him place a finger against my lips. He held my gaze as he ran it down the middle of my chest, stopping just above my navel. Somehow the shiver he evoked centred me.

"We can't do more than our best. We must trust our team an' each other." He turned, rolling onto his side to face me.

Trust each other.

I swallowed the faithless words I'd rehearsed, unable to ask for reassurance. His unwavering attention needed to be enough.

He smiled, resting his hand on my hip and making small circles with his thumb. Willing me to smile back. I did, toying with his hair instead of tugging my own.

"I want to do something we'll always remember anyway. If nothing changes, it's not like we'll regret it. But if..." I let the sentence dissolve.

His penis fluttered to life. I hadn't done anything to warrant its regard, yet it swelled in the most fascinating way.

Elton cleared his throat.

His arousal put me in mind of a cicada emerging from its exoskeleton.

"Uhm, I wasn't talking to you," I told it. Except now I was. Curiosity stirred within me. Not desire, but not repulsion either. Bringing him joy made me happy. Or at least the idea did. When I glanced up, he wore his mortified expression. Perhaps I wasn't supposed to address it?

Elton's penis twitched again, and he rolled onto his belly and buried his face in the pillow. "It does that by itself!"

I waited for him to stop holding his breath, my lips pressed tightly to hold in my mirth. He was delightful.

"Dare I ask what you've got in mind?"

I took his muffled question as an invite to touch him, running my fingers over the lines and curves of his speckled back. "It might sound silly, but there's this spell I know. Like a lesser version of handfasting, almost." I stopped to take a few breaths and overcome the awkwardness. Meddy once asked how I didn't feel ridiculous talking about magick and leading rituals, and I'd said it came with practise. Truth be told, I was acutely aware of how different I was. I got on with being myself because morphing into someone else wasn't an option. That's how I wound up in uncomfortable situations like asking my boyfriend of thirty-one days to perform a spiritual marriage with me.

Elton pushed up onto his elbows. "Please continue."

"It's a connection ritual. It'd make it so wherever we are, we'll be able to sense each other."

"You would know then, how you enchant me?"

I fought with my grin, but it won. "Something like that, yeah."

"Would you also feel my arou—" He broke eye contact, as though the books lining the wall were the most interesting thing he'd ever seen. "—uh, my physical attraction to you?"

I hadn't thought of that. "Maybe? I don't know. I've never done it before." There hadn't been anyone I craved. I wanted to curl around his mind; meld into him.

He sat up, grabbing a pillow to cover his lap. I almost made a joke about how I didn't want my pillow smelling like crotch but caught myself. Now wasn't the time.

"Hopefully no," he said. "I wouldn't want to change you."

I kissed him for that. How could I resist?

"I don't think it would," I reassured him. "Even if I felt echoes from you, they wouldn't be mine." He couldn't fix me because I wasn't broken.

A candle directly behind him haloed him in gold. "Oh Morrigan, I cannot comprehend how deeply my love for you flows."

"I love you, too." My voice dropped to a whisper, but I persisted. "I can't imagine not loving you forever."

"To have your heart wherever I be? Yes!" He kissed my third eye. "Shall we cast circle to include our nest?"

I nodded and got up to gather the things we required. Elton followed, bravely doing away with his pillow. I'd left a pair of boxers on one of the covenstead sofas for him, but he declined. He'd offered his reasoning, too, but I hadn't understood what he said.

While I constructed our altar, he drew a passable circle with red chalk, then we moved on to marking the quarters.

I lit Jasmine incense for the element of air. He was inspecting the contents of a cabinet lining the wall. "Are quarter candles preferable?" he asked.

I shook my head. "Everyone thinks candles equal romance, but fire is the element of lust, not love." I poured rose water into the western quarter cup. "It's water that presides over emotion and intuition."

A potted Prince of Orange marked the south. Prince Orange didn't live down here full-time, of course. The junior members of Elouera cycled the covenstead plants with a sunny spot upstairs; a job I was immensely happy to delegate.

Elton placed a little something extra at each quarter. Rose quartz for earth, a pigeon feather for air and a shell for water. He hovered by the lit red pillar to the north, passing one of my parents' couple candles between his hands.

"Do it," I said. "It's perfect."

I was glad he thought of it; it would never have occurred to me to select wax lovers from the candle cupboard. I tried to keep my elation low-key, but it had be a good sign that he felt comfortable customising our circle.

When everything was ready, Elton sat in our nest at my feet while I invited every spirit of love and devotion I'd ever heard of to witness and empower our ritual. Finally, I rang the bell to declare our circle cast.

I knelt beside him, our altar off to my left. "Let us acknowledge the custodians of the land upon which we worship. Blessed be the Wangal people of the Eora nation."

"Blessed be," Elton intoned.

"Next we state our intent," I said. "It's the most important part, so we'll each need to do it separately."

"Like vows?" The weight of commitment didn't seem to faze him.

"You could call it that." I didn't require a mirror to know my face matched the fire of my hair. "Just say how you feel and what you hope for."

"May I go first, then?"

"Uh, yes. For sure!" I schooled my surprised expression but wriggled with excitement.

"What you say may sway me, and that would be for shame. I want my declaration wholly mine, untamed."

"Fair enough. Well, go ahead. The Gods are listening."

He swallowed, then shifted from cross-legged to kneeling. After a moment he took both my hands in his.

"Hail Venus, Hathor and um, Branwen," he stumbled to a stop.

I resisted the urge to feed him an opening line or to tell him it was okay, not to worry about the address. He could vow to the nameless universe or speak to the sea, it would work the same.

Elton's voice held gravity as he started over, "Lo' Goddesses with many names; sky father high above, Eros, god of love, spirits gathered here tonight. This woman, Morrigan, brings me delight." He cast his eyes to the beamed ceiling. "Bless our devotion with a conscious tether of emotion, connecting us throughout the days, thwarting miles, across the waves. Above, below, without, within—" He mangled the Hermetic Principle beautifully. "—mark my words, make Morrigan kin." He squeezed my fingers and gazed into my soul. "So mote it be."

"Blessed be." I responded out of habit. Nothing I could say—nothing I'd prepared in the hopes he'd agree to this ritual—came close to his declaration. I slid my hand from his to press my lips and blinked my vision clear. He was perfection.

I shut my eyes to centre myself. "My Lady and Lord, guardians of the elements, and assembled spirits, bear witness." My heart swelled and I opened my eyes, giving him my bravery. "Layer your blessings upon us, I beseech you. Tonight, we kneel in your sacred temple to create an enduring bond. Every day Elton teaches me new things about myself and shows me greater wonders. He is my home, safe and comforting, but also embodies wild adventures and unexplored horizons. His love was my life's missing piece. Join us, so we might know each other more intimately."

Instead of selecting cords, as I would for our handfasting, I bound us with smoke and breath, wine and saliva.

I kissed him as passionately as I knew how. Kissed him with the intent of fusing our souls for eternity, begging him to never leave. And he answered, pushing into me until our skyclad chests stuck together and our breathing came short. My head spun as we tumbled into our nest, limbs as tangled as our hearts.

When we drew apart, gasping and laughing, tears streaked past the edges of his swollen smile. I kissed them away.

I whispered my last line. "Bind us."

"We are bound." He caught my lips again, pushed past them hungrily, spurred on by my caresses. His glorious body reacted to the slightest touch. Desperation filled my chest. I needed to keep him. To have all of him. To consume and exist inside of him and coat myself in the devotion he showed me. I pressed closer. Breathed deeper of his scent.

"Morrigan, please," he moaned into my mouth. "I crave you."

Goosebumps raced up my arms.

We rolled, spilling the rose water. His hair tangled with mine in the puddle. His hands burned against my skin. Together we fell into the magick of the night.

EIGHT OF WANDS

ELTON

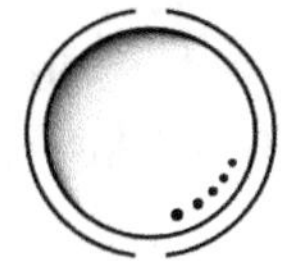

The drive to Tamarama Beach was charged. Full of bravado. Popular faeries, or perhaps witches who'd been in the industry decades, bounced from group to group, chatting in the bus isle. Old friends squeezed each other's fingers for reassurance. New ones cracked jokes. Arms were slung across shoulders.

Not Matthias though. The greying witch spoke in hushed tones, no nonsense, his knuckles white on the steering wheel. Where AI had hired the buses and whether their drivers were licenced for the task remained a mystery.

Matthias didn't so much as crack a smile when he discovered Brooke's sigils on the underside of the bus radio. She'd turned the vehicle into a club with a bathroom on the right instead of a bad moon on the rise. I smiled lest my nerves devour me. Our faces reflected in the black windows, vibrant with life.

Ahead, the bus carrying Felicia and Ms Moontread snaked along the coast. Our destination neared.

Parking would challenge us before the Muldjewangk. Our bus was carrying fighters, it didn't much matter if we had to walk a few blocks to the rendezvous point in Tamarama Park, but the one following ours carried everything necessary for a makeshift infirmary and needed to park as close as possible.

Up the back, Dave—I was reasonably certain the middle-aged man with the metal in his face was Dave—threw himself and his air guitar into the aisle. On the radio, a rock-and-roller from yesteryear belted out, "It's a long way to the shop if you want a sausage roll."

Oberon chuckled at Dave's antics. "We've got the best people."

Morrigan and I sat near the driver's seat, ensconced among her coven.

Matthias radioed the driver behind us, telling him to park in the no stopping zone—AI could absorb the cost if they got a fine—but the voice on the other side worried they'd draw unwanted attention.

"Park across those garages on the opposite side," Ms Moontread's austere voice broke in. "There's ample room for a bus. Feign engine trouble if you need to."

Whyever not? Residents weren't going anywhere at midnight on a Wednesday.

"I suppose the extra ten metres won't matter," Matthias muttered to himself. No way he believed that. Every step would count to the injured.

Matthias turned down Gaerloch Avenue, a thin dead-end single-lane driveway particularly perfect for parking a bus, and killed the engine.

We alighted as quietly as possible. Small groups broke off, heading toward Tamarama Park. How many were amateurs like myself? Had they any battle experience?

I tucked my child-sized baseball bat into my waistband, hiding it for the walk. The metal chilled my thigh. We weren't encouraged to bring traditional weapons, but many of us felt more comfortable with their presence. My makeup kit was spread throughout the pockets of my cargo shorts.

I hung back with Morrigan and the others, waiting while Matthias locked the bus and bound it with sigils, making it less conspicuous. AI hadn't requested people dress a certain way, but we'd all wound up in black clothes that covered as much skin as practicable, myself included.

Clinging to Astrid in the shadow of a bottlebrush, Medusa was all but invisible with her black niqab. She wore a dagger in a sheath at her waist and her eyes were round, as if she were permanently startled. Brooke resembled a videogame ninja; formfitting garb and a belt with multiple pouches. Glassy black nail polish. Intense smoky eye makeup not unlike a mask. Long golden hair tied low. Ready to fell evil; or pose for a photoshoot.

I shifted my weight from foot to foot, feeling disconnected. Outside myself, removed from it all.

Matthias finished with the bus. "Let's go."

The old vegan would assist the medical team, coordinate squads, and lead our reinforcements if necessary. To my relief, Raeyn would stay with him. Astrid and Trinity too. I scanned the crush for my sister to wish her well, but didn't see her.

People arranged themselves into units, beginning their warm-up exercises.

Felicia rushed over, pulling Matthias and Morrigan into an embrace. Every line on her face begged her daughter not to fight, but she held the words. Matthias kissed Morrigan's forehead and his wife's lips. "You're my entire world. Don't shatter it."

Felicia returned to her guards. Medusa and Astrid disentangled themselves. I shook Matthias's hand, then we left them there, setting up trestles.

Wispy clouds obscured the sky over the beach, but on the horizon, beyond the reach of light pollution, the night was clear and the stars twinkled. My unit consisted of myself, stoic Morrigan, Brooke, Eliss, Oberon, Faun, and Medusa. For all she looked on the brink of soiling her pants, having Medusa at my side brought an unanticipated comfort, despite the knowledge she wasn't to use her formidable power.

"Wait!" The shout bounced off the sleeping homes, freezing Morrigan and I on the ramp down to the beach. An Indian guy, probably in his teens, jogged toward us. He wore a black and silver rash guard and long board shorts, either trying to dress inconspicuously, or knowing so little about our mission that he thought it involved swimming. There was a light pack on his back and, like me, he carried a bat. His was wooden though.

Morrigan ran to him and pulled him into a hug. "You came."

She continued to embrace him, his chin nestled neatly into the curve of her shoulder. Our unit reached the bottom of the ramp, and they were still holding each other. Who did he think he was? I swallowed the urge to clear my throat, unlacing my sneakers instead. The mobility it would give me outweighed the risk of injury.

Morrigan drew the stranger closer, "Elton, this is Indra. Indra, this is my boyfriend."

I stood a hair straighter at that.

We shook hands, then proceeded to the beach.

Indra surveyed our forces. "I should've come to the practises."

It was so obvious it was hardly worth saying, yet Morrigan didn't agree with him as I was tempted to do.

"You're here now, that's what matters," she said. "Look for the crystal on each monster's shoulder. It enables them to camouflage and aids in their ability to hold their shape on land. They don't react to pain, so destroying those crystals is crucial."

The day's heat lingered underfoot. I tucked my shoes behind a garbage bin.

Morrigan continued. "And don't let them touch you."

"Got it." Indra tapped his bat against his hand.

We rejoined the rest of our unit, heading to the southern side of Liam's shack, which was invisible from this distance, cloaked in magick as it was. The waves splitting around the jetty's posts betrayed its presence, but you had to know to look.

If Liam attempted an escape, his best bet would be to cut from the fire escape at the rear, swim the short distance to the southern headland, and either wait it out there, or continue around the point toward Bronte. We and the unit accompanying us were to apprehend him if it came to that.

We passed a witch muttering about how there was no one here. Not that they hadn't been warned. But they trusted their fallible eyes over what they knew to be true.

"Move into place," someone else snapped.

They weren't talking to us, but we picked up the pace. When we reached the algae carpeted outcropping, I scrutinised every patch for the gleam of crystals, or any indication that the flotsam was animating. I pulled out my compact, gripping it in my left hand. The fifty shattering bursts contained within were theoretically sufficient to take down a fifth of Liam's projected force. More than enough, I hoped.

Our army were in position. On Ms Moontreads' signal, we advanced.

Static rippled over what little skin I'd left exposed. My hairs stood at attention.

Medusa hissed, stomping. Something broke under her heavy boot but my query as to what shrivelled in my throat. I stumbled. An endless forest of Liam's seaweed creatures actualised where there had only been desolate coastline before. Rank upon rank of them, in greens and browns all muted by the moonless night. Eerie for their sound-less communication and the sameness of their empty glass eyes. They shuffled and conferred, bending their heads toward each other. Concert attendees before the opening act, waiting.

Time felt sluggish. For several seconds, the Muldjew-angk remained motionless. Some had fully formed legs. Others stood on stiff tentacles, or what appeared to be gnarly mangrove roots. So many more of them than I'd imagined. A living heap of kelp and slime behind which my foe cowered.

"Oh my ancient gods," Morrigan murmured.

Brooke cupped shaky hands around her mouth and hooted, signalling to the others on the beach that we'd breached the boundary of Liam's magick.

Other hoots echoed along the sand, a counterpoint to the flicker-flash of witches loosing gusts of fatal energy. Each had enchanted their compact in accordance with their personality, with differing bursts of light and sound. The splatter of seaweed blown asunder was akin to the first, fattest drops of rain before a thunderstorm.

Eliss and Indra spun, their backs to ours, observing the scuffling of our accompanying unit. I kept my eyes on the enemy, searching for that which animated them. Not a single monster wore a pauldron, or if they did, it went undetected in the gloom.

They surged, flicking time into fast-forward. A wave of them washed in, seeping into the cracks between AI's units. I raised my bat and smacked a dripping, reaching, deathly hand away from Morrigan.

Someone nearby shrilled, "I don't see the crystal!" Either I didn't know them, or fear distorted their voice.

"Use your brush then," Morrigan snapped.

Sweat rolled from my lip into my mouth. My bat produced a wet splat each time it connected. Using the bronzer would require getting awfully intimate with the enemy.

Security lights flicked on at the warehouse, haloing slimy heads and lengthening shadows. Had Felicia's unit made it to the door? I dared not hope.

A creature reared in front of me. As I prepared to strike, Morrigan's compact made a satisfying click; the safety of a gun turned off, as if this were a gangster movie.

The Muldjewangk exploded.

I popped my mirror and shot a blast, testing. The invisible force took a six-armed Muldjewangk mid-skull. Goo sprayed out over the masses of seething fin folk behind it. Unfazed, it reached for me. A harmless gesture, inviting me to shake, or give over the mirror. Light glanced silver off my bat as I bashed it aside.

I swung for the monster on its left, who'd come uncomfortably close. It toppled easily, which made me note it's legs, or lack thereof. Its tail resembled that of a seal. I bared my teeth at the mockery.

Beside me, Morrigan jabbed about with a driftwood stick, keeping the flood of animated seaweed back long enough to snap and trigger her compact again. She was speaking, but her words garbled in the din. Brooke's golden head darted past on my right and I barely corrected my next blast to avoid her. An arm tore off a Muldjewangk several ranks deep. Its face gaped open at the affront, resembling nothing like the shock or defiance of a soul-possessed being.

Muldjewangk swarmed over their seal-tailed comrade, an inexorable tide. Where were the damn crystals?

Indra lost his footing on the uneven stone outcrop and fell into me from behind, throwing me forward.

My face squelched into the seaweed abomination's stomach. Acid splashed into my open mouth. We slid together, the three of us. Indra on my back, pushing me deeper into the burning, screaming sludge. It didn't matter that I'd chosen a long-sleeved shirt with a high collar. It burned me through the oppressive fabric. My skin boiled up, straining under the cloth. I didn't need to see the blood blisters to know they swirled with the same poison as Viri's. My lungs would burst. My eyes, seared, would never see again. I would kill Indra. If only. The pain! My thoughts were hardly mine, spluttered observances awry in my skull. Naught I could do with them.

A wave broke beneath me; the Muldjewangk disintegrating. I hit the unforgiving stone. Delicious cold soothed my cheek. Someone hauled Indra off me. A breeze caressed my lips.

"Elton?" Morrigan tried to lift me. I struggled to raise my eyelids. Somehow, the Muldjewangk curse hadn't burnt out my sight. She'd saved me. I managed to stand.

Medusa was crouched a foot away, drawing a hasty circle around our unit with Rendezvous eyeliner. Or attempting to. Faun and Eliss covered her.

How did she focus through all the shouting? None of them were defeating the monsters, merely holding them at bay.

"My liner is out." Medusa scrambled to me, fishing in my pockets. "I'm borrowing this." She filled in the last foot of boundary.

The Muldjewangk hesitated, repelled by her magick.

Morrigan exploded a monster, undoubtedly hitting its crystal.

"How?" My voice felt raw.

She popped another and another, her brow furrowed in concentration. It made no difference, the surf teemed with them.

I tried again. "Where is the crystal?"

"Don't know." Morrigan squinted, obliterating another. "But I know there is one, and what it looks like."

The shadow of Indra's bat flickered in my peripheral. The blows he landed achieved naught.

Eliss had zir bronzer brush in hand. Ze just needed to get close enough to use it. I tucked my bat into the waistband of my shorts to follow zir lead, retrieved my brush and reached for my compact. No way I could focus how Morrigan did.

My compact wasn't in any of my pockets.

I'd been holding it when Indra knocked me down.

"I've lost my mirror," I said, scouring the uneven ground.

Behind me there was a splatter. Brooke cheered. "Got one!"

I glanced her way and my heart went cold.

We were surrounded. They had severed us and the accompanying unit from the main force. How?

Shrieks rent the air. Had Matthias anticipated those? Were Arcane Industries working spells to dampen the noise or were residents peering through curtains, on the phone to the police?

I spotted my mirror between a Muldjewangk's feet in the same instant I remembered Medusa stomping; Kendren must have summoned additional forces behind us. We'd walked into his trap.

I had to retrieve my mirror before it either got broken or turned against us. Cries of agony weaselled into my soul. The ocean thumped. Bodies jostled mine, seeming a mile away.

"Cover me," Eliss demanded. Ze darted over Medusa's line. Indra and Oberon surged forward, flanking zir. Ze swiped with the brush. Light flashed.

Medusa's circle was smudging. She regarded me for a moment. The surf was loud, drowning out the screams. She said something. Tilted her head to the side. The ocean sang louder. Muldjewangk kept exploding and being replaced. Too slow. We were too slow. An inert pile of seaweed covered my compact.

I was floating. Falling.

Crumpling under the sound of people dying in agony.

Dying for me.

How had it come to this, from one girl's mistake? One man's ambition.

Medusa punched me square on the shoulder. Pins and needles shuddered under my skin. "Do something!" she demanded.

I leaped over her line and scrounged in the muck for my mirror, unleashing a blast as I stood. The Muldjewangk looming over me paused, rocked by the force, but remained whole. I summoned an image of the crystal to mind. Popped the compact again. Same dismal result. Swinging my other hand, I made a sweep with the bronzer. The cold radiating from its body cramped my knuckles.

It made a grab for my face. I dodged. Its crystal was at eye level, in the centre of its chest. Glowing through layers of animated seaweed. Another giant hand came at me. I unleashed a blast. It hit true with a gratifying splatter.

I retreated into the circle, all but washed away on my edge. Muldjewangk pressed close, fouling the air.

I fell into a pattern with Brooke and Eliss. Swipe with the brush. Blast with the compact. Brush. Blast. It didn't matter if a burning wet tentacle took hold of me. Brush. Blast. I knew the pain now. Anticipated it. I mashed the trigger all the same and my foes blew to pieces.

Kelp and puddles of stagnant water became our new circle. Though my nose adjusted to the stench, on my tongue lingered a taste reminiscent of childhood. That time I'd taken a bite of chicken wing and got a mouth full of maggots.

The magickal device was uncomfortably warm in my palm and I wished I'd had the foresight to count blasts. I'd charged it not expecting to face an uncountable army, nor considering some of my surges would miss their target entirely.

Dave from AI materialised beside me, his lips drawn back in a snarl. Light flashed off his piercings. Our movements synchronised. I sensed his regard, a quirked lip or friendly wink unacted upon. Brush. Blast.

Mine hit. Dave's did not. His target flowed to one side, then back again. I snapped my mirror shut, ready to go again. The Muldjewangk reached past Dave's guard and dug its fingers into his eyes, penetrating his skull. I swiped its arm with my brush. The crystal glowed yellow through its weedy torso. Blood boiled within Dave's brain and oozed from his eye sockets. I blew the Muldjewangk apart. A fountain followed the creature's fingers as they ripped from Dave's face, spraying me as both dropped.

Dave's feet scuffed the stones where he lay. I retched and cast my gaze away. There were more enemies. Always more.

I fought on, friends and strangers appearing in my peripheral from time to time. The hinge of my compact squeaked.

Brooke took my wrist. "We need more fighters!"

I tried to sight a path through the battle to the camp uphill. The witches on the sand were having a better time of it than us. Their left flank was vulnerable, but no Muldjewangk had spawned to their rear.

If we fell, however, the monsters covering the southern outcropping would crush them. Looking from the top floor of his warehouse, Liam would note what I had: that once his forces cleared the southern rocks, he'd be able to surround AI's army from three sides.

What remained of Dave's unit merged with ours. Morrigan and Eliss picked Muldjewangk off one by one, but the rest of us were largely useless.

"Stay behind me!" Medusa pulled a chunk of salt from her pocket. "Indra? You still here?"

He pushed past me, heading toward her voice.

A witch I'd trained beside rushed by with their brush. A Muldjewangk grabbed their arm before they landed a stroke. Their face contorted and swelled, as though the searing touch pooled in their chest, neck, and jaw. Deafeningly close, their scream erupted, needling into my neck. I hadn't taken the time to learn their name but their cry stayed with me, eating into my ears.

"We need help," Brooke repeated.

I fought to clear my head. My fists clenched around my weapons. Anything to stop the screaming.

I cast my eyes to sea. She was a black sheet, whispering in the darkness. Promising comfort.

Indra smashed a salt statue with his wooden bat. Shards stung my cheek. Medusa turned another. It was a slow process. Another slimy lump lurched forward. I needed away from this horror.

"Elton!" Brooke shook my arm. "If we open a path, can you run?"

Surely there was another more suited to the task? How on earth would they create an opening?

Her eyes were huge.

I nodded.

She tugged me through the pressed bodies, barking orders. I wasn't the only person to have lost their wits. Several witches were befuddled by the broken bodies. Many had been torn asunder.

Brooke scrawled a sigil on the palm of each witch she recruited and formed an arrowhead around us. "Sigils out! Hold them up."

We inched forward.

The Muldjewangk leaned back. Not giving ground, but not attacking.

"Move!" Brooke barked.

As one, we shuffled.

"Focus," Brooke said. "Elton, be ready to go invisible."

I couldn't see clear of the monsters. I'd never hold my soul on the outside long enough to reach the grass. "It's too far."

She didn't respond.

We penetrated their mass further.

In our wake, Morrigan directed the remaining witches, her voice loud and steady. "Don't let enemy ranks close between us!"

The bedrock was uneven. I stepped up.

It yielded in a way rock should not. It was soft. I kept my eyes straight ahead. Getting clear was all that mattered. Getting help.

A witch in front of me checked his footing.

His hand dipped and he moaned.

I wanted to scream at him—at all of them—not to look down. But it was too late, his focus was broken.

A Muldjewangk pulled him into their writhing bulk. Others convened.

We lost him to the kelp forest.

"There!" Someone shouted. "On its back!" A burst of light rendered me sightless.

Humans cheered.

Brooke shoved me through the gap left by the witch who'd looked down. "Go!"

I wrenched my soul, flipping inside-out. Invisibility washed over me, icy and refreshing.

I ran.

Foul water and green chunks sprayed overhead.

"Yeah!" Faun's voice was higher than I remembered. "Eat it!"

I dodged through the Muldjewangk, guided by the fitful shine of mirror blasts.

Bedrock under my feet turned to sand. The green of the park spread before me, lit by a solitary streetlight.

I dropped my invisibility and focused on running across the cold grass.

Up the unforgiving concrete to the street.

Matthias hailed me as I crossed the road. His mouth opened. I filled it with my own words.

"Need reinforcements on the southern side." I scanned the activity in the park. There didn't appear to be many wounded. Perhaps they were in the bus. "Are there reserves?"

Raeyn rushed me, pulling my body to hers. "Little brother."

"We've not won yet," I said.

Matthias gathered two units of reserves and re-joined me.

He met my gaze. "Morrigan?"

If she'd fallen, I'd have lied.

"She's keeping her head." *Oh.* How poorly I'd spoken confronted me. "I mean, she directs our unit competently."

We loped across the grass. My spirit lifted. Most of the dark forms now dotting the sand were witches. Well before our unit had, they must have discovered the crystals hung from cords, sitting in the middle of each monster's back, not suspended inside the abominations.

Matthias jogged on one side of me, Raeyn on the other. Trinity kept pace with us. Astrid too, skimming her white cane across her path. She'd covered the entirety of her skin with runes and sigils, a ferocious sight to behold. We angled south, our fighters fanning out as we ran.

Matthias grabbed my hand, as desperate as I to sight Morrigan.

The Muldjewangk knotted close around those on the outcropping, too tall to see past.

We put the cliff to our backs.

Matthias scrawled a light bulb onto his fist and raised it high. Crystals glimmered.

"Bring them down!" he roared.

Rendezvous compacts fired, clicked shut, and fired again in unison. I broke to the side, for room to swing my metal bat in case they rushed us. Raeyn shadowed me. Her hooked teeth shone. She'd not only lit her shots but coloured them. They exploded ash, reminiscent of fireworks.

Astrid wound up at the end of the line too. She was tying the bronzer brush to the bottom of her cane.

"We have your flank," I said.

Her smile was as thin as the rest of her. "What am I seeing? Are there people in front of me?"

The witch standing in line before Astrid shoulder checked, alarmed.

"Not if you side-step toward us," Raeyn said.

Astrid did.

"Okay, shoot," said Raeyn. "We've got sea-zombies for days."

Astrid swept the sand as if to confirm what Raeyn had said, then held her compact at arms' length, facing the ground, and triggered it.

A burst of energy exploded from the device, pushing shells, sand, and debris ahead of it as it fanned out 180 degrees. The wave hit the Muldjewangk in what passed for their ankles and a score of them toppled, their legs thrown from under them.

"That ought to get their attention," Astrid observed dryly. "Yell when they get back up, I can go again."

The Muldjewangk turned toward us. Half of them, anyway.

Matthias, his blasts remarkable for the bullet shape of them, peppered not the monsters regaining their feet, but those behind. I glimpsed orange through their ranks. Morrigan! My throat constricted.

The Muldjewangk charged.

"Astrid, again!"

They went down in a line.

Astrid swung her cane and every crystal blazed with rainbow light, chiming loudly.

Where had she been when we needed her?

She let off three shots. I managed four.

Raeyn and Matthias's witches felled the rest. Not a single monster reached us.

Down the line, another witch unleashed an area of effect spell. It wasn't quite as impressive as Astrid's, but it opened a hole in the enemy's mass as a group of Muldjewangk fell into their kin. My heart stuttered, Morrigan and our friends huddled tight, fighting ruthlessly. Had they all survived?

A quintessentially human scream ended abruptly in a shower of salt. Medusa was fine, then, and whomever she'd rescued.

Matthias was still trying to clear salt from his eye when another explosion sounded down on the sand. Blue-green smoke billowed.

A twang from the direction of the jetty heralded another explosive incoming.

"Spread out," Morrigan yelled. Then, "Move!"

The dark wad arced through the sky.

Someone struck me with their shoulder as they barrelled past. Astrid whacked me in the shin with her cane.

Raeyn scrambled up a boulder. "Brother, this way!"

I grabbed Astrid by the wrist and pulled her along.

Not fast enough.

The explosive landed, spraying chemicals and billowing gas. Something bit my calf. I stumbled into the boulder. Astrid slammed into my back.

"Boost her up!" Raeyn told me, then said to Astrid. "We've got you. Climb." Astrid pocketed her compact and hung her cane from her arm by the strap. I spared a glance over my shoulder.

Through the smoke, witches broke madly and clawed at their eyes. Muldjewangk shambled after them. Our ranks broke, every witch for themselves, any semblance of order forgotten.

Astrid put her foot in my linked hands.

I searched for the people I knew.

Matthias was surrounded but outclassing his enemies. He performed a sideways tumble, coming up beyond their reach, then threw them to the ground through pure will. Every second a new bullet emerged from his compact and another monster fell. Brooke and Eliss remained together. They'd raced toward the sea and were fighting with waves breaking over their feet.

Where was Morrigan?

Another dark mass arced high. It would smash on the cliff.

"No, jump!" I wrapped my arms around Astrid's waist and threw her aside. Raeyn leapt over me. She hit the uneven rocks hard and crumpled. I didn't have time to run. I tucked myself low under the boulder as Liam's homemade bomb shattered above. Gas hissed. Crouching, I ran to Raeyn. My eyes wept of their own accord.

She reached for me, and I hauled her up. "Can't walk." She spoke through clenched teeth. Her foot was twisted unnaturally, in need of medical aid. I was grateful for the darkness, shielding me from the gore.

"I have you, sister."

Coda

MORRIGAN

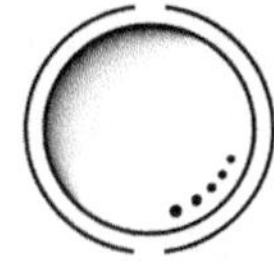

Ten odd metres away, Dad passed through a spray of seaweed, sand, and gas. It may as well have been fifty. Then he was gone. I headed in the direction I'd seen him last. Meddy appeared at my side, flowed away, and returned, serpentining over the outcrop. When I gave a direction, she followed without question. We destroyed every Muldjewangk we crossed as we ran.

Behind us, Brooke and Eliss made their own pattern, staying clear of the toxic explosions Liam Kendren lobbed from his warehouse. It seemed unlikely he'd attempt to flee now. We'd reduced his force enough that his retreating form would be obvious despite the pervasive dark. I needed to gather any remaining AI fighters from the southern headland to regroup at the beach.

Meddy pointed off in the opposite direction, where the cliff and the rocky outcrop met the sea. The Muldjewangk had clustered there. Great billows of steam rose from the ocean's spray.

"It's Astrid," Meddy called.

How did she know?

I scanned the area once more for Dad, then veered toward the cluster.

A comet of green smoke arced over us from the warehouse, aiming for the same target.

I stumbled to a halt as it hit.

A girl screamed.

Muldjewangk blown aside by the force rose again, their crystals undamaged.

Smoke replaced the steam.

Astrid scrambled to her feet and resumed her spell.

I closed in, opening fire. The Muldjewangk would turn on us. We'd have to outrun them, draw them away from Astrid.

Beside me, Meddy let loose, her eyes slits. At some point she must have looted one of our fallen. She fired a compact from each hand. Personally, I wouldn't have trusted a stranger to have enchanted their mirror with safe, useful spells. Meddy either hadn't thought of the risks or didn't care. Her own blast shot out, grey and glittering darkly. A moment later three purple missiles pew-pewed from the other compact, making exactly the sound I expected. Whoever the witch had been, they played the video games my dad liked.

"Mad!" Eliss said. Ze fired from Meddy's other side, a crowbar in zir off-hand. I wished I'd brought mine. On the far side of zir, Brooke scrawled a rune onto a broken bottle she plucked from between two rocks, then lobbed it overhead. The sigil corrected her throw, guiding it true. Her target and makeshift ammunition shattered.

My fingers cramped around my weapon. I kept firing.

Meddy's next shot sent her hurtling backwards. Her squeal ended abruptly with a wet splat. She shrieked, the surprise in her voice replaced by agony.

As I turned, she slid to the feet of the Muldjewangk she'd collided with. I snapped my compact shut, reloading.

Brooke was already there.

She sprang lightly over the rocks, relieved Meddy of her athame, and spun upward, using momentum to compensate for the blade's bluntness. She hooked it under the cord around the Muldjewangk's neck, snapped it, and caught the crystal as it fell.

The Muldjewangk grabbed at her.

Brooke was faster. She whipped the twine, cracking the crystal against the ground.

I left her to get Meddy up, returning my attention to the cluster.

They lumbered our way, giving Astrid space. She was alone; or had been. I was glad we came.

Halfway between us and Astrid, the Muldjewangk paused. Their bodies emitted a hissing sound. Again, steam rose, leaking out of them. Astrid was a fearsome sight. Utterly covered in runes and sigils, a warrior of ages past. Her face was set with grim determination. She raised her hands and the hissing intensified. Bubbles rippled over the shoulders of the Muldjewangk nearest to me.

They boiled. Pieces of seaweed pop-corned from them.

Meddy whimpered her mantra of no's. In between blasts, I glanced her way.

She held both compacts in one hand. Salt crystals scattered from her other, caught in the wind. She'd fallen on the clump in her pocket. The salt didn't resemble a rock now.

Logically, Meddy could use even the tiniest speck to turn someone. If she'd had more experience, she likely wouldn't need reagents at all. But magick worked more on belief than logic. She had to believe she'd create salt instead of the featureless grey stone her curse dictated. I doubted Meddy would risk experimenting here. The cost was too high if she got it wrong.

She wiped her hand on her pants, took a breath, and resumed firing, wresting the Muldjewangks' attention from her girlfriend. For creatures of decay, they'd been quick to figure out who was evaporating them and appeared torn. Instinct—or Liam Kendren's magick—bade them to work together, but they couldn't decide who posed the greatest threat. They shrivelled, deprived of moisture. Eliss made fast work with zir crowbar, slamming them in their backs.

Meddy inched around the side until she reached Astrid.

I glanced toward the warehouse. The catapult jerked, it's load directed at the main part of the beach. Perhaps we weren't as visible here as I'd feared.

I cast around for my next target, panting. Only the waves moved.

Meddy took Astrid's hand. "Come on."

We were the only people on the outcrop now. The shapes meandering were distinctly not human. A shiver prickled my skin. "Look for survivors."

"They're not so scary, spread out like that," Brooke said.

"I beg to differ," Meddy replied.

One caught wind of our group and stormed in our direction.

Eliss clutched zir brush, muscles tense.

I visualised the rhombohedron. My eyes ached. Were my parents okay? Why hadn't Mum made the arrest yet? I brought my mind back. The crystal. It's perfectly flat faces and waxy texture. I triggered my compact.

The Muldjewangk's chest burst, its feet taking a few independent steps before they too broke apart.

Brooke side-eyed me. "Getting tired?"

"As if." I took down another several metres ahead. "Bit worried about my parents is all."

Eliss veered away, checking bodies for signs of life.

"Isn't that your dad there?" Brooke shot glitter from the tip of her finger, making a sparkle arrow as if to prove she also wasn't tired.

The man she indicated stood on the cusp of rock, sand, and grass. He was back-lit. Just a silhouette.

"Hold up," Eliss called. Ze supported the weight of another witch across zir shoulders. Brooke ran to assist. The injured witch lifted their head. Faun.

She heaved a sob. "The burning. It stopped." A wet hiccup escaped her. "I thought it never would." Tears left clean trails down her cheeks.

"It's over now," Meddy assured her.

I wished that was true.

The man appeared to be instructing witches on the sand. We made our way toward him.

At the water's edge and on the jetty, the fight raged on. Too close for Liam Kendren to lodge explosives, if any remained.

We stumbled off the rocky outcrop.

"Morrigan?" The man resolved into my dad. He crushed me to his chest. "Morrigan," he spoke into my matted hair. "Are you okay?"

When I could speak through my relief, I gave my report.

Dad and I slapped together a plan, rallied the remaining AI forces on the beach, and sent word to the healers that they were clear to send a crew. Most of Elouera was accounted for amongst the diminished AI force. Meddy and Astrid, Brooke, Eliss, Indra, Faun, Oberon, and Trinity bolstered me. Each had their own brand of wired exhaustion. Their eyes uniquely haunted. Dad hadn't seen Elton, whose life still pulsed through our connection, or his sister. Brooke's aunt Annis was also missing. Dad said he'd seen her apologising profusely to someone in the toilet block not long before, but it was hard to know if that was Canadian humour intended to alleviate Brooke's anxiety.

I prayed they were all okay; there wasn't time for anything else.

"We need confirmation that there are no dormant Muldjewangk on that bluff." Dad pointed to the northern headland, where a ramp meandered from the exposed bedrock at sea level to the Surf Life Saving Club on the cliff top.

My guts jumped into my throat. I couldn't do it. I glanced at the southern outcrop where my friends and I had been surrounded. Where people I'd known my whole life had been shredded. A fresh unit stood there now, just in case.

The explosions had ceased. Mum's unit were keeping Liam Kendren busy, but they hadn't hauled his arse out of there yet.

My hands shook. I clenched them into fists. "I'm going into the warehouse."

Dad's eyebrows said the northern outcrop was the safer, smarter job, but he nodded once and waved a different unit in that direction.

"Do you still have your Rendezvous brush?" he asked.

"I have all my weapons. Reckon my mirror's about out of charges but."

Around me, witches checked their pockets, pouches, and bags.

"All right. I'll see that you aren't in direct combat." Dad's gaze fixed on the warehouse. "It's about time we recovered those furs. Dawn's too close for my comfort."

How long would the shack remain undetectable to the general population once we removed Liam Kendren?

Dad's Adam's apple bobbed. "Your mum's got things under control, of course."

"No doubt." If he could swallow the worry, I could too. "But she can't do everything herself."

"Right you are." Dad cleared his throat. "Miss Larue, you'll take a team to the upper level of the warehouse." He nodded to Ronnie from AI. "Mx Ronnie, get the wagons down here. Ask if any of the injured can ferry skins to the bus. And we're going to need this area combed for magickal artefacts; can't have any Rendezvous weapons falling into civilian hands."

Ronnie's palm-tree-tuft piggie tails flapped as they nodded, tagged a bunch of people, and dashed away.

Dad surveyed the team left to him, knowing Elouera would stick by me. "The rest of us will clear out the ground floor and provide Mrs Larue assistance if she requires it."

I turned to go.

Dad gripped my shoulder. "Give my unit a few minutes to clean up before following."

"Okay."

He gestured with his head and about forty witches responded, tightening their gear, and jogging to the warehouse.

I ought to have asked for a bigger team. Suddenly we were just tired kids, milling on a littered beach. Smaller, less competent, and less experienced than AI needed us to be. I hoped Elton was okay. Ten of Swords flashed into my mind. The card wore his face. I shook the image out of my brain. The Muldjewangk didn't have swords.

Footsteps thundered on the jetty. Dad's team entered the building to no resistance. How long did I need to wait?

Meddy's voice seemed disembodied coming out of her niqab; stones and bones rubbing together. I needed a moment to make sense of her words.

"Shouldn't we use the fire escape? Enter directly where the skins are stored?"

"That's where they're processed."

She blinked at me. Slowly. Waiting.

I hadn't answered her question.

"You're right," I said. "Let's enter through the back." I wouldn't be any help to Mum that way, but we'd serve the mission overall. We'd get the skins we'd come for.

I took the lead. Brooke strode beside me down the jetty, but there wasn't room to walk two abreast alongside the warehouse. I lead them right, around the southern end of the building. At the corner, it surprised me to find Oberon with me, not Brooke. I rubbed my eyes and bounced on my toes a few times, reviving my focus.

With the building blocking my view of the beach, there was nothing but the shush shush of the fathomless waves and the wide-open sky above. We were the horizon.

The fire escape created a single zigzag with the jetty; the rickety stairs shadowing the narrow strip of boards we were crossing. I mounted the lower steps and pressed my back to the corrugated wall. Oberon and Eliss passed me. I wanted all nine of us here before I opened that door. Chances were the processing room would be deserted, but instinct warned me to keep my coven close.

Trinity watched the water, placing her feet carefully. She looked a whole lot more alert than I felt. Indra and Brooke came behind her, chatting. I lifted my sweaty curls and let the pre-dawn breeze cool my neck. A powerful urge to sit tempted me. Astrid appeared around the corner next, followed by Meddy. I wished I could see her expression. Was she coping all right?

At the top of the stairs, Oberon swept his bronzer brush over the lock and conferred with Eliss. "I'll give it a go, I've been practising."

"Unlock it, sure," Eliss answered. "But leave it closed till Morr gives the all-clear."

Trinity joined me, waiting on the step below while the others inched over to us.

She gasped and pointed.

Coming last around the corner of the warehouse, Faun screamed.

I lurched forward, searching for the cause of their alarm. My eyes flicked so fast, the jetty blurred into the sea.

Indra, who'd been speaking over his shoulder to Brooke, stumbled as a mass broke the water.

I gripped the railing in front of me. Forced myself to focus. The Muldjewangk hauled itself onto the wooden planking. The way it moved needled my logical mind. It made no sense. It stood taller than Indra but had no legs. No tail or feet. Just an oozing pile of seaweed that elevated its torso despite its spread. Brooke retreated into Astrid.

Astrid stepped back and clenched her fists, corralling her energy.

The Muldjewangk began to steam and hiss.

My compact was in my hand.

Indra, having misplaced his baseball bat, threw a punch. His fist sank into its shoulder as it turned from him, seeking Astrid.

Indra let out the kind of yelp that accompanied cursing when you bumped a hot frypan. He jerked away, arms windmilling.

I shot a wild, unfocused blast at the monster as Indra lost his battle with gravity and went splashing into the bay. I missed. The Muldjewangk regarded me with its unreadable expression.

Brooke lunged with her brush.

The Muldjewangk decided she was the greater threat.

My eyes were gritty with fatigue. I shut them. The crystal was a rhombohedron filled with Selkie derma cells and peacock ore. Brooke's scream brought tears to my eyes. I imagined the crystal exploding, opened my eyes, and hit the trigger. My bolt of energy flew harmlessly out to sea. I flexed my jaw.

Billows of steam shrouded Brooke. Her shriek stuttered as she fought to free herself of the Muldjewangk's grasp. A flash of light illuminated the crystal on the monster's back.

Trinity, Faun and I fired at the same time. Our bolts collided, veered off course and struck its cheek. Chunks of goop sploshed in all directions. Seaweed splattered up to my shoes.

It didn't look any worse for having half a head.

"Sorry," Trinity said.

"Not your fault." It was mine. I could end this. I had to concentrate.

From the top of the stairs, Oberon threw a shoe at the Muldjewangk. It didn't seem to notice. He dropped his other on it for good measure. Faun fled around the corner.

The Muldjewangk wasn't dehydrating fast enough. It was too saturated. Too large for Astrid's magick.

Humidity thickened the air. I grit my teeth. Dug deep into my power. I'd blown apart a hundred of these creatures. This monster would fall too. I pressed the trigger.

Nothing happened.

I pressed again.

Nothing.

Brooke pleaded for help.

The Muldjewangk stepped over her crumpled form.

Indra rushed around the northern edge of the warehouse, barefoot and dripping. He wielded a hunk of driftwood.

Using the wall for support, Brooke dragged herself up and grabbed the crystal. Her choking sobs punctuated the hiss of the steaming Muldjewangk. Trinity screamed at Astrid to work faster.

"Stone it!" Eliss yelled at Meddy.

Meddy backed up to the edge, pulling Astrid with her. The Muldjewangk's hands clawed at the air in front of Astrid's face. She'd be able to smell its salt-death stench.

Brooke restrained the beast by the cord around its neck, one of her arms bubbling. It turned toward her.

Eliss leant over the rail, crying. "Medusa!" Zir voice cracked.

Meddy would be crying too. At any moment she'd order us to look away. She'd rip off her niqab and save us.

Possibly dooming Viri in the process.

No. Meddy knew not to use her power.

The Muldjewangk reached for Brooke.

She whimpered. Hauled on the crystal.

Indra thrust his driftwood into its face, over Brooke's head. Stalling it a mere second, the time it took to snatch the stick and toss it to sea.

I rushed past Trinity, using one hand on the railing and my weight as propulsion to swing toward the fight. I didn't consider how I'd help, only that I needed to.

The cord holding the crystal sank deep into the monster's neck as Brooke scrambled backwards into Indra. He returned to the water.

Meddy's whimpered no's cut though the cacophony, matching my footfalls. Waves slapped the platform. The wood was slick. Brooke took heaving gasps.

"No no no."

The Muldjewangk's hands turned to thick grey stone. It stumbled forward, unbalanced by the sudden load.

My fingertips caressed Brooke's shoulder; an inch short of the grab I'd intended. Chills prickled my skin.

The Muldjewangk raised its stone fists as a mace, blocking out the faint stars.

In one powerful motion, it drove them down through Brooke's skull. Grey matter and blood plopped against the wooden decking. I pressed the back of my hand to my nose.

Momentum pulled the monster down. Brooke's bones snapped. The sound echoed through my frozen joints.

Trinity hauled me away as the boards below shuddered.

The Muldjewangk smashed its own crystal, still clasped in Brooke's slender hand. Its eyes went wide.

It gurgled.

Then it was gone.

Steam lingered in the space where it used to be, its remnants running down the wall of the warehouse.

My shirt was wet. Bloody. I saw it as though through a stranger's eyes. I laid my palm over it, this piece of my friend who'd become Medusa's newest victim.

The last wisps of steam cleared on the sea breeze. I took a deep breath, a wordless prayer for strength, and crouched beside Brooke's beaten body.

Medusa was at Brooke's feet, having somehow passed Astrid. She was blubbering. I set my jaw. *Murderer.* No, that wasn't fair. But why did I always have to be fair?

Brooke's skull was caved in. Her chest impossibly broken. I checked for a pulse anyway. Put my cheek by her mouth to feel for breath. Mine caught in my throat. Pressure built behind my nose.

"Help me move her," I ordered.

We laid her down. I put her hands on her belly in peaceful repose. Her eyes were already shut.

I swallowed again and again but still felt like I was choking.

We had to keep going. My unit expected me to lead.

In case another team recovered her body before I returned, I wrote on her arm with my eyeliner. *Brooke Milson. Hero.*

Someone vomited into the water.

A grey, squishy glob clung to my palm. I tucked it in beside her, not allowing myself to think about it. I pushed myself up and had the odd sensation of watching myself stand from a distance.

She'd have hated this. Her hair matted with gore. Her fingernails torn and her drab clothes covered in seaweed. Her petite face ruined.

"I will remember you beautiful," I promised her. To the others, I said, "Medusa, Astrid, loop around the building." I turned. Trinity and Indra were there. "Move. Please."

I clomped up the stairs, opened the door, and switched on the light. The processing room was how I remembered it, Selkie skins in stacks along one wall. I pointed at them. "Get these to Robbie's team."

My coveners hastened to obey. I couldn't look at their ravaged faces or bear their accusatory gazes. This was what we'd come for. This time, there was no thrill as my friends rushed Selkie skins out the fire exit. No sense of achievement. Nothing. But we were our actions, not our thoughts. I'd come to retrieve Elton's skin and it was as good as done, no matter how I felt about it.

I wasn't interested in feeling right now.

Across the room was a coat rack and two doors. One accessed a small landing at the top of the staircase where we'd been apprehended on our previous visit. I strode over and wrenched the other. A walk-in pantry sat beyond. Within, tea chests and wooden shipping crates were stacked three containers high. Some were damaged, their corners crushed, the boxes above leaning. Open crates beside the door confirmed what I suspected—these too held skins. How many abominations had Liam Kendren thought he needed? How many lives was he willing to ruin in the process? I stepped into the narrow room groping for a light switch that wasn't there. How deep did this closet go? I worked my way into the shadows, my heart sore. Surely these weren't all furs. There were too many. I'd have to open each crate and box to check.

The outer wall of the warehouse shook. A member of AI heading up, no doubt. This storeroom also opened onto the landing. If unlocked from my side, some of Dad's force could be reassigned to clear and sort this stash.

Muffled voices reached me, either from downstairs or the main processing room. I thought I heard my name.

"Here," I said, bumping someone as I turned.

No, not a person. Just crates, stacked higher than my head.

They swayed. My first instinct was to steady them. I thrust my hands out to stop the avalanche and found myself inadequate, again.

The darkness completed itself.

The weight on my shoulders drove my already loose consciousness through the floor. Closer to the voices. I squinted in an effort to hear them better. The odour of frying bacon permeated the air.

I lay on plush burgundy carpet. That wasn't possible.

I pinched my nose shut, testing reality. My breathing continued, though not easily. I was dreaming. Where was the sleeper? I sat up and glanced around. When I fell into another person's dream—or entered willingly—the dreamer was usually nearby.

As I surveyed the room, I was aware of distant pain. My neck strained when I turned it to the right. My chest hurt abominably. Why? Was I getting old, walking into rooms and forgetting what I came for?

No. My body was unconscious in Liam Kendren's storage room. Brooke! My vision darkened as awareness twisted within me. My mind had jumped the hedge to escape. To find help. Not dreaming then. Astral travelling. The mumble of voices scratched at my psyche. Perhaps the goddess demanded something of me.

The teak desk I leaned against dominated my view. I tipped my foggy head.

Smoke swirled around the ceiling, the result of cooking in a poorly ventilated office. It hung low over a false window, below which was an electric kettle. Closer to me, there was a Victorian chaise lounge and a plastic plant.

I moved in the way of dreams: I decided to stand and so I was standing, as if I'd never lain on the floor to begin with.

"Hardly," Liam Kendren scoffed.

I jerked away from him, but he wasn't looking at me. He was speaking to my mum. Why was she here alone?

"...trotting in here, declaring I'm under arrest," Liam Kendren said. "You have no such power."

A laptop sat open in the centre of the grandiose desk, and at the corner a single gas burner perched, flames unattended. He held the frypan flippantly.

Mum's expression said someone was about to get grounded for life. "My power should be the last thing you question."

His chuckle snaked behind his teeth. "The least of my concerns you mean?" He put the frypan back on the burner and threw a couple of limp rashers in beside the remaining cooked slice. "It is."

Did he see the tick in her cheek?

Mum squeezed her cauldron amulet. "I'd prefer not to use force, Liam. Please come along in a civilised fashion."

"Civilised?" He pinched the cooked rasher with his tongs and fanned the air, breathing deeply. "Denying a man his breakfast is hardly civilised."

Mum's retort died as he bit into the pig flesh and moaned. A droplet of grease glistened on his chin.

My connection to my body weakened. The room became more vivid.

Knuckles white, Mum wove a binding spell. I recognised the incantation. She'd used it on me once, when I was particularly young and stupid. The cauldron made all the difference though, amplifying her strength. Thick, silken cords unspooled from its core, grasping for Liam Kendren.

"Oh, stop that." He flapped his hand, splashing her with magick. Despite my incorporeal form, the cold shock of his flippant spell splashed over me; poorly directed in a deliberate display of power.

He turned his back on her and parked his rump on the edge of the desk, savouring his bacon. The contents of the frypan began to burn. Mum's eyes watered.

She began another spell, a silent ritual of gestures I didn't recognise. Power built quickly, humming through my astral body. I backed up, afraid I'd become entangled in it.

Liam Kendren sounded bored. "Leave, Felicia."

She danced faster, weaving near-visible brambles through the air.

"Your daughter needs you. The rest of your piddling army are so busy looting, they haven't noticed her missing."

How did he know? Wards? Security cameras?

She ignored him, continuing her spell with one hand, readying her compact with the other.

"I don't have any ill will toward Morrigan. She amuses me." He plucked a stick of charred bacon from the pan. "She might have been my daughter, if things had gone differently." He took a tentative bite. "If you don't listen to me, she'll suffocate."

Lips pressed into a tight line, mum popped her compact, caught the magick in her other hand and seamlessly directed it down the lines of her spell. The cage of vines she'd woven cast stark shadows on his pasty skin.

He sighed theatrically and withdrew his athame from a desk drawer, leaving his greasy tongs to stain the desktop. A V of concentration wrinkled his brow, then he thrust the knife between the bars of the cage, dispelling it. He slid off the desk to face her, his expression dangerously neutral. Without breaking his gaze, he passed the ritual dagger from his right hand to his left and reached into the drawer for his wand.

A surge sucked at me as he drew energy from every direction and shot it out of his wand at Mum. It knocked her backward over a travel trunk, landing her on her rear.

With the speed and hip-swish of a dancer, he rounded the desk. She inhaled a lungful of smoke. Violent coughs wracked her body. Her eyes watered. He stood over her, sucking the vibrance from the room as he gathered more energy. My powerlessness choked me.

She grabbed her cauldron, aiming the opening at him as she hacked into her elbow.

I envisioned acid shooting out, green and eerie. Or perhaps lightening to stun and blind. Pink jiggly chunks spewed forth instead.

Liam Kendren laughed so hard I thought my body on the upper story would feel the vibration. He scooped a lump off his expensive carpet and waggled it at her, his tools clasped in one hand. Droplets of moisture caught the light. It was flesh. Raw pig.

She dry-heaved. Something about the bacon had unhinged her.

"Bizarre." He flapped the pork again. "I expected more from you, Felicia."

Blood sprayed from the cauldron, thick and sticky. It saturated his suit and forced him back a step. Then more pig parts came. A trotter. A snout. He dodged the solids. She retched. I would've too, if I had a stomach to do it with. A gob of gore stuck to his face, right beside his lip.

Standing over her, close enough their shoes almost touched, he reached out his tongue and licked the globule.

Every mention of pathogens Meddy had ever made rolled through my mind. Hopefully parasites would destroy him from the inside while he rotted in ICR's prison.

He dropped the hunk of meat. The carpet absorbed the sound, but his intent hit the mark, disempowering her. This was why she'd rejected the job the first time AI offered.

She ripped the long chain off over her head, disgusted. With herself more than him, I was sure.

Liam coughed discretely into his elbow, then ducked below the heavy smoke and leered at her. "I always loved you best when you played coy and begged."

"And I always said your cruelty would damn you." She held his gaze, but the way she fidgeted with the chain, twirling it around her hand, betrayed her fear.

"Atonement? The bridge of souls at the end of my days? Please." He leant forward from the hips. "Will you beg for me tonight?"

She sat straighter, thrusting her face upward defiantly. The haze softened their profiles.

"Yes," he cooed. "Your passion lights you up."

I willed myself toward the gas burner, ignoring his word play. I had to turn the flame off. Or remove the pan from the heat. Save Mum from asphyxiation.

My hand went through the dial. I tried again. The spitting fat ought to have stung. I focused on it, trying to ground myself. I'd never affected the waking world when

I'd astral travelled, but if I could do it in dreams, this was possible. It had to be.

Liam Kendren's voice simmered. That, at least, I felt the heat of. "You miss me," he said.

Visions of burning to death with this building chewed at my mind.

"I do," she said.

I gawked over my shoulder.

Mum reached for him. Slowly. In defeat. "I didn't want this job. We don't belong in opposition."

My stomach twisted. They'd have made an interesting couple. His willingness to risk it all and her eye for detail. His cunning paired with her brawn. She'd make a fine crime boss, dressed as she was.

"You miss a hardened man."

"Sometimes, yes."

I covered my mouth. They *had been* an interesting couple.

She kept her hand extended, waiting for him to help her up. "You never know how the choice pans out until you make it."

I gaped.

The quality of his smile changed. Less sneer, more victory. He took her hand, bracing himself.

Her gaze softened.

She'd barely tried to fight him!

A soft woof rippled from the frypan. Flames engulfed it.

He pulled her up, using his weight for leverage. His eyes never left her face. Orange light flickered over every surface.

I clutched my own arms, holding myself tight. My mother... She'd tried to warn me. She knew if she came here, she'd betray us all.

Her lips parted. There was a slight quiver in her pout. A tenderness. She put a foot back to steady herself.

He tossed his tools to the side. They clattered against the closed office door as he reached to caress the curve of her hip.

Her breath caught in anticipation of the kiss.

I couldn't blink. Couldn't breathe.

Mum let go of his hand. His stumble was barely noticeable—a shift I'd have missed if I hadn't spent weeks training in my backyard.

A streak of black whirred toward Liam Kendren's temple. The smoke parted. Mum's miniature cast iron pot thunked into his skull.

"Ah fuck!" Liam Kendren brought one hand to his head and thrust the other out to catch himself.

It didn't help.

Mum's cauldron spun from her fist, a new age chain lock. She clubbed him with it again, neatly missing his intercepting wrist, changed stance, and struck the other side of his head.

A breathless huff escaped me. What. A. Legend.

The momentum turned him.

She hooked her foot around his ankle. Grabbed his wrist in her free hand. Brought him down.

He fell face first onto the floor, where she pinned him under her black moto boot. "I love my soft husband. I choose him every day."

A roll of wide tape ejected from her cauldron.

"You never stood a chance, Liam. And you're under arrest."

Ten of Quavers

ELTON

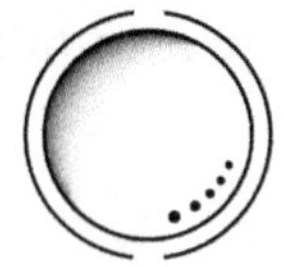

My text went unanswered. Forgotten, perhaps. Morrigan's misery pulsed through our connection, the rawness of it threatening to steal my breath. But she was steady as a marksman's hand; that she might let me down was inconceivable. It was 2:45 in the afternoon. I pushed last night's horrors from my mind. Arcane Industries' office tower bristled at the end of the block. I'd see my beloved soon, and she'd unite me with my future. Exactly as she'd promised. I slipped my phone into my pocket.

When I reached AI, I stepped up to the glass door and rang the intercom. No point in waiting outside for ten minutes.

The receptionist opened the door personally instead of buzzing me in.

I smiled and bowed my head. "I'm early."

"Not to worry, Mr Abercrombie. I'll let Ms Moontread know you're here." She gestured to a wooden bench half buried in flowers. "Take a seat, if you please."

I sat, carnations to my left, rows upon rows of gladioli standing sentinel behind me, their bell-flowers tipped in sadness. There hadn't been abundant flowers in the foyer before, had there?

Oh. A cold touch cramped my chest, forcing heat to rush upward into my face. There were photos displayed amidst the sprays of flowers. Sitting offended my sense of self.

I walked through fields of air-conditioned lilies, starting by the door and following the curve of the room. Some photos had cards nearby. This one had a copper plaque—*Dorothy Windrider. Fly free*—and a handcrafted witch's broom leaning alongside. Besom, Morrigan would call it.

Most of the faces sparked only a vague recognition. Until Dave. I picked up the frame holding what was clearly his work ID photo. The solid metal of it pressed on my spirit. I shut my eyes and he died again. My breath cut its way into my lungs and sawed out. I gulped and swallowed and blinked as hard, the edge of the photo frame aching my palm. I ought to say something. Acknowledge him.

I replaced the frame atop its cardboard display column. "Good man," I choked out.

Past the bench and an impossible spray of baby's breath bordering the window, I found Brooke's pillar. She was, by far, the youngest. I was at once grateful I'd already known. That I hadn't found out about her death within this room.

Morrigan broke the news to me on the bus home from Tamarama. In true Larue style, she and her parents were the last to leave, having made sure every person and weapon was accounted for prior to giving Kendren's shack over to the ICR. After assisting Raeyn to the healers', I'd joined those who'd sustained minor injuries in combing the beach for lost Rendezvous weapons, until Matthias heralded the battle won.

During the drive home, Morrigan alternated between hysterical—which I hadn't understood at first—and catatonic, unable to respond at all. She pulled at her hair, crying one moment, blank and soulless the next. Felicia and the healers murmured about possible concussion. Long-term effects. Shock. They'd wrapped her in a silver first-aid blanket.

"Muldjewangk got Brooke," she whispered.

I blinked away the memory. I hadn't cared who'd seen my tears on that bus, but today was different. Victorious. Should I not be happy? Perhaps it was too soon. Success came at a price. These people had paid that for me. For my community.

Brooke's photo was displayed in a gaudy glitter frame. Her flowers were black and purple tulips. Beside them sat a bell. I rang it. Did she—her spirit, rather—hear the crisp notes? The chimes reverberated throughout the foyer, inviting me to feel self-conscious. Somewhere behind me was the receptionist, and possibly others. I rang it again, pealing my remorse into whatever lay beyond. Let her hear my feelings.

I held the bell for a while after, cradling the curve of it. I wanted to thank her. But that was hardly enough. Though I hadn't touched her photo, my palm shone with glitter.

Ms Moontread waited at the end of the display.

Morrigan still wasn't here. I visited the rest of the memorials. When next I raised my head, an apprentice I didn't recognise stood with AI's CEO.

I drew a deep breath and joined them.

"Our pride equals our grief," Ms Moontread said in way of greeting.

I nodded. "Of course."

She beckoned me to follow her to the elevators.

When the doors shut, I said, "Do forgive me for being forward, but is Morrigan not here?"

"The Larue's are on leave. They deserve it; I'm sure you agree."

"Indeed."

And yet, how could Morrigan miss this? Didn't she want to say a proper farewell?

Her sadness entwined with my own, tugging at me.

Perhaps it was too much. She'd told me once how she hated goodbyes.

Arrogantly, I'd thought that didn't apply to me.

Two guards were stationed outside the door to which Ms Moontread led us.

Within were four more sitting on folding chairs, one to each corner. AI weren't taking chances this time.

Ocean scents enveloped us.

The hairs on my arms rose. A monumental stack of Selkie furs waited in the middle of the floor. Mine called to me. My mind registered that I ought to tell Ms Moontread it was here. They'd definitely recovered it. But speech failed me. I lurched, a grunt ripping from my throat.

My knees hit the carpet with a dull thud. I reached into the mass and a murmuring crowd surrounded me. The furs pulsed with life and boasted of memories.

I found my parents' first and set them aside. I couldn't have rightly said which was Mother's and which belonged to Papa. The larger one made sense as Papa's, but if it were that simple, Raeyn wouldn't have accidentally donated mine. I had to explain to AI that these were my family. These would enable a fur to be curated for my sister. Sweat broke over my skin. I leaned in and sniffed. Shoved an old grey fur away. It was here. It was here. So close.

Greed and hunger surged up my arms, elbows swallowed in the pile. I held tight, pulling and shaking my fur free. It was glorious. Charcoal with a white belly.

Humans edged around my peripheral. The elder had her hands out, gesturing caution. The guards were on their feet. Would they try to stop me leaving? I gripped my fur harder, hugging it to my chest.

Instinct told me to get to the water first, where it'd slide on easy. I'd be the most majestic creature in the ocean.

I rose.

The old woman smiled.

Ms Moontread.

CEO of Arcane Industries.

I tried to remember how to talk. "My thanks," I managed.

"You're most welcome." She gestured to the furs I'd set aside. "And these?"

"Raeyn." My fur weighed pleasantly in my arms. I cleared my throat. "Ask Raeyn... Confirm my family wish to proceed. My sister will know to which parent each o' these belong." If it mattered to their scientists. If my parents declined to withdraw. Over breakfast this morn, they hadn't been sure.

"Thank you, we'll let them know immediately." She pulled a digital notepad from her blazer and scribbled with a stylus, then smiled at me. "We'd like to offer you this carry-bag, too." She gestured at the apprentice, who took a shaky step forward, holding a large gym bag at arm's length. "It's watertight."

I made an effort at levity. "Holds in the goo, you mean? Thank you." I accepted the bag and crouched to stuff my fur inside.

In the doorway, Ms Moontread conferred with another employee and passed off my parents' furs, then she turned back to me.

"May I escort you to the tearoom?" She guided me into the hall and the door closed behind us. "You're welcome to explore the tower or relax here as long as you like."

I'd intended to head to The Devil's Den—a nearby creatives café—to finalise my affairs, but AI's tearoom made as much sense. Weightlessness infused me. I floated through the witch's tower.

In a few short minutes I was alone with a cup of hot cocoa, the gym bag on a chair beside me, zipped shut around my wrist. I suspected the apprentice hovered in the hall to act as my escort should I wander, but I neither saw nor heard her, and they would pay for her time.

Staying in contact with my fur tempered the urge to shift and kept oidhirp anabarrach at bay. Barely. Stroking it soothed my nerves. I didn't doubt for a moment that I could withstand the storm as my parents had done. I could train myself to resist the whims of the heavens.

But I didn't want to. Morrigan, at least, understood.

She'd be happy for me. When the fatigue ebbed and Viridis awoke and her grief for dearest Brooke stopped consuming her—then she'd be happier for me than even my family had managed. It wouldn't just be relief, as it was for Raeyn, or the grudging acceptance of my parents. Morrigan was capable of the selfless joy true friends experienced.

When the time came, I'd feel it. She'd given me her heart.

I double-checked my bank details, ensuring that the money I'd squirrelled away wouldn't be eroded by fees, then went over my checklist. I'd left my room clean, with my car keys on my bed next to the signed paperwork Papa would need to sell or regift the vehicle. My phone service would cease tomorrow. My gym membership next week.

I'd said my goodbyes to everyone except Morrigan. And her coven. I'd email the latter.

I shifted uncomfortably on the metal stool and scratched at my face. They'd wonder, rightly, why I wasn't at Brooke's funeral. But to wait for that? There'd forever be things happening ashore and people to miss. A thousand reasons to delay. There was never a perfect time to start over. No one disappeared without being mourned. I phoned AI's florist, assuming they'd provide flowers for Brooke's funeral, and organised an arrangement to be sent on whichever date Brooke's Aunt chose.

Next, I drafted an open letter to the coveners, thanking them and recognising each individual's contributions, or sharing a fond memory I had of them. I scheduled the email for tomorrow at dawn.

What to say to Morrigan? Words weren't sufficient. I sipped my cocoa and scrolled through the photos on my phone. Screenshots of cute messages she'd sent. Selfies we'd taken on our dates. Her laugh captured so perfectly, I almost heard it. There was nothing to ease the sting of parting for either of us. Leaving her empty handed didn't sit right though. I tapped my phone against my chin until it came to me.

This I'd give to her! I'd carried it with me every day—useful for a witch. And I'd record the full version of my song so she'd have that and our photos and my love. I quickly ordered a replacement charging cable delivered to her house, then ducked into the bathroom off the tearoom to make my recording. Lastly, I uninstalled all my apps, signed out of my accounts, and removed the pass code, making the phone clean and accessible.

Lingering in the hall, as I predicted, was the apprentice. She appeared to be studying calculus.

I waited until she looked up. "If it's no trouble, might I see Morrigan's office please? Something small I'd like to leave as I'm heading out to sea."

"No problem." She scrambled to pack and got to her feet. "This way."

A security officer joined us at the elevator, discreetly following to the Private Investigators' suites. AI had learnt a hard lesson.

The apprentice approached a middle-aged woman. "Belinda? Uh, Ms Coolman? This is Elton Abercrombie, Miss Larue's partner. He wants to put a gift on her desk."

"How sweet," Belinda said. "Come through."

Morrigan's desk seamlessly blended her earth-loving, nature witch aesthetic with business functionality. Her keyboard, a high-end light-up affair, was scrupulously clean, with sigils on the macro keys. Her desk plant sat in a terracotta pot painted with Celtic knotwork, next to a wire pen holder and a bottle of hand sanitiser. I took a pump before touching any of her belongings. Morrigan would appreciate that.

She had regular yellow Post-It notes, and blue ones. I went with blue.

My beloved Morrigan, I wrote, *to take you to sea is my greatest fantasy. That I must renounce my heart leaves me maimed.*

With gratitude undying,

yours forever,

Elton.

I wished I had the time to fashion a poetic message, but the presence of Morrigan's workmates forbade that. I stuck the Post-It to my phone and tucked it behind her keyboard.

"My thanks." I turned to my escort. "I'm ready."

MORRIGAN

Meddy wrapped her arms around me. We sat together on the edge of her bed. She'd called me the moment Elton's group email arrived, offering me refuge. I'd already been a sobbing mess; didn't need to read it to guess its contents.

I sank into her. A snake shifted under my weight. I jerked away, felt guilty for jerking away, and cried anew.

We should have been walking the Bondi esplanade, having this conversation with ice cream melting over our knuckles. A few weeks from now. Instead, we were in her bedroom with a ridiculously healthy platter of sliced vegetables, chilled fruit, and fucking tahini dressing. Across the room, Meddy's collection of elegant perfume bottles mocked me with their romantic undertones. She'd made love to Astrid in this bed and described it to me in detail the next day.

The one time he'd come here, Elton and I had stolen a kiss framed by the ensuite door, light pouring through the curtains and turning the dust motes into daytime fireflies. This was not where I needed to be. Yet it was the safest. Meddy was no stranger to devastation.

"I've got you," she said, pressing the glass of water into my hands.

I took it. Observed it shake; the water threatening to leap the rim. "Water isn't going to do it."

Meddy's eyelids drooped a moment and she nodded, as if in silent communication with someone, but unless Poe'd taught her how, she didn't have telepathy. Maybe she did. I'd been so absorbed over the past month, she could have sprouted a second pair of arms and I wouldn't have noticed. I checked for extra arms, like a fool, but all she had was a bottle of Baileys Almande.

"It's not cold, but I can get ice."

"You don't even drink."

"It was a gift."

She was studying to be a nutritional scientist. She didn't do unhealthy, aside from white bread. I shook my foggy head, then realised that would read as rejection. "I mean yes. Let's do this!"

She turned the bottle, looking for instructions on how to make it go.

"Ice will do, right?" I said, "No need to dilute its healing properties."

"Mum adds milk." Meddy scrutinised my ravaged face. "Or just ice. Ice sounds amazing." She ducked out of the room.

Was it even after midday? It didn't matter. Nothing mattered. How awful I'd feel later wouldn't shadow the abyss inside me.

The glasses Meddy brought were so full of ice, I doubted we'd fit any grog in there.

"Figure this way we'll get several rounds and won't have to stagger back to the kitchen," she explained.

Her glass had a spoon and bit of milk in the bottom. She poured.

Sniffing the beverage, she asked, "How'd he tell you?"

"Didn't." I dug his phone from the pocket of my jean-shorts and slapped it against my thigh. "Left this on my work desk."

"Serious?"

"My supervisor dropped it off last night. Didn't want it derailing me when I return next week." I shrugged. "He texted, too. Before. Saying that he was going to pick up his skin and he'd see me there, but I was asleep. I can't believe he expected I'd be at work." I tapped the heart icon, centre screen. Elton's song rippled through me, uppercutting my core. A gasp burst from my mouth. I downed half my drink.

When the music ended, Meddy said, "Do you think it works?"

"What?" The alcohol? Not yet. I drank again.

"The song. It's instructions for contacting him."

"What do I care? I wasn't worth staying for." Was I unreasonable? Probably. But I didn't owe him a scrap of virtue. He'd given me zero time to grieve the death of my friend before abandoning me.

My last memories of him—clear ones, at least—would be fighting alongside each other on Tamarama beach. To-gether we were unstoppable, just as I'd written in my letter to the gods. But those memories were fragmented and tinted with fear. He'd left me yearning for him when we should be honouring Brooke as a couple.

Did I even deserve to mourn him when he'd gone in pursuit of happiness?

Meddy refilled my glass without prompting.

Elton was everything I'd asked for. Everything. But I'd never said selfless. That'd been my jam. I embodied that. Didn't need others to sacrifice themselves for me. What thirteen-year-old knows to ask the gods for altruism?

No, I'd longed for impractical qualities. Who needed every step to be a dance? Or timeless ancestry? As much as I loved his rich voice, was it more important than a man who would stay? Who'd choose me? My glass ran empty. Stupid ice.

Meddy topped me up. I glared at her drink until she took a swig, making me less alone.

"It's not like I didn't know. I was warned." I clenched the disconnected phone. "It isn't as though he lied. I wish he'd lied." The creamy drink left a trail of fire through my hollow chest. "It'd be okay to be angry then. If he'd fooled me. But nope, I can only resent the lies I told myself."

"It's okay to rage. Normal even." Meddy sat statue still, as if she might scare me off. "I hoped too, you know."

"That he'd stick around?"

"You're beautiful together. Like pecans and sweet potato. Utterly different but perfect paired."

Trust her to make it about food. "Yeah, well, at least he won't be cooking any of his stinking fish in my house!" It should have been empowering to say. Instead, I lost grip on my glass, tumbling pieces of ice onto Meddy's carpet.

She set hers down to retrieve mine and renew it, leaving the ice to melt into the floor. A cube died slowly, turning into a miniature wave and rolling away from me. Disappearing.

I swallowed, but my throat remained dry. "Don't I deserve more?"

Meddy chewed her cheek. Released it. Sucked it in again. "Tell me to shut up if you like, but you've learned you're lovable from this. You spent ages afra—"

"Shut up."

She did. We drank.

Drinking watered the seed she'd planted. "Shut up," I told her voice in my head. The insinuation he'd never rejected me. "He didn't love me enough to stay."

"But he knew you loved him enough to let him go." She whispered, invited me to be proud.

"Fat lot of good that's doing me now."

Meddy poured.

"How long's this shit going to take to work?" I snapped.

She raised her empty hand; *How should I know?* or maybe, *What's the hurry?*

"You've never drunk to escape?"

She shook her head.

"Not even when... ?"

"I was a minor."

Like that mattered. My soul stung; I should have asked ages ago. "How'd you do it? Cope, I mean."

It was her turn to search for answers in her cup. "Well, my best friend is awesome, so that helped." She grinned, but it was tired and faded fast. "Truth is, I didn't realise how bad it was while it was happening. I was too busy surviving. It was only later, when the worst was past, that I had time to process it. School let out, I had no obligations because of my legs. I fell apart then. Privately." She swirled the liquid in her glass. "I cried and cried. 'Why me?' Like I wasn't the moron who jumped off that damn bridge. I blamed Eliss. Blamed Astrid. Blamed Aurora. But in the end, I made that choice. Knowing what it'd do to me, I'd jump again. Even though my legs ache when it rains." She wiped condensation from the bottom of her glass on her baggy ripped jeans. "I've never told anyone, but I'm terrified of falling now. Sometimes when I'm climbing it paralyses me. I get stuck up there, clinging until it passes."

"But you still climb anyway?" It wasn't really a question.

"Yeah of course."

I stood to pace, but the floor wasn't where I expected and I stumbled. Then I caught sight of my face in her mirror, all red and blotchy. Sitting had been working better. I flopped back down. What would Elton think of me like this? I huffed. It wouldn't change a thing. Nothing I did—nothing I could have done—would have made a shred of difference, because he hadn't stopped loving me.

Worried I'd crack the glass in my aching fingers, I drained it again and set it down on the damp floor between my feet. "I want to be happy for him."

"Really? I want to punch him in the face."

I snorted. Classic Meddy. She would too. I took my bracelets off one at a time. The gemstones clicked. The metal charms rattled. Wooden beads clacked. He'd have called that a kind of song. My head swam. I snapped a gem-chip bracelet against my skin. Garnets; good for healing the heart, apparently.

"You want some music? Something loud and angry?"

Did I?

Meddy activated her Bluetooth speaker. "It's worth a shot."

There were markings on the side. At first, I thought they were a sigil from Brooke, but no. Just Meddy's phone number, in case she lost it. A song started automatically. She paused it a few beats in to search for a suitable playlist.

I picked up my glass again. Brooke would have put ice cream with this Baileys and wouldn't give a flying batshit about being under drinking age. The thought choked me. She hadn't made it to her eighteenth birthday. Wouldn't.

An angry woman belted out of the speaker on Meddy's immaculate desk. Condemning the world and some man and his stupid ute.

I didn't have someone to blame.

I grabbed Meddy's wrist and squinted at her as my vision warped. "Sorry about anything mean I said on the bus. You didn't deserve me lashing out."

She sipped her drink, then patted her lips dry so as not to smudge her lipstick. "Nothing you said was worse than what I think about myself."

I shook my head. "I'm the common on denom... de..." My tongue tripped over itself. I glared. "I'm the thing that is there in all our miseries and even I'm not at fault." My eyes grew heavy with the effort of speaking straight. "At least, that's what all them therapists at work reckons."

The singer howled. Might have been the same woman or not, but I had the urge to howl along with her. Meddy's parents weren't home.

"You're the common denominator for all the wonder in our lives too, Morr. How much have you got to achieve before you give yourself credit?" She leaned forward to lock eyes with me. "You are enough."

"I'm an idiot. I made a complete fool of myself. For a guy!"

"Nobody thinks you're stupid."

I snorted a little too forcefully and snotted on her carpet. "Sorry," I took the tissue box she offered and cleaned my mess. The floor heaved toward me. I tucked the dirty tissue into my pocket and collapsed back on Meddy's bed, hands suspended in the air because I couldn't fathom looking for my sani.

Meddy sprayed my hands with hospital freshness. "Drink's working, I take it?"

Everything I cared about was drifting on the far side of a hazy wall as I lay on the ocean. A wave rolled under me, then through my guts. I pressed my lips together. When the queasiness passed, I said, "Doesn't feel how I'd imagined."

"Mm. I'll get a bucket."

Another wave came. The music faded.

"Do you think Viri's awake yet?" I asked.

No reply.

"The curse lifted. Did I tell you?" I'd cried my way through endless reports and text messages; I didn't know who knew what anymore.

"Come again?" Meddy sat back down. "Bucket at the end of the bed. Roll to your right."

I held onto the bed like it was a raft. Poe told me once 'True love cleans your spew. It's not in his kiss at all—it's in the bucket.' I wanted to pass that on to Meddy, but words defeated me. Hopefully I'd remember when I thanked her later.

An odd sense of freedom rushed over me and was gone as my stomach roiled.

Meddy put cucumber slices over my swollen eyes. And stayed. She'd sit here beside me until the world turned to stardust.

I reached for her hand. "Play his song again for me?"

Last Christmas

MORRIGAN

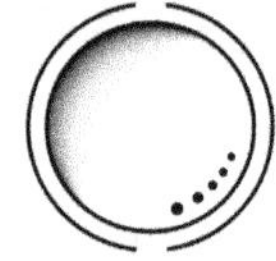

Poe and I stood at my parent's kitchen sink, washing vegetable juice off our hands. Beside us, Mum put the finishing touches on a matching platter for her coven. We waited on the hot food. Most of her coven were already downstairs in the covenstead, relegating my mates and I to the garden for our less-formal gathering. Tasmin was visiting Sydney for the weekend.

Poe shook her head as she watched Meddy and Astrid though the window. I didn't have to look to know what they were doing. Alone out there, waiting for Eliss and Tasmin to arrive, they'd be making out.

"Is it weird for you?" Poe lifted her chin in their direction.

"How do you mean?"

She fetched a tea towel from the third drawer and dried her hands. "You know, like…" She rolled her wrists, stirring the air as if to generate the correct terminology. "It's like when I see photos of me eating meat as a kid. The thought of eating corpse now is unfathomable, but I did it. And I enjoyed it."

Mum paused her scrap-gathering to consider that.

Beyond the windowsill knickknacks and the potted parsley gone to seed, Astrid squealed with joy as Meddy devoured her neck. Elton and I had canoodled like that, but the memory did feel weird now, with the distance between us. "You'd think that experience would allow me a better understanding," I said. "More compassion for allos."

"Who?" Mum sealed the compost bucket and then grabbed a cloth to wipe down the bench.

"Allosexuals. You know, normal people."

"Hey, don't call me normal! It's insulting." Poe crossed her arms and stuck her nose up comically. "Seriously though, it didn't help?"

"Not really. If anything, I understand myself less." A whisper of stubble prickled my collarbone, chased away by my own chilly hand. "I would've liked to make him that happy." He was still there, touching my life in small ways.

A cold splash out of nowhere. A warm presence behind me in bed at night. The knowledge that if he came ashore, he'd find me, but that could be in forty-odd years.

I worried that if he took a lover, I might feel it.

"And what happens when I want to date again?" I mused, so caught up in my thoughts that the sound of my voice startled me.

Mum thrust her head into the oven, studiously inspecting the yum cha.

Poe gave me less grace. "He didn't strike me as the type who'd expect you to wait."

"Same." Maybe we shouldn't have bound ourselves together with magick. It had been foolish. And yet, I wouldn't change a thing. It was like having a guardian spirit. A carefree one that never offered advice.

"She's turned out well." Poe let me off the hook. "Astrid, I mean. Really held her own over the summer."

"She fits in nicely," Mum agreed as she pulled the tray from the oven. "These are done. Would the twins like some?"

"Yes, but be stealthy." Poe said. "Let's not remind them we exist when they are playing quietly." She grabbed two plastic plates and put some veggie sticks on them to go with the yum cha. "Thanks Felicia."

Mum tiptoed into the lounge room with the twins' snacks.

I picked up our platter. Poe followed me down the hall, bringing the drinks. "I vote to initiate her next Imbolc."

"I was thinking the same, if Meddy's ready. That'll probably be Indra's last circle with us, right?" I scrutinised my mental calendar. Initiations were held at Imbolc, in early August, before the HSC trials.

When Poe didn't respond, I glanced over my shoulder. She had her disapproving-parent face on.

"I want to say he'll reconsider, but my judgement is garbage." We stepped out into the thin winter sunshine. Poe shook her head. "Not to be harsh, but we won't miss him. He hardly attends as it is." She set the drinks down on the lawn. "Gonna peek on the kids one last time and grab a jumper. Bit nipply out here." She nodded to Meddy and Astrid. "Either of you need anything?"

"Heeey sibbies!" Eliss skipped past Poe, brandishing a paper-bag-wrapped bottle. "Knew you teetotalers wouldn't have anything fun, so I brought my own."

Tasmin approached slower, carrying a worn cardboard box—a croquet kit, if the label was to be believed.

I snorted. "Yes, well, I've never drunk a cup of tea and then vomited into my bestie's designer bouldering shoes. We enjoy different things." Poe would say nobody drank tea and went home to flog their daughters; I was glad she was missing this conversation.

"I'm not holding a grudge," Meddy said. "But everyone, note how restrained I'm being; not reminding anyone of alcohol's health risks or how even one dr—"

Eliss hit Meddy with the balled up paper bag. "Thanks, Grandma."

"Yous should be grateful," Tasmin said, as she pulled six wire arches from the box. "Eliss is the master at this game, ze'd wipe the floor with your arses if ze stayed sober."

"This is grass." Meddy stated the obvious. "Not floor."

Astrid took a spring roll and aimed for Meddy's lips. "Shush you!"

I focused on the contents of the box, diligently ignoring their wrestling. Their ridiculous, untamed love and the empty space beside me. The croquet balls blurred. I blinked hard.

Poe delivered Astrid's coffee, then joined me, rubbing her hands together. "Wasn't Kendren's trial today, Morr?"

"This morning," I said, glad for the distraction. "I didn't go, but Dad reckons it was straight-forward. He pleaded guilty. Not that he got a lighter sentence out of it. He still had his magick bound, has to pay massive damages, twenty years of community service... The works. ICR will be up his arse for life."

"They aren't locking him up?" Astrid asked.

I selected a mallet. "Turns out ICR doesn't have a prison. Neither does AI."

"Probably because incarceration is a broken system," Tasmin said. She dragged the cardboard box aside and grabbed a mallet. "All set to play, whenever."

We tapped balls through arches until our shivers grew unbearable; first just the six of us, and then with the twins and my parents after their coven departed. Poe took her kids home to be bathed, dropping Tasmin and Astrid off on the way.

As the sun set and Mum plugged in the electric heater, the rest of us clustered around the kitchen table. Meddy produced an itemised list from her planner, detailing everything I'd need—including a budget—for moving in with Eliss and Oberon.

"What would we do without you?" I asked her.

"Wing it," Eliss answered. "And fail dismally."

Dad rested a hand on my chairback. "Morri isn't in the business of failing."

No, I was in the business of secrets. Of long nights and mysterious bruises, friendship, and sacrifice. Love was my jam, even when it was hard. Especially then.

I rested my head against his forearm and smiled at my coven. "Not with all of you looking out for me, anyway."

Afterword

If you enjoyed this book, please take a moment to tell the internet. Good reviews keep authors writing when all else fails.

Found typos? Great! This is an indie published novel, so I can fix it. Just shoot me an email at miriamcumming@gmail.com, and if it's a mistake (not a quirk of Australian/British English) I'll credit you in the acknowledgements.

Love free stuff? I have a freaking amazing newsletter: https://mailchi.mp/8c1ed308f871/moonlitgathering

Other Titles in This Series

Namesakes (2018)

Namesakes Three Fold Return (2019)

Blessed Prey (2020)

Celtic Dreamer (Newsletter free novella)

The Ferryman (Coming 2023)

My Thanks

It takes a team to produce a quality book and once again I've been blessed to find the best people by my side.

My biggest thanks to Crit Club members Michele Howell, Sarah Katyi, Yvone Williams, Jenea Tallentire, and Jenn Pook. You kept me showing up to my desk every day. Thank you for highlighting everything you hated about this novel so I could make it suck less. Jenea - Who knew there was a difference between discrete and discreet or persecuted and prosecuted? Thanks for saving my dyslexic arse. You're all invaluable to me. Let's keep making books together!

Dustin Cumming, you're not just the love of my life, you're also my sponsor and consistency reader. May we one day be as cool as Morrigan's parents.

Thanks to Rebbecca Janson, both for watching my kids one day a week back in 2019 so I could focus, but also for giving your own kids cool names to inspire my stories. I love that you're my biggest fan.

Thank you to Kathy Johnson and Peter Mieras for the brainstorming and the critique, and for deepening my love of the ocean in general. I hope I did your ideas justice.

Cade Everly – you're the best ever; better than all the other evers. I cannot thank you enough, nor do I think you'll ever really know how much your solid presence in my life has meant these past couple of years. If it weren't for you, this novel would literally just be characters breathing on each other. We're all in your debt.

Ken – Every version of you is beautiful and talented. Thank you for everything.

A huge thank you to Michelle Custerson and Katie Va-clavek for your undying loyalty to Elouera and your pure enthusiasm for each book I release. Knowing that you'll read and love my work fills me with the greatest joy. And Katie? I can't wait to start doing in-person events with you!

www.ingramcontent.com/pod-product-compliance
Lightning Source LLC
Chambersburg PA
CBHW060811120726
47909CB00006B/1871